gorgeous Nordic backdrop that had me itching to visit. If Iceland's tourism agency doesn't pay Megan, I'll sue."

—Katie Naymon, author of *You Between the Lines*

"Megan Oliver is an instant star; *Secret Nights and Northern Lights* shines as brightly as the aurora borealis itself, and the expertly crafted layers of longing and history between Mona and Ben sparkle, simmer, and then blaze in this stunning debut about what it means for two people to each do the work necessary to love each other well."

—Audrey Goldberg Ruoff, author of *Hopelessly Teavoted*

"The sexy, swoony, angsty, second-chance romance of my dreams. Megan Oliver perfectly weaves together lush atmospheric settings, complex characters, and tender emotions in this wise, perceptive romance about taking chances and stepping into the lead role of your own life. An absolute triumph of a debut."

—Heather McBreen, author of *Wedding Dashers*

"*Secret Nights and Northern Lights* is a gorgeously written love letter to Iceland and second chances. . . . Megan Oliver hit this out of the park."

—Heather Frances, author of *Chase Me If You Can*

TITLES BY MEGAN OLIVER

Secret Nights and Northern Lights
Hate and Other Acts of Fiction

Hate and Other Acts of Fiction

MEGAN OLIVER

Berkley Romance
New York

BERKLEY ROMANCE
Published by Berkley
An imprint of Penguin Random House LLC
1745 Broadway, New York, NY 10019
penguinrandomhouse.com

Book design by Laura K. Corless

Library of Congress Cataloging-in-Publication Data

Names: Oliver, Megan author
Title: Hate and other acts of fiction / Megan Oliver.
Description: First edition. | New York : Berkley Romance, 2026.
Identifiers: LCCN 2026015452 (print) | LCCN 2026015453 (ebook) |
ISBN 9780593952429 trade paperback | ISBN 9780593952436 ebook
Subjects: LCGFT: Romance fiction | Novels
Classification: LCC PS3615.L58663 H38 2026 (print) |
LCC PS3615.L58663 (ebook)
LC record available at https://lccn.loc.gov/2026015452
LC ebook record available at https://lccn.loc.gov/2026015453

First Edition: November 2026

Printed in the United States of America
1st Printing

For my husband,
who has been by my side
encouraging me every step of the way.

Hate and Other Acts of Fiction

CHAPTER 1

Every good scandal has a few defining qualities: public intrigue, sex appeal, and enough staying power to monetize the hell out of it. The one inconsequential detail: whether or not it's all fiction.

Sadie Stockton swept her arm in a graceful motion down the length of a solid rosewood table, set with enough patterned dishware and polished silver and sparkling crystal to serve twelve, though no one had eaten a meal at this table in half a century. "All right, everyone, this is what you've waited all night to see—*the* infamous dining room where Hazel Wilmont's first husband chased her soon-to-be second husband around the Easter ham with a shotgun."

The antique table was part of the spectacle now. The showstopper that drew her tour to a close. The piece that sold out two groups of twenty, five nights a week.

Well, that and some decades-old rumors.

Under Sadie's direction, the historical tours at the Wilmont House had become the second-most-popular tour in Sutton Island, Georgia—a tourist hot spot due to the city's picturesque downtown and proximity to numerous beaches. Her runner-up status was nothing more than a technicality, however, because the top spot always went to some ridiculous, *highly* overrated pub crawl, which wasn't even a real tour and therefore shouldn't qualify.

Then again, maybe she was just bitter.

As the night's sold-out group *ooh*ed and *aah*ed and circled the very spot where soon-to-be deceased William Eubanks confronted Hazel and her beloved, Sadie chirped out her usual reminder. "No flash photography, please."

The Wilmont House was stocked with priceless artwork and antiques. Artwork and antiques that she knew way too much about, just as she knew way too much about every minute detail of this mansion.

But Sadie also knew what these visitors actually came for, and unfortunately it wasn't to hear her talk about the paintings or the furniture or even the books that long-deceased, world-famous children's author Hazel Wilmont brilliantly created within these walls. That was all a guise. What people really came for was the gossip and scandal still interwoven with Hazel's legacy. It was why Sadie's tours were performed at night, and why this room was saved for the grand finale.

Of course Sadie didn't believe any of the nonsense she spewed on these tours. Still, she infused some mystique into her voice and began the same old theatrical spiel to the night's group of tourists ages sixteen-plus.

"As most of you probably know, this is the very room in which Hazel Wilmont's affair came to a shocking climax on Easter Sunday in 1940. As we touched on earlier, this house was built by William Eubanks, Hazel's fiancé at the time, as a vacation home and wedding present in 1935. The two were married a year later, despite their fifteen-year age gap, when Hazel was only nineteen years old. Both families ran in the same social circles up in Charlotte and, needless to say, Hazel never had a choice when it came to her marriage."

"Until she poisoned her husband." The snarky whisper of some college-age kid rose over the hushed crowd. "I'd say that was *a choice*."

Ignoring the remark, Sadie pressed onward. "It didn't take long before the cracks in the marriage began to show. William was incensed by the amount of time Hazel spent here on the island, penning the children's stories that would one day make her famous all across the world. And Hazel, well, she didn't really care what William thought at all."

Sadie slowly strolled to the head of the table, just as she did every night, the room so quiet she could hear the toll of the grandfather clock in the library announce the arrival of the eleven o'clock hour. "As the marriage continued to deteriorate, William spent more and more time drowning his marital woes in the local women and the tallest bottle of brandy to be found. This went on for several years until, as is often the case in the South, word spread that Hazel had begun her own affair out here on Sutton Island with a young man she befriended at the local print shop."

"John Wilmont," the crowd murmured in unison.

"Correct," she confirmed. "Now these rumors spread all the way back to William in Charlotte, and despite his own *numerous* indiscretions, he became infuriated. It was nothing for a man to cheat on his wife back then—happened all the time and was never spoken of—but for a *woman* to cheat on her *husband*? Unfathomable."

Sadie dramatically tsked her tongue and shook her head. "So William journeyed down to the island, hell-bent on putting an end to this dalliance and taking his wife back home to Charlotte for good. Arriving in town late Easter morning, he kicked in the front door with a shotgun in one hand, bottle of brandy in the other, to find Hazel in her silk robe at this very table, with none other than John Wilmont, who happened to be in the act of carving the Easter ham in his undergarments."

The group hung on her every word, like children hearing a ghost story around a summer campfire. "Thanks to that brandy habit, William was too drunk to aim the shotgun, much less fire it. But that didn't stop him from chasing John Wilmont, who still clutched the carving knife, out the front door and all throughout the square. Just as the church on the corner was letting out. Talk about a scandal."

A wave of titters and whispers rolled through the crowd.

"Luckily, one of the town's patrolmen happened to be walking through the square and intervened. He didn't place William under arrest, because high society and all that, but he did take William to sleep it off in the county holding cell."

"Should've stayed in jail," the same college-age kid piped up once again.

Annoyed, Sadie made a pointed effort to hold the kid's gaze. "*No one* knows for certain what happened next, though people have spent decades speculating and spreading false accusations. All we *know* is that William was eventually released, and he returned to this very house where sometime after a dinner of leftover Easter ham, Hazel sought help from the neighbors, saying William had collapsed. His death was later determined to be from natural causes. Cardiac arrest, to be precise."

"Come on, Sadie!" Apparently College Kid was the confident type who had no problem calling her by her first name as he interrupted her tour, yet again. "Everyone knows Hazel poisoned the Easter ham!"

Sadie wasn't unfamiliar with hearing these rebuttals. People had made up their minds one way or another when it came to Hazel Wilmont's story, and nothing she said on a ninety-minute tour was going to change that. Even so, she refuted. "That has *never* been proven. With his heavy drinking habit, William Eubanks wasn't the exact picture of health."

"Yeah, okay, maybe." Some of the smugness faded from College Kid's voice. "But she married her lover *two weeks* later. Don't you think that's a bit suspicious?"

"They were very much in love," she replied. "And they remained married until John's unfortunate passing . . . a year later."

"Oh, what a coincidence," College Kid deadpanned.

"It *was* a coincidence," Sadie, very much losing her patience, insisted. "A tragic coincidence because Hazel loved John very much. So much so that she spent the remainder of her years alone, shut off from the rest of the world here in this home, writing the twenty-three children's books that were published between 1945 and 1965. Those books are still read by children worldwide today."

This was the part of Hazel's story that Sadie longed to delve into. She could talk for hours about Hazel's books and how the faraway lands with magical fairies and unicorns transported her to another time and place when she was a kid. A place far away from her lonely childhood bedroom, a time when her parents weren't arguing in the kitchen under the false assumption she'd been asleep for hours.

"Hey, Sadie," College Kid said, and she internally sighed. It wasn't unusual to have one person on a tour who wouldn't ever shut the fuck up, but this kid was really pressing on her last nerve. "Remind me what John Wilmont died from again?"

"Cardiac arrest."

A self-satisfied grin broke out over College Kid's stupid face as another wave of murmurs rolled through the group.

Suddenly exhausted, Sadie wasn't about to get into any deeper of a debate with this kid, so she rushed to her closing commentary, more than ready to wrap up the night. "All right, everyone, I'm sad to say we've now reached the end of our time together." She wasn't sad in the slightest. "I'll give you some time to take any last photos—remember, no flash—and I'll be waiting in the front courtyard if you have any further questions. And please remember, the estate is open for self-guided audio tours during the day, as well as the gift shop located in the guesthouse where we sell Hazel's books and an assortment of souvenirs."

She didn't mention one of those *souvenirs* was a Christmas ornament shaped like a platter of sliced ham, a travesty she could barely stomach let alone speak of.

Making her way toward the black-and-white-checkered floors of the grand foyer, Sadie smiled politely as she passed by a silver-haired man who enthusiastically snapped multiple photos of the dining room table with his phone.

Outside, the night air was thick and muggy, dampening her skin with sweat before she reached the wrought iron gate that separated the estate from the public sidewalk. Late September, Sutton Island had yet to receive any respite from the sweltering summer heat, and the humidity—well, the humidity was always off the chart in the South. Retrieving the hair tie she wore around her wrist, she twisted her long auburn hair into a low bun at her nape, but it provided only brief seconds of relief before the stifling air converged upon the small slice of freshly exposed skin.

Reaching one of the redbrick pillars composing the entrance gate, Sadie leaned against it and closed her eyes, waiting for the group inside to slowly trickle back to their hotels or B and Bs or beachside condos so she could lock up and retreat to her studio apartment on the second floor of the guesthouse.

"Well, well, well." A deep Southern drawl interrupted her fleeting moment of peace. "Look who we're lucky enough to spot tonight. Sutton Island's very own Sadie Stockton."

Unfortunately, Sadie didn't need to open her eyes to place the voice that haunted her nightmares, but she did anyway, pushing off the brick pillar as dread filled her. How she'd managed to miss the approaching footsteps of an entire group of fifteen-ish, she wasn't sure, but it was too late to run, too late to hide.

From *him*.

Ryan Fucking Pearson.

His tall, athletic frame came to a stop about ten feet in front of her, his face partially shadowed as the dark night clashed against the well-lit mansion at her back, though somehow his forest green eyes still managed to reflect vibrant pools of color. His sandy brown hair curled slightly at the ends, and he wore the familiar attire she was accustomed to seeing him in whenever their paths unfortunately crossed: white Nikes, dark jeans, black T-shirt with *Pearson's Pub Crawls* printed across the chest. She didn't need to see the back of the shirt for it to annoy her, too. From previous encounters she already knew it boastfully taunted: *Sutton Island's #1 rated tour.*

God, she hated that shirt.

Loathed it.

Wanted to rip it off his stupid chest. (Not for sexual purposes, obviously.)

Casting a glance down at her creamy silk blouse, perfectly tailored dress pants, and black kitten heels, Sadie decided her outfit was one hundred times more professional than Ryan's arrogant T-shirt. Because she led a *real,* historical tour. About a *real,* exceptionally talented writer. Not some glorified excuse to get drunk strolling from bar to bar throughout the city.

"Sadie here leads the Wilmont House Tour," Ryan said to his followers, a smirk twisting his lips. "Sutton Island's *second*-most popular tour. Y'all should try to fit it into your schedules while you're in town. If you have the time, of course."

To the members of his pub crawl—mostly twenty- and thirty-somethings clutching plastic cups filled with colorful concoctions—Ryan probably sounded sincere. Friendly even. He was one of those people charmers with charisma for days—likely why his tour was so damn successful. And Sadie would know. She'd been on the receiving end of his attention once before. But that was forever ago, and it had ended exactly as she'd predicted it would.

Shoving that thought to the back of her mind, she smiled at the strangers gathered behind Ryan. "Yes, we'd certainly love to have you visit us here at the Wilmont House."

"You're all probably familiar with the story of Hazel Wilmont and the famous Easter ham," Ryan continued, though his eyes stayed locked on hers, irritating smirk firmly in place. "And her two young husbands that mysteriously died in that house. Question is, Would Hazel Wilmont ever have become a household name if not for the scandal?"

"*Hey!* That's not—" Sadie stopped herself, realizing as Ryan's smirk split into a full-wattage smile that she was playing right into his hands. Lowering her voice, she addressed the group again. "Hazel Wilmont was an incredibly talented writer whose accolades had nothing to do with any ridiculous rumors. If you'd like to learn more about Hazel, the house is open for self-guided audio tours during the day, and yes, I lead *historical* tours five nights a week at seven and nine thirty. We cover everything from the mansion's impressive collection of artwork to Hazel's brilliant literary career."

"Hey, Sadie!" College Kid's voice beckoned from somewhere

behind her, and she tried not to cringe. "Do you know if that Easter ham was ever tested for arsenic? Or lead?"

Oh, for fuck's sake.

She spun around to see College Kid leaning over the front porch railing. "Really not sure on that one."

With a disappointed nod, he disappeared back inside the house.

Turning back to Ryan, Sadie loathed the satisfaction gleaming in his woodsy-green eyes.

"All right, y'all," he said, "I'm sure you've grown bored of Sadie's self-promotion by now so let's keep it moving." Walking backward, he led the pub crawlers down the sidewalk, the group falling in line behind him like baby ducklings, likely already filling out their raving Tripadvisor reviews. "Our next stop is this really cool bar with an absinthe cocktail that will blow your mind."

Sadie watched them go, but as the group reached the corner of the square, Ryan glanced her way one last time with that same ever-present smirk.

Since no one else was paying her any attention, she returned his smirk, along with her raised middle finger.

Mouth easing into a grin, Ryan subtly shook his head a few times as if her gesture was amusing to him. Then he fucking *winked.*

So instead of enjoying the glowing satisfaction of her vengeful response, Sadie was further distressed. Heat flamed in her cheeks, a sweeping flush that spread down her neck and across her chest. Thank god Ryan was too far away to see how he'd gotten under her skin, literally. Because one thing was certain: Ryan Pearson had firsthand knowledge of all the places she flushed. And he knew precisely how to make it happen.

Spinning toward the mansion, Sadie stomped up the brick pathway. Time to get rid of any lingerers and lock up. She was officially over this fucking night.

CHAPTER 2

"Well, don't keep me in suspense here. What do you think?"

Sadie snapped her attention back to her friend. Though more often than not she wondered if perhaps just friend*ly* was a more accurate description of their relationship in Eric's mind. She didn't have many friends, so maybe it was a low bar, but as far as she was concerned it counted.

Eric Andreas (her friend *and* daytime boss) had been a local celebrity ever since he starred as a contestant on the popular reality TV series *Runway Wars.* Though he'd finished in third place overall, during one of the weekly challenges he'd discovered that submerged in his already unfairly deep talent pool lay a special forte for wedding gown design. When his time on the show was up—unfairly so, but one dickhead judge had it out for him from the beginning—Eric returned to his hometown of Sutton Island and opened Eric Andreas Designs, a bridal boutique that carried his own line of wedding gowns and bridesmaid dresses, as well as those of a few designer friends.

Seven years later, the store was thriving, with brides traveling across the country for one of the few coveted consultations with the one and only Eric Andreas to select *The Dress* for their special day. And for VIPs, celebrities, and a few lucky others with that enigmatic quality that deemed them *worthy* in his eyes, Eric would design a custom gown.

Sadie had watched it happen on several occasions. A bride standing on a platform in front of the trifold mirror in the fifteenth dress of the day, Eric circling behind, rubbing his chin. Sadie could almost predict it now, the moment his brow would furrow and he'd proclaim, "Something isn't quite right." The bride's face would fall in utter devastation—was there no perfect dress fated to be hers? Then Eric would smile, tilt his head, and announce, "I think we need to go custom on this one."

The bride would emit a high-pitched shriek (Sadie's cue to grab the Kleenex), oftentimes collapsing to their knees in a state of euphoria. It was as if they'd just won the lottery. *The Wedding Dress Lottery!*

Anyway, Sadie worked the register.

No, that was reductive. She also handled the consultation bookings and assisted the customers who wandered in without an appointment.

Now Eric cleared his throat in a way that suggested he was losing his patience as he clutched a wooden hanger that held one of his latest creations.

"It's gorgeous," she assured him. "Your designs are always gorgeous. You know that."

Arm extended above his head, Eric lifted a brow into a *That's all you've got?* arch.

"No, really!" She swept her fingertips over the ivory material, barely touching. "I love the elegance and simplicity of this one."

"And the train?" He flipped the hanger around and maneuvered the dress so that the train fanned out across the store's wide-planked hardwood floor. Silk-covered buttons trailed down the back, leading to a sweep train with intricate light pink floral embroidery.

"Literal perfection."

"You mean it?"

"Would I ever lie to you?"

Nearly seven years working together and Sadie still didn't have the slightest clue why Eric insisted on getting her opinion whenever he had a new design. Until he came into her life her closet consisted of mostly leggings and basic T-shirts, occasional jeans, and some strappy sandals if the occasion called for something nicer.

Early on in their relationship, Eric had taken one look at her sandals and declared them *atrocious*. Sadie had pointed out that they were highly functional—*waterproof even!*—to which he'd asked if she had plans to wade through a river later. She hadn't worn those sandals since, but she kept them shoved in the back of her closet in case circumstances ever called for a beach day.

Anyway, Eric was, bare minimum, one thousand percent cooler than her.

Today he wore a white, deep V-cut shirt that revealed a large portion of the smooth, dark skin of his well-muscled chest (and likely cost an amount that would make Sadie nauseous), paired with trendy (but not *too* trendy) high-waisted trousers and some type of organic canvas shoes that Sadie kept hearing (from him) were highly versatile and perfect for any occasion (though not waterproof). His long, braided hair was tied back over his shoulder, and a tiny gold stud on the left side of his nose glinted in the light.

In comparison, Sadie was pretty certain her fashion opinion

was null. Still, she'd give him her thoughts if that's what he wanted. "It may be one of my all-time favorites," she added, fully taking in the subtle floral detailing.

"I thought this one felt special." Eric nodded, her words seeming to confirm something he already knew.

Satisfied, he headed for the back sewing room where he created his custom designs, returning a moment later minus the gown. With a to-go coffee cup in hand—courtesy of Sadie—he slumped onto the wooden stool behind the glass countertop at the checkout area. This was their typical morning routine; Sadie arrived around nine thirty with their coffees, then they spent the half hour until the store opened caffeinating and gossiping about whatever plethora of drama was occurring with their current brides.

Peeling off the lid, Eric lightly blew across the steaming surface. "Tell me about this meeting you need to leave early for."

"Are you *sure* it's okay?" she asked for the umpteenth time since her arrival. "We've been so busy lately."

The last thing Sadie wanted was to disappoint him. She still remembered her interview here six months after graduating from UGA with a bachelor's degree in history—one that did *not* end up paying for itself in value and practicality. Working at a bridal boutique hadn't appealed to her in the least, but she needed a job. *Any job.* Desperate, she laid it on thick in her interview, spouting nonsense about how much she loved romance and weddings, even going as far as uttering the humiliating phrase, *I just really* love *love.*

Seated in a folding chair in the back room, Eric's expression remained inscrutable as he'd studied her, finally replying, "I don't think you believe a word of that bullshit."

Her hope sank on those very words. At least until his booming laugh filled the room and he'd added, "But I don't believe in this bullshit, either."

He'd hired her on the spot, and they'd been a team ever since. Eric was even supportive when she'd taken the second job at the Wilmont House a couple years later because he seemed to understand, without any real explanation, how much the place meant to her. She imagined Eric, like herself, thought eventually she'd end up leaving the bridal shop to work solely at the mansion, but her rent—though heavily discounted—and student loans didn't get paid on a part-time tour guide's salary alone.

So she'd kept her day job at the shop, running herself ragged for the past five years. But staying busy was good. It left less room for erroneous decisions.

Sadie tuned back in as Eric was saying that of course it was okay if she needed to cut out early and that he could handle the customers "just fine, thank you very much."

A worry arose in her mind then. One that bothered her frequently, though she always tried to dismiss it. Yet every time it recurred, it lingered a little longer, buried itself a little deeper. Was her hesitancy to leave her job at the shop solely about money? Or was it about the deep-seated concern her friendship with Eric might slip away if she didn't see him every day? After all, relevance in another's life goes hand in hand with visibility, and the thought of her one friend fading from her life made her sick to her stomach.

"I thought you might have a hot date with Charity tonight," she said, reburying her doubts for another day. "I don't want my meeting to ruin your plans."

Charity was the supermodel Eric had been on-again, off-again with since they met on *Runway Wars*. The past few months they were very much on again, and she'd been staying at his beachfront home for the past six weeks.

"Oh, I do," he confirmed. "Just not at six p.m., Grandma."

Ignoring the slight—because okay, fair—Sadie said, "I wish I knew what this meeting was about." Taking her usual latte along, she ambled toward the pink velvet sofa across the room. The boutique was filled with pops of pastel pinks and purples and blues. It was like being spun into a cone of cotton candy or falling into the cover of Taylor Swift's *Lover* album. She sank onto the sofa, the crushed velvet always a pleasing texture under her palm. "Evelyn's text only said that staff was to report to a mandatory meeting at five this evening. And Evelyn's not the type of person to call a meeting that could be an email. In fact, the only times she's ever texted me are when the mansion closed during the hurricane a few years back and when I got that terrible case of food poisoning and had to call out sick."

"Ah yes, the great food poisoning of 2023." Eric sipped his coffee with a mirthful grin. "A rough time for us all."

"Joke all you want, but what if I'm getting fired?"

"And she's calling a staff meeting to fire you?" His dark eyes narrowed. "Come on now."

"Perhaps that's a bit of a stretch." Worrying her lower lip between her teeth, Sadie stared out the glass front of the shop. Evelyn Myers had worked as the director of the Wilmont House for the past forty years. Since Hazel Wilmont never had children, her home fell into the hands of her sister after her death, and upon her sister's passing, it went to Hazel's niece. A niece who quickly realized the monetary advantage of capitalizing off Hazel's fame by turning the home into a visitors attraction as opposed to selling it. The family had no desire to run the estate, however, and that's when they hired a director to oversee day-to-day operations. Only the second person to hold the position, Evelyn was business savvy and well respected among staff. Now the estate was under the ownership of Hazel's great-niece, Mindy, whose appearances at the mansion were few and far between.

"Maybe she's giving you all raises," Eric joked with a little snort-laugh. "Or maybe she's retiring."

Straightening, Sadie pointed her index finger in his direction. "Do *not* play with my emotions like that."

No disrespect to Evelyn, but Sadie had been daydreaming of that very possibility since her first day on the job. If Evelyn's position came open, Sadie would surely be the frontrunner to take her place, having worked at the mansion longer than anyone else other than Evelyn herself.

"Who knows? Maybe it's your lucky day."

"I don't think I have those."

For no particular reason other than the mention of her nonexistent luck, last night's encounter with Ryan Pearson popped into her head, unprovoked and unwelcomed. Ryan always brought his pub crawlers through the square to share the story of Hazel's home, using the house she loved as nothing more than a gimmick on his tours.

She needed to be more cognizant of avoiding the square after eleven p.m.

"What has you blushing over there?"

When Sadie glanced up, Eric's back was turned as he filed an invoice away in a drawer. A task she probably should have done when she came in. "I'm not."

"Yes, you are. I can hear your awkward silence from here."

That was the downside of allowing someone to know her as well as Eric did—it was an inconvenient fact he knew all of her tells.

"I'm not blushing," she corrected. "I'm fuming. There's a distinct difference." She averted her gaze out the storefront again, watching a group of tourists duck into a locally made candle shop as the shopping district came to life. "I had another encounter with

Ryan Pearson last night. He's literally the worst. For the life of me, I cannot understand why his pub crawl is so damn popular."

"Oh really?" Sarcasm rang loud and clear in Eric's voice, and Sadie knew he was definitely watching her now. "I'd think you of all people would understand his appeal. You were the one sleeping with him."

"It was college!" she barked, abandoning the couch with such haste that some of her latte sloshed through the cup's mouthpiece and splattered against her hand. She stopped on the opposite side of the display counter stuffed full of sparkling, jewel-encrusted garters and headbands and tiaras. "And hooking up for a few months does *not* mean I fell victim to his charms. Even then I knew exactly what we were and what we weren't."

Eric grabbed the nearest box of Kleenex. There were a multitude stashed in strategical locations throughout the store for the tears of joy—well, *mostly* joy—often shed during try-ons or custom wedding gown lottery proclamations. He passed her three. "Look, I'm not judging. Just putting it out there that maybe your current distaste might be rooted in a bit of past resentment."

Begrudgingly, Sadie accepted the tissues and patted at the coffee pooling near her thumb. While it was true she and Ryan had a short-lived fling during freshman year at UGA, Eric was making more of the relationship than what it actually was. "I'm not resentful. Not over the college stuff anyway. Over his pretentious attitude and snide remarks about his number one–rated tour, yes, I am resentful. Everything's just so easy for him, you know? I worked hard to make my tours at the Wilmont House a success, then he comes along a year later and steals my title of top-rated tour in Sutton Island with some *pub crawl*. Which, frankly, shouldn't even count as a real tour!"

"Sure, sure." Eric glanced down at his gold watch. "As much as

I'd love to delve into this more, and trust me, we *will* circle back, right now it's showtime." As he went to unlock the door, he added, "If I don't get to check in with you later, let me know how the meeting at the estate goes."

Shit.

The meeting.

Busy stewing over Ryan Pearson, Sadie had almost forgotten about it.

Chapter 3

One of the many things Sadie loved about Sutton Island was the downtown area, which was relatively compact and walkable, designed in squares similar to those in Savannah. On the days she worked both at the bridal shop and at the Wilmont House, she'd walk the half mile or so between the two, weather permitting. On her way back, she'd stop at her favorite deli for a chicken salad croissant, which she always enjoyed from the wooden bench in the square across from the mansion. It was the exact spot she used to rest with her mom when they'd escape to the island, seeking solace in the shade of the nearby mossy oak while finishing off their dripping ice cream cones.

Now Sadie sat on that same bench and attempted to clear her head before Evelyn's mysterious meeting began. This was where she'd fallen in love with the Wilmont House and, more specifically, Hazel's stories, though she wasn't sure which came first. There weren't a lot of visits here, maybe a handful over the course of a few years, a few *tough* years, but each trip burned bright in her memory.

The first visit came after one of the bigger arguments between her parents. Sadie was in second grade at the time; she remembered because her mom let her skip school and it felt like the ultimate naughty treat. Instead, they made the forty-five-minute drive from their small hometown out to the bustling island filled with loving families on vacation and travel groups full of smiling faces.

In retrospect, she realized her mom was likely attempting to assuage her own guilt as the arguments became more frequent, more heated. Or maybe she just needed a goddamn skip day, too.

Sadie couldn't recall what that particular argument had been about. Perhaps money, perhaps the amount of time her father spent at the local bar, perhaps another new woman her mom found out about. Perhaps nothing at all. Funny how some details are solidified in one's memory like cement, while others remain as impressionable as wet sand.

Head tilted back, broken sunlight washed over Sadie's face, filtered through the twisted branches of the oak tree. That first trip to the Wilmont House, her mom bought her three of Hazel's books from the gift shop. Over the next months, Sadie read them so many times the bindings wore out and the books would flop open to the middle of the story, barely held together in one piece.

The second trip occurred about a year later, after her dad had an affair with the neighbor. Three more books.

The third visit came after her father announced he was moving to Florida with his pregnant girlfriend. Again, more books.

A couple more visits to the estate happened over the next year or two. One when Sadie returned from a court-mandated, two-week visit to her father's new house in Florida over summer break. Another when he made no effort to see her at Christmas at all.

The trips to the city halted soon after that, as her mom, a nursing assistant at the local hospital, picked up more shifts in order to financially support them. It was fine, though. By then Sadie was probably getting too old for those books anyway.

Because it's impossible to separate those unpleasant times from the Wilmont House itself, some might have assumed Sadie wouldn't ever want to return here, much less work and live on the premises. But no matter what bad news preceded or followed the visits to Hazel's home, those trips with her mom were some of the happiest memories she had from her childhood, and the stories discovered here were what saved her when she needed saving the most. Even after five years at the mansion, whenever Sadie stood in the second-floor writing room and ran her fingertips along the smooth grains of Hazel's desk, she still got full-body chills. Every single time.

Shading her eyes with a hand, Sadie went to check the time on her phone, instead glimpsing something familiar across the street. Or *someone* familiar, rather.

Ryan Pearson strolled down the sidewalk nearing the estate, his casual pub crawl attire replaced with navy pants and a fitted white button-up, brown leather oxfords the same shade as his belt, and effortlessly fashionable aviator sunglasses. It was a stark contrast to the T-shirts and baseball caps Sadie was accustomed to, not that both looks didn't perfectly suit him. Not that she was noticing.

But when Ryan turned into the gate of the Wilmont House and quickened his pace up the brick pathway toward the home, *her* home, Sadie definitely took notice. Heart suddenly pulsing in her throat, she slung her nylon tote over her shoulder in a rush, stumbling over her own feet in her haste to hightail it across the street and find out precisely what the hell was going on. If she'd already had a bad feeling about this meeting, seeing Ryan Pearson stroll through the gate only amplified that feeling by one hundred.

Seriously, what the actual fuck was *he* doing there?

Darting across the street to find out precisely that, Sadie forgot about the measly little thing known as traffic until a horn blared and a hood came to a screeching halt approximately three feet from her hip. But even that did nothing to deter her, and she threw up a customary *my bad* wave as she continued to the other side.

It wasn't until she hurried through the gates and neared the cherub fountain that split the brick pathway in two that she looked up and saw the small group gathered on the front porch, all watching her with horrified looks.

Evelyn was there. So was Mindy, current owner of the estate, along with a man Sadie hadn't met in person but knew from following Mindy on social media (Mindy didn't follow her back) was her new husband, Jerry. Both in their forties and on their fourth marriages (so much in common!), they were dressed like middle-aged twins in solid-white tennis athleisure as if they came straight from a doubles match at the country club.

Alongside the newlyweds stood a dark-haired stranger in thick-framed glasses and a tweed vest over a long-sleeved button-up. And beside that person stood Ryan *Fucking* Pearson, whose alarmed expression suggested she'd just run into traffic.

Oh right . . .

"Sorry, sorry, sorry!" Sadie shouted her apology to the stunned group for her almost demise, as if getting run down in the street would have somehow been worse for them than for her. "I didn't want to be late."

A double-sided staircase led up to the raised front porch, and she hurried up the set on the right to join the others. Sweat gathered at the small of her back, and she could only hope it wouldn't soak through her blouse.

"You okay there?" Ryan asked once she reached the top, because of course he'd take the opportunity to call her out in front of everyone.

"Dandy," she replied without looking at him. "Shall we go inside and cool off?" Was everyone else sweating, too? She wasn't sure.

"Yes, let's do that," Evelyn said, also eyeing her with concern before leading the way through the front door.

Lingering behind, Ryan curled his fingers around her elbow as Sadie went to follow the group. "Really though, Stockton," he said low enough only she could hear, "you good?"

Even through her sleeve the pressure of his fingertips stirred something oddly familiar low in her stomach. "Perfectly fine. Although I'd be better if I knew why the hell *you're* here." Never particularly quick-witted with retorts, she added, "Or if you weren't here at all, actually. Then I'd be great!"

"Aww, I didn't know I still had such an effect on you," Ryan rasped, close enough behind her that she felt his breath on her ear. "I'm honored."

"Please," she scoffed. "The only effect you have on me is making me question a society that ranks your juvenile pub crawl higher than my historical tour about a world-famous author."

"Yes, it is truly *baffling* you aren't winning over the crowds with your radiant personality." Releasing her arm, Ryan moved through the doorway. "You joining us for the meeting sometime today, Stockton?" he loudly inquired over his shoulder. "Thought you didn't want to be late."

God, he was smug.

Inside, the group gathered around *the* dining room table, each person hovering behind an antique chair but not daring to sit and disturb the preserved furniture.

The mansion was eerily quiet. Not unusual, per se, since all daytime visitors had to be out by five p.m. so the house would be empty for Sadie's tours. But something was definitely off.

Evelyn had called this a staff meeting, but none of the staff other than Sadie were present. None of the gift shop employees, or the groundskeepers, or the daytime staff who passed out audio devices for the self-guided tours. Not even Matt, who doubled as Sadie's backup whenever she took time off (never) or had food poisoning (2023 was not her year).

"Let's get started," Evelyn said from the head of the table.

"Shouldn't we wait for the others?" Sadie spoke up. "I thought this meeting was all-staff."

"Yes, well, I meant all staff that this matter pertains to," Evelyn clarified.

"Oh."

Sadie wasn't a particularly anxious person, but when it came to this house it was possible she cared a little too much, and a heavy sense of foreboding filled her chest.

Evelyn went clockwise around the table as she introduced everyone, all of whom Sadie already knew except the person in the tweed vest, who was soon announced as "Simon Winchester, former actor in the New Orleans production of"—adjusting her wire-rimmed glasses, Evelyn read from a clipboard clutched in the opposite hand—"*Dinner and Demise.* Did I get that correct, sir?"

Simon Winchester gripped the V of his vest with both hands. "Yes, Evelyn, that's correct."

Sadie hadn't the slightest clue what was happening, but watching Evelyn in her pink skirt suit trace her fingertips over her pearl necklace while struggling to maintain proper decorum was entertaining, even if worrisome.

Evelyn's lips pressed into a tight smile. "I'll let Mindy and Jerry take it from here to discuss their new plans."

Sadie shifted her attention to the owner, or owner(s) now, she supposed, and tried to maintain a neutral expression. Rarely had Mindy so much as visited the estate in the past five years, now she had *plans*?

"Hello, everyone. And thank you, Evelyn." Mindy was so soft-spoken that Sadie stepped closer to better make out her words. "As you all know, Jerry and I recently got married." She lifted a hand and wiggled her fingers back and forth, a massive square-cut diamond catching the light and proclaiming *wealth!* loud and clear. "Since then, we've been discussing some of our . . . investments."

Investments? It was downright delightful to hear the house Sadie had loved nearly her entire life reduced to just another slice of the couple's portfolio.

"Bunny, why don't I take over?" Jerry chimed in with a condescending chuckle.

Meanwhile, Sadie debated if Jerry's sunburned nose and forehead were the result of too much time on the tennis courts or too much time in a tanning booth. Either way, he clearly didn't take SPF protection seriously. Maybe he'd never been told to reapply every two hours.

"Of course, darling," Mindy replied. "You're so much better with this business stuff than I am." Dipping her head bashfully, she batted her eyelashes like a schoolgirl talking to her crush.

Sadie wanted to vomit.

"That's right, Bunny." Jerry flashed his smile, perfectly straight and shockingly white in a way that could only be veneers. "Now, here's what I'm—sorry—*we're* thinking. I've heard the historical tours here have become a huge success—"

A jolt shot through Sadie at the mention of her tours, and she bit down on the inside of her cheek, that neutral expression harder and harder to maintain.

"—and we want to expand upon those tours to create another income stream. So we've come up with an idea we want to test out. We'll leave those nightly tours as is, but for those guests who want a bit *more*, we've decided to trial an overnight murder mystery experience. It will run from midnight to five a.m. on Friday and Saturday nights for three weekends in a row. Depending on how the trials go, and if they're as successful as I—*we*—predict, we're hoping to make these a permanent weekend option."

Sadie's heart sank, even as relief swept through her. If her historical tours weren't changing, she wouldn't be involved with this nonsense. Yet Hazel's legacy was once again being exploited for all the wrong reasons.

"I've brought in two expert consultants to ensure my vision is carried out correctly and these trial weekends go off without a hitch." Jerry motioned toward Simon Winchester, who still maintained a death grip on his tweed vest. "Simon will head up the murder mystery portion of these tours, and he'll ensure our guests have an unforgettable experience."

The question remained what Ryan Pearson had to do with any of this, but good ole Jerry managed to clear that up with his next sentence.

"Since the primary challenge with something like this will be to separate ourselves from the multitude of other tours and experiences Sutton Island offers, I've brought on Ryan Pearson of Pearson's Pub Crawls as our second consultant. I'm not sure if everyone is aware, but Ryan's company is consistently voted the top-rated tour in all of Sutton Island."

Oh, she was fucking aware.

Annoyance swept up the back of Sadie's neck in a hot flush. At this rate, she'd likely be covered in hives by the time they got through this meeting.

"Mindy and I had the opportunity to partake in Ryan's pub crawl a while back, and I was blown away by his ability to captivate and hold the attention of an audience. Not to mention his incredible knowledge of the city and the bars and the cocktails." One side of Jerry's mouth lifted as he hitched a thumb in Ryan's direction. "I knew right then and there I needed this guy on our team."

"Thank you, Jerry." Ryan humbly shook his head. "I appreciate that."

Gross.

But Jerry wasn't finished.

"Ryan is a mixologist in addition to leading his very successful company, and I know he'll be able to create a cocktail lounge right here in the mansion that will provide the perfect ambience and setting for a murder mystery. We'll call it the Clues and Concoctions Tour." Jerry spread his hands through the air as if unveiling the name written on an invisible marquee. No one said anything, apparently not the response he was hoping for. He dropped his hands and cleared his throat. "Or something snazzy like that. So that's the overview. We want to test the market, but I'm"—he coughed—"*we're* sure this idea is a real winner." He tossed a quick glance at Mindy, who fervently nodded in support. "With that being said, we expect these trial tours to be up and running in two weeks to take full advantage of the Halloween season."

Sadie nearly laughed aloud, only managing to suppress her reaction at the last moment when she realized he was serious. *Two weeks?* Putting something like this together that quickly was, well, almost impossible. Evelyn was going to have her hands full overseeing Jerry's little pet project.

"I'll toss it back to Evelyn now," Jerry continued. "The missus and I have a dinner party to get to. But Sadie—"

She nearly jumped at the mention of her name.

"—we'll be checking in." Extending an arm, Jerry flicked his fingers at Mindy, summoning her to his side as if recalling a hunting dog. Mindy gave the group a dainty little wave, then slipped her shoulder under Jerry's awaiting arm as they saw themselves out.

Checking in? What did that mean? And what did any of this have to do with her?

As soon as the front door closed, Sadie addressed Evelyn. "I have *so* many questions."

"I'm sure you do." Evelyn approached while Ryan and Simon broke off into their own conversation across the room. "Let me start by clarifying why you're here today."

"Uh, yeah. Let's start there, please."

"What Jerry failed to mention is that I've decided to retire at the end of October. Therefore, I'm not the one overseeing this project. You are." Evelyn sounded so completely unbothered that Sadie thought surely she'd misspoken. But then she kept talking. "As of this very moment, Matt will be taking over your nightly tours so you can solely focus on this trial murder mystery project."

"*Excuse me?*" Sadie had heard Evelyn just fine. But she was truly at a loss. Wishing for Evelyn's retirement had come back around to bite her in the ass. Talk about karma.

"You can say no if you want, but you're the only person I trust to take this on." Evelyn glanced around as if the other estate employees might overhear, though none were in the room. "And consider this, Sadie. If you succeed at this project, you'll show Mindy and Jerry that you're the only logical choice to take over as director."

Well, there was that. The job she'd coveted since her first day as a tour guide. Though truthfully, probably long before that. Probably since she sat on the bench in the square with her mom and laid eyes on the mansion for the very first time. If overseeing this ridiculous project was the way to land her dream job, she'd bite her tongue and do whatever it took to make it a success. "Yes, I'd love that opportunity," she admitted. "I mean, I'm sad to see you go, of course."

Evelyn waved away her niceties.

"There is a slight problem though." Sadie lowered her voice to a hushed whisper. "Or more like an *inconvenience* of sorts."

"And what's that?" Evelyn asked.

At that exact moment, the *problem* loudly cleared his throat from just over Sadie's shoulder. She startled, hand clutching her chest.

"I think she means me." Sidestepping around her, Ryan proffered a hand to Evelyn with a beaming smile. "*I'm* the inconvenience."

CHAPTER 4

Evelyn shook Ryan's hand while her gray eyes stayed narrowed, suspiciously, on Sadie.

"Stockton and I have a bit of a *history*, that's all." Ryan's gaze bounced between the two women, his amusement evident by the spark in his deep green eyes.

"Ah, so you two are familiar then?" Evelyn asked.

Sadie shook her head. "No, I wouldn't say—"

"*Familiar* is certainly one word for it," Ryan cut her off. "Although it would seem she doesn't look back on those times very fondly. Can't say I blame her, they were certainly no walk in the park for me, either."

Oh god.

Sadie's heartbeat reverberated throughout her entire body.

Ryan was trying to get under her skin again. And it was, unfortunately, working.

Ever poised, Evelyn replied with a thin smile and a succinct, "Sadie, we'll continue this later. Right now, I'll let you get acquainted, or *reacquainted*, with your new partners." She gave them both another once-over before exiting the room.

And then there were three. Though Simon remained on the far side of the room, intently examining the ornamental gold-framed mirror that hung above the fireplace mantel.

"What *the hell* was that?" Sadie whisper-shouted at Ryan. "That's my boss, for Chrissake!"

"What?" Ryan gave a half-hearted shrug, tongue sweeping across his lower lip as the corner of his mouth twitched. "All I said was that we had a history. I didn't specify that history took place in your bed."

Squeezing her eyes closed, Sadie pressed her fingertips to her temples and attempted to massage away both her current predicament and the memories of that very *history* he referred to.

It had all started freshman year at UGA when Ryan stumbled into class five minutes after it had begun (a tardy on the very first day, no less) and earned himself a swift look of disapproval from Professor Dickinson (not what the students called him) as he took the only open seat left, which happened to be the one right behind Sadie.

All semester long he just kept *talking*, and even then he was charismatic as hell. For some reason he seemed determined to get Sadie to interact with him. Or maybe he just wanted to cheat off her work. Either way, she'd started looking forward to Fundamentals of American Government, of all things, and by the end of the semester that December, she found herself a little sad their semi-friendship was drawing to a close.

Then on the last day of class before finals, Ryan leaned forward and whispered, "Listen, Stockton, you should probably give me your number so I can annoy you over Christmas break, too." He discreetly slid her his phone, which Old Man Dicky (what the students actually called him) still insisted students place in a box by the door when they entered his classroom.

Nevertheless, Sadie, feeling rebellious, took the contraband and typed her number into his contacts. But as she passed it back, Ryan's fingers brushed over hers and caused her stomach to cartwheel. She dropped the phone onto the worn linoleum floor with a clatter, drawing the attention of their classmates and their professor.

Old Man Dicky, mid-lecture, was none too thrilled about the disruption. "Mr. Pearson," he'd said in the condescending tone he used when catching someone breaking one of his numerous rules—likely the exact type of behavior that earned him his unfortunate nickname. "I'll see you in my office after class."

"Happy to, sir," Ryan replied, unfazed.

Once the professor was back at his lecture, Sadie turned and grimaced. "Sorry," she'd mouthed.

Ryan simply smiled and mouthed back, "Worth it."

Charming bastard.

That kicked off a weeks-long texting spree over break, and when they returned to campus in late January, the tension was a rubber band pulled taut and ready to snap. Ryan immediately began sleeping over in her dorm room since Sadie's roommate was always at her boyfriend's place. But they were never a couple, and they didn't acknowledge each other when they'd pass on campus and he was surrounded by his vast group of friends. Which was perfectly fine with Sadie. She didn't want a relationship anyway.

Then spring rolled around and Ryan surprised her by asking her to attend some frat formal with him. Ryan wasn't in a fraternity, but he was friends with everyone on campus and scored invites to every event. Sadie put off giving him an answer for weeks. She had her reasons. Then one night when they were lying in her bed,

Ryan abruptly said, "You're not gonna go to the formal with me, are you?" When Sadie shook her head, he got up and left her room. The next day she heard he was going with Lauren Scott instead. Lauren was everything Sadie wasn't—popular, outgoing, wealthy-with-a-capital-*W*. So it all made sense. The obvious choice, really.

Now Sadie took some slow, measured breaths and tried to convince herself this wasn't real. Ryan Pearson wasn't actually standing in front of her, and he certainly hadn't made suggestive comments alluding to their shared past in front of her *boss*! Maybe she accidentally ingested some sleeping pills and this was an all-too-vivid nightmare. She'd wake up any moment and have a good laugh over the absurdity of this dream. Her palms framed her cheeks, and yep, hot as a thousand suns. Oh! Maybe it was all a fever dream!

"This isn't happening," she muttered quietly to herself. "It doesn't make any sense."

"What doesn't make sense?" Ryan's slow drawl pulled her attention back to the unfortunately very real moment.

She opened her eyes to glare at him. "*You.* You don't make sense. Why are you here? You have a job. A whole company. Why would you even entertain this . . ." Her hand flitted wildly through the air as she sought the right word, eventually settling on, "Malarkey!"

The smirk-ish grin Ryan wore split into a full smile, revealing his obnoxious dimple that formed only on the right cheek.

The fact he was enjoying her frustration made her all the more incensed. "Do you know *anything* about Hazel Wilmont? Or her books? Or her life? And I don't mean the fabricated bullshit you spew on your tours, by the way."

"Oh, you want to talk about my pub crawls, Stockton?" His

eyes shone with amusement and humor and the spirit of Lucifer. "The number one–rated visitors experience on Sutton Island? Sure, we can talk about that. Did you know the *Sutton Island Gazette* is doing a profile on me next month? If you want, I'd be happy to toss in a few words about *your* tour. I'm all for extending a hand back down the ladder."

"You know what? It's not even a fair competition!" Her pitch rose as she grew more frazzled by the second. "I am one person doing two tours a day. You have multiple guides working for you—if you can even call them that—doing multiple tours each day. Brunch crawls. Midnight crawls. Themed crawls. The numbers aren't in my favor. You're simply too big for me!"

"You know I love it when you talk dirty to me, Stockton."

A frustrated groan rattled through her chest. Then a thought dawned, causing her to suddenly switch gears. "Wait. Is your company actually struggling? Is that what this is about? Did you mismanage funds or something and now you're left with no choice but to take on this project to stay afloat? But that still doesn't make sense, either. *What are you getting out of this? How much is Jerry paying you? Why would you—*"

"Jesus," Ryan interrupted as he rummaged a hand through his tousled brown waves. "Might I suggest at least taking me to dinner before you pry into my personal life with such vigor."

Jaw snapping shut, Sadie folded her arms across her chest.

Ryan copied her pose.

They glared at each other in a low-stakes standoff in the middle of the dining room for a solid ten seconds.

Ryan broke first, and Sadie took an inordinate amount of satisfaction in that.

"Look, I have my reasons for agreeing to do this," he said. "And trust me, I realize it must be hard for you to believe that someone like me is capable of running a successful company, but I'm doing just fine, thanks. The rest is really none of your business."

"*Everything* that happens in this house is my business," she countered. "This is my job. I don't need you here messing things up for me. Especially when I have a shot at the director position when Evelyn retires."

"Why would me being involved with this project mess that up for you? I'm certainly not interested in Evelyn's position, and I, too, have a vested interest in making sure these tours go well."

"Yeah? What's that?"

Ryan's mouth opened and closed a few times before he said, "I already told you, it's none of your business."

"Hey there, friends!" Simon, whom she'd met less than an hour ago, approached with his hands clasped underneath his chin. "I think we're all on the same team here." His placating tone resembled that of someone negotiating with toddlers who refused to share their toys. But this house was a lot more than just some toy, and Sadie didn't want to share. "Maybe we should all try to get along since we're going to be spending *a lot* of time together over the next month. I believe we all want this project to be a success."

"You're right," Ryan huffed. "I'm sorry."

"Sorry, Simon." Sadie deliberately directed her apology to Simon only since deep down she knew this was all Ryan's fault.

"That's better." With a smile of approval, Simon's hands fell to grip the V of his vest. Sadie wondered how often he wore vests in order to have developed this habit. "Now, Sadie, if you would be so generous, perhaps you could give Ryan and me a quick tour to become more familiar with the mansion?"

She glanced back and forth between the two men, swallowing down her irritation and pasting on the practiced smile she used every night on her tours. "Of course. Right this way."

* * *

The old stairs creaked and moaned as they made their way up to the third-floor ballroom. The open space with polished wooden floors and elongated rectangular windows was intended to be the place William and Hazel hosted the high-society vacationers who once flocked to Sutton Island for the summer season. Problem was, Hazel had no interest in doing any such thing, and the space sat empty and unused, the fancy velvet drapery and ornate crown molding going largely unseen.

Next came the second floor, which consisted of Hazel's and William's separate bedrooms for the times they were together here, as well as Hazel and John's shared bedroom during her second marriage. There were a few more guest rooms on this floor which, like the ballroom, never saw any use. But the showstopper—at least for Sadie—sat at the end of the long corridor. Hazel Wilmont's writing room, the place she had penned every one of the stories Sadie could still recite line by line to this day.

Slowing her step, Sadie hesitated as they approached the closed door, not wanting to share the place that meant so much to her with the man who was her sworn enemy. It felt too significant, too private. Like peeling back a stage curtain and revealing a magician's secrets. But what choice did she have? She twisted the brass knob and pushed through the door. And just like every other time she entered the room, goose bumps raced down her arms.

To an outside observer who didn't know Hazel's history, there wouldn't be anything special about this room in particular. It was open and spacious, likely intended to be another bedroom. Centered in the middle of the floor was a simple oak desk with Hazel's typewriter placed on top—a gift from John on their first wedding anniversary (unfortunately, the only anniversary the two shared). Behind the desk, a window overlooked the back courtyard, framed by the same rich, wine-colored drapery that matched the ballroom's on the floor above.

A bookshelf ran the length of the far wall, floor to ceiling, and was filled with not only Hazel's works but other classic children's titles such as *The Secret Garden*, *The Tale of Peter Rabbit*, and *Mary Poppins*. These stories must have been especially meaningful to Hazel since she kept them nearby and not in the main library downstairs. Sadie often wondered if these were the books that meant to Hazel what Hazel's books had always meant to her.

Now she watched as Ryan made his way to Hazel's desk and ran his fingertips along the grains. The urge to yell, *Don't touch that!* was nearly irrepressible as she waited for some childish comment such as, *So this is where the magic happened*, which she'd heard countless times on her tours.

But Ryan stayed quiet, respectful even, as he placed a finger lightly over a typewriter key. Then his eyes lifted, catching with hers for the briefest moment before she cleared her throat and blinked away.

"This is Hazel's writing room," she began. "It was here that she wrote all of her— *Oh, watch out!*"

Ryan's hand slammed against the corner of Hazel's desk as his upper body pitched forward. Thankfully, he caught himself, and once he regained his balance, he ran the toe of his oxford over the upturned edge of a floorboard.

The warped piece was normally covered by an antique paisley area rug that resided underneath Hazel's desk. However, after a guest blatantly ignored the posted NO FOOD OR DRINKS signage and proceeded to drop an open bottle of Dr Pepper on the rug just last week—giving Sadie an intense light-headed feeling she had assumed to be an aneurysm—they'd shipped it off to a specialty rug restoration place for proper cleaning.

"Old house," Sadie explained. "It has some quirks I should've warned you two about."

Simon wheeled around with sudden interest. "Quirks?"

"Yeah, for example, on the back staircase leading up to the third floor, only the odd-numbered stairs creak, even-numbered are fine. And the water in the restroom will only come out ice cold no matter how many times we've tried to have it fixed."

A sinister grin played over Simon's lips. "This house is creepy as hell. Literally the perfect place for a murder mystery."

"Just so you know," Sadie said harshly, "Hazel Wilmont never poisoned *anyone*. Those rumors are pure fiction created by people who were bored with their own lives and had nothing better to do. People like Pearson."

Ryan promptly flipped her off, attention still on the floorboard.

"I mean . . ." Simon tapped his chin, contemplating. "There's a little truth in all fiction, isn't there?"

"Not in this case."

After leading Simon and Ryan through the first floor—the kitchen, formal library, and the infamous dining room—Sadie opened the door off the grand foyer, revealing the steep stone staircase that led down to the cellar. "We don't need to go down there unless you really want to," she explained. "It's just an empty space with a utility closet where we store cleaning supplies and holiday decorations."

Truth be told, Sadie didn't care for the cellar. Similar to most houses built close to sea level, the cellar wasn't fully underground. Dissimilar to most houses built close to sea level, the builders chose not to install a single window; therefore, it sure felt like being fully underground. The windowless stone and mortar walls gave off some real dungeon vibes, and the temperature was always at least twenty degrees colder than the rest of the house. Also, there were only two lightbulbs that hung from the ceiling, and one was in the closet. Plus the air was consistently damp, making her feel sweaty even though she was usually shivering. Overall, it wasn't a place she cared to spend a lot of time.

Yet, at Ryan's and Simon's requests, down the uneven steps they went.

Once they descended into the dank, musty space, Sadie took exactly eleven paces and then reached overhead and tugged the pull chain that hung from the lone bulb, illuminating the surrounding area in a harsh yellow glow she knew from prior experience made her appear sickly.

Before she could say, *I told you we didn't need to come down here*, she noticed the looks exchanged between Simon and Ryan in their odd little circle.

Rubbing his palms together as though a buried treasure had been revealed instead of a creepy dungeon/cellar, Simon said, "I believe we've found our cocktail lounge, friends."

"Down here?" Sadie's gaze drifted around the depressing space. "No one ever comes down here."

She looked at Ryan, who turned a slow circle with his hands on his hips. "He's not wrong, Stockton. This space is perfect for a murder mystery cocktail lounge. We'll need furniture and lighting, of course, but this will definitely work. Hey, is that an elevator?"

He pointed to the far corner where the gray stone gave way to two ornate matte gold doors that stood in stark contrast to the rest of the dreary cellar.

"That *is* an elevator," Sadie replied. "Good job, Pearson."

He looked back her way long enough to roll his eyes. "Can we use it?"

"You can. I don't get in it."

"Why not?"

Sadie pictured the rich wood paneling and the polished brass buttons of the interior. Like the rest of the mansion—other than the cellar—the elevator was created with an emphasis on design meant to showcase wealth. It was elaborate. It was flashy. It was also . . . tiny. "I don't know, guess I don't love the prospect of getting stuck in a confined space when an almost century-old piece of machinery decides to fail us. Can we get back to the point?"

"Well, I think the point is that we've found our cocktail lounge," Ryan said.

"For sure, for sure," Simon agreed.

A shiver rolled through Sadie's shoulders, so she tugged the sleeves of her blouse down as far as they would go. "I don't know. What about the ballroom? It has way more space and actual windows."

"*Too much* space," Ryan said as if this was the obvious answer. "Trust me, I know cocktail lounges. I'm telling you, this is perfect."

"If I recall correctly," Sadie argued, "*I'm* the overseer of this project."

"And if I recall correctly, *I* was brought in as a consultant for this very purpose," Ryan shot back.

"*A consultant,*" she snorted. "Okay, well, you've been consulted. But I think we should go with the ballroom."

"We could always ask Jerry whose expert opinion he would prefer to go with on this one." Ryan grinned smugly, both of them knowing exactly who Jerry would side with and that it wouldn't be her.

Irritation climbed her spine notch by notch like ivy spreading up a lattice. "Simon." She spun on her heels. "What do *you* think?"

Simon blanched. "Uh . . . I mean . . . I think either option would work." Just when Sadie thought that was all he was going to contribute to the conversation, he said, "But . . ."

"But what?" she prompted.

"But if I *had* to choose . . . like knife to my throat, gun to my temple kind of thing . . ."

"Yes, Simon?"

"I, uh, I think Ryan may be right about the cellar." He winced. "Just because it matches the vibe, you know? Creepy, dark, mysterious. And the ballroom's vibes are more grand piano and foxtrot and . . . *ballroom*."

This was clearly not a battle she was going to win. "Fine. The cellar it is."

It *was* fine. Perfectly fine.

Spending her weekend nights in the cellar with Ryan Pearson wasn't ideal, but she'd manage. It was temporary, after all. And it would be well worth it when she was named the next director of the Wilmont House.

Three weekends.

Six overnight tours.

She could handle that.

Above her head the lone lightbulb blinked off and darkness overtook the space.

"Everything's fine," she announced, though no one had spoken. "Faulty electrical."

Sadie waved her arm frantically through the air in search of the chain but came up empty. She scooted to her left. Nothing. Back to her right. Still nothing. She shuffled forward and the tip of the chain brushed her middle finger. "Ahh, found it!"

As she took another step, the toe of her heel wedged against something that felt like a shoe, causing her to stumble sideways and collide with a body. A lean, well-sculpted body with a lean, well-sculpted forearm, which was now the sole support that kept her from falling backward to the ground.

Please be Simon. Please be Simon. Please be Simon.

The hope was hopeless though, because unless she'd somehow turned completely around in the dark, the person on her right had been—

"First your inquisition into my personal life . . ." An air of annoyance echoed through Ryan's voice, now cast from somewhere above her. "Now feeling me up like this. Honestly, Stockton, I'm not sure if I should file an HR complaint or make plans to meet the family."

The bulb shone back to life directly above them. Without a flicker. Without a sound. Maybe even brighter than before. Like it was taunting her.

Simon looked their way and his lips turned inward as he bit away a smile.

They surely looked ridiculous, Ryan holding her in a poor portrayal of a ballroom dancer's dip, the bulb above them now functioning as a spotlight.

Sadie cleared her throat, loudly. At the prompting, Ryan pulled her up, his hand remaining on her waist until she fully regained balance. Then the three stood in silent, shared bewilderment, a circle of suspicious glances exchanged.

Simon eventually piped up, eyes filled with the excitement of a child hearing the telltale melody of an ice cream truck on a hot summer day. "This tour is gonna be *so* sick."

Sick was one word for it.

Chapter 5

Sadie reluctantly entered the pub where she had agreed to meet up with Ryan and Simon late Sunday afternoon.

With the nightly tours soon to be in full swing back at the mansion—without her at the helm, which alone made her feel some type of way—the three needed somewhere else to officially get started on this project. Evelyn's tiny office in the guesthouse was hardly more spacious than a closet, and Sadie certainly wasn't willing to invite the two men—one she barely knew and one she didn't care to—up to her apartment. Ryan had suggested a quiet pub he claimed was popular with locals but off the radar of tourists, and they'd agreed that while not ideal, it was the best option.

As soon as Sadie walked through the door, however, she saw that *quiet* wasn't a fitting descriptor. A large, rowdy crowd gathered around the bar, most donning UGA jerseys or T-shirts, most yelling four-letter obscenities at a long row of television screens lining the wall. Within seconds, Sadie unwillingly learned that the "so-called refs" were not calling the football game correctly or fairly—likely paid off by the "College Football Conglomerate"—as this was pointed out repeatedly and in less polite terms.

Spotting Ryan—and only Ryan—seated in a booth in the far corner, she took a cleansing breath and made her way over. Bypassing the ruckus at the bar, she reached the booth and dropped her tote bag onto the padded maroon bench as she slid in opposite him. "This is your idea of quiet?"

"I didn't realize they'd be replaying clips of last night's game." Ryan stopped scrolling and set his phone aside. "My bad."

Sadie motioned to the bar. "*This* is over a game they already know the ending of?"

"Unfortunately it wasn't a good ending. And I wasn't really thinking about it being a weekend when I made the suggestion."

As a fellow tour guide, that was something she understood. When every weekend was spent working, they easily blended in with the rest of the weekdays. To best accommodate the most popular times for tourists to visit the city, Sadie's nights off from the Wilmont House fell on Mondays and Tuesdays. The bridal shop was also open on Saturdays, closing on Sundays and Mondays instead. That left Mondays as Sadie's one blessed day off from both jobs, which she spent on her couch catching up on *Jeopardy!*—her comfort show—before meeting up with her mom for their weekly dinner date.

Picking up a laminated menu, Sadie pretended to peruse it, but her gaze kept sneaking above the top edge. Ryan sat with one arm propped on the table between them, the other stretched long over the back of the booth. Never afraid to take up space. Always confident. *That* was Ryan Pearson.

Another wave of *boo*s and other imaginative curses rang out from the bar.

Sadie projected her voice over the noise. "Guess we'll just yell at each other."

The corner of Ryan's mouth lifted just enough to showcase his singular dimple. "Great. We won't need to deviate outside your comfort zone then. They have a great beer selection if you're interested."

"I don't drink beer."

"Wine then?"

She scrunched her nose as if he'd said something offensive, though she was, in fact, a wine drinker. She placed the menu back down. "Have you heard from Simon?"

"Not yet. Hopefully he isn't lost. He only moved from New Orleans a few months ago when his husband was transferred here for work."

Of course Ryan already managed to find out all about Simon's life. Nothing could have surprised her less.

A frazzled waitress approached their table as someone in the crowd behind her shouted, "You call that *interference*? Fuck you and your mom, ref!" and the rest of the group burst into raucous cheers. The waitress smiled apologetically and took their drink orders—some local IPA for Ryan (typical) and, willing to bow to her pride in exchange for a slight wine buzz in this terribly awkward situation, a glass of Moscato for her.

Alone again, Ryan leaned forward in the booth, setting both exposed forearms on the tabletop. Sadie stared down at the sinewy muscles and the ropy veins that shifted underneath summer-tanned skin. For someone with such a pleasing physical aesthetic, wearing short-sleeved T-shirts could be considered a hostile act. No matter how fortified her defenses were, she couldn't prevent the swoop low in her stomach. She quickly averted her eyes back to Ryan's face, but the jawline alone was equally dangerous territory.

"Can we get the obvious out of the way?" he said suddenly. "I know you weren't thrilled to see me in that meeting yesterday. And I'm positive you're not thrilled to be sitting across from me now. I'm sorry my involvement in this project is so upsetting for you."

Wow. The audacity of this man was next level. So upsetting for her? That wasn't an apology, that was yet another way of fucking with her. But that's what Ryan did. He loved to watch her get flustered and angry and break out in a flush. There were countless times he'd made teasing comments as he'd passed her by on the street or given her that infuriating smirk when distance separated them.

There was also the very first time she saw him in the city. It was years ago, but she could still recall every little detail. She was in line at a local coffee shop, mindlessly scrolling on her phone as one does. When the line moved forward and she glanced up, there he was, about five people in front of her. His back was to her, but she'd know that six-one frame—the broad, rounded shoulders, the trim waist, the slightly curled brown hair—anyplace, anytime. She'd immediately ducked her head, debated walking out altogether. But she hadn't seen him since sometime sophomore year, and she found herself frozen in place, fumbling to come up with any reason he'd be in *her* city.

Ryan must have spotted her before she'd spotted him, because when she reached the counter, the barista informed her that her *friend* had already ordered and paid for her. She moved to the side, awaiting whatever she was about to receive with a sense of dread. Moments later, they called for "Stockton," and Sadie made her way to the counter and collected a blueberry muffin and an iced caramel coffee. It was her weekly treat to herself during her college days, usually to survive Old Man Dicky's early-Friday-morning lectures. Sometimes she'd even split her muffin with Ryan before class if he was being especially flirtatious and bothered to show up on time.

Some people might have found the move charming, but Sadie found it irritating. As if he were tauntingly throwing in her face what happened between them back then. Throwing in her face that he'd gotten to know specific details about her. Throwing in her face that she'd actually—*foolishly*—let him in. Not wanting to look rude in front of the staff, she'd smiled and made her way outside with her iced coffee and muffin, but as soon as the coffee shop door closed behind her, her smile vanished.

In the following weeks, she started spotting Ryan around the square and learned that he'd started a pub crawl business. It made sense that he'd chosen Sutton Island—the walkable downtown was full of breweries, pubs, and yes, cocktail lounges, too. But Sadie wasn't thrilled to be sharing her city, especially when the very next year Pearson's Pub Crawls knocked the Wilmont House out of its spot as the number one–rated tour on the island.

And now, all these years later, Ryan remained egotistical enough to assume she still thought about him, probably convinced himself those three months they spent hooking up were the highlight of her entire existence. Giving her some cop-out apology no better than the typical male go-to *I'm sorry you feel that way,* vain enough to think she was thrown by their short-lived, meaningless past. Well, he was wrong. She didn't think about their history at all. Ever.

"It's really *not* a big deal." Sadie lifted her menu again, hiding her face behind the print she wasn't reading. Then her thoughts suddenly snagged on a detail she hadn't considered before, and she slowly lowered her menu once more. "Do tell, Pearson. How *long* exactly have you known about this project?"

The waitress returned before Ryan could answer, placing Sadie's wineglass and Ryan's beer bottle on flimsy coasters then swiping her hands on her apron. "Can I get you two anything else right now?"

"Thank you, kindly." The full force of Ryan's attention and impish smile focused on the pretty young woman with deep brown eyes. "But we're still waiting on one more. I think he might be lost."

"Oh no!" the waitress chirped, eyelashes batting at a speed that made Sadie wonder if she had something stuck in her eye.

"We'll give him a few more minutes to figure it out before we order, if that's okay," Ryan continued. "I know you're quite busy."

"Of course!" The waitress tapped a bright red fingernail with a bulldog art design against the bottom of Ryan's beer. "Let me know if you need another one while you wait. I'm Georgia, by the way. Georgia from Georgia, should be easy enough to remember."

"Georgia from Georgia," Ryan repeated in his slow drawl. "I like that. Very unique."

Very unique? Good god. It wasn't like her name was Birmingham.

The waitress's cheeks tinged pink. "Just yell if you need anything."

"Thanks so much, Georgia from Georgia," Ryan said.

Sadie's eyes rolled of their own accord as the waitress nearly skipped away from their table.

"What?" Ryan lifted his beer to his lips, which twitched with a grin.

"*Thanks so much, Georgia from Georgia,*" she mimicked, making her own accent extra thick. "Back to the point," she continued, definitely not distracted by the way Ryan's throat moved when he swallowed, because that would be weird. "How long, Pearson? How long have you known about all of this?"

"Uh . . ." He set his beer back on the coaster. Sadie took a sip of Moscato while he considered what was apparently a difficult question. "A couple months maybe."

Months?!

She nearly spat out her wine.

Instead, she swallowed it too quickly and got choked up. Thrusting her glass onto the table, she grabbed the rolled silverware and unfastened the paper napkin, pressing it to her mouth as she coughed.

Ryan's brows pinched, but not in concern. More like he was annoyed by her gall to choke in public.

"Went down wrong," she eventually sputtered, not that he'd asked. In the past two days alone, Ryan Pearson had caused her to walk into traffic and nearly choke to death. Working closely with him for the next five weeks might actually put her in the grave. "If you've known about the project for that long, why did you never mention it *to me*?"

Another loud uproar broke out at the bar, this time something about a fumble that was obviously an incomplete pass and further irrefutable proof of the referees' complicity in the cover-up. When it died down, Ryan said, "When was I supposed to mention it, Stockton? We don't really talk. Did you want me to fill you in on the street as I passed by on my pub crawl?" Okay he had a point there. "And I figured you already knew. Evelyn knew. She applied for a liquor license back in August."

"Wait. So *everyone* knew but me?" She was the ultimate fool. "Was yesterday's meeting all a show? Just for me?"

"Someone's feeling particularly vain," Ryan muttered, absently rotating the bottle in front of him. "I think the meeting was to bring everyone together for the first time and make it official."

Sadie dropped her forehead into her palm. All of this had been in the works for months and no one, not even Evelyn, had bothered to tell her until yesterday. She was humiliated. And furious. "Okay, what else don't I know?" She lifted her head again. "Have you and Simon already planned everything behind my back?"

Ryan shook his head in a quick jerk. "No, I only met the guy yesterday. Right before you walked into traffic. Which we should definitely discuss, by the way. I mean, what *was* that about?"

Sadie downed the rest of her Moscato (carefully) and motioned at Georgia from Georgia—all too eagerly eyeing their table—for another. "Well, imagine my shock when I saw *you*, of all people, turning into the gate."

Amusement sparked in Ryan's eyes, his tongue darting out to wet his lips. "Jesus, Stockton, I get that you aren't my biggest fan, but throwing yourself into traffic over me seems a bit much."

"I don't know, Pearson, I imagine the desire to play in traffic is the exact effect you have on women." Her saccharine smile grew as she internally congratulated herself on that top-notch zinger. But then it was back to business. "Look, let's just cut the bullshit. We both know you're not any happier about this situation than I am."

"I honestly don't know what you're talking about." His easy grin and sexy dimple teamed up to mock her. "I'm *thrilled* to have the opportunity to catch up with my old college pal."

"Really? Let's catch up then. How's Lauren Scott these days?" The words fell out of her mouth unplanned, and she could see the surprise she felt simultaneously play out on Ryan's face. They hadn't spoken about this since the night he'd shown up at her dorm room, *after* she'd already heard the news on campus, *after* he'd been in her bed just the night before.

When she'd opened her door, Ryan stood on the other side wearing a wrinkled T-shirt and a look of uncertainty, and she'd stepped into the doorway to make it clear she wasn't inviting him in. "You don't need to say anything," she'd immediately prefaced. "I already know about you and Lauren."

He'd had the courtesy to act remorseful. "I wanted to talk to you before you heard. I'm sorry."

"It's fine." Sadie had pushed down any shred of emotion that felt even the slightest bit like anger or hurt, wholly aware that they were never a couple and he didn't owe her anything.

"I've been begging you to say yes for two weeks," he'd justified, hands buried in his hair, frustration threaded through his voice. "Last night you made it clear that was never going to happen. Today, Lauren asked me, and I . . ."

"You said yes. Got it." Sadie certainly couldn't admit to him the amount of effort she'd gone to over those past two weeks hoping she'd be *able* to say yes. It was far too embarrassing. "You really don't need to explain. We aren't anything to each other."

"Come on, Stockton." His brows had knitted. "We're *something* to each other."

She'd swallowed, throat unexpectedly tight. "We're fuck buddies, Pearson. And now, we're no longer that. So you should probably go."

"Fuck buddies," he'd repeated, gaze boring into hers as though she were the guilty party. "Right." Then he'd turned and walked away, calling over his shoulder, "See you around, Stockton."

If she'd thought for a second that her comment might have affected him in any way, she was proven wrong when Ryan and Lauren not only went to the formal together, they also became the hot new couple on campus afterward, and Sadie got the pleasure of witnessing their adorable displays of affection multiple times throughout the remainder of freshman year.

Now, years later in a different city, the smug expression was wiped entirely from Ryan's face. Good. "What the fuck is that supposed—" He leaned in over the table, gaze fixed on hers the exact way it had been outside her dorm room that night. "You said no, Stockton." Though his voice was low, there was a biting edge to it. "You said *no*."

"It doesn't even matter." Sadie swallowed, then redirected. "If you want to talk, let's talk about your reason for working on this project."

Groaning, Ryan sank back in the booth. "How many times do I have to tell you it's none of your business? I don't have to divulge details of my life to you. We're not friends."

Despite the truth of the statement, Sadie bristled at its bluntness. No, they weren't friends and they never would be. But Ryan was yet another person who likely had tons of friends and never struggled to form relationships, and she couldn't help but wonder if he could somehow identify whatever was lacking in her that made her unable to do the same. "Definitely not friends," she replied, quieter.

"Hey there, partners! So sorry I'm late."

Simon's chipper voice cut through the tension as he scooched into the booth beside her. A line of perspiration dampened his forehead, his navy sweater vest slightly askew.

"I think I took a wrong turn or two," he continued. "I don't really understand maps, and these one-way squares are for the birds, you know. Anyway, what'd I miss?"

Sadie returned her glare across the booth to Ryan. "Nothing. You didn't miss anything."

"Nope," Ryan echoed, lifting his beer as he blinked away. "Not a damn thing."

Georgia (from Georgia!) returned with Sadie's much-needed second glass of wine and then took their orders. Then Sadie pulled out her legal pad and a pen. "Okay, the objective for tonight is to determine a precise schedule for the tour. We need to fill *five* long hours with our guests and ensure they stay entertained for that extended period."

"Interesting." Ryan rubbed a hand along his jawline.

"Interesting?" she repeated. "What could possibly be *interesting* about what I said?"

"I think our first objective needs to be more logistical. We need seating. A bar. Lighting. We have an entire cellar to transform and less than two weeks to do it." He shrugged. "I think that should be top priority."

"You think that because the only part of this tour you care about is *your* cocktail lounge."

"That isn't true. But we can plan the greatest murder mystery tour ever created and it won't matter if the guests don't have anywhere to sit or are wandering around aimlessly in the dark."

Of course. *Of course* he was trying to undermine her once again. "Simon?" she huffed.

"Uh . . ." Simon took a long swig from his Cherry Coke before answering. "I could be wrong, of course, but *perhaps* we should look at furniture and lighting options tonight and focus on the tour schedule tomorrow? Getting furniture delivered in time is already going to be tough with this deadline."

Deep down, Sadie recognized that they were right. But that didn't mean she wasn't annoyed about it. "Fine. But I at least need an overview of how this *murder mystery* thing works."

"Ah, okay." Simon angled his body to better face her in the booth. "Essentially, everyone will have a role. At some point during the night, our *victim*"—he mimicked air quotes—"will fall to the floor. Chaos will ensue. Everyone will search the mansion for clues and interview their fellow guests. At the end of the night, everyone will come together again to present evidence and make accusations. With a little guidance from me, the killer will be revealed and the mystery solved. I'll write a few different scripts so that we can change it up each weekend to keep it from being repetitive."

"And you're confident you can pull this off?" Sadie asked.

"I was a lead actor at *Dinner and Demise* for ten years." Simon scoffed as if Sadie should understand the prestige associated with that title. "We had fifty nightly guests and a consistent four-point-three-eight-star rating. I've got this."

He sounded confident enough, so she moved on. "Do you have any ideas for what the storyline will be?"

"Well . . ." Simon looked at Ryan and then back to her. "I was thinking since this is the Wilmont House, I should write the script to mirror the rumors about Hazel."

"No," Sadie said flatly.

"I thought you might say that," he sighed. "I'll come up with a different angle. But can I at least use the poisoned ham? Maybe we even serve some biscuits and ham? Ohhh, that would be so—"

"No."

"Fine." Simon sank against the back of the booth, shoulders slumped. "I'll go a different direction."

Soon enough, Georgia (interesting fact: She's also *from* Georgia) dropped off their food. While they ate they each perused local furniture store websites on their phones, composing a list of prospects to check out in person the following day. By the time they finished, they had decided on seven shops to visit.

When the check arrived, Georgia handed it directly to Ryan and quickly slipped away.

"Here, I'll take that," Sadie said, digging through her tote for her wallet. "I have the estate's credit card for business expenses."

Ryan opened the check presenter, eyes scanning the inside. "I've got it."

"Don't be ridiculous. I have the credit card for this very reason."

"We had alcohol. That's not a business expense. Really, I don't mind."

"Trust me, it's fine." Now she was suspicious. Clearly he didn't want her to see the bill, which made her all the more determined to get her hands on it. "Now give me the check."

Ryan passed her the leather folder.

As soon as Sadie opened it, her eyes dropped to the loopy scrawl at the bottom of the check.

So nice meeting you!

If you're single, give me a call sometime.

—Georgia from Georgia, 912-555-0777

"Really?" Sadie huffed, annoyance heating her cheeks.

Ryan raised both hands in defense as if he were a mere bystander to his flirting game. As if it just couldn't possibly be helped that masses of women wanted to fuck him.

Sadie rolled her eyes. Again. "Here, you want the check so bad, have at it." She slid the folder back across the table. "Wouldn't want to stand in your way of getting laid." Tucking her legal pad away, she pulled the straps of her tote bag over her shoulder. "Simon, could you let me out? I think I'm done here for the night."

Without a word, Simon slid from the booth, and Sadie made her way through the animated crowd at the bar and straight out the door.

CHAPTER 6

Tuesday morning, Sadie perched on the edge of the sofa in the bridal shop, her left foot tapping incessantly against the hardwood as she awaited Eric's arrival. She needed to talk to him about this project at the mansion and how it would affect her job at the shop. More specifically, that it *wouldn't* affect her job at the shop. She wouldn't let it.

After some debate yesterday, Sadie and her new partners had agreed the most reasonable plan would be for the three to meet up on a nightly basis to work on the tour. There really wasn't any other choice unless she took time away from her day job, which she refused to do. Ryan finally caved and agreed to have one of Pearson's many pub crawl guides (because he's *so* successful and in demand!) cover his tours temporarily. They'd also steal time during the day whenever Sadie's schedule allowed, like yesterday when they spent no less than eight hours traipsing from furniture store to furniture store, eventually agreeing on several chaise longues and sofas and high-top tables for the cellar.

A soft vibration buzzed at Sadie's side. Setting her caramel iced coffee on the table—okay, maybe those college memories had given her a craving for something other than her usual latte—she picked up her phone. Guilt whirlpooled in her stomach before she finished reading the text.

Mom: Hey, it's Mom! Missed our dinner last night. You think next week will work? Fingers crossed!

Why her mom felt the need to identify herself at the start of every text conversation—as if Sadie wouldn't have the number of the woman who birthed her stored in her contacts—she would never understand. But years ago she'd given up trying to convince her it wasn't necessary.

Thumbs poised over the screen, Sadie hesitated. Getting this murder mystery tour off the ground was going to consume every minute of every day for the next couple of weeks. There would hardly be time for sleep, much less anything else. She'd canceled last night's dinner and stayed up till two in the morning designing promos for social media because the advertising needed to go up ASAP if they wanted anyone to actually buy tickets to this thing. Only seven hours later, she was exhausted and guilt-ridden over standing her own mother up on such short notice.

Sadie: Can I let you know this weekend?

Sadie: I'm going to try and make it. Promise.

As she hit send, the clatter of a key turning the front door's lock caught her attention. A second later, Eric made his way into the store with his eyes concealed behind a pair of gold-framed sunglasses.

Her phone buzzed again.

Mom: Of course, sweetie! I know you're busy. No worries either way.

Somehow her mom's understanding made her feel worse. Sadie was well aware that other than their longstanding Monday-night dinners, her mom's social life was slim to none. Outside of working too many twelve-hour shifts at the local hospital, Ann Stockton didn't have any hobbies that occupied her time. Probably because her number one priority had been to financially support them after Sadie's father left. Once Sadie was grown and financially supporting herself, she imagined it was challenging for her mom to try to find new interests and meet new people. Sometimes Sadie felt like she was the only thing her mom had in this world, so canceling the one night a week they met up for a nice dinner made her heart physically ache.

"You're here early." Eric slipped the strap of his olive green messenger bag overhead and tucked it away behind the counter. The bag was stuffed full of design sketches, and he carried it almost everywhere he went, never knowing when inspiration might strike. He even sketched a breathtaking gown just last week while he waited in line at the DMV, somehow creating beauty among the fifth circle of hell.

"I thought I'd get a head start on the workday." It sounded like a complete lie, evidenced by the fact she wasn't filing invoices or straightening dresses on the rack or checking the consultations on today's schedule. Nope, she was lounged on the sofa, staring at her phone.

Eric's eyes narrowed over the lid of his coffee cup. "Everything okay? You never texted this weekend about the meeting at the estate."

And there it was, the subject she'd tossed and turned over all night.

"About that . . ."

Sadie launched into the details of the meeting, filling him in on everything from Simon Winchester the murder mystery actor to Evelyn's retirement announcement to Ryan Pearson somehow being thrown into the mix because life was especially cruel and very unfair.

When she finished, Eric tilted his head, considering. "Sounds like you have your plate full."

"Okay, yes, but I need to make something very clear." Sadie crossed the store to the counter. "My job here is of the utmost importance to me, and I will *not* let my duties here slip. I swear it."

Just making the declaration out loud lifted some of the pressing weight off her shoulders.

Until Eric replied, "Okay, let's take it down a notch. You don't work for Miranda Priestly. It's okay to take some time off if you need to. You know that, right?"

Then the weight was back, with a few extra pounds for good measure. Eric's *reassurance* did the opposite of its intended effect. Suggesting she take time off screamed one thing and one thing only: She was expendable. "I don't need time off," she insisted. "Why would I need time off? I've managed both jobs for five years now. This doesn't change anything. I'll make it work."

"Just saying." Sadie had always thought Eric's calming presence and soothing tone could have earned him a job as a hostage negotiator, tactics he now employed on her. "I know you pride yourself on being reliable, and I admire that quality. But sometimes, let's just say when you have a horrid case of food poisoning for example—"

Shivering, Sadie automatically recalled those three days she neared death back in 2023. It was the dark days of winter. The kind where it's pitch black outside by five thirty p.m. and the sun is nothing more than a myth. She'd tried her damnedest to make it through her shift, not wanting to leave Eric in a bind. But when she'd thrown up for the third time in less than an hour, Eric promptly closed the store. When she'd reemerged from the bathroom, barely able to stand on legs weaker than a newborn fawn's, he'd insisted on driving her home, and though the guilt was real, she hadn't been in a position to turn him down.

He'd spent the next three days showing up both morning and night with take-out chicken soup and reusable grocery bags stuffed full of saltines, Sprite, and Gatorade. Most likely, he was the singular element that kept her hydrated enough to escape death's clutches. Yet every time she thought about those three days, more than anything else she was overwhelmed with shame for how irresponsible she'd been to cause Eric to close the store that day. It was his livelihood, after all, not something to be taken lightly.

"—it's perfectly okay to take some time off," he continued. "No one can do it all."

Perfectly okay? But didn't he *need* her? "I don't need time off because I'm more than capable of doing both. Besides, the planning stage of this project is only for the next couple weeks. Once it's up and running, I'll only need to be there overnight on the weekends."

There was no need for Eric to state the obvious. It was written in the depths of his skeptical, copper-flecked eyes. If she worked all day at the shop and stayed up all night for the murder mystery tours, when would she sleep? She didn't have an answer for that, *yet*, but she'd figure it out.

"I'm only putting options out there." Then, clearly sensing her

Praise for

Secret Nights and Northern Lights

"This contemporary romance is engaging, well written, and realistic. With well-developed characters who have immediate, almost tangible chemistry and a well-described atmospheric setting whose details pull readers into the landscape of Iceland, Oliver's debut is unputdownable."
—*Library Journal* (starred review)

"An exceptional romance debut that doubles as a love letter to Iceland. . . . Oliver's debut is a stunning achievement, full of unresolved emotion and angst that results in feelings simmering to the surface, as well as proof that the embers of true love can never fully die down."
—*Kirkus Reviews* (starred review)

"Oliver pens a moving second-chance romance against the vivid backdrop of Iceland."
—*Booklist*

"Oliver's debut novel is a love letter to Iceland, rekindled relationships, and a sweet reminder that sometimes we need to leave to find the place that feels like home."
—#1 *New York Times* bestselling author Jodi Picoult

"I loved visiting Iceland with Mona and Ben—richly descriptive about the joys and frustrations of travel and falling in love."
—Kate Clayborn, *USA Today* bestselling author of *Georgie, All Along*

"Megan Oliver's debut, *Secret Nights and Northern Lights*, is childhood-sweethearts, friends-to-lovers, second-chance romance perfection. I believe so strongly in Ben and Mona's love for each other back then—when he had a cute nickname for her that only he would use; when he stood up for her with her brothers; when she was always there for him even when he had struggles she didn't know about. And I believe so wholeheartedly in their happily ever after now, even if it took traveling all the way to Iceland to break the ice between them. Oliver excels at tender moments, relatable characters, and stunning scene descriptions in a book that had me completely immersed from beginning to end. Oliver is a gorgeous new voice in romance!"

—Alicia Thompson, *USA Today* bestselling author of *Never Been Shipped*

"What a splendid and magical debut from Megan Oliver! *Secret Nights and Northern Lights* captures all the beauty and heart of traveling the world, falling in love with new places, and finding your way back to the people you're meant to love. Ben and Mona are so authentic and heartfelt, and exactly why I'm so weak for second-chance romance. Iceland may be freezing cold, but this romance is scorching!"

—Mallory Marlowe, *USA Today* bestselling author of *Love and Other Conspiracies*

"Lush in both its prose and [its] setting, *Secret Nights and Northern Lights* swept me away. I adored these characters and their second chance at love, and felt completely immersed in their story and in Iceland! An absolutely swoony and special debut! Megan Oliver has a forever fan in me!"

—Naina Kumar, *USA Today* bestselling author of *Flirting with Disaster*

"A love letter to wanderlust and risk-taking, *Secret Nights and Northern Lights* is my favorite kind of second-chance romance: simmering with tension, banter, and well-earned growth—with a need for a subject change, he added, "So, Ryan Pearson, huh? How's that going?"

"Not great, Eric. Not great." Sadie made her way back to the sofa. "We're bickering over every decision and Simon is forced to act as our mediator. And of course the two of them are like BFFs already 'cause that's how Ryan operates, you know. Always making you feel special because that's how he sucks you into his little web of charm, then before you know it, you're stuck and there's no escape. I mean, I could play that game, too, if I wanted, but I have enough pride and enough maturity—"

She stopped short as one side of Eric's mouth lifted higher and higher. "What are you smirking at?"

"Okay, don't freak out on me for saying this." Circumventing the counter, he came to sit at her side, elbow propped against the back of the sofa and head resting against his fist. This was exactly how he sat whenever they were about to get into some *salacious* gossip. Like the time he overheard one of their brides on a not-so-innocent phone call with the best man. "Is there *any* chance you two might still . . . you know . . . be into each other?"

"Oh. My. God." Sadie slammed her cup down on the coffee table with such force the lid popped off. "No. *Hell no.* No possible way at all, sir!"

"Just hear me out." The devious spark in Eric's eyes was the same one he got the time he told her that a married mother of the bride was hooking up with her daughter's young, sexy wedding planner, and the two women were definitely more interested in *planning* steamy rendezvous than a sit-down dinner for five hundred. "The dynamic you're describing sounds like two schoolchildren teasing each other at recess to cover up their gigantic crushes on each other."

Gigantic crushes? No fucking way.

The insinuation alone made her cheeks heat, which she knew Eric would interpret as—

"See? You're blushing!"

"I'm not blushing!" She silently cursed both her fair skin and her overachieving circulatory system for being so transparent. "And no, I'm not into Ryan Pearson. He's literally the last person on earth I would go for. Besides, I don't even know if he's single."

Fuck. Now she'd implied that she'd thought about Ryan's relationship status. Which she definitely hadn't. Although . . . Okay, *maybe* she'd wondered about whatever happened with him and Lauren Scott. But she wasn't bitter. Just curious. Ryan Pearson dropped off the map during sophomore year.

"We can certainly find that out in about two seconds." Eric pulled his phone from the back pocket of his black denim jeans and started swiping.

In all the years they'd been running into each other, Sadie had never once looked up Ryan's social media accounts. Mainly because she couldn't fathom the horror of inconveniently fumbling her phone and accidentally hitting the follow button. Forget being naked in public or getting chased by a monster, Ryan receiving a notification that she'd followed him was the stuff real nightmares were made of.

"Hmmm," Eric mused, continuing to scroll. "If he's in a relationship, he isn't posting about it."

Sadie realized she'd been holding her breath, which was *Ri-dic-u-lous!* because she didn't care. Or maybe she did a little bit, but *only* because the idea of Ryan being happy and in love on top of his career success ate at her.

Seizing the opportunity—a device that couldn't be connected back to her—she grabbed Eric's phone and scrolled through the posts. There were photos of Ryan with other Pearson's guides—all in those matching, aggravating, boastful T-shirts—and some of Ryan with different pub crawl groups, taken in front of numerous bars throughout downtown.

What she hadn't expected were the scenic photos taken from various locations on the island. The old, abandoned lighthouse on the coast. A sunrise at the shore with a gull soaring over the horizon. The sprawling branches of a mossy oak at sunset. These weren't photos snapped on a whim, but ones taken with the intention to showcase the irrefutable beauty of the city.

Sadie didn't want to be impressed by yet another thing Ryan had a talent for, so she passed Eric his phone back. "It doesn't matter to me in the slightest if he's single or not. Neither of us has any interest in the other. The only thing between us is a mutual, respectable, long-standing hatred."

"Sure thing, darlin'." Eric tucked his phone back into the pocket of his jeans. "Keep telling yourself that."

CHAPTER 7

"Tickets are now live." Sadie would have sounded more celebratory if she hadn't been speaking through a yawn. Flipping her laptop closed, she rubbed at her burning eyes. It was late Friday night, or technically early Saturday morning now that she glimpsed her watch. *Shit*. She had to be at work again in eight hours, and there was still plenty to be done here at the mansion.

"We should celebrate," Simon declared with a chipper note of enthusiasm that was uncalled for at this hour.

Next to her in the circle they'd formed on the ballroom floor, Ryan stretched his arms overhead, the short sleeves of his T-shirt displaying the slow extension of his biceps. Sadie blinked away.

Despite the differing opinions she and Ryan had on nearly every topic, they'd managed to accomplish a good amount in the past three nights, but there was still so much to be done it made her nervous to think about it all. Tonight's tasks involved getting feedback from Ryan and Simon on the social media promotions she'd put together and enabling ticket purchases on the official website of the Wilmont House. She could now check those off her list, but that was only *her* agenda.

On Ryan's task list, he needed to finalize the layout for the furniture that was being delivered on Monday. And Simon's task for the night involved further exploring the mansion to determine the best places to plant clues.

"Simon," Sadie said through another yawn, "I appreciate the sentiment, but the only celebration I'm interested in at the moment is getting home to my bed."

Emphasizing her point, she reclined back against the hardwood floor and closed her eyes, not giving the slightest care to the dust that would surely cling to her black silk camisole, which she'd paired with wide-leg jeans and heeled slingbacks. It wasn't the usual button-up blouse and dress pants she wore every night to give her tours, but there was no harm in switching up her wardrobe while she had the opportunity. Because a change of routine would do her good. Not because of Eric's wildly off-base suggestion that Ryan might be "into" her.

She shoved all thoughts of her wardrobe selection out of mind. "I have to be back at Eric's shop in eight hours and we're not close to being finished here yet."

Begrudgingly opening her eyes, Sadie noticed Ryan had also stretched out on the floor. One large hand rested over his sternum, his luxuriously soft-looking shirt lying flat against his chest and abs, revealing every dip and groove of the muscles underneath. A thin slice of tanned skin was exposed between the hem of his shirt and the waistband of his jeans.

It was indecent.

Borderline pornographic.

"Why don't we split up then?" Simon suggested, and Sadie tore her gaze away from the X-rated display in front of her. "I'll check out each room while you two head to the cellar, okay?"

She didn't love that prospect. "Why don't I come with you instead?"

Simon's answering smile looked partly like a grimace. "I feel like you might . . . impede my process a little. No offense."

A low snicker from Ryan drew her attention back his way.

"And Ryan probably needs your help anyway," Simon rushed. "Right, Ryan? Don't you need Sadie's help?"

"*Desperately*," Ryan muttered, eyes still closed.

Sadie didn't have the energy to argue. She just wanted to get home as soon as possible. "Fine. Just let me know when you're finished so I can lock up."

"Of course. I won't leave without letting you know." Simon rose to his feet and headed for the nearest door.

"And remember," she called to him, "Hazel's writing room is off-limits!" Once he was gone, she sat up and dusted off her hands. "All right, Pearson, let's get to it so we can get to bed."

Lips sliding into a grin, Ryan pushed up onto his elbows. "My, my, Stockton. I don't remember you being that forward in college."

"You know what I meant," she sighed. "Can we just get this over with so we can both go to our *individual* beds in our *individual* homes?"

Standing, Ryan proffered a hand down to her. Purposely ignoring it, Sadie gathered her laptop, legal pad, and cell phone, then stood on her own.

* * *

Two stories below, Sadie's fingertips floated over the cool stones of the cellar wall as she made her way down the treacherous staircase in the cast-off light from the floor above, Ryan so close on her heels that she could smell the sandalwood scent of his soap.

It wasn't an unpleasant experience, but that wasn't the point. "Can you maybe give me a little space here?" She jostled her elbow backward, making her point when she connected with his ribs.

"Forgive me for wanting to ensure you don't fall down the dark staircase," Ryan replied.

"I'm the one who knows this place like the back of my hand. If anyone's going to fall down the steps, it's you."

"Then you'll be close by to break my fall."

"Does anyone ever tell you how infuriating you are, Pearson?"

"I'm not going to apologize for being chivalrous, Stockton."

"Can you apologize for breathing down my neck then?"

Ryan blew out a gusty sigh, the skin on the back of her neck pebbling in response. "I'll feel better once the lighting is installed. I can't believe you all haven't bothered with it until now. This place is a hazard."

Sconces for the stairwell along with a plethora of floor lamps would be delivered Monday with the furniture, and with the first tour scheduled in exactly a week, the timeline was tight. Proper lighting was one thing they couldn't function without, as they certainly couldn't risk any guests falling to their demise. Although, however morbid, that would likely make the house more popular to the murder mystery crowd.

Sadie shook off the thoughts of dead guests. "No one ever uses this space. And to be fair, I highly advocated against using it for this tour. This was all you and Simon."

Her foot met the bottom landing, and she counted off eleven paces before reaching above for the pull string to the single bulb. A second later, the grating yellow light illuminated their surroundings. Their gazes met, and Sadie wondered if Ryan, too, was thinking about when she'd stumbled into him the last time they stood in this spot. His reflexes were surprisingly quick to catch her full body weight in the dark. His forearm strong and sturdy around her waist. The ease with which he'd yanked her upright with the exact amount of force that was gentle enough while also confirming he'd have no problem being a little rough if that's what she wanted.

Ryan cleared his throat.

Sadie snapped out of it.

"Where's the tape measure?" he asked, voice raspier than normal. "I, uh, want to double-check we have room for all six high-tops over here." Turning away, he motioned to the open space to his left. "If not, we'll put the couches and chaises there and the tables on the other side."

"I don't have a tape measure," she replied, confused. "Why would *I* have a tape measure?"

He looked back at her with an equally perplexed expression. "Because *you're* the overseer of this entire project. As you have reminded me at least a dozen times thus far."

"And yet, I don't carry around a bag of random tools to whip out for your convenience. How shocking that must be."

Ryan bit down on his lower lip, though it was his tousled waves that took the brunt of his frustration as he buried a hand there. "I don't expect you to have a tape measure *on your body*." His eyes briefly skated down her before he cleared his throat again and jerked his gaze back to her face. "I assumed there would already be one here. At the mansion. Do you all keep tools anywhere?"

"Oh." She considered this. The groundskeeping tools were stored in a fenced-in shed at the far end of the courtyard. But maybe . . . "We can check the utility room. Follow me."

Sadie led the way to a nondescript gray door decently camouflaged into the surrounding stone wall, eyes slowly readjusting to the low light the farther away they traveled from the center of the cellar. The brass knob turned easily in her palm, and once inside she maneuvered her body around stacks of boxes as she reached overhead for the lightbulb. As light shone down on the cramped, cluttered space, the unmistakable click of the doorknob catching the latch made her stomach drop.

Spinning, she loudly demanded, "Don't let that door close!" though it was too late.

"*What? Why?*" Ryan asked with reactive alarm.

"The knob gets jammed from the inside." She pushed past him, barely able to thread herself between his body and a stack of plastic totes labeled CHRISTMAS in red Sharpie. "If you're in this room, *never* let the door close."

"A little warning would've been nice."

Reaching for the knob, Sadie hoped this would be the exception and not the rule. But she met resistance immediately. *Shit.*

"Well, I hope you're happy," she sighed, turning and squaring off against Ryan. "Now we're stuck here. Why would you close the door?"

"I didn't *close* the door. I just didn't prevent the door from closing. There's a difference. And how are we stuck? Knobs don't randomly not work for no reason."

Irritation spewed from her lips. "Please, *please* mansplain to me how this house works. I've only spent nearly every day here for the past five years."

"Then I'd think you'd know where a tape measure would be," he mumbled flatly.

Sadie's back teeth clenched. "If you would like to try and get us out of here, please be my guest."

Ryan studied her like the offer was a test.

It was.

One he failed miserably when he said, "Fine, move out of the way."

Sadie complied, although it was easier said than done. They performed an awkward shuffle that involved the brushing of their chests as they swapped places. Then Ryan bent forward and examined the knob, attempted to twist it several times. It didn't budge.

Eventually, he conceded, "It's stuck."

"Yeah. No shit."

When Ryan gave up and turned back her way, they were so close in the tightly packed space that Sadie folded her arms across her chest, needing *something* between them. "I left my phone upstairs," he said, "but if you have yours we can call Simon to let us out."

If only . . . "Mine's upstairs in my bag. Wouldn't matter anyway, there's no service down here. The stone walls are too thick."

"That makes sense." Ryan eyed the shelves stuffed with spray bottles and lightbulbs and other household items. Then his gaze fell to a vacuum cleaner whose handle pressed into her hip, and he subtly shifted to lean against a shelf at his back and open up more space for her.

"Thanks," she acknowledged, putting a couple steps between herself and the Dyson. "I guess now we just wait. Simon won't leave without us."

"Right." Ryan propped his hands on the shelf at his hips, his long legs stretched between them with nowhere else to go. "Since we have some time on our hands, tell me, you're really not happy about this murder mystery thing, are you?"

"No, I'm not," she admitted. "I think it's a shame that Mindy, and now Jerry, are using some fabricated scandal to profit off Hazel's legacy when the whole poisoned-Easter-ham rumor is the least interesting thing about her."

"Yeah?" The toe of Ryan's sneaker pressed against the tip of her heel. Sadie wasn't sure if it was intentional or a consequence of their lack of space. "Then tell me something about Hazel Wilmont I don't know."

"Why? So you can use it on your pub crawls?"

"No. Because I want to know. For myself."

Sadie hesitated, unable to determine if this was a genuine request or another way for him to toy with her.

"Come on, Stockton," he urged. "Share your knowledge with me. *Please?*"

"Fine," she relented, fully aware she might later regret it. "Let me think . . ." Whenever she had the opportunity to talk about Hazel's life—the part that didn't involve offensive rumors of poisoned ham—there was so much to say it was hard to narrow down. "Okay, did you know that despite publishing twenty-three children's books, Hazel had more than *fifty* unpublished projects in various stages of completion?"

Ryan's mouth curved into a grin. "I did not."

"Hazel began creating stories as soon as she learned how to write. Her parents assumed she was a daydreamer type and would eventually grow out of it, settle down, and take on the role of a proper housewife and mother. And her first husband, William Eubanks, wasn't exactly thrilled with her writing, either. He hated that she spent her time here on the island at their vacation home instead of their main home in Charlotte, caring more about her stories than her so-called *wifely duties*. He thought he should be the sole focus of her attention."

Ryan smirked. "What a dick."

"Oh, for sure. But Hazel never gave in to the pressure from him or her family. She knew exactly who she was and what she wanted to create, and she did just that, no matter what anyone else thought."

"Have you read them?" Ryan asked. "The unpublished works."

"Every word," Sadie proudly replied. "We put them on display once a year in the formal library to create buzz for ticket sales."

"Can I ask another question?"

She shrugged. "It appears we've got nothing else to do at the moment."

"It's not hard to see that you care, *a lot*, about your job here." He paused, as though he knew whatever he said next might be pressing his luck. "But what is it specifically about this place that gets to you?"

This conversation was venturing far deeper than Sadie cared to go, and she imagined Ryan had knowingly hesitated for that very reason. But there was a curiosity in his green eyes that pulled her in, a dangerous riptide in an otherwise serene ocean. "Hazel's books were my escape as a kid."

"Escape from what?" he asked, no hesitation this time.

"Oh, you know . . ." Sadie infused indifference into her voice. "Two parents who were always arguing. A father who constantly cheated on my mom and wasn't exactly good at hiding it."

After another moment, Ryan said, "I'm sorry."

With another casual shrug, Sadie dropped her gaze to where Ryan's sneaker still pressed against her shoe. "On the nights they'd start up about the hair clip my mom found in his truck, or how he was being a little *too* welcoming to the new neighbor, or how he'd had the audacity to flirt with the organist the one time he'd come to church all year, I'd sneak a flashlight and one of Hazel's books under my comforter. The stories she wove on the page were captivating enough to block out everything else. At least for a little while."

Blinking up, she realized how much she'd revealed about herself and swallowed hard, cheeks blooming with heat. One of her struggles in social situations was never recognizing the line between sharing and oversharing, but wherever or whatever it was, she was pretty sure she'd just crossed it.

"You, um, never told me any of this." As Ryan spoke, he ran a hand along the back of his neck and then up into his hair. "Back then, I mean. When we were—"

"Yeah, I know." Sadie didn't want him to finish that sentence. If she'd made it awkward by oversharing, he'd upped the ante and made it unbearable. Heat pumped through her body, veins transforming into boiling jet streams. The space was too cramped, too confined. Usually freezing cold, tonight this stone dungeon was a furnace. "Anyway, it was a long time ago. My dad moved away when I was in middle school."

Ryan appraised her in a way she wasn't sure she cared for. "That must have been really tough for you."

"It's fine. I wouldn't expect you to understand." She hadn't meant to sound combative, necessarily. Or maybe on some level she had. The fact she was engaging in a personal conversation with Ryan Pearson was unsettling, and it was better if she set them back on the right track, the familiar track. They were adversaries, after all, not friends—something Ryan himself had been quick to point out. No more falling for his mind games.

"What's that supposed to mean?" Ryan matched her antagonistic tone, and for some reason, that set her at ease. "Because my parents are still married my life must be nothing but rainbows and butterflies?"

"Well, that *and* the fact your family is loaded." Maybe Ryan's life wasn't perfect, but in college he'd always had nice clothes and money to go out despite not having a job. If there was one thing gained from growing up without a lot of money, it was the ability to instantly recognize those who had it in abundance. Those who never thought about it, because they had the luxury of never *needing* to think about it.

Ryan folded his arms over his chest, briefly drawing her attention to his forearms. "I don't know if 'loaded' is the right word."

Sadie narrowed her eyes. "Do they own a boat?" she asked on a hunch.

"What does that have to do—"

"Do your parents own a boat, Pearson?"

"I mean, yes, but—"

"Then they're loaded."

Ryan shook his head, and a frustrated groan tore from his throat. *This* was more like it. "So because my parents are married and have a *fucking boat*, I've had it easy my whole life. Is that right?"

"I assume one's troubles must look pretty far away from the deck of a yacht."

Another groan. Then, "And here I was actually trying to get to know you again. But you always have to be like this."

Sadie might have felt a tad remorseful if she didn't know better. "Please. To get to know me *again*, you would've needed to know me in the first place. Which you didn't. We used to hook up, that's it. You just want this project to go well for *you*. For whatever reason you're still keeping a secret from me, by the way. So it works best if I'm under your spell. That's all this is."

"My *spell*?" Anger flashed in Ryan's eyes. Pushing away from the shelf, he stood to his full height, bringing their bodies within inches as he towered over her. "What the actual fuck, Stockton? I assumed after all these years that maybe you'd changed. Clearly, I was wrong."

The words plucked a nerve, even if she wasn't sure what he

meant by them. But the only response she could muster up was, "Yeah, well, neither have you."

Ryan scoffed. "Let's just wait for Simon to find us."

"Fine by me."

"Fine."

And it was fine. More than fine. It was a welcome relief, really. She could stand in that utility closet and stare at her feet without uttering a single word for hours if necessary.

It was a solid plan.

At least until an odd hissing sound cut through the silence and the lightbulb shut off, leaving the cramped space completely dark.

Chapter 8

Startled, Sadie grabbed what felt like Ryan's forearm on pure instinct as déjà vu swept through her. "I, uh, I told you, the mansion has some faulty electrical . . . stuff. No need to be alarmed."

Despite her words, Sadie was a tad alarmed. It was the middle of the fucking night, after all, and they were stuck in a closet with three feet of shared floor space and a darkness so consuming she couldn't make out the shape of Ryan's body across from her, which was close enough to touch. And she was . . . touching. But Ryan hadn't pulled away, either, so she was perfectly willing to pretend it wasn't actually happening while continuing to clutch his forearm like a security blanket.

"So, how long do you suppose Simon might be?" she asked. "Can't be that long, right?"

"It's a twelve-thousand-square-foot mansion. We might be here awhile."

"No, no, no!" Desperation seized her in a vise grip. It was one thing to be stuck in a cramped closet. But stuck in a cramped closet in the complete dark . . . *with him? Un-fucking-acceptable!*

Releasing Ryan's arm, she flailed her own arm overhead, intent to pull that fucking chain as many times as it took to get the light back on. But before her hand connected with the chain, her elbow connected—*hard!*—with something that felt an awful lot like a face.

Ryan's face?

"Fucking hell!"

Yep, it was Ryan's face.

"Oh my god, oh my god, oh my god!" she exclaimed. "Are you okay?"

A slow hiss cut through the air in response, one that sounded like Ryan pulling his breath through his teeth.

"That was a total accident. I'm *so* sorry!" Arm now free of obstacles—at the expense of Ryan's face apparently—Sadie located the chain and pulled repeatedly. Somewhere around the twentieth desperate tug, the light flicked on again. Once her eyes adjusted, she gasped.

Ryan's hand covered his right eye, the left blinking rapidly. In her desperation to not be stuck in the dark with Ryan Pearson, her elbow had made direct contact with his orbital bone. Now Sadie was stuck in the light with an injured, brooding Ryan Pearson, which was *way* worse, and from the look in his one healthy eye, she was in for it.

"What the hell, Stockton?" he accused.

"It was an accident!" She covered her grimace behind her hands. "I didn't realize you were like, *right there*. Sorry."

Leaning his body weight against the shelf at his hips, Ryan again created the maximum amount of possible space between them. Probably for his own protection.

"But, hey, look." She pointed upward. "Light works now. See?" *Look* and *see* perhaps not the best word selections at the moment.

Ryan swallowed, and there was the tiniest twitch at the corner of his mouth.

"Can I take a look?" she asked, jutting her chin in his direction.

"I suppose," he replied, not sounding any more thrilled about it than she was. But she needed to make sure he was actually okay. Though if he wasn't, she certainly didn't have any medical training to lean upon other than a babysitter's first aid course taken when she was thirteen. Somehow that skill set didn't seem applicable here, and she couldn't recall the exact steps for making a splint out of household objects anyway.

With Ryan halfway sitting on the shelf, they were at eye level, his legs sloped between them. For Sadie to get where she needed to be, the only option . . .

Watching the dilemma play out over her face, Ryan spread his feet apart. "No need to get shy on me now. We've been a lot closer than this before, sans clothing."

The bold reminder both infuriated her and made her stomach swoop, and goddammit, where the hell was Simon?

"You look a little flushed," Ryan continued, the cadence of his voice fully restored to the teasing tone he always seemed to have for her. "You okay?"

"Perfectly fine." Sadie maneuvered herself between Ryan's denim-clad thighs. "It's just sweltering in this fucking closet."

But it wasn't fine, not really, because once in place Ryan's face was mere inches from hers, his legs bracketing her sides, his chest and shoulders *right there*. Memories flooded her mind at once: Ryan's specific knock on her dorm room door, his mouth on hers the second she pulled it open, the way he'd walk her backward to the tiny bed they barely fit in while they clutched and groped at each other in a game of who could undress the other quickest.

But they'd been young at the time.

It hadn't meant anything.

Yet, this close together, they both fell silent, and Sadie knew without a doubt that Ryan remembered it all, too.

Then Ryan's hand fell away from his eye, and Sadie cringed as guilt rippled through her at the sight. His chiseled cheekbone was marred with an angry red blotch, but it was his swollen lower lid that worried her most. Water accumulated at the corner of his eye, clumping his lashes.

"Oh dear god!" she exclaimed. "*I broke your face!*"

Despite his gruesome injury, Ryan let out a short, raspy laugh. "Don't give yourself that much credit. My face will be just fine."

The way he struggled to keep the wounded eye open made her doubt the validity of that statement. "I feel *awful*. I promise it was an accident."

"Despite your deep hatred of me, I don't believe you'd resort to violence." When she didn't make any snarky comeback, his expression sobered. "Hey. I promise I believe you. I'm okay."

"I just . . . I wasn't thinking." Still not thinking, Sadie grazed the pad of her middle finger underneath his cheekbone. "Does this hurt?"

When Ryan shook his head, the sandpaper texture of his jaw brushed against the soft curve of her palm, and it was oddly pleasant.

"And here?" Her finger trailed up along his temple. "It just occurred to me— Is it possible I gave you a *concussion*?"

"No," he said through another raspy laugh. "I don't have a concussion from your elbow."

"Okay, good. That's good." Just to be thorough in her exam, and not because awareness was slowly overtaking her concern, she stroked her finger above his brow. "All good up here, too?"

Ryan swallowed. "All good."

With no other plausible reason to keep touching him, her arm fell away, along with her gaze, and that's when she noticed Ryan's hands gripping his thighs, fingertips blanched white. Perhaps he was in more pain than he was letting on.

"Hey, Stockton." His voice was a gravelly whisper. "You look really nice tonight."

Sadie's head jerked up. "*What?* What does *that* mean?"

Brows drawn together as though he was the confused one, Ryan replied, "It means I think you look really nice tonight." He tugged at the side of her camisole. Just once, but it was enough to send her stomach into free fall.

"I . . . um . . ."

"Just take the compliment," he sighed. "And I can't see all that well at the moment, so I could be totally off base."

"You jackass." Her palm forcefully met his shoulder as she shoved him backward, not that there was anywhere for him to go.

Smiling now, Ryan captured her wrist and swept it behind her body, pinning it against the small of her back in one smooth motion. He didn't let go, but his grip was loose enough that she could pull away at any time if she wanted. The problem was that her body didn't seem all that interested in extracting itself from her current placement.

"It was a joke," Ryan said as his eyes swept the low-cut neckline of her camisole. "I actually noticed how good you look long before you maimed my eye."

"Oh."

Suddenly all Sadie could think of was Eric's insinuation that there was still some kind of attraction between her and Ryan. Ever since he'd brought it up, the suggestion lingered in the back of her mind, stuck like the remnants of chewing gum one can never completely scrape from the bottom of their shoe. Was the idea so off base? She was standing between Ryan's thighs. He had her wrist pinned behind her back. She wasn't pulling away. Neither was he.

Her heart raced. Could Ryan feel it in the pulse point on her wrist?

"You know," he rasped, and god that voice was starting to do things to her. Half of Ryan's charm might've been from that Southern drawl alone. "We're gonna be working together for the next month. Closely. Maybe we should make a friendly truce. For the sake of the project."

"What are the terms?" Her heart rate was beginning to feel dangerously high, and she had no idea how to slow it. Again, something that babysitter's course skipped right over.

"I didn't draw up a contract. Just saying." His thumb swiped across her inner wrist, and she nearly moaned. "I can play nice if you can."

Warmth pooled between her legs.

Ryan's gaze fell to her mouth.

This was quickly spinning out of control. Had he intended for his offer of a truce to sound that provocative? Was he flirting with her or fucking with her? There was no way to know.

His grip on her wrist tightened, and his forearm flexed around her waist, drawing her even closer to his chest. Then he dipped his head and whispered next to her ear, "Tell me to let go, Stockton."

Breaths heavy, she inhaled the sandalwood scent that only made her desperate to get closer instead of farther away. So she couldn't tell Ryan to let go. Partially because she didn't trust what might come out of her mouth if she opened it, but mainly because she didn't *want* him to let go. Which was definitely a predicament.

When she didn't respond, Ryan eased back until their gazes caught. And Sadie wondered if the heat in her eyes was as obvious as the heat in his.

"Yeah," he said. "That's what I thought."

Suddenly the closet door flew open and Simon appeared in the doorway. "Friends, I've been looking *everywhere* for you two!"

Sadie jerked out of Ryan's grasp, moving as far away from him as she could in the cramped space. And *fuck*, she could only imagine what their positioning looked like to Simon.

If Simon noticed though, he didn't say anything, instead taking in the more pressing issue of Ryan's face as his eyes went wide. "*What happened?!* I swear to god I leave you two alone for a few minutes and *disaster* strikes? I'm—"

"It's okay," Ryan assured him. "Small accident. No disaster. It's all good."

Simon looked back and forth between them. "Well, come along then. I need to show you both something."

* * *

Upstairs, Simon led them to the dining room.

"I was up here doing my thing, because obviously we have to plant something in the dining room. I mean, come on." Stopping in front of the fireplace, he turned to them. "Then I remembered that when I was here for the meeting something felt off about *that* mirror." His arm flailed in an upward diagonal motion as he pointed at the gold-framed mirror above the mantel.

Sadie exchanged a glance with Ryan, mystified as to where this was going.

"Then I got to looking at it again," Simon continued, turning on his heels to pace the length of the fireplace. "Sure enough, my suspicions were confirmed."

"Um, what suspicions?" Sadie asked.

"That things aren't as they appear in this house."

"I have no idea what you're talking about."

"I shall enlighten you then." Turning to the mirror, Simon spread his hands along the bottom of the massive frame. Then he began rocking each side back and forth. "It doesn't lie completely flat against the wall. See?"

"Simon, please be careful." Visions of the priceless antique shattered on the dining room floor sprang to Sadie's mind. "That's original to the home."

"Oh, I could've guessed that. Because there's something hidden behind it."

"I really don't think—" Sadie stopped speaking as Ryan stepped up to examine the mirror, too.

"I think he's right," Ryan said, attempting to slide a hand behind the frame. "There's only a few centimeters of space, but there's definitely something behind this mirror."

"We need to take it down," Simon said. "Ryan, help me lift it."

"I'll take this side." Ryan moved into position, bracing one hand to the bottom and the other along the side of the frame. "You get that one."

"Wait, wait, wait!" Sadie exclaimed. "That is a very heavy, likely priceless mirror you two want to casually remove from the place it's hung for decades. If that mirror is harmed in any way, it's going to be *me* who has to explain it to Evelyn and Mindy and Jerry."

"I swear we'll be careful," Ryan said earnestly. "We won't let anything happen to it."

Simon added, "Don't you want to know what could be behind here?"

If something was behind that mirror, then of course she wanted to know. Even if it was likely nothing of importance. "Fine. But if something ends up broken, don't think I won't drag you two under the bus with me."

"Fair enough," Simon replied, getting into position again. "All right, Ryan, on the count of three. One . . . two . . . three!"

The two men hoisted the mirror upward, and Sadie closed her eyes and held her breath until Simon exclaimed, "I knew it!" When she opened her eyes again, the mirror was safely propped against the wall and Simon clutched a thick envelope in his hands. "This was tucked into the back of the frame. Look, Sadie!"

He passed the envelope to her.

Stunned into silence, Sadie carefully opened the folded-over top, then pulled out a stack of papers. Yellowed around the edges and softened with age, they felt as though they might disintegrate under her touch. And all she could do was stare at them in wonder, eyes refusing to focus on any specific words.

"Simon, why don't you help me get this mirror back up?" she heard Ryan say in the background, followed by the shuffling sounds of the two men hefting the mirror back to its proper location.

Yet, she couldn't look away to ensure they were being cautious with the precious antique. All she could do was stare down at the papers in her hands, the typewriter font legible if only she could focus. After a few deep breaths and some hard blinks, her eyes caught on a sentence midway down the page.

Once Alice found Harriett's journal, she would have her proof.

"Uh, you guys . . ." Sadie's focus remained on the delicate pages as she carefully flipped through them. "I think I'm holding one of Hazel's unpublished manuscripts."

"Oh wow," Simon said. "That's . . . unexpected."

"Were any of the other unpublished ones hidden like this?" Ryan asked.

"No," she answered, bewildered. "The others were stored in her writing room." So why would Hazel purposely hide this one? "And this appears to be the middle of the story. There's no beginning or end. From what I know about Hazel, she was a linear writer."

Mind whirling, Sadie's thoughts were like flying debris in a tornado. Here for a nanosecond before disappearing into the chaos. "Can we be done here for the night? There's no way I can focus on anything else until I read these pages and figure out what's going on."

Tearing her eyes away from the manuscript, Sadie caught Simon and Ryan exchange a glance. And she knew what they were thinking. They were up against an almost impossible deadline, and every hour, *every minute*, was precious. But they'd possibly just discovered brand-new words from Hazel Wilmont more than a half century after her death, and Sadie's hands shook from the need to be the first person to ever read those words.

"Sure," Ryan eventually said.

"Yeah, of course," Simon agreed.

"Thank you," she sighed in relief. "We'll get it all done. I swear."

Then Sadie gathered her belongings, along with the precious pages, and led them to the front porch to lock up, not bothering to do a walk-through to turn off the lights.

CHAPTER 9

After a restless night, Sadie's heels clicked down the sidewalk toward Eric's shop, their coffees clutched precariously in her hands, the sun high above in a cloudless blue sky, the heat already bearing down on her skin. She'd stayed up way too late reading and rereading the pages they discovered at the mansion, and it was clear they were the words of Hazel Wilmont—Sadie recognized her voice on the page immediately. But what wasn't clear was the storyline. Without a beginning or an ending, all Sadie deciphered was that one sister was searching for the other sister's diary.

Reaching the store, Sadie shifted both coffees to one hand to dig her keys out of the bottomless pit of her tote bag—a feat mastered thanks to years of waiting tables throughout college. Today, though, her coordination was sluggish, and as she pulled her key ring through the tangle of pens and lip glosses, she lost control of her balancing act.

The next moment, she stood on the sidewalk with two empty to-go cups at her feet and napkins scattered around her like fallen leaves. Coffee swirled underneath her heels, was splattered up her gray slacks, and formed a very large, very hot, dinosaur-shaped blot that soaked through her favorite silk blouse.

"Fuck, fuck, fuck!" Hunching her shoulders forward, she yanked the fabric away from her skin so it wouldn't burn.

Through the glass Sadie watched Eric approach, stop as he took in the scene, then double over with laughter, not even trying to hide his amusement. Or offer any help. From the other side of the glass, she flipped him off.

Eventually, he composed himself and pushed through the door. "Rough morning?"

"You could say that."

"Uh, is this a bad time?" a familiar voice asked from behind her.

Sadie spun around in the coffee puddle.

Simon, a shy smile on his face, stood on the sidewalk before her. Next to him was Ryan, hands shoved deep in the pockets of his jeans, face partially concealed by a navy baseball cap pulled low.

What the hell?

There was no escaping this man lately.

"Uh, no, not a bad time." She managed a smile as she fanned out her blouse. "Just a bit of clumsiness on my part. What are you all doing here?"

Stepping forward, Ryan extended a hand toward Eric. "Since Stockton clearly wasn't going to introduce us, I'm Ryan, by the way. So rude of her."

Sadie ignored the way Eric's eyes flashed back to hers as he shook Ryan's hand. "I was going to introduce you, Pearson. You didn't give me time." Her back teeth ground together but her smile held firm.

Also not giving her time, Simon stepped forward and introduced himself next. "I watch every season of *Runway Wars*," he told Eric. "It's an honor to meet you."

"You as well," Eric replied. "You want to see the store?"

Simon's face lit up. "I'd love to!"

"Come on in." Eric held the door open as Simon carefully stepped around the puddle.

"Don't mind me," Sadie muttered. "I'll just clean this mess up."

"I'll help," Ryan offered, kneeling and reaching for some paper napkins.

"Thanks, but I don't need help." Giving up on fanning her blouse, she crouched down and scooped up a plastic lid.

"Really?" Ryan tilted his head back, sunlight illuminating the side of his face enough to reveal the dark purple bruise highlighting the curve of his under-eye. "Because you certainly looked like you could use some help when we arrived."

"Well, I don't." Unfortunately, she leaned too far forward to stretch for a red stirrer and ended up planting her palm in the middle of the coffee puddle to maintain balance.

"Sure about that?" Ryan asked.

From above, Eric asked, "Are they always like this?"

"Every day," Simon replied with an air of defeat. "Every. Single. Day."

"Bless their hearts," Eric uttered as the shop door closed behind them.

Ryan picked up a sopping wet napkin. "Why do you always insist on being so stubborn? I'm only trying to help."

The truth of the matter was that Sadie was more than a little off-kilter today. Between the found pages of Hazel's manuscript and the moment in the closet with Ryan, it was all she could do this morning to focus. Her mind was all too busy recalling the way Ryan's thighs parted to let her close, the suggestive tug of her camisole between his fingers, how easily he'd pinned her arm behind her back. She'd even headed out her door this morning with two different shoes on before realizing she was walking lopsided and hightailing it back inside to change.

So seeing Ryan in the flesh was definitely not what she needed right now, nor was the heat that stirred inside her all over again. Alas . . .

Once the mess of litter was tossed in a nearby sidewalk trash can, Sadie nodded toward the shop. "Come on, I'll show you where we can clean up."

She led Ryan through the showroom to the single employee bathroom in the back of the building and held the door open with the back of her hand, indicating it was okay to follow her inside. They made their way to the sink, Ryan's hands held aloft like a scrubbed-up surgeon entering the operating room. As he twisted the faucet on to wash his hands, Sadie pulled a handful of paper towels from the dispenser and dabbed at the massive stain on her blouse.

"No one answered my question," she said. Despite her efforts, her favorite blouse was likely ruined. "What are you two doing here?"

Ryan shut off the water and reached around her to pull a paper towel from the dispenser. "Jerry didn't text you?"

A pit opened in her stomach. She paused her pointless cleanup effort, catching Ryan's gaze in the mirror. "Um, no, he didn't text me. About what?"

After tossing his balled-up paper towel in the trash can, Ryan turned her way with a clear expression of discomfort. "Jerry pulled some strings and got the electricians moved up to today to install the outlets we'll need in the cellar. I assumed he texted you, too. Simon's riding over with me 'cause his car's in the shop, and we were stopping by on our way to see if you had any specific instructions you wanted us to pass along."

The pit in her stomach filled with fury. "Nope. I had no idea about any of this. And how is that going to work? The mansion opens to the public at ten, they can't have electricians traipsing around with people there."

"Jerry said he's closing the estate until the electricians are done for the day."

The Wilmont House wasn't opening for the first time since the hurricane four years ago and nobody bothered to inform her?

Sadie dabbed at the stain on her blouse again, this time with much more force. "Well, that's lovely no one told *me*. I'm only the overseer of this entire project. That's just fan-fucking-tastic." Frustrated, she discarded the useless paper towels and then roughly yanked the corner of her blouse toward the faucet. A loud groan rumbled deep in her throat when it wouldn't reach. "You've gotta be fucking kidding me!"

Releasing the wrinkled, wet blouse, she leaned against the counter and dropped her head, inhaling slow and deep.

After a few seconds, she heard a low "Hey, Stockton, look at me."

Embarrassed and angry, that was the last thing she wanted to do. But she lifted her eyes anyway.

"If it makes you feel any better," Ryan said, "I swear I'll make sure everything gets done correctly."

"Thanks, but that doesn't really help." She turned on the faucet and washed the coffee residue from her hands. As she dried them, she caught Ryan grinning in the mirror. "What? Why are you smiling?"

"Give me your number."

"Why?" Up until that point, they'd agreed on meeting times and locations and there hadn't been a need to exchange numbers. She'd planned to continue that for the duration of the project.

But Ryan pulled his phone from the pocket of his jeans and

thrust it toward her. "I'll text you photos and updates the whole time. If anything doesn't look right just let me know and I'll have them change it."

"I don't get it." She narrowed her eyes suspiciously on the device. "Why are you being nice to me? It's disorienting."

"Don't get carried away, I'm not that nice." For some reason that statement sounded far more sexual to Sadie than it should have. "Again, I have a vested interest in making sure this all goes well."

An interest he still hadn't shared with her, and she was determined to figure it out sooner rather than later.

"Just give me your number," he pressed. "I'm sure I'll need it at some point over the next month anyway."

Being that he was likely right, Sadie took Ryan's unlocked phone, ignoring the sense of déjà vu that swept over her as she typed her number into his contacts. Until, just like freshman year, his fingers brushed hers when she passed it back, and a spark ignited across her skin.

"See, told you I can play nice," he said, a suggestive tease in his tone that she swore hadn't been there only a moment ago.

Warmth rippled through her. "I—I can play nice, too," she replied, voice tripping over the bass drum in her chest.

"So we agree then?" Ryan stepped closer, their bodies nearly brushing, and Sadie's head fell back to look up at him. "We can be *friendly* while we work together?"

Maybe it was the way his earthy green eyes focused on her mouth, or the way he pulled his plush lower lip between his teeth as they did. Or maybe it was the way heat throbbed at her pulse points, shooting fire through her veins with each beat. But she heard herself match his suggestive tone and reply, "How *friendly* would you like to be?"

A low groan rose from Ryan's throat, but that was the only

reaction she got because at that exact moment Simon burst through the door unannounced. Ryan took three steps back as Sadie straightened her posture.

"Guess what?" Simon's eyes danced behind his glasses. "Eric invited us all to that new haunted house next week for Charity's birthday. *Supermodel Charity Chase!* Can you even believe it?"

* * *

That afternoon when there was a lull in the store's traffic, Sadie found Eric between rows of gowns, sorting dresses back into place after being pulled for try-ons. "What's this about a haunted house?" she asked, skipping any preamble.

Earlier when Simon barged into the bathroom, Sadie had been so caught off guard she'd simply replied, "Sounds great," and then ran away as if her life depended on escaping those four walls. Now that she'd managed to (mostly) shove the bathroom encounter into the deep recesses of her brain alongside the closet encounter, she realized she had no earthly idea what he'd been talking about.

"Charity's birthday party." Eric placed a sheath-style gown back on the rack in front of him. "Some of her model friends are flying down from New York so we're grabbing drinks and then checking out that new haunted house that opened last weekend. She's been talking about it since she saw an ad weeks ago. You know how she loves anything horror-related."

Sadie did know. In fact, she'd been conned into catching a movie with the couple once before, only to find herself covering her eyes through the majority of some grotesque slasher film. "Okay, but why invite Simon? You just met him."

Eric moved farther down the row. "I'm just trying to help you bond with your new coworker."

Sadie stood with her arms crossed over her chest until he finished straightening a long-sleeved lace number and finally looked her way. "That's bullshit."

"Okay, maybe a little bit," he admitted with a sly grin. "But since I invited Simon, it wasn't weird to also invite Ryan Pearson."

"And why would you invite Ryan?"

Instead of answering, he asked, "Why were you two in the bathroom for so long?"

"Nothing happened."

"Sure, sure."

"It didn't!"

"Well"—he had the audacity to wink at her—"maybe it will at Charity's party."

Sadie's jaw dropped. "You know what? I'm not even sure I can make the party. I have work to do at the mansion."

"Please be serious," he scoffed. "There's no way you aren't showing up for Charity's birthday."

It had been an empty threat from the get-go. Sadie was quite fond of Charity, even if her supermodel schedule meant they'd never had a chance to get to know each other all that well. "When is it?"

"Wednesday night."

"*This* Wednesday?" That was two days before opening night. She'd probably be drowning trying to get everything finished at that point. "And you're just mentioning this now?"

The chime on the front door alerted them that they had a customer. Eric straightened another hanger on the rack then took off toward the front of the store, his last words trailing over his shoulder. "Can't wait to tell Charity about this latest development. And by the way, wear something hot."

CHAPTER 10

Ryan Pearson was in her *apartment*.

All of twenty feet from her *bed*.

An occasion that definitely called for alcohol.

True to his word, Ryan had texted her updates throughout the day, which she appreciated. And when Sadie had returned to the estate after work, she'd found Simon and Ryan chatting in the courtyard, the electricians all finished up. Ryan had suggested a few restaurants for their nightly meetup. But Sadie was exhausted and had been wearing her coffee-stained blouse so long it had partially adhered to her skin. Instead, she suggested they go up to her apartment in the guesthouse, and Simon and Ryan had ordered delivery while Sadie changed into her favorite matching sweats.

"This place is so cool," Simon commented as Sadie pulled three wineglasses down from the open shelves in her kitchen.

"Thanks," she replied, grabbing an unopened bottle of sauvignon blanc from the fridge. "It's small but it works for me." She slipped the glass stems between her fingers and carried them to the table, then passed one to Simon and one to Ryan.

"It gives me chills to think about Hazel living her everyday life here." Simon's round eyes drifted along the wooden beams that ran the length of the ceiling. "All that history . . ."

Sadie looked past Simon to the living room area, where the shelves of her media console were filled with her personal copies of Hazel's books. Ones so worn the titles were no longer legible on the spines. "Yeah, I know what you mean."

But it was a different history that made her stomach pull uncomfortably tight. The shouting that echoed off the walls of her childhood home. Pulling her comforter over her head as if that might absorb the noise. Switching on the flashlight she'd stolen from the kitchen's junk drawer—not that anyone ever noticed—and repeating the words from the page aloud to herself. *Keep your courage close. Keep your courage close. Keep your courage close.*

"You want help with that?"

At Ryan's voice, Sadie blinked back to the present, and to the wine bottle in her hand. "Sure. Let me grab a corkscrew."

Sometime after midnight, Sadie dropped her pen onto the legal pad in front of her and rotated her wrist to relieve the aching burn from hours of note-taking. They'd formulated an hour-by-hour structure for the tour (something she thought they should have done *long* before now, but whatever), though it wasn't without disagreement.

The murder mystery experience—which they were now calling the Wilmont House Mixtures and Murder Tour—would begin at midnight in the grand foyer with introductions, a welcome cocktail, and Sadie slipping each guest a notecard with information about the character they'd each play that evening. From there,

Sadie would lead the guests on a sixty-minute tour through the mansion so they all became familiar with the layout and history of the home.

Sadie's portion would end in the cellar for cocktail hour, where Ryan would provide a couple more drinks and share some of his mixologist knowledge along with recommendations for bars and pubs in the city.

Next up would be showtime. This is where their plans diverged and sat at a current standstill. As lead on the murder mystery, Simon insisted he needed both Sadie and Ryan to fill roles in the game in order to make it a success. Sadie was not about that. It was one thing to oversee this project, it was another to role-play a sexy museum curator whose affair with a local antiques dealer gets her offed at the end of cocktail hour. Or whatever Simon had planned.

"I promise you, Simon," she stated her case for at least the third time, "you *do not* want me acting in anything. And I'm going to be way too busy ensuring our guests are taken care of to participate in this . . . game."

"I prefer to call it an act of fiction," Simon retorted, tone sharp. "'Cause we're *acting* and it's *fiction*."

"No matter what you call it, I'm not doing it."

"I can't make this work without a few other actors," Simon insisted. "What am I supposed to do?"

"Why don't you ask *him*?" Sadie pointed her index finger directly at Ryan, whose brows shot up like *What did I do*? "As I recall, I wanted to have all of this sorted the very first night we met, but no, no, no. You two are the ones who put this off until now. Now opening night is in a week, and you're telling me you don't know how this is going to operate?"

"I know *how* it operates," Simon countered. "I just need a couple other actors. That's all."

"Well, it isn't going to be me," she reiterated. "If Ryan wants to participate in this game—"

"Act of fiction," Simon huffed.

"—that's up to him."

Simon looked to Ryan, desperation in his eyes.

"Uhhh . . ." Ryan winced so hard his eyes crinkled at the corners. "The thing is, I'll be serving drinks right up until the *murder* happens. I don't think I can be both bartender and actor."

Simon slumped in his chair.

"So, what now?" Sadie asked gently. Disappointing Simon really did suck.

"I guess I can ask some of the actors from my improv group," Simon said. "I don't know any of them that well though."

"That sounds like a great idea!" Sadie wanted to lift his spirits in any way she could. "Surely a couple of them would want to participate in a paid gig, right? How many are in your group?"

"Four."

Oh.

"Not including me, though," he added.

The numbers were not in their favor. "Okay, why don't you check with them tomorrow and let me know," she suggested. "If it's a no, we'll figure something else out."

Simon nodded, but his normal cheery enthusiasm was long gone.

Across the table, Ryan pulled off his baseball cap, ran a hand through his matted hair, and replaced the hat with the brim turned toward the back. He looked as tired as she felt, even more so with the dark purple shadow her elbow had left imprinted under one eye. Yet somehow, he was still gorgeous. Unfairly gorgeous. The kind of gorgeous that made her stomach flip every time his knee bumped hers underneath her too-small kitchen table.

Ryan caught her watching then, and her stomach bottomed out once more as she blinked away. If they were going to spend the next month working together, she had to find a way to tame this internal roller coaster or she was going to spend every day nauseated.

"I think it's about time to call it a night," Ryan said, stretching his arms overhead.

"Agreed." Sadie stood and collected their empty glasses. "We got a lot accomplished tonight," she added to sound optimistic and hopefully erase the frown from Simon's face. "There are always a few hiccups in planning something like this, but it will all work out."

It better work out. Her job likely depended on it.

"Yeah, I guess." Simon made his way around the table, the usual pep in his step notably absent. "I'm gonna get going. I'll see you all tomorrow." He slow-walked out her apartment door, even his footsteps sounding melancholy as they echoed down the staircase.

Ryan moved around her tiny table, mouth slightly tilted. "At some point, he's going to realize I'm his ride home." He gathered their remaining plates and set them in the sink.

Now that they were alone, tension curled between them, slinking its way up her body like a boa constrictor intent on its next kill. "I feel like I really let him down."

Turning from the sink, Ryan's eyes settled on hers. "You're right, though. There's no way you can make sure all the guests are taken care of and take part in the game. It's too much."

"Thanks for saying that."

He lifted a shoulder. "It's the truth. I should go check on him, though. I'll see you tomorrow."

Sadie followed him on the short journey to the door, anticipating the moment she could lock it behind him and her stomach could settle. Unfortunately, Ryan stopped short and she collided with the broad expanse of his back. Immediately, she backed up, but not before getting a hit of sandalwood from his T-shirt. The scent was familiar from college, but there was something more sophisticated about it now, something more adult. "Sorry about that."

He rounded on her. "My fault. Shouldn't have stopped like that. It's just . . ."

"What?" Her heart thudded in anticipation of whatever he was about to say, but Ryan let the moment linger between them. When she couldn't take his piercing green eyes anymore, she urged, "Get on with it, Pearson."

"It's just . . . The closet . . . Then the bathroom—"

No, no, no, no, no.

"—Is something happening here?"

She feigned confusion. "I don't know what you're talking about."

"Pretty sure you do." A knowing grin played over his lips. "I think you may have been flirting with me."

Her face was scorched by now, no doubt a shade of scarlet reserved for clown noses or medically alarming sunburns. "I wasn't flirting with you. I was simply agreeing to maintain a friendly decorum while we're forced to work together."

That hadn't been what she'd meant at all. She had one hundred percent been flirting with him, as hard as that was to admit. But he had flirted with her, too, and he wasn't owning up to that little fact, either. Ryan Pearson had gotten the best of her once before—she wasn't about to let him do it again.

"Really?" he asked, clearly skeptical. "Because it felt a lot like a conversation we had once before."

Oh dear god. How her skin wasn't melting by now, she didn't know.

What she did know was the exact conversation he was referring to, the very first time he'd come to her dorm room in their college days. They'd watched one of those *Final Destination* movies and eaten popcorn in the glow of a tiny Christmas tree she hadn't yet put away. She'd been so nervous she couldn't pay attention to the movie, and when he'd started to leave afterward, she was gravely disappointed. After flirting with her mercilessly all semester and texting her nonstop over break, *that was it*? He wasn't even going to kiss her?

As they stood by her door about to part ways, she'd gathered her courage and said, "So I guess we're just going to be friends then."

Ryan had tilted his head, expression somewhat perplexed. "You're not exactly easy to read, Stockton, and I'm trying to be a gentleman here. I'll be okay with being just friends if that's what you want. If you want more, I need you to tell me."

"No, I want to be . . . *friends*." It had taken every ounce of bravery she'd possessed back then to add, "But I also want you to be way less of a gentleman right now."

Ryan hadn't left her dorm that night.

Now that he'd brought it up, she saw the similarities.

So Ryan had taken her comment in the bathroom to mean—"So you thought we were just going to start *hooking up* again?"

"No, I wouldn't be quite that presumptuous," he clarified. "But I don't know, it seems like maybe you want something from me. And just like back then, I'm trying to figure out what that *something* is."

Called out, Sadie shook her head emphatically, as if that could erase the past thirty seconds like an Etch A Sketch. It was quite the leap from a flirtatious comment to assuming she wanted to reignite their old sexual relationship. And why was he making it sound like it was all on her? *He* started it! "I think you misread the situation." *Did he?* "I wasn't flirting with you. And, frankly, the idea of going down that path again is just . . . *asinine*."

Ryan's jaw tightened. "Asinine, huh?" Looking away from her, he nodded once. "Of course."

Without another word, he left her apartment.

But as his footsteps thudded down the staircase to the gift shop below, Sadie didn't feel vindicated, or even relieved. All she felt was the overwhelming sense that somehow she'd majorly fucked up.

CHAPTER 11

"Sadie Marie, that's the third time you've yawned in the past two minutes. Are you sure all of this isn't too much for you?"

It was late afternoon, and Sadie sat next to her mom on the very bench they'd been sitting on for twenty-plus years now. Overhead, the sun was obscured by a continuous cycle of rolling, puffy gray clouds that threatened to spill rain at any moment. The air smelled like a thunderstorm was imminent, and for the first time since early spring, the temperature had finally dropped below eighty.

"I'm fine, Mom. I swear."

By yesterday afternoon when Sadie still hadn't gotten back to her about their weekly dinner plans, her mom had called seven times in a row while Sadie was working, prompting Sadie to believe someone must be dead or close to it by the time she saw the numerous missed calls on her silenced phone. Freaking *the fuck* out, Sadie hurriedly excused herself and stepped outside the coffee shop where she'd set up with Simon and Ryan, hands and legs trembling with the fear she was about to get devastating news of some variety.

Instead her mom answered on the second ring, voice as breezy as a perfect spring day. "Oh, no need to fret, Sadie-bug," she'd dismissed. "I just wanted to get your attention. Now that I have it, what about tomorrow night's dinner?"

Maybe Ann Stockton was slightly manipulative, but she was also a genius. There was no way Sadie could cancel their plans again when she was so relieved her mother was alive and well after such a scare. Yet despite the well-played mom guilt, Sadie couldn't miss today's furniture delivery and setup at the mansion, either. When she'd relayed that information, her mom agreed to bring dinner to her.

Now Sadie ate her chicken salad croissant while her mom threw alternating accusations and questions her way like a seasoned police interrogator.

"You don't look fine," she noted. "You look like you're not getting enough sleep. And are you eating at regular intervals?"

"Mom, only you could be worried about how much I'm eating as I'm currently eating." Sadie took a large bite for emphasis.

"One meal does not make a nutritious diet."

"Jesus." Sadie wiped her mouth with the back of her hand. "Yes, I'm eating. And yes, I'll admit there's not a lot of time for sleep right now. But the tour will be up and running this Friday. I'll catch up on sleep after that."

"So I assume you won't be working at Eric's on Fridays and Saturdays while this tour is going on."

Shit.

Sadie had hoped her mom wouldn't make the correlation between her hours at the shop and the overnight tours, but that wishful thinking didn't pan out. "Mmmm . . ." she mumbled noncommittally, as if she couldn't possibly answer with a full mouth.

"Sadie Marie!"

"It's only three weekends. And I'll get a few hours of sleep between jobs. It'll all be fine."

As her mom wrapped the remainder of her own half-eaten sandwich in wax paper, Sadie considered pressing her on how much *she* was eating. "You're going to burn yourself out working these kinds of hours. It's not healthy."

This from the woman who worked every overtime shift she could pick up during Sadie's middle school and high school years. "I think you're overreacting. It's temporary. And I'm not going to bail on Eric last minute."

"Okay, sure. And then what?"

The wind kicked up, whipping loose strands of hair from Sadie's ponytail across her cheeks. The rain was coming any minute now, and she was far more concerned about the delivery guys getting the furniture inside before the storm came than the conversation at hand. "If everything goes to plan, I'll get promoted to director."

Her mom gathered their trash into one bag, likely in case they needed to make a sudden run for it when the downpour started. "Hopefully that's exactly what happens. You definitely deserve it. But if it does, you also know that will mean you'll have to leave your job at the bridal shop."

"I'm aware." The last thing Sadie wanted was to be irritated with her mom when they'd spent so little time together lately, but she also didn't need her to point out all the things she was purposely avoiding thinking about.

The idea of Eric slowly fading from her life as exchanged texts and promised dinners became fewer and farther between until, eventually, inevitably, he was just someone she used to know . . . it made her chest collapse in on itself until taking a breath felt like pushing a boulder uphill.

Other than the woman sitting beside her, Eric was the one consistent person in her life. She'd always been better at making connections with books than with people, and she was self-aware enough to recognize her lifelong struggle to make friends.

When she was young, there was no way she'd risk inviting a friend over and have them witness an argument between her parents. Or worse, have her father take an interest in a friend's mother. That had actually happened once with the mom of a neighborhood kid named Elizabeth that Sadie used to play with. She'd heard her parents arguing over her father making excuses to spend time at the woman's house. A woman whose husband was overseas for work, and Sadie's father was simply "helping out" with some "repairs" at their home. Which apparently required late-night visits to her house because of course that was the best time to fix a broken porch light. Sadie quietly stopped playing with Elizabeth out of loyalty to her mom, and as soon as the woman's husband returned, the family quickly moved out of the neighborhood.

Once Sadie was older and her father was out of the picture, mistrust already filled the hole where her desire for companionship should've been, and it was easier to keep to herself. She wasn't a social outcast or anything. She had "friends" she sat next to in class and the cafeteria, ones she'd team up with for lab partners or the dreaded group project. Ones that would invite her places and she'd be forced to come up with an excuse not to go. Those relationships were carefully constructed and contained to school hours, Monday through Friday. Any time beyond that, she'd rather be lost in a book, escaped to a world that existed between pages.

It wasn't until college when, of all people, Ryan somehow wormed his way into her private life in a moment of personal weakness. But even then she'd compartmentalized him as well, aware their relationship existed only behind the locked door of her dorm room.

Then Eric came along.

Seven years working side by side with someone has the potential to tear down anyone's walls, and Eric was a proficient wrecking ball. Even as complete opposites they'd clicked from the very beginning. Yet despite their years-long history, Sadie had a deep-seated fear that she didn't mean to Eric what he meant to her. He was her only friend, she was one of his many. The worst thing she could imagine was to slowly be forgotten.

It was her major flaw: Once she cared about a person, she cared *too much*. There was no halfway about it, and losing Eric would be devastating.

Right now, she had too many other things to stress about. "Look, Mom, I'll cross that bridge when I get to it. Right now, I have this entire project to worry about, and I don't need anything else added to the list."

A low roll of thunder rumbled in the distance.

"Okay, okay." Her mom's expression softened as she patted Sadie's knee. "I'm not trying to stress you out. I just worry about you, okay?"

"I know. But I've got everything under control. I promise." Sadie took in her mom's sleek auburn bob, her deep blue eyes framed by a few crow's-feet that made her look wise, never old. "Let's talk about something else. What's new with you? How's work? Is that married neurologist still screwing his resident?"

Normally the hospital was always a topic with an ample supply of gossip-worthy subjects, so much so that at times Sadie questioned who was actually doing the important work of saving lives.

"About that . . ." Speaking softly, her mom sounded almost . . . *shy?* "That's one of the reasons I wanted to see you today."

"Because of the cheating neurologist?"

"No, no, no, sweetie, not that!" A lighthearted chuckle floated through the air before her expression turned . . . *timid?* Something was up. "You asked what's new with me, and well, there is something new . . . I met someone."

"Met someone?"

For the first time Sadie had ever witnessed, a blush blossomed across her mom's cheeks. "As in, I'm dating someone."

Dating someone? That didn't make sense. Ann Stockton didn't date.

"His name is Doug," she continued, filling in for Sadie's silence. "He's an accountant."

Sadie heard the words, she just couldn't process them.

It's not that she didn't know her mom was a catch, that was obvious. Smart and beautiful and wickedly funny, any man would be lucky to be with her. But her mom hadn't been with *anyone* since her father left. Not so much as a single date. Hell, she hadn't even mentioned the topic. Not once. Her parents' marriage had been such a colossal disaster that Sadie assumed her mother had no interest in ever going down that path again, that she was happier alone rather than taking the risk of giving her heart to another man. So this . . . *Now* . . . It was the last thing she could have predicted.

"I—I don't know what to say," Sadie managed. "Where did you meet? How long have you known him? Did you check into his background?"

This time when her mom smiled, her eyes were lit from within. She looked happy. Really happy. "We met on one of those dating apps and we've been seeing each other for a few months. I didn't mention it until now because I didn't know if it was going to be anything worth mentioning. And no, I didn't *check into his background*, whatever that means."

A fierce gust of wind stirred both the leaves at their feet and the thoughts in Sadie's head. *Doug. Accountant. Dating app?!?* "Mom, you still identify yourself on your texts to me. You made a dating profile on an *app*?"

A raindrop pelted Sadie's forehead, but a monsoon could've sprung up and she wasn't leaving that bench until she'd wrung every last detail out of her mother. Doug. Douglas. What kind of name was that?

"Kayla, the new grad nurse on my floor, made the profile for me one night at the hospital when it was unusually dead." Tilting her chin, she clarified, "Not patients dead, work dead. Which, ironically, means the patients are alive and thriving. Anyway, Kayla found this one app for ages fifty-five-plus and said that since I barely met the age requirement, I'd be a hit. Sure enough, I had ten messages within twenty-four hours. Ten! Can you believe it?"

"Of course I can believe it." Maybe Sadie should have a talk with this Kayla person. Let her know that Ann Stockton already had a daughter. One who understood the dangers of the World Wide Web. "I just wasn't aware you had any interest in dating."

"For a very long time I didn't. But as the years pass, it felt like it was time."

Guilt unfurled in Sadie's chest like smoke from a wildfire, thick and heavy and consuming everything in its path. Had she been too busy to see that her mom was lonely? Perhaps Kayla should be composing a lecture for her entitled Shitty Daughters 101. Hell, Kayla probably knew about Douglas from the first DM while Sadie was finding out months later.

"Listen, I can come around more," Sadie offered. "I won't miss any more dinners, and I can make time to drive up to the house more often. And what about that respiratory therapist you always gossip with? Maybe you two could get coffee or hang out outside of work. I would, however, highly advise keeping your distance from Kayla. Something feels off about her."

Her mom's smile turned strained, as though she was holding back laughter. Which was odd because Sadie couldn't find even a morsel of humor in this situation. "Sweetie, you have your own life to live, and you don't need to feel guilty about that. Even when Kayla made the profile, I never thought I'd meet someone I had any real interest in. But then I met Doug, and we've been having a lot of fun together."

Sadie couldn't help but notice the way her mom's eyes lit up each time she said his name. It's not that she didn't want her mom to be happy, *of course* she did, but with happiness came the risk of losing it, and the last thing she wanted was for the fate of her mom's fragile heart to be left in some random guy's hands. If her mom ended up heartbroken again, it would break Sadie's heart, too. Just as it had the last time.

"Are you sure about this?" Sadie pressed. "I mean, how much can you really know about someone you met on an app? What if he has a whole secret life you don't know about? A wife. Kids. No pets because he's *supposedly* allergic, but really it's just another lie and he doesn't even like dogs. Not even golden retrievers. And excuse my language, but who *the fuck* doesn't like golden retrievers?"

Her mom's brow arched. "Doug isn't like that."

"Think about it, though. There's a reason so many *Are we dating the same guy?* social media groups exist. And an accountant? Seems awful generic. Almost like he's purposely come up with the most unsuspicious career possible."

Deep down, she realized the odds of Douglas having a secret identity were probably low, but even if he didn't have a fully fleshed-out double life, he could still be a serial cheater like her father had been.

Instead of responding to the very logical concerns Sadie had laid out, her mom slipped an arm around her shoulder and pulled her close. "Listen, Doug is a good guy. I understand you're worried, and that's why I want you to meet him. It will put your mind at ease. I know you're busy right now, but soon, okay?"

"I guess . . . If that's what you want." With her head resting against her mom's shoulder and the scent of vanilla perfume mixing with the smell of oncoming rain, Sadie could have stayed in that exact spot for hours. The gusty breeze on her cheeks. The sound of leaves scattering across the sidewalk. It all soothed her soul.

But there was work to be done across the street, and, as if on cue, Ryan walked through the estate's front gates with one hand on his hip and the other pressing his phone to his ear. Pacing down the sidewalk, he turned, spotted Sadie, and hesitated before giving a little wave. They'd mostly kept their distance since he'd left her apartment the other night, and when forced to speak it had been clipped and awkward. Still, she waved back because she couldn't be rude in front of her mother.

Unable to keep avoiding her responsibilities, Sadie sat up straight. "I should go. I've got a million things to—" She stopped when she saw her mom staring across the street at Ryan with hawkish eyes and pursed lips.

"Sadie-bug, who is that?"

"Um, that's Ryan. Ryan Pearson. I've mentioned him to you before."

"*That* is Ryan Pearson?" Head tipping back, her mom let out a loud, animated cackle. Then she regarded Sadie accusingly. "*That* is the Ryan Pearson I've heard you talk about as though he were Lucifer himself?" Totally unbothered, she waved eagerly at Ryan as though they were long-lost best friends.

Still on his call, Ryan's lips shifted into that charismatic-as-hell grin of his, single dimple popping. He waved back.

What in the actual fuck?

"Yes, Mother." Sadie's head twisted back and forth between them. "That's him."

"Not to point out the obvious here, but that man is *hot*. Are you certain you two can't settle your differences in a healthy way? Perhaps one that involves a mattress."

"*Mom!*" First Douglas, now this. There was only so much Sadie could handle in one visit. Another clatter of thunder vibrated through the cement beneath her feet. "Can we maybe not discuss my sex life?"

Shrugging off the question, her mom flicked a hand lackadaisically. "Just a suggestion, dear."

Working in the health care field, the subject of sex to Ann Stockton was no different than talking about the weather. As such, she'd ensured there wasn't one singular birds-and-bees discussion Sadie had to endure as a teen—that would've been far too easy. Instead, her mom had more of an open-ended approach to sex ed where every few months over dinner she'd randomly scar Sadie's brain with topics ranging from OPRAH being a helpful acronym for remembering how to properly put on a condom (Open, Pinch the tip, Roll down the penis, And Hold at the base) to the neurological symptoms of late-stage syphilis.

"Mom, I think we better wrap this up."

"I'd be more concerned with getting *him* wrapped up."

"*Mother!* Please. Stop."

Another burst of laughter surrounded Sadie as she was pulled into a goodbye hug, and even with all the disturbing talk of the past few minutes, the lighthearted sound soothed her on a deep level.

They parted ways with Sadie's promise that she'd find the time—*soon!*—for a nice sit-down dinner to properly meet this person who had her mom so enchanted. But *soon* was relative, and she had every intention of stretching that nonspecific timeframe as long as possible.

As Sadie crossed the street to the mansion, the slow sprinkles of rain dotted her white top with round, wet splotches. She stepped onto the sidewalk in front of the entrance gate at the same time Ryan ended his call.

"Hey," he said.

"Hey," she replied.

And yeah, it was awkward.

Ryan tapped the corner of his phone against his palm. "Your mom seems friendly."

"How'd you know she was my mom?"

His immediate grin released the tiniest bit of tension between them, like air escaping an overfull balloon. "You look exactly like her. Same dark blue eyes. Same nose." His gaze dropped to her lips. "Same smile."

"Oh." If she was going to repair the damage she'd done between them—for the sake of the project—now was the moment. "Listen, I'm sorry for what I said in my apartment. I didn't mean—"

"That having any interest in me would be, what did you call it again? Oh right. *Asinine.*"

She cringed. "Yeah. That. I didn't mean anyone being interested *in you* would be asinine. I was trying to say that you and me . . . I mean . . . we don't even get along, you know."

"It's fine." His focus briefly dropped to the brick sidewalk between them. "I'm not your favorite person to be around. Trust me, I get it."

For some reason, Sadie felt compelled to say, "Actually . . . Working together hasn't been as terrible as expected."

Ryan huffed a short, surprised laugh. "Not as terrible as expected. Thank you for that glowing recommendation. Let me go update my website right now."

A grin pulled at her lips. "Oh, I never agreed you could put it in writing."

"Right," he said, still smiling. "Of course."

"If you want the full truth, you're pretty good at all of . . . *this.*" Sadie motioned to the mansion as sprinkles continued to pelt them both. "I'm glad you're here, even if you won't tell me why you're here."

"*Really?*" Eyes narrowing as though he couldn't comprehend what he was hearing, Ryan seemed at a loss for words. Finally he settled on, "I . . . I appreciate you saying that. Thank you."

As he studied her, the furnace inside Sadie roared to life. But what was she supposed to do? She couldn't control it. Thanks to her mom's sex ed talks, she was all too knowledgeable about the body's physiological response to arousal. The only thing she *could* do was not give in to it.

She tilted her head up to the foreboding skies. "We should get inside. It's only gonna get worse."

As if the heavens heard her, a jagged streak of lightning flashed above the mansion and the downpour began. No easing into it, just sheets of rain suddenly soaking her hair, her face, and her clothes all at once. With a quick glance at Ryan, she pulled off her heels, and together they sprinted back through the front gates, down the brick pathway, up the steps, and into the Wilmont House.

Sheltered inside the grand foyer, Sadie leaned back against the heavy oak door to catch her breath. But when she glanced down, she was mortified to discover that her nude bra was blatantly visible as her soaked top clung to her skin.

"Here, take this." Ryan shrugged off his sweater—a heather gray quarter-zip—and held it out to her while he straightened the white T-shirt underneath and purposely avoided looking in her direction. She stared blankly at it for a moment until he said, "Just take it, Stockton. You're drenched."

Reluctantly, she accepted the sweater and pulled it on over her shirt, not hating the delicious woodsy scent that surrounded her. The sleeves were too long, and it was also just as wet as her top, but it was a warm, knit material, and her chest was no longer on full display. She cleared her throat. "Thank you."

Ryan looked at her then, pink staining his cheeks. Likely from the exertion of sprinting inside. "You're welcome."

After an extended moment of quiet that somehow wasn't uncomfortable, Sadie said, "I should probably go find some towels and clean up these puddles."

But as she walked away, she swore she heard Ryan softly add, "Looks good on you."

CHAPTER 12

Sadie lay in bed that night wearing Ryan's sweater. But *not* because it was his. It just so happened that she didn't care for most sweaters, sweatshirts, and/or hoodies—they were usually too bulky and pulled at her neck in a way that felt like she was slowly being strangled. However, Ryan's sweater was soft and oversize, and the quarter-zip feature meant it was never too snug around her neck. The fact that it smelled of the warm, woodsy notes of a summer campfire didn't hurt, either. She'd definitely return it to Ryan, *soon*, but in the meantime there was no harm in being comfy.

As Sadie sniffed the collar again and inhaled the delicious scent into her lungs, her phone lit up on the nightstand, casting a soft glow over her apartment. Giving up on sleep, she grabbed for the device, and a new notification badge from Instagram greeted her. She tapped on it, then bolted upright faster than if she'd been struck by lightning.

Holy. Fucking. Shit.

AnnStockton.007 is now following you.

Her thumb couldn't smash the username fast enough and, lo and behold, there was a grid with exactly one post, the same picture that matched the profile photo. Her mom on the beach in a floral-print sundress, cheeks pink from the heat, face aglow with the radiance of her smile. Reactively, Sadie smiled at the joy on her mom's face, even as wisps of unease curled beneath her ribs.

Her mom joined Instagram.

And a dating app.

And her username made her sound like a Bond girl.

Was this what a midlife crisis looked like? Sadie assumed that happened in one's mid-forties, but people lived longer these days, so maybe. Or perhaps this was more intrusive meddling by that new grad, Kayla. If so, Sadie needed to put a stop to this nonsense before she found her mom smoking marijuana or launching a YouTube channel.

Fuck. Now sleep was definitely out of the picture.

Just as she pressed the follow back button—she'd need to monitor this page closely—a text notification popped up from a Ry.

The first time Ryan had texted her, the bridal store had been extremely busy and she'd been interrupted by a customer while typing his name into her contacts, hitting save after only the first two letters.

Sadie tapped the notification, and her phone popped open their text thread.

Ry: Hey, you awake?

Well this night was proving to be full of unexpected twists and turns. And at one a.m. his particular wording kind of sounded like . . .

Sadie: If this is your refined version of a middle of the night "u up?" text to instigate a sexual encounter, I'm not interested.

Ry: Give me some credit, I have a little more finesse than that.

Ry: If this was a middle of the night attempt to "instigate a sexual encounter," I'd at least ask what you're wearing.

A snort burst from the back of her throat, so unexpected that she fumbled her phone, which lodged itself between the bedframe and the nightstand. After an unreasonable amount of effort to retrieve it, she saw her furniture had responded on her behalf.

Sadie: ttnb

A barrage of responses also filled her screen.

Ry: Is that an acronym the youths use these days?

Ry: tiny thong, no bra.

Ry: tight t-shirt, no bra.

Ry: Surely I'm at least right about the bra part?

Ry: Come on, Stockton, the suspense is killing me here.

Maybe she should be annoyed, probably mildly offended, but she opened up this line of conversation the second she mentioned middle-of-the-night sexual encounters. And for a reason she couldn't explain, she found herself smiling at her phone.

Sadie: You're a menace. It was clearly an accident. Sorry to disappoint.

Ry: No worries. I already know what you're wearing.

Oh god. Could he somehow sense she was still wearing his sweater?

Sadie: Is that so?

Ry: You always sleep in an oversized shirt that absolutely does not touch your neck, little pajama shorts, and, for reasons I'll never understand, knee-high socks.

So he remembered. Warmth swirled through her belly, and her toes curled in the knee-high socks she was, in fact, wearing.

Sadie: What's wrong with my socks?

Ry: Nothing can touch your neck but you're okay suffocating your toes? Make it make sense, Stockton.

Sadie bit the corner of her mouth to suppress what was surely a ridiculous smile. Why are you even texting me, she typed, then erased it before she hit send. That sounded harsh, and despite her better judgment, she didn't want the conversation to end. Maybe this was the distraction she needed to get her mind off her mother's newfound habit of giving into peer pressure from new grad nurses.

Sadie: My toes can breathe just fine and are perfectly cozy. Why are you still up?

Ry: I'm a creature of the night. Comes with the job, I guess.

Ry: Shit. I just realized you work tomorrow morning. Seriously, did I wake you?

Ryan Pearson had her work schedule memorized. It was a small thing. It was a trivial thing. Yet a thrill vibrated through her chest like a plucked guitar string.

Sadie: I wish. I've become a creature of the night lately, too. Not by choice, just can't sleep.

Ry: Is it the project?

Was it the project? Sure. But it was also her job with Eric that could be drawing to a close, her mom's sudden love of the internet and nonchalant attitude regarding stranger danger, and the fact that her daily routine as she'd known it for the past five years had been upended. So yeah, it was more than just the project. It was as though someone had shaken her life like a snow globe, but instead of leaving her with a sense of magic and whimsy it was dizzying, and she wasn't sure what the world would look like when all the pieces settled.

Sadie: Among other things.

Three blinking dots appeared and then disappeared.

Sadie wasn't trying to be closed off, she just didn't know how to be a conversationalist like Ryan. That elusive quality of captivating someone's attention was something she'd never possessed.

Ry: I wanted to say that I realized it's not fair to you that all my cards aren't on the table with this project. I know how much you have invested in this, and you deserve to know why I'm invested, too.

Ry: Presuming you still want to know why I said yes to Jerry?

Sadie: 1000%

She waited with bated breath through those teasing dots. But when the next message materialized, it came in the form of a voice note. For reasons unbeknownst, her heart skipped a beat. She pressed play, and Ryan's voice filled the silence of her apartment.

"It's probably easier to say it than to type it all out, so I hope you're okay with listening to my voice at one a.m." Not only was Sadie okay with it, his sleepy, slightly husky cadence at the late hour was kind of . . . soothing. She wondered if Ryan was also in bed, curled on his side and unable to sleep in his dark, empty apartment, his face illuminated as he stared at his phone with anticipation for whatever may happen next. No, she decided, that was probably only her. "So here's what I haven't told you. I want Jerry to invest in my pub crawls. I've made plans to expand to Charleston if I can convince him to write a check. I thought doing him this favor might make him more inclined to come on board. But I'm waiting until these trial tours are over before I pitch the idea."

Well. That was unexpected.

Ryan's business was thriving here—as the very person (unsuccessfully) chasing at his heels for the title of Sutton Island's most popular tour, she'd certainly know—so why risk an expansion? And why now?

As she pondered, another voice note popped up. Again, she pressed play.

"I tell you my secret and get no response. That's kind of disappointing, Stockton."

After some debate on whether or not it would be weird or off-putting to reply via text versus a return voice note—since apparently they were doing that now—she hit record and spoke into her phone. "Sorry, just processing . . . Okay, don't take this the wrong way, but why do you need *Jerry* to invest? I'm all too aware you happen to be the owner of the number one–rated tour company in Sutton Island—loathe that T-shirt, by the way. And your family does have a yacht so . . ."

Ryan's return note began with a raspy chuckle, and then, "First of all, let's leave my tastefully designed, screen-printed T-shirt out of this. It's never hurt anyone. And yes, the company does well. But not risk-it-all-on-an-expansion well. As for my family, and this will no doubt come as a complete shock to you, I haven't received a dime from my father since he cut me off when I dropped out of college sophomore year. We're not on the best terms. I'm not even invited on the *yacht*—which is actually a small fishing vessel—anymore."

Oh shit.

This was exactly why Sadie didn't hold personal conversations with people outside of her mom and Eric. Now she felt terrible, truly. For years she'd assumed Ryan had the perfect life. With a single conversation, he'd shredded her imagined portrait of his picture-perfect family. Now what was she supposed to say? If she couldn't handle small talk, she certainly wouldn't thrive at big talk. *Fuck!* What to say . . . What to say . . . Minutes passed while her mind remained a blank Word doc, judgmental cursor taunting her with each blink.

Another voice note popped up. Startled, she nearly dropped her phone a second time.

"Don't you dare go silent on me now, Stockton."

Finally, Sadie replied with the most honest response she could come up with. "I'm really sorry, and I don't know what to say here. I have questions, but I'm not sure they're appropriate."

"There's nothing for you to be sorry about," Ryan said in his next message. "I just thought it's time you knew my life isn't as perfect as you thought." Humor entered his voice as he added, "And you can ask whatever you want. We've already discussed middle-of-the-night sexual encounters. I don't think a few questions about my old man is gonna cross a line."

Fuck. Hearing Ryan utter the words *sexual encounters* in his late-night drawl threatened to drag her mind straight to the gutter. But she was a mature adult, so she listened to it only three more times before refocusing.

"So what exactly happened between you two?" she finally asked, curiosity taking over. "And why cut you off just because you didn't finish college? And how did your mom feel about that? Also, I'm kind of being a nosy bitch so feel free not to answer any or all of the above."

"It's fine," Ryan replied, "I don't mind talking about it with you. We had a falling-out when I decided college wasn't for me. My father is a highly regarded professor in a graduate business program at a private—*aka pricey*—college upstate, and my mom is a law professor there, too. Coming from a family who values academia above all else, I was enough of a disgrace when I couldn't make the grades in high school to get accepted to undergrad there. But then dropping out of a state university to become a bartender . . . That didn't go over well. He cut me off financially, which was fair. But to this day he's never let it go, and his disappointment in me has never faltered."

Sadie's automatic response was, "What a complete and utter dickwad!" Then she realized that probably wasn't the emotionally supportive response Ryan deserved. She went to delete the note and try again, but her finger accidentally hit send. *Shit.* Left with no other choice, she quickly recorded a follow-up. "That was uncalled for. I apologize for calling your father a dickwad. What I should have said was I'm sorry he didn't support your decisions."

When Ryan's next note popped up, she held her breath and hit play. "No, complete and utter dickwad is accurate. Probably one of the more generous things said about Preston Pearson."

Smiling in relief, Sadie shifted in the covers. While baffled this conversation was taking place, she was even more baffled she longed for it to continue. Maybe she was just really, really lonely. For some reason, in her quiet bedroom in the dark of night, it was easier to let her guard down. As if tomorrow in the daylight, none of this would have ever happened. The same way those heated nights in her dorm room led to mornings of awkward avoidance and furtive glances across campus.

"Do you two have *any* relationship now?" she asked.

A few minutes passed before his next recording appeared in

their thread. "'Relationship' is a strong word. We tolerate each other for the sake of my mom and sister. He loves to point out everything I'm doing wrong with my business. Even made me a PowerPoint about it once. Holidays are super fun."

Sadie started to ask another question, but a message popped up before she could send it. A text, not a voice note.

Ry: I'm keeping you up. You
should get some sleep.

Oh.

Disappointment settled over her like another blanket added to her covers. Had she messed up somewhere? Had the dickwad comment gone a smidge too far? Or was Ryan truly cutting off conversation because of the late hour? She couldn't ask those things, obviously. Instead, she thought up a casual enough response.

Sadie: Yeah, I am pretty tired.

Sadie: I'll see you tomorrow.

She stared at the screen as a full three minutes ticked by with no trace of the promising three bubbles. Maybe that was it. Somehow she'd messed up and Ryan couldn't end their conversation fast enough. Giving up, she plugged her phone into the charger on her nightstand, then collapsed back in bed and threw her forearm over her eyes.

It was *fine.* There was no reason to be in her head about a late-night conversation with Ryan Pearson. Perhaps working in such close proximity was getting to them both, but as soon as this project was over, they would return to exactly what they had been before—enemies. Although, as the word floated through her head, it didn't summon the kind of lip-curling disdain it used to when she thought about Ryan.

Then she heard it.

The low vibration of another text.

Sadie hurled her arm in the direction of the nightstand, and as soon as it connected with her phone, the screen lit up with the message preview.

Ry: Sleep tight, Stockton.

CHAPTER 13

Ryan Pearson may no longer indulge in the family riches, but from the location of his row house condo bordering the city's park filled with old oak trees, Sadie knew the man was doing just fine for himself.

Tonight's plan was to meet at Ryan's place so she and Simon could taste-test some cocktails for the tour. When Sadie discovered Ryan lived less than a mile from her own apartment, she'd decided to walk over since the October evening was warm enough for a denim shirtdress and a pair of strappy sandals that wouldn't leave blisters on her feet (but were *not* waterproof). After last night's unexpected conversation, she was extra nervous about being in Ryan's home. Luckily, Simon would serve as a buffer, and she'd arrived exactly five minutes late in hopes he'd already be there.

Starting up the porch steps, Sadie gave a friendly smile and nod to an elderly man sitting on the stoop next to Ryan's, a gray cat purring in his lap. It was odd to greet Ryan's neighbor—someone in his everyday life who had a very different relationship with him than she did. Did Ryan offer to look after this man's cat or water his plants when he went out of town? Did he purposely play his music low as to not disturb the man's sleep? Ryan was so good with people, she bet he did all those things and more. The two probably went for a friendly breakfast together at least once a month.

Coming to a stop next to two wooden rocking chairs, Sadie rapped her knuckles against the door, nerves sparking under her skin like live wire. Would they acknowledge last night's conversation once they were face-to-face, or would they pretend it never happened?

Footsteps approached the opposite side of the door, and her heart pulsed faster.

Simon will be here. Simon will be here. Simon will be here.

Two seconds and at least ten heartbeats later, Ryan opened the door and leaned his shoulder against the frame, cell phone in hand, lips twisted in an expression of uncertainty. He wore a thin, long-sleeved black shirt and dark jeans. "Simon texted us. Did you see it yet?"

"No . . ." Her phone was currently buried in her tote bag. But the hesitation in Ryan's voice told her she wasn't going to like whatever the text said.

"The good news," Ryan started, "is that two of the actors from Simon's improv group agreed to help with the tours. The bad news is that they need to go over the script tonight, so he isn't going to make it. Looks like it's just the two of us, Stockton."

* * *

Ryan's kitchen was something straight out of a cable TV design show. More specifically, one where the quirky host specializes in Southern rustic meets modern minimalist and ends each episode with a tall glass of sweet tea in hand and cheerfully declares, *We'll see y'all next time.* It was all butcher-block countertops and white subway tiles and a custom island large enough to easily fit both Jack and Rose had it been found floating in the ocean that doomed night instead of the controversial door. Hell, this thing could have saved half the crew.

Centered in the middle of the island, on the side Ryan now leaned against, there was a sink deep enough to bathe in. On Sadie's side opposite him, there were four wooden barstools, one of which she sat in, another of which she placed her tote bag in. A rustic fixture hung above the island, composed of smooth wood and twisted black metal with a horizontal row of Edison bulbs. A soft breeze blew through a propped-open French door leading to a small courtyard out back.

None of that surprised Sadie. What did surprise her was how *clean* everything was. Even the French doors lacked a single fingerprint or smudged blemish on the square glass panes. For a single, thirty-year-old man's condo, it was an unexpected discovery.

On the countertop directly in front of Ryan, a rectangular serving tray was filled with an assortment of fancy-looking cocktails of all colors and garnishments. Some were topped with speared fruit, others twigs of fresh herbs—and yet, the only clue he'd mixed all these drinks in *this* kitchen was the low hum of a dishwasher.

"Your kitchen is *really* clean," Sadie remarked. "Like impressively so."

"Thanks," he replied, adjusting a spear of fruit just so. "I hardly ever use it."

"Still. You're a bit of a neat freak, aren't you, though? This kitchen is way too clean for someone who just mixed . . ." Leaning onto her elbows, she performed a quick count. "Twelve! *Twelve* cocktails?"

"To be fair, there are two of each. One for you, one for Simon. So technically six. But since Simon won't be joining us, I'll take his. And we're only tasting here." Ryan pulled a kitchen towel from somewhere behind the counter, wiped his hands, then draped it over his shoulder. "And yes, I do prefer things to be orderly. There's nothing wrong with that."

"Not judging. I just didn't know that about you."

His eyes rose and met hers, the deep green irises enhanced by his black shirt. It was the kind of green that felt like falling into a forest, surrounded by leaves and moss and grasses of every subtle shade, all of them reflected back at her with a few flecks of golden sunlight breaking through the canopy.

For a moment it seemed Ryan was going to say something about last night. But then he cleared his throat, and those gorgeous eyes fell back to the tray, and the moment flickered out like a candle on a gust of wind.

Well, Sadie had her answer then. They weren't going to talk about it. Likely, he regretted opening up to her in the first place.

"I went ahead and mixed these so you wouldn't have to watch me experiment." Ryan picked up a martini glass topped with speared green apple slices and placed it in front of her, careful not to spill. "It's been a long time since I've been behind a bar. I'm very rusty."

That was doubtful. Based upon the presentation of the cocktails alone, it was obvious he was talented. And she felt a pinch of disappointment that she hadn't arrived earlier to watch him work. It would have been nice to see him a little messy, a little less than perfect.

"Don't judge me too harshly." Ryan lifted the martini glass that mirrored hers, and Sadie clinked her glass against his.

After removing the spear of apple slices, Sadie tilted the rim to her lips, smelling the sprinkles of cinnamon before she tasted them, along with the undeniable apple flavor and a hint of caramel. The smooth burn of vodka slid down her throat, transforming the drink into the adult version of the caramel apples she used to make with her mom every Halloween.

"This tastes like candy." She downed another gulp. "This is definitely one of the three for the tour."

Ryan's eyes sparked as he slowly sipped from his own glass, but after her third long swig he stretched across the island and pulled the drink from her hand. "Slow down, killer, we've got a long way to go."

Sadie couldn't keep the smile off her face as Ryan rinsed their glasses in the huge sink while she pulled each thin apple slice from the spear and popped them into her mouth one by one. There hadn't been time to eat dinner before she came over, so the fruit would have to do.

"Remember, you can tell me if you don't like something." Ryan placed the second drink in front of her. "It won't hurt my feelings."

"Please," she scoffed. "Have I ever been afraid of hurting your feelings?" The comment was intended to be a teasing ode to their status of mortal enemies, but as soon as it left her mouth she regretted her choice of words.

Confirming it was the exact wrong thing to say, something far from humor echoed in Ryan's voice when he replied, "No. You certainly have not."

Shit. Why did she have to be so terrible at normal human social interaction? This territory of not-friends but more than strangers was incredibly daunting. Unsure what to say next, she picked up a drink that looked like hot chocolate in a martini glass.

"This is an espresso martini with shaved dark chocolate," Ryan explained.

The coffee flavor swirled on her tongue, the addition of chocolate sweetening the drink in just the right way so it wasn't bitter. "Okay, it's also really good, but I'm not sure we want to pump our guests full of alcohol *and* caffeine."

"That makes perfect sense." Ryan reached for her glass. "Good call."

Next up was a bloodred rum punch, and it made the top-three list the moment Sadie had her first taste. Followed by a second, third, and fourth taste in rapid succession. Just to be certain.

"Again, you're supposed to be tasting not drinking." Coming around the island, Ryan pried the stemless wineglass from her fingers. But he did it with a grin, and Sadie was relieved they'd found their way back to this easier, playful place. Maybe it was the alcohol, but she much preferred these moments to the times they were constantly bickering.

"You're not the boss of me, Pearson," she teased, perhaps enjoying a little too much the way his fingers plucked at hers until the glass was out of her grip. "What else you got?"

Next up were a pumpkin-flavored old-fashioned and a tall, ghost-white mixture with rum and coconut cream. They were both expertly crafted, but it was the last cocktail on the tray—something bubbly with a hint of cranberry—she couldn't put down. It packed a strong punch but was remarkably smooth, and before she knew it, her glass was empty.

Ryan's back was turned as he wiped down the serving tray and placed it in a cabinet, chatting away about champagne and absinthe.

Sadie had trouble concentrating on his words though—for some reason they sounded muffled and far away. Instead, she focused on the back of his neck just above his collar—the smooth, taut muscles a far more captivating subject—and wondered what it would feel like to walk up behind him and sink her teeth there. To taste the salt of his skin with her tongue.

She abruptly pushed her glass away as heat wound its way into her cheeks.

It had been a fairly long time since she'd been tipsy. Probably last New Year's Eve when Eric convinced her to attend a party he and Charity threw at his place. She partook in one too many Jell-O shots and found herself in the corner making out with some Scottish model named Callum. Sure, Callum may have had a narcissistic personality that rendered him incapable of talking about anything other than himself, but he also had a swoon-worthy accent and a jawline that could double as a cheese grater so it hadn't been all bad.

"Stockton, you still with me?"

Sadie dialed her attention back in as Ryan promptly confiscated her glass. "Sorry, just zoned out for a second." Which was certainly one way to describe daydreaming about licking his neck.

"So do we have our three?" he asked.

"I believe we do." She nodded her head, which felt wobbly on her shoulders. Like a Sadie bobblehead. "You're really good at this, you know. A-plus for sure."

Leaning over the counter across from her, Ryan's eyes narrowed at the compliment. "Thanks."

Gaze straying to the towel thrown over his shoulder, then to the pushed-up sleeves of his shirt, Sadie envisioned herself tucked between Ryan's body and the gigantic island. His forearms trapping her in on both sides. His green eyes capturing hers from above. His hips pressing into hers.

Drinking this much was clearly a huge mistake.

The cocktails were toasting her insides like a chocolate chip cookie baked to melty, gooey perfection, and those goddamn green eyes only cranked up the heat until it was nearly broiling in this kitchen. Add in a heaping dose of competence porn and the remnants of vulnerability from last night's conversation, and maybe she *wanted* to get burned.

Sadie slid off her stool, taking a moment to ensure she had her balance before making her way around the island, Ryan's gaze trained on her every move. As she approached, he pushed off the counter and stood to his full height, curiosity etched in the single line formed between his brows.

"I shouldn't have let you drink so much," he said as she came to a stop directly in front of him.

Propping her hip against the island, she scoffed. "*Let* me?"

"Yes. *Let you,*" he unapologetically replied. "As the one serving it's my responsibility to make sure you stay safe."

Sadie ran a finger along the smooth edge of the butcher block, quiet for a moment before she peered up at him through her lashes. "I wasn't aware I was in danger."

Eyes flashing in surprise, Ryan wet each lip with a sweep of his tongue. "Careful, Stockton. I might assume you're flirting with me again, and you made it painfully clear the other night you would never do such a thing. An asinine notion even. Remember?"

Sure he was calling her out, but she was too warm, too fuzzy to care about things like her hypocrisy at the moment. Those champagne bubbles had infiltrated her bloodstream, making her veins fizz with electricity, arousal, and the desire to make bad decisions. She ignored his comment. "You should still do this."

"Do what?"

Her hand traveled to his shoulder, fingertips brushing over the towel that resided there. "Bartending. You should still do it."

"Yeah? Why's that?"

"Because it's clear you enjoy it, and you're good at it." As she toyed with the towel's edges, her fingers nearly grazed Ryan's chest, and she fought the compulsive urge to just give in and touch him. "Therefore, you should still do it."

"And what?" he prodded, eyes tracing her movements. "Give up my company to bartend again? Christ, that might actually kill my father."

"No, you shouldn't give up your company, silly goose." *Silly goose? WTF.* "Unfortunately for me, you're really good at that, too. You're really good at everything you do. It's actually kind of rude." That made Ryan smile, and her gaze snagged on his lips. The desire to taste-test those was almost irrepressible. *Almost.* "But you could find a couple nights now and then to still do something that inspires you. It could be just for fun."

Ryan inched closer, bringing with him that intoxicating scent she'd grown accustomed to from sleeping in his sweater. "If I convince Jerry to invest in Pearson's, there won't be time for fun."

"Right." Something inside her deflated like a popped balloon. "'Cause you'll move to Charleston."

"Right."

A light breeze swept through the French door, and Sadie cast her attention to the courtyard outside. It was the perfect spot for morning coffee, and she pictured Ryan out there reading a book or working on his laptop. Then she recalled the photos on his Instagram.

"Do you even want to expand though?" she asked. And now they were doing it. They were discussing the things they'd only talked about late last night. Real things. "I mean, you love *this* city. I can tell."

Ryan tilted his head. "I won't deny that. But isn't that the way life works, to always aspire for more, never stay complacent?"

"I don't know, that seems kind of sad to me," she answered. "If you've found a way to be happy *and* successful in a place you love, what more is there to achieve?"

"Tell that to my father."

For a man she'd never met, Sadie had a few choice words for his father already picked out. But as she considered those choice words and precisely which order they would come in if ever given the opportunity, something else clicked into place. "Ah, I get it. This expansion is to prove a point to him."

Dropping his head, Ryan didn't respond other than a muffled scoff, and Sadie became all too aware that, once again, she was encroaching into territory she had no right to enter.

"I'm sorry," she blurted. "I have no right to insinuate . . . I just think . . . Never mind . . . I'm just—"

"Drunk?" Ryan lifted his head, eyes gleaming, easy grin curving his lips in a way that gave her the strongest desire to—

Oh god.

She was doing it.

As if her hand were no longer attached to the rest of her body, she was cupping Ryan's face and running the pad of her thumb over his pouty lower lip. Realization (horror!) dawned quickly, and she jerked her rogue hand away like she'd just caressed a hot iron instead of a hot man's face. Although the damage was done, evidenced by the aching pulse between her thighs.

"I'm not drunk," she lied.

"Oh yes, you are. Wanna know how I know?" With a slight turn of his body, Ryan boxed her in against the counter. She'd gotten what she'd wished for only moments ago and it was almost too much. She could barely breathe with him this close, oxygen harder and harder to come by as her lungs were compressed by her racing heart. Yet the closer he came, the closer she wanted him. A torturous dilemma.

"How?" she breathed.

"Because you're flushed high on your cheekbones and across the bridge of your nose." His index finger traced a slow line starting near her ear, up over her nose, and across the opposite cheek.

A shiver rolled through her shoulders. "So what? I get flushed easily. It doesn't mean anything."

"Sure it does. Because when you're annoyed or irritated, it starts here." He lightly touched her neck, just over her pulse point. "And when you're turned on, it moves from your cheeks all the way down here." His finger trailed down the column of her throat to trace the outline of her collarbone over her dress.

"I guess you have me all figured out then, Pearson."

Ryan swallowed. "Not even close."

It was all so overwhelming. The flutters in her stomach. The thrumming of her heart. The wet heat between her legs. Every sensation amplified by the liquor sloshing through her veins. Suddenly she was dizzy. Not in a good way.

Sadie gripped Ryan's forearm, hard, and his expression transformed the same instant. "Stockton, you good?"

A wave of nausea ripped through her. "I might be *a little* drunk."

"Shit." Ryan straightened, hand moving from the counter to her waist. "This is my fault."

"I decide how much I drink, Pearson. I'm my own person." Although at the moment her *own person* was dangerously close to puking in his immaculate home, so maybe she should blame him.

"I'm the one serving you, though. It's my responsibility to know better." Keeping one hand sturdy on her waist, he took an empty glass from a cabinet behind him and filled it with water from the fridge's dispenser. "Drink this."

Holding the glass in both hands, Sadie swallowed half the contents before setting it on the counter. "Sorry about this. I think I should head home now."

"Ha," he huffed. When she stayed silent, his head cocked to the side. "You're *serious*? You can't leave like this. If anything, you need to lie down and sleep it off."

Sleep it off in Ryan Pearson's condo? *Nope. Nope. Nope.* "Calm down. I'm slightly inebriated, not dying. I just need some fresh air. Which I'll get on my walk home."

"Stockton, you *cannot* walk home like this."

It would certainly help her case if the island at her back and his palm on her waist weren't the only things keeping her vertical. "Well I'm not staying *here* so . . ."

Sighing as though she were exhausting him, Ryan rubbed his jaw. "I can't drive you home. I've been drinking, too."

"I'll take an Uber."

He looked at her like the suggestion was utterly absurd. "There's no way I'm putting you in a stranger's car in this condition."

"You're worried I'll get taken." Her heart warmed at his concern. "That's kind of sweet of you, Pearson."

"*Taken?*" he huffed. "I'm afraid you'll vomit in some unlucky driver's car and get us both banned."

Sadie knocked his arm away from her. "You know what? I'll be just fine, thank you very much. Already feeling tons better." As she moved away from the counter, the room tilted in her peripheral vision. But if she kept her focus on one stationary object at a time, surely she could get the half mile back to her apartment.

"You're impossible, you know that?" Ryan was already at her heels, palm on the small of her back.

"I'm not going to be your prisoner, Pearson."

"My *prisoner*? Jesus H. Christ. So we're doing this again, are we?"

Truthfully, Sadie didn't want to fight with him. But it was so much easier than admitting she'd screwed up and had way too much to drink and was now silently praying to the gods of drunk women everywhere that those drinks didn't reappear. Worse, she didn't want to admit that she needed his help to get home. Or that she needed anything from him at all.

She hobbled toward the door, arms splayed in a low V at her sides as if that would provide her better balance. But she wasn't a penguin, so it didn't help.

"Just stop for one goddamn second." From over her shoulder, Ryan's hand pressed against the door before she could open it.

She spun around, jaw clenched tight.

"Look," he said, lowering his voice, "if you insist on walking home, *please* just let me walk with you."

Energy quickly dissipating, she leaned against the door and nodded.

Ryan's expression visibly relaxed. "Okay. Let's get you home."

CHAPTER 14

The fresh night air reinvigorated Sadie, and she speed-walked down the sidewalk as if the faster she moved the more she'd burn off the alcohol igniting her. She was a rocket ship, blasting back to her apartment.

And more than *a little* drunk.

Before long she caught up to a young couple pushing an old-fashioned baby carriage and taking the term *stroll* quite literally. Unable to bypass the couple on the stretch of narrow sidewalk, she was forced to slow down.

Ryan, practically jogging at her side, asked through heavy breaths, "Are we in some kind of race I didn't know about?"

"Not anymore." She jerked her head in the direction of the couple. "Is there anything worse than slow walkers taking up the *entire* public sidewalk? Like, go faster or scooch over, you know?"

Ryan's eyes flared. "You might want to lower your voice, Stockton."

She shrugged. "Meh."

They continued down the block, painfully slowly, and Sadie couldn't keep her eyes off the couple. The blond woman looked to be in her late twenties, effortlessly cool and extremely fit in an expensive athleisure dress, while the man at her side wore a sweatshirt and running shorts and had calves that screamed, *I'd love to tell you about my marathons!*

Without fully seeing their faces, Sadie already knew they were both gorgeous, surely wealthy, likely even happy (for now). Their baby was probably gorgeous, too. Probably already making a name for themselves in the baby modeling world and giving all the other not-as-gorgeous babies self-esteem issues.

"Cute family though," she muttered. "Wonder how long daddy of the year up there will stick around before he abandons them both for his coworker with a penchant for miniskirts and see-through blouses."

Ryan's arm landed firmly around her shoulder, pulling her close until his breath was on her ear. "There's a lot to unpack with that statement, but for right now, I am *begging* you to lower your voice."

Sadie jerked her shoulder out from under his arm. *Fine.* If he didn't want to converse, she'd be completely silent. Like a mime. Or a man experiencing an inkling of emotion.

Craning her neck, she tried to glimpse inside the carriage at the blessed, beautiful child.

And when she saw it, a piercing scream tore from her throat.

Instead of the expected face of an angelic infant, what greeted her was the face of a maybe-dog, maybe-rodent, maybe a mixture of both. It had black, beady eyes, one single strand of hair (fur?) that originated on its forehead where a unicorn's horn should reside, and its mouth gaped open, baring the tiniest teeth that looked sharp as hell. It was the ugliest creature she'd ever laid eyes on. And it was wearing a puffer vest.

"She's fine! Totally fine!" Ryan announced to the passersby on the street who had all come to a standstill at her harrowing scream, including the attractive slow-walkers. "Just deathly afraid of dogs. Bad encounter as a child." She had no idea where he was coming up with this. "Very cute fellow, though."

"I don't think *that* is a dog," she tried to tell him, but his arm was back around her shoulder and he cradled her against his chest. To others it probably looked like he was comforting her, but Sadie knew better. *He was silencing her!*

"We're just gonna take a different route." Sliding his hand into hers, Ryan tugged her in the direction of the nearest alleyway.

When she glanced back over her shoulder, the rodent snarled, and she let out another high-pitched yelp. "That thing's staring at me," she told Ryan as he dragged her away from the couple. "It has the eyes of a demon."

Halfway down the alley, Ryan wheeled around. "Hand to god, I'm never serving you alcohol again." His gaze flicked past her, and she whipped her head back in the direction they'd come. There was a group still gathered on the sidewalk, the attractive woman now holding her little beast and smoothing down the tail growing from its forehead. "Since you clearly can't be trusted around the public right now, we're taking a different way back."

Ryan sounded awful preachy for her liking, but she had just raised public alarm so maybe now wasn't the time to protest.

They traipsed onward in silence, the alleyways mostly deserted except for an occasional shop or restaurant employee out for a smoke break. This way was definitely longer, but with Ryan still holding her hand, she didn't really mind. In fact, she savored the warmth of his skin against hers. Of course he was holding her hand only because she was a danger to society in her current state, but it still felt nice, and every so often, he'd run his thumb up and down the length of hers and she'd break out in goose bumps.

Sadie tried to recall the last time a man held her hand. Probably around six months ago when she'd gone to the movies with some guy who had taken her tour and asked for her number afterward. The date had gone okay-ish, but his hand had been oddly sticky, which was (justifiably) enough reason for there not to be a second date. But Ryan's hand wasn't sticky at all. It was dry and slightly calloused and strong enough to keep her tethered when it felt like she might float away.

Eventually they emerged back onto a street only a few short blocks from the estate. Ryan stayed with her all the way to the guesthouse, releasing her hand only so she could punch in the four-digit code to unlock the door. She expected him to say good night (and good riddance) there, but instead he asked, "Can I come up? I'd feel better knowing you get settled okay."

"Uh, sure." She must be in really pathetic shape if he didn't have faith in her ability to make it up a single staircase and through her apartment door. But she proved him wrong when she led him through the shop and up to her apartment, only stumbling once on the stairs.

Safely inside her kitchen with a tall glass of water in hand, she defiantly stated, "See? I made it. You don't have to babysit me any longer."

Ryan's mouth pinched into an expression she was familiar with, one of annoyance. "That's not what I'm doing."

"Really? What are you doing then?"

He drew closer until he was mere inches away, and her heart rate spiked as he swept one side of her hair behind her ear. Then he took the glass from her hand and set it on the counter behind her. Leaning in, he whispered, as if telling her a forbidden secret, "I had a really good time with you tonight. Maybe I wasn't ready for it to end."

All of her insides melted into liquid. Hot, swirling liquid. "Careful, Pearson," she whispered back, pulling away just enough for their eyes to meet. "It sounds an awful lot like you might be flirting with me now."

"Yeah. Obviously." Dark green eyes skated over her cheeks, traced the line of her jaw, hung on her lips. "You know I blatantly hit on you *first,* right? Both when we were in that closet at the mansion and at Eric's store. I was only surprised you seemed to be flirting back. When I brought it up the other night, I guess I wanted confirmation it really happened. Not to worry though, you set me straight pretty quick."

So Ryan hadn't been calling her out, he'd only been trying to determine what she meant by her comment. And now he was admitting that he started it. Whether it was his honesty or the alcohol, she felt the urge to make a confession of her own. "If you want to know the truth . . . yes, I was flirting with you, too. And I knew what I was insinuating."

Ryan's brows rose, something devious lighting his eyes. "And what was that?"

There wasn't enough alcohol in the world to get her to admit *aloud* what she'd hinted at.

"Never mind," he said upon seeing her surely stricken face. "You don't have to say it."

For the second time in as many hours, Sadie found herself backed against a kitchen counter, trapped between Ryan's forearms. "I don't?"

He shook his head, elbows bending to bring him closer again.

"I'll say it," he said in a low, raspy whisper against her ear. "I think we both know exactly what this is, Stockton. I want you. I think about it, about *you*, all the time. The night we were trapped in the closet, I wanted to touch you so badly I had to grip my thighs to keep my hands off you. You have *no idea* what you do to me. Or the things I want to do to you."

A desperate ache throbbed between her thighs, her breaths heavy and deep. And perhaps it wasn't the best idea, but her inhibitions were long gone, and she heard herself suggest, "You can touch me now if you want."

Craving some type of movement, some way of releasing even a fraction of the energy building between them, she placed a hand on his chest and kneaded the soft material of his shirt between her fingers.

Ryan's eyes fluttered closed, and her hand rose and fell as he took a deep, deliberate breath. Opening them again, he said, "Trust me, I absolutely *want* to, but I absolutely *cannot*."

Disappointment swelled like a sponge inside her chest. "If you're worried about how much I've had to drink, you could just stay and hang out. Nothing has to happen between us."

"I'd like that." Covering her hand with his own, he gave it a small squeeze before easing the material from her grasp and returning her hand to her side. "But given our history, I'm not sure even that's a decision you'd make if you were sober. The last thing I want is for you to regret anything tomorrow, even just hanging out with me."

He stepped away from her, and the loss of his body heat felt like being plunged into an ice bath. "But now you know where I stand," he continued. "So the ball's in your court." Moving toward the door, he called over his shoulder, "Get some sleep, Stockton. Drink lots of water and don't forget to set your alarm for work in the morning. And lock this door behind me."

Then he was gone, and Sadie was left drunk and alone in her kitchen, wondering if the whole night had been a fever dream.

* * *

It had not been a fever dream.

That much was evident by her dry, swollen throat and throbbing headache the following morning. She'd swapped her morning latte for four Ibuprofen (directions be damned) and copied Eric's coffee order—black with two extra shots of espresso—despite hating the bitter taste. Now Sadie pushed through the doors of the boutique, oversize sunglasses firmly in place despite the morning's overcast skies. The welcome bell chimed from above and reverberated deep in her brain.

From behind the counter, Eric took one look at her and cringed. "Dear god."

"Could you maybe lower your voice?" she rasped, her vocal cords likely burned away by the vodka or absinthe or whatever devil's concoctions Ryan served her last night.

"The *hell* happened to you?" Eric shoved a sketch pad to the side, her haggard appearance taking priority.

She placed their coffees on the counter, then nudged her sunglasses up to her hairline, squinting as the store's lights invaded her corneas. "Ryan Pearson happened."

"Oh shit." Eric tucked his pencil behind his ear. "Tell me *everything*."

Sadie swallowed a small sip of her too-hot, too-bitter coffee and tried not to pull a face as she filled him in on the cocktail taste test gone wrong, Eric's grin growing remarkably similar to the cartoon version of the Grinch with each embarrassing detail she provided.

"The night ended with Ryan walking me back home," she reported. "The details are a bit fuzzy, but I'm pretty sure I saw some type of rodent in a baby carriage and screamed in the middle of the street like a victim in a slasher film."

"You always make the worst decisions when you drink," Eric so kindly pointed out. "Remember Callum? I'd even warned you about him ahead of time."

"To be fair, I didn't sleep with him."

"Callum? Or Ryan?"

"Either!" A sharp pain shot through her skull from one temple to the other, and she lowered her voice. "Anyway, when we got back to my apartment, I may have embarrassed myself further."

Eric's eager grin returned. He ate this shit up. "What'd you do?"

Ryan's words from the night before played in her head. *I think we both know exactly what this is, Stockton.* The real question was if he actually meant the things he'd said, or if he, too, had been inebriated and making bad decisions. "I may have asked him to stay." She cleared her throat. "In a slightly flirtatious manner."

"Oh, this is *too* good. So, did he?"

"No. He said something about me not being sober and then left."

Stroking his chin, Eric contemplated her drunken night with Ryan like a complex word problem. "It sounds like he's a decent guy. Leaving was the right call."

"Yeah, I get that." Sadie understood why Ryan made the choice he did, but that didn't make her feel any less foolish for putting them both in that situation in the first place.

"Here's the question I'm most interested in," Eric continued. "Did you ask him to stay because you were drunk? Or did you ask him to stay because maybe you don't actually dislike him as much as you pretend to? Because I imagine that's the question Ryan couldn't sort out, either."

Her head was in too much pain for this line of questioning, so she went with the only answer that made sense. "There's a physical attraction between us. But that's all it is. It'll fizzle out."

"Tonight should certainly be interesting." Sliding off the stool, Eric made his way to the door.

It took a few seconds for Sadie's sluggish brain to remember Charity's birthday party. "Oh god, Eric. There's no way I have the energy for that tonight. Look at me." There was no way she could survive another late night of drinking when she was still hungover.

"Oh, you'll be there." He flipped the lock and held one side of the door open. "Because I'm sending you home."

"Excuse me?" Another knife sliced through her forehead. "Don't be ridiculous."

"I'm not. And you heard me. You're going home to sleep this off." Eric stood firm, propping the door with an elbow. "I'll see you tonight."

Was he *mad*?

He didn't sound mad.

But he had to be mad, or at least disappointed, which was possibly worse, in order to send her home.

Sadie had never once gotten in trouble at any job. She was prompt, hardworking, reliable. She'd exceeded expectations on every employee evaluation she'd ever had. This felt like a brand-new kind of low.

"No, wait!" she protested, hurrying to join him at the door. "Don't send me home. I get that it's unprofessional of me to show up hungover. It will *never* happen again. But I'll be okay. Really. I can work, I swear."

"It isn't that," Eric sighed. "I want you there tonight. Charity wants you there tonight. Things between us have gotten really serious lately, and I . . . it's just important to me that you come, okay? So please go home, get some sleep, and come out with us later."

She wasn't ready to relent. "I can do both. Forget what I said. I have plenty of energy. Let me get all this godawful espresso in me and I'll have even more. I'm totally energized and ready to go!"

His eyes flicked to her cup. "Okay, I'm going to be frank here. You sound like you're speeding toward some type of Jessie Spano caffeine addiction meltdown." He pulled the coffee cup from her hand. "Go home. I'll see you at eight."

With no other choice in the matter, Sadie shamefully walked back to the counter and collected her things, then left through the door Eric held open.

She made it halfway down the block before she burst into tears.

CHAPTER 15

Ten hours later, Sadie tugged open the heavy door of a hole-in-the-wall dive with neon signage on the walls and colorful Christmas bulbs strung across the ceiling. Patrons sat scattered at high-top tables throughout the one-room establishment, and gathered around the bar was the group of unbelievably gorgeous humans she was looking for.

Eric stood in the middle of the crowd—looking extra handsome in a navy blazer—with his arm slung around Charity, who wore a minidress as sparkly as a disco ball that displayed her mile-long legs perfectly. Some people were so attractive it was borderline rude.

Speaking of rudely attractive people, Ryan was seated at the bar with Simon. Next to them was a wiry, dark-haired man she assumed to be Simon's husband, Adam.

Sadie had a decision on her hands of which particular brand of awkwardness she'd prefer to deal with first. Eric, whom she owed a massive apology to for having to be sent home earlier. Or Ryan, whom she'd drunkenly embarrassed herself in front of the night before. Decisions, decisions.

Mulling it over, she hung in the shadows of the entranceway until a face she almost didn't recognize cut through the crowd, headed in her direction.

And, oh, what fresh hell had she fallen into?

None other than narcissist Callum approached, an extra drink in hand. "So we meet again," he said, extending a champagne flute her way with a wink.

"So we do." She waved off the drink. "Thanks but I'm not drinking tonight."

Callum's features contorted as though he were mentally doing the math on how much that one sentence decreased his chance of getting laid tonight. But he recovered quickly, never one to count himself out.

A solid fifteen minutes later, Sadie remained trapped in conversation—albeit her only contribution was a series of nods—about Callum's latest photo shoot for a popular men's magazine. He never offered the name of the magazine, however, so she had doubts about its *popularity*. Since Callum had cornered her near the entrance, she had yet to make eye contact with anyone other than Ryan, who had looked her way once, smiled, then noticed the male model in the dark corner with her and went back to sipping his drink and hadn't looked her way since.

The problem was that Sadie was far too socially awkward to know how to extricate herself from this conversation gracefully, and Callum was far too self-centered to notice the subtle indicators that she didn't want to be in this conversation in the first place. So they were stuck. Possibly forever. This could be where she died.

But then a miracle occurred and Charity's beautiful brown eyes met hers through the crowd. Charity whispered something to Eric, who also looked Sadie's way and then chuckled behind his beer glass. Then Charity made her way across the room in what was surely, hopefully, a rescue mission.

"Sadie, love, you look absolutely stunning." Reaching them, Charity leaned in and air-kissed each of Sadie's cheeks.

"Happy birthday!" Sadie replied, the first words she'd spoken since she turned down the drink from Callum. "And if anyone looks stunning, it's you. That dress is amazing."

"This old thing?" Charity spun a little circle, graceful as a ballet dancer even in sky-high stilettos.

Knowing there was no way to compete with professional models, Sadie had selected a simple mid-length black satin slip dress and heeled ankle boots for the occasion.

"Callum, darling, give us a few to chat?" Charity batted her thick eyelashes in his direction.

"Sure, I guess." Callum sounded disappointed, but then he winked and said to her, "Catch up to you later."

They watched him make his way back to the bar, then Charity whipped around. "I am *so* sorry about that." Her dark, bouncy curls framed her angular face, deep red lipstick enhancing the glow of her flawless skin. "I wanted to warn you he'd be here, but Eric said you'd never show if I did."

That was entirely accurate. "It's fine. It was my own inebriated mistake." She seemed to be racking those up lately. "Anyway, how are you? Excited for the big two-eight?"

"Ugh. Don't remind me," Charity groaned. "Every year older is one year closer to the end of my career."

"Please." Sadie did a blatant once-over from the model's head to her toes and back up. "Look at you. You're more beautiful than ever."

"Oh, please keep going," Charity teased, tossing her curls.

"Don't get me wrong, I'm not calling it quits anytime soon or anything, but I do think I'll be spending more time in Sutton Island than New York this year." She glanced over her shoulder to Eric, who caught her looking and instantly smiled. "But there are other reasons for that, too."

Sadie watched the exchanged glance between the couple. "You two seem really great together lately."

In the earlier years of Eric and Charity's relationship, the off times had been far more frequent than the ons. They'd been so young when they met on the show—Charity only twenty and Eric twenty-two. Add in two high-pressure careers, a certain level of fame, and the long distance, and it was no wonder they'd had their share of ups and downs.

On some level, their years-long struggle to make it work had always been confirmation to Sadie that all relationships were doomed from the start. Eric and Charity were both incredible people, and neither of them were cheaters or treated the other with anything other than respect and admiration. The times they'd called it quits, it was never dramatic or done in anger. Rather, it was because they thought they were doing the best thing for each other. Yet, that didn't stop Eric from being heartbroken each and every time, and Sadie had watched that quiet, stoic hurt play out on multiple occasions over the years. If two people who loved each other that much couldn't make it work, it was pretty obvious no one could.

"Yeah, we're really good." Charity turned her attention back on Sadie. "He's worried about you, you know."

Her heart fell. "Did he tell you about today? I can't believe I was so unprofessional. He has every right to be worried about my job performance."

"He's not worried about your job performance." Charity

booped the end of Sadie's nose as if she were a lovable household pet. "He's worried about *you*."

"Oh. Well, I'm busy but I'll survive."

Charity's eyes could be as assessing as Eric's, and Sadie shifted uncomfortably in her heels. Maybe she should have stuck to conversing with Callum—there was zero chance of him deciphering her inner thoughts.

"If you say so," Charity eventually said. "Now let's go have some fun."

Looping her arm through Sadie's, Charity pulled her in the direction of the bar, pausing before they were fully absorbed by the crowd to lean in and whisper-shout over the music blaring from a jukebox. "By the way, that guy who's here for you . . ." Her eyes cut to Ryan at the bar. "Hotter than three hells."

Sadie shook her head. "Oh no, he isn't here for me."

"Yeah, okay. Then who's he here for?"

Sadie glanced at Ryan, currently sipping from a glass while Simon animatedly chatted away to the small group gathered there. She opened her mouth to respond, then noticed Charity was already gone, now throwing her arms around some blonde in a red leather miniskirt.

Continuing on her own, Sadie made her way over to where Simon and Ryan were in conversation with Eric and Adam and two other well-dressed men, alongside another gorgeous brunette whose face Sadie recognized from makeup ads.

As she entered the circle, Eric tossed an arm around her shoulder and leaned down to say, "Glad you made it."

"Thanks," she said with a half smile up at him. "Sorry again about earlier."

"Don't even start," he warned, wagging a finger back and forth.

Proper introductions were made to those gathered she didn't

know, and after pleasantries were exchanged, Sadie made her way to the bar while the group fell into conversation about *Runway Wars.*

Leaning against the counter, she waited for the bartender's attention. Ryan, seated at her side but turned toward the group, propped an elbow back on the bar and asked, "Can I get you a drink?"

At the memory of him tracing her alcohol flush with his fingertip, her skin heated. "I'm just drinking water tonight."

"Me, too." He swirled his glass, apparently filled with ice water. So he likely had been as drunk as she was last night, and the things he'd said probably meant nothing.

Tonight he wore a light blue button-up with navy pants, sleeves rolled to mid-forearm and wavy hair tousled to an expert-level of perfection. His green eyes showed no evidence of a hangover, and for the first time since she'd accidentally elbowed his face, there was no lingering trace of the purplish bruise under his eye. He looked good. *Really* good. Or as Charity phrased it, hotter than three hells.

Standing from his barstool, Ryan encroached into her space and angled his body to make their conversation private from the group gathered behind them. "That, uh"—he rubbed the back of his neck—"that guy you were talking to earlier, he a friend of yours?" His chin jutted in the direction of Callum, currently chatting up a high-top table of women seated near the jukebox.

"Uh, no. We met at Eric's New Year's Eve party last year. That's all."

Sadie didn't offer any more detail than that, and to his credit, Ryan didn't ask anything further. Instead, his eyes roamed over her dress, down to the toe of her boots. "You look really, *really* good tonight."

Captivating Ryan's attention would make anyone feel special, but in a room full of literal supermodels, having his eyes solely on her made that feeling all the more potent. "Thank you. You look pretty good yourself, Pearson."

Once she secured a glass of water, they turned back to the group, where a lively conversation was taking place about a contestant who sabotaged one of Eric's designs hours before he had to present to the judges. Sadie couldn't fully focus on the story, though. Something was shifting between her and Ryan, that was undeniable, but she didn't understand in what way or what any of it meant. If it meant anything at all.

With their history, acting on whatever was brewing between them would be a terrible idea. A surefire way to pull her head from the game when she very much needed her head *in* the game to secure the promotion at the estate. Another slipup like being sent home from her job was unacceptable. And the very last thing she needed was one more upheaval in her life right now anyway.

Peering at Ryan in her periphery, she swept a discreet gaze along the line of his broad shoulders, up the shifting column of his throat, over his sharp, freshly shaved jawline, pausing on his lips—curved into a grin at whatever was being said in the group—then up to his eyes, which flicked over to meet hers. She didn't blink away. Neither did he. And yeah, acting on anything would be disastrous.

The night moved on, and after delivering a heartfelt toast to Charity, Eric announced the arrival of the cars he hired to chauffeur everyone to the haunted house.

"This is gonna be so much fun!" Simon commented as he finished off the last of his drink.

"Aye, Sophie," a loud Scottish accent inquired from somewhere behind her. "Wanna ride over together?"

Shit. Despite getting her name wrong, Callum was clearly talking to her. Sadie pasted a smile on her face and whipped around just as he approached. "Thanks for the offer, but I'm riding over with my friends here."

"Oh." Callum's gaze traveled from Adam to Simon to Ryan, who—purposely or not—moved closer to her side. "You didn't introduce me."

Okay, this guy was being kind of pushy for someone she'd made out with months ago and couldn't be bothered to remember her name. And he wasn't taking her subtle hints, so she quickly formulated a new plan.

"I'm sorry, how rude of me," she apologized. "Callum, these are my friends Adam and Simon Winchester. And this"—she slipped her hand into Ryan's—"is my boyfriend, Ryan Pearson."

Silence fell over them, except for Simon, who choked on his drink at Sadie's announcement, then walked away hacking and beating his chest with a closed fist.

Sadie squeezed Ryan's hand in an effort to communicate, *Please just go with this.*

Entangling their fingers, Ryan extended his free hand toward Callum. "Nice to meet you."

Callum shook his hand, but an immediate disinterest clouded his eyes and he soon drifted off in the direction of the woman in the red leather miniskirt. Sadie had to give him props for maintaining a confidence level she could only dream of.

She released Ryan's hand once Callum was out of earshot and said, "Thanks for that."

Ryan smirked. "Definitely not a problem."

Finally recovered, Simon returned to them. "Your *boyfriend*? What the hell was that? Are you two a thing?" Adam shot his husband a stern look that said, *That's none of your business,* but Simon ignored him. *"Are you?"*

"No," Sadie answered. "I just needed Callum to think that."

"Oh." Simon's voice returned to its normal pitch. "Okay, that makes sense. I get it now."

The four began walking toward the entrance where Eric stood directing people into cars.

"'Cause I mean, *you two*?" Simon chuckled. "I'd expect hell to freeze over before you two became a couple."

Sadie knew he didn't mean anything by it, that it was a statement anyone who had witnessed her and Ryan together would make. But for a reason she didn't want to examine, it stung a little all the same.

CHAPTER 16

Gus's Ghostworks was housed in a run-down strip mall ten minutes from downtown, and the parking lot was packed even at ten p.m. on a Wednesday night. The windows were blacked out with spray paint, and an assortment of creatures—a blow-up zombie, a skeleton at least twenty feet tall, a vampire lying in a coffin—flanked the entranceway, providing a glimpse of what was to come inside.

They crossed the parking lot, and the closer Sadie got to the grotesque decor, the more she questioned how she'd written this whole thing off as laughable. Because if she wasn't mistaken, that vampire looked—

The very *real* vampire sprang up in his coffin, eyes popping open to reveal soulless black holes.

Stumbling backward, Sadie screamed and clutched her chest.

"Hello, beautiful, you look like a perfect midnight snack." The vampire threw his head back and let out a roaring "*Muah-ah-ah.*"

As quickly as he'd sprung alive, he closed his iris-less eyes and lay back in his coffin, arms folded in an X over his chest.

"Jesus Christ! We're not even inside yet!" Sucking in gulps of air, Sadie realized her chest wasn't the only thing she was gripping. In her terror, she'd stumbled backward into Ryan and pulled his arm around her waist like a seat belt. Now she felt the press of his chest against her back, the soft shake of suppressed laughter.

"Well, it *is* a haunted house." Simon held the entrance door open. "What'd you expect?"

"I'm sure she didn't expect *that*," Adam spoke up in her defense. "I didn't think that fucker was real, either, Sadie."

"Thank you, Adam." Composure somewhat regained, she released Ryan's arm. "Sorry about that."

"It's funny, I don't remember you being such a screamer." Ryan's arm slid away from her, but he squeezed her hip before contact was lost, and her stomach dove like a seagull spotting a fish in the ocean.

Falling in line, Sadie let Ryan take the lead behind Adam, following closely at his heels in case any more shit went down.

Entering the lobby, Eric spotted her. "There you are. Why were you fucking around in the parking lot for so long?" As Sadie went to explain that having the bejesus scared out of her was not the same thing as *fucking around*, he waved away any explanation. "Never mind. We're all here now."

The last part was addressed to a teenage employee with braces who stood behind a countertop display of Gus's Ghostworks T-shirts and bumper stickers and other assorted memorabilia for those who might want to remember their time here. Sadie certainly did not.

As the teenager delved into a memorized spiel on the list of medical conditions that would prevent a patron from going any farther, Sadie's gaze traveled over the group lined against the wall, pausing briefly on Callum, his nostrils flaring at each medical condition ticked off the list. Skating past him, her eyes landed on Charity, tucked protectively under Eric's arm. Charity glanced her way, discreetly pointed to Ryan, then mouthed, "So hot," while fanning herself.

Blushing, Sadie blinked away, dialing back into the teenager's instructions. There were five rooms they would *experience* tonight, each act designed *to put the true meaning of horror back into Halloween*—a line delivered with the enthusiasm of a teenager who would rather be literally anywhere else.

Next the group was directed into a large room in a single-file line, the teenager instructing them to line up with their backs against the wall and "enjoy the show" before shutting the door behind them. Then the lights faded until they were immersed in darkness. Sadie and Ryan were the last of the group, and she was grateful she'd chosen the spot between Simon and Ryan so she wasn't the last person in line and nearest to the door. Just in case.

It was so quiet Sadie could hear Simon's breaths beside her, and a heavy sense of foreboding settled in her stomach as the seconds ticked by and the anticipation became stifling. Sadie shuffled closer in Ryan's direction, stopping only when their shoulders brushed. Why had she agreed to this again? Oh yeah, because Eric knew she never stood a chance against any type of peer pressure.

The tension rose to a climax as a set of double doors on the opposite wall slowly opened, a creaking-door sound effect simultaneously playing through speakers that must've been hidden around them. Sadie's heart beat faster as everything went silent again. Then all at once a spotlight illuminated the doorway. A second later, a doll with long black hair and thick black eyeliner appeared out of nowhere. It wore a frilly white dress, and it just *stared* at them.

Taking another sidestep in Ryan's direction, Sadie leaned closer and whispered, "I'm not sure this is really my kind of scene."

The musical notes of a child's lullaby blared through the speakers before she got any response, and the thing in the doorway moved toward them, limbs bending and snapping at odd angles like broken tree branches.

Fear swept through Sadie's veins like ice water, even as she tried to rationalize with herself. It was an adult actor, heavily made up to look like a porcelain doll, an acrobat or contortionist of some type. There was no reason to be afraid. It wasn't going to touch her. And yet, none of those self-reassurances did a damn thing to keep the hairs on her arms from standing on end.

The contortionist approached the group and paced down the line, staring at each of them in turn. The only light spilled through the open doorway on the opposite side of the room, providing just enough illumination to see the show. Over the lullaby, a shrill voice asked, "Do you want to play with me?" and it was by far the creepiest shit Sadie had ever witnessed. At least until the doll stopped directly in front of her and Ryan, smiled, and blood oozed from its mouth.

"Oh dear god." Revolted, Sadie spun and buried her face against Ryan's shoulder. What kind of scar-you-for-life attraction was this? Gus's Ghostworks was a deceivingly innocent name for this kind of doll-demon, mind-terror shit. She sure hoped Eric was prepared to fund the therapy sessions she would need to ever sleep again.

Somehow, the scent of sandalwood drifted past the damage being inflicted on her brain, and her terror subsided long enough to realize she was snuggled against Ryan's chest, hands clutching the sides of his shirt.

Sadie took the briefest second to enjoy the comfort of another human body, *Ryan's* body, pressed against her. But as she started to step back and apologize (again) for using him as a comfort object, Ryan's arms came around her, hands splaying protectively over her back and holding her in place. Dipping his head, he whispered, "Stay."

One single word and Sadie forgot the contortionist horror show and became hyperaware of Ryan's hands on her, of his thumbs pressing between the notches of her spine, of the goose bumps ignited from her nape to her toes.

Was it possible to be aroused in a house of horror?

Absolutely it was, she decided when the pressure of his fingers sank deeper, clutching her over the top of her slip dress.

Loosening her grip on his shirt, Sadie trailed her fingernails lightly over his abs, lingering just above his beltline, skating in from his hip and then out again. With her forehead buried against his collarbone, she heard Ryan's deep sigh, felt his breaths come faster under her touch.

After last night, this little bit of physical contact had her nearly ready to explode. Arousal pulsed between her thighs as her satin dress was crushed against her skin, Ryan's grip bordering on desperate now. She hadn't the slightest clue what was happening in the background, and she was fairly certain Ryan didn't, either. The only thing she was aware of was him. Her only thought was his raspy admission the night before, *You have no idea what you do to me. Or the things I want to do to you.* Maybe he hadn't meant it. Maybe he had. Maybe it was time to find out.

But Ryan would leave this up to her, she knew that. He'd told her the ball was in her court, so if they were going to cross a line, she'd have to cross it first.

Fuck it.

Tilting her head up, she pressed her lips against Ryan's neck in a featherlight kiss, then opened her mouth and tasted his skin with her tongue.

She felt Ryan's sharp intake of air as his chest rose, as his hands fell to her hips and gripped her roughly. His head fell forward, and a strangled, "Don't fuck with me, Stockton," brushed against the shell of her ear. A plea or maybe a warning. Either way, she pulled back to get a read of his expression, but it was too dark to decipher anything beyond the intensity burning in his eyes.

Sadie shook her head, hands sliding up his chest and hooking around his neck. "Not fucking with you. I want you, Pearson."

"Prove it."

Rising onto her tiptoes, Sadie pressed her mouth to his almost before he got the words out. If she surprised him, though, it lasted only a split second before his mouth moved over hers, confident and greedy. Cupping her face, he tilted her jaw to deepen their kiss, and she couldn't contain the low moan that rose in her throat when his tongue swept against the crease of her lips.

But somewhere in the back of her mind she registered their proximity to Simon and Adam, and that they might be visible despite the dim light. Ryan must have felt her sudden hesitation because he broke their kiss, whispered, "Come here," and pulled her into the dark corner a few feet away. Then his hands slid into her hair as he brought her mouth back to his.

Over the years, Sadie hadn't let herself think too much about what a great kisser—among other things—Ryan was in college. But as she tasted the spearmint on his tongue and her nipples tightened in response, all those memories came flooding back. If his skill set was impressive then, it was expert-level now.

Desperation taking over, she arched her back and pressed her hips into him. Struggling to keep them both steady as she clung to him, Ryan turned and pinned her back against the wall, pressing his full weight against her. She gasped.

"Too much?" he asked against her lips.

"Not nearly enough," Sadie replied before sinking her teeth into his luscious bottom lip.

But all too soon, Ryan interrupted their kiss again. "I think we're about to move rooms," he said in broken breaths. "Music's fading."

Breathless herself, Sadie glanced over his shoulder. The contortionist crawled back in the direction of the double doors on the opposite side of the room, one leg draped over her own shoulder with a foot dangling near her face. If this was room number one, who knew what fucked-up shit lay ahead.

Sadie released Ryan, and they straightened their clothing and moved back in line just before the lights rose. Another door opened at the front of the line, and the teenage employee reappeared to lead them into room number two.

As they followed the line ahead, Simon turned to her. "Wasn't that an incredible performance?"

"Indeed," she replied.

Unimpressed with her answer, Simon turned back to Adam, chatting away.

Drop-kicked back to the real world, Sadie was afraid to check Ryan's expression in the harsh light of reality. Was he as dazed as she was? Had she been too forward in coming on to him? God, that kiss was something though.

Before they crossed the threshold into the next room, Ryan's arm snaked around her waist. "Do *not* get weird on me now, Stockton," he said, voice pitched low.

"People can see us now," she replied over her shoulder.

Confirming her point, Eric looked their way as they entered the next room, his eyes doing a quick double take at Ryan's arm around her waist. Then his mouth broke into his devious-Grinch smile that promised, *We'll definitely be talking about this tomorrow.*

"So what?" Ryan challenged. "You're my girlfriend tonight, remember?"

Flutters invaded her stomach. Her heart rate accelerated to a speed that could likely break the sound barrier. And the heated flush that already burned through her cheeks, her neck, and her chest, spread down into her belly.

As the lights faded once more, Ryan stopped short near the door they'd just entered, keeping a fair amount of space between them and the rest of the group. "Besides," he continued, leaning against the wall at his back. "I don't think there's any way to keep this a secret. I'm wearing more of your lip gloss now than you are."

As if determined to break her (already missing) resolve, he swept her hair forward and kissed the back of her shoulder. The sticky residue of her lip gloss lingered on his lips, and yeah, that did things to her.

Sadie turned in his arms, whispered, "Okay, but just for tonight," and then kissed him again before the next horror act even began.

CHAPTER 17

"So how was the sex?"

Those five words from Eric were the exact reason Sadie spent half the morning scheming up an excuse to be late to the shop, ultimately deciding a tardy wouldn't be the best look the very day after she'd been sent home with a hangover.

"No sex was had, thank you very much." At least not with another person, but that was neither here nor there.

She settled her bag and their coffees on the counter while Eric's hawkish eyes followed her movements, searching for some type of tell.

"You're telling me that you two got freaky in a haunted house—not here to kink-shame, by the way, but I never knew you had it in you—and you didn't take him home with you?"

Sadie straightened her short-sleeved, fuzzy gray sweater then smoothed wrinkles that didn't exist from her black pencil skirt. "It's not a kink, it just kind of happened. It was only kissing"—*and* so *much touching*—"nothing more. So, no, he didn't come home with me."

It was the truth. Just an abbreviated version of the truth. The full story was that she made out with Ryan Pearson in every single room of that haunted house. To the extent that she couldn't provide the theme of the last few rooms even if she were forced to take a multiple-choice quiz, though she vaguely remembered some clowns with chainsaws. However, she could now pass any in-depth written (or oral . . . *definitely* oral) exam on Ryan Pearson's mouth. Hell, she could write a thousand-word essay on the shape of his lower lip alone.

But when the night had ended, they again split their car with Simon and Adam. Between the three drop-offs, Sadie's apartment had come first, and it's not like she could invite Ryan to her place with Simon and Adam sitting *right there*. Simon had been dazed enough after noticing Sadie's lip gloss smeared on Ryan's mouth after room number three, and she wasn't about to confuse him further when she didn't understand what was happening herself.

So Sadie went home alone and spent some quality time with herself. And her fingers. And her vibrator.

After relieving some *tension*, she'd picked up her phone to see a single text.

> Ry: I enjoyed every single
> second of tonight. Get some
> sleep, Stockton.

He really was being entirely too nice, on top of being entirely too hot. It was disturbing. How was she supposed to resist him when he was attentive and thoughtful and could kiss like it was the sole thing he was put on this earth to do? Then again, she'd thought he was all those things when they were in college, and in the end, he still let her down just like everyone else.

"I can't say I'm not disappointed." Eric's voice pulled her back to the conversation at hand. "I was rooting for you."

"How sweet of you to care about my sex life."

Huffing a laugh, Eric picked up his drink. "Let's be honest, I'm not sure you have enough sex to call it a *sex life*. And of course I care. I also care about the hundred bucks I just lost to my girlfriend."

Her jaw fell open. "You made a bet on if I'd get laid? You're an asshole."

"Never claimed otherwise."

"Switching topics," Sadie said, desperate to talk about anything other than her lackluster sex life, "anyone interesting on the schedule today?"

"Actually, I have a prom dress consult coming in at four."

Sadie pulled the lid off her latte to let it cool. "Since when do we do prom dresses?"

"We don't. But we're doing this as a onetime favor."

"Is this some VIP celebrity thing?"

"Not exactly." Reaching into his messenger bag stashed behind the counter, Eric removed a stack of folded papers and laid them out in front of her. Sadie picked up the first one, eyes quickly skimming what appeared to be a letter.

"This high schooler, Jade, wrote to me," he explained as she read. "She wants to be a designer one day, and she sent me these sketches she made for her prom dress. But it sounds like her family doesn't have a lot of money, and I don't think she can afford the materials."

Sadie put the letter down and picked up several drawings.

"I emailed her and told her to come by after school today. That we'd take one of these sketches and figure out how to bring it to life here in the shop. I can't stand the idea of this kid skipping her prom because she can't afford a dress."

Sadie's breath caught behind her sternum.

She knew all too well what it was like to grow up always worried about expenses, never wanting to ask for anything above and beyond basic needs. Her mom worked long, *hard* hours, but nursing assistants didn't make a salary anywhere near what the job deserved, and money was always scarce.

Sadie worked part-time jobs through high school in an effort to help out, but the older she got the more expenses came along. It seemed they were always behind, the stack of overdue bills piled on the kitchen table as consistent as the days of the week.

While grants and a few scholarships covered some of her college tuition, and she was able to secure loans for the rest, she also waited tables at a local restaurant every night and weekend throughout her undergrad years, spending her tips on necessities and saving any scarce extra for whatever emergency might lay ahead. A problem with her car. An unexpected trip to the doctor. A needed repair on her years-old laptop. There was simply nothing left for the extras most college students enjoyed—a night out at a bar or getting her nails done or purchasing the latest trendy makeup product.

Or buying a fancy dress to attend a formal on campus.

"Hey." Eric spoke gently, brows lowered. "You, uh, you good?"

Tears welled at the corners of her eyes as she handed the sketches back to him. "Yeah, it's just . . . sometimes a dress is *really* important." She grabbed a Kleenex from the stash near the register and dabbed at her eyes. "You know?"

"I do," he said with an odd look. "It's kind of the whole reason behind what we do here."

"Yeah. I guess it is." Sadie knew Eric didn't have to bother working in this store every day. After *Runway Wars*, he could have lived more than comfortably off his designs alone, or catered to only a celebrity, high-couture crowd. But more than anything, Eric's true passion was helping others feel beautiful and confident in their own skin. And while he also didn't buy into the bullshit of happily ever after, watching a bride try on a gown that made them radiate with joy was a truly special experience—even Sadie could admit that.

Thankfully before Eric could further inquire into her sudden emotional state, her phone buzzed against the countertop.

Mom: Hey, it's Mom! Dinner Monday? Doug really wants to meet you.

It was as though Ann Stockton could sense her tears from miles away and knew precisely when to strike. Nothing like a heady dose of daughter guilt to top off the morning.

Sadie: Not this week. Overnight tours start tomorrow and my schedule is packed. Soon though. Love you.

Then Sadie tucked her phone in her bag so it was out of sight.

* * *

"Shhhh! We have to keep it down."

Sadie had warned Simon and Ryan multiple times about the

nightly tour still going on a floor above, yet both men were in an animated mood tonight, exchanging jokes and bursts of laughter like currency. But Sadie wasn't animated, and laughter was something she couldn't afford.

Nearing eleven, the only thing she felt was stressed. And tired.

Having worked diligently since they'd arrived earlier that evening, every last detail of the cellar was set up for tomorrow night's inaugural Wilmont House Mixtures and Murder Tour. Upholstered sofas and armchairs lined the perimeters of the space, and floor lamps with art deco shades dripping in crystals illuminated the area in an inviting, low-lit glow. Clusters of chubby white candles were scattered atop the half-dozen high-top tables and cast shadows that danced upon the stone walls like a puppeteer putting on a show. All Sadie could think of as she took in the space was that Ryan was right—the cellar was now the perfect cocktail lounge oozing both mystery and sex appeal.

Now they waited for her old tour to wrap up upstairs so they could perform their practice walk-through. The actors from Simon's improv group were scheduled to show up at midnight, and this was the first and only glimpse Sadie would get into how this was all going to play out. So as much as she'd love not to have a single care in the whole world just like her partners, she instead felt the weight of that world placed squarely on her shoulders. It was finally happening. In twenty-four hours.

"I don't think they can hear us down here, Stockton," Ryan said from where he was lounged on a sofa.

Sadie spun in his direction. "*You* don't know what they can hear, Pearson, and I don't know how many times I have to say it. Matt is up there working very hard to ensure his guests have a good experience, and the last thing he needs to contend with is a bunch of noise and—"

The creak of the cellar door at the top of the stairwell cut her monologue short, followed by Matt's voice echoing down the stone walls. "All done for the night, Sadie. Mansion's all yours."

"Thanks, Matt," she called back. Both Simon and Ryan watched her expectantly. "What? Why are you both staring at me?"

Simon rose from a burgundy velvet wing-back chair. "I'm just gonna run up to the restroom before we begin." He took the stairs two at a time.

Instead of fleeing her wrath at warp speed, Ryan sheepishly approached, hands raised like he might sneak up on an injured wild animal. He was dressed down for the walk-through in a fitted gray T-shirt and jeans, his baseball cap pulled low. But not low enough that she couldn't make out his earthy green eyes under the brim.

"You okay tonight?" he asked.

"Fine. Why wouldn't I be? It's you two who don't seem to understand that we have a lot of work to do."

He slowly lowered his hands. "Okay, I get that. But we were at a standstill." One corner of his mouth lifted, and there was that dimple. "Look, I know you're under pressure with the project, but if it's more than that, and if you want someone to talk to, I'm here."

Sadie nodded, a thick cloud of emotion billowing in her chest for reasons she couldn't explain. While she appreciated the gesture, she couldn't talk to him about something she couldn't put into words. Everything in her life was changing in one way or another, and each day that passed brought her closer to the point of no return. Even if the outcome of these tours was what she hoped for, she'd still lose something in leaving her job with Eric. And then the only person she would have left would be her mom, who might get her heart broken again by an accountant named Douglas. She longed to hit a pause button, to slow everything down and deal with one issue at a time. But life didn't work that way.

"I appreciate that. Really," she managed. "But I'm okay."

"Should we . . ." Ryan scrubbed a hand over his jaw. "Should we maybe talk about last night at least?"

"*Should we?* Probably," she admitted. "Do I have the capacity for that at this exact moment? Not really."

"That's fair." As he twisted the brim of his hat to the back, Sadie felt the familiar swoop in her stomach the simple action always brought on. "But I had a really good time with you. I want you to know that at least."

Cheeks warming, she softly replied, "I had a really good time with you, too."

Simon's footsteps thudded down the stairs once more. When he returned to them, they went over the tour schedule one last time before heading upstairs to begin the walk-through. In the foyer, they briefly discussed introductions and when Ryan would serve the vodka appletinis. Next, Sadie led them through a revised version of the tour she would give, and they made their way to Hazel's writing room.

"This will be the only time throughout the night we invite guests into this room." Sadie cast a deliberate look at Simon. "*Agreed?*"

"Agreed," Simon sighed wearily.

Over the past weeks he'd fought hard making his case for planting a clue in this room, but if Sadie nearly had an aneurysm over a spilt Dr Pepper, there was no way she was allowing their guests to rummage through this sacred space unsupervised.

"*Christ!*" Ryan shouted.

When Sadie turned her attention in his direction, he was

gripping the edge of Hazel's desk, steadying himself after tripping over the same bump in the floor.

"Y'all should really fix this," he said.

A soft smile came to her face. "It adds character."

Ryan returned her smile. "It's going to add a fracture to my neck by the time this is all over."

"All right, Pearson," she teased. "If you're done fucking around up here, we can continue."

A bark of laughter as he held her gaze. "Fucking around? Is that what you call it?"

Simon cleared his throat. Loudly. "Should I go to the restroom again or . . ."

Both of their heads snapped in his direction.

"Nope," Sadie said quickly, feeling like a middle schooler getting called out for liking a boy. "Sorry, Simon."

Ryan scratched his forehead. "Yeah. Sorry about that."

Simon motioned toward the door. "Let's proceed then."

CHAPTER 18

The massive library on the first floor had always reminded Sadie of *Beauty and the Beast*. Shelves of old, dusty books ran floor to ceiling, complete with a rolling wooden ladder that always tempted her to reenact her favorite scene. She never did it though. Even when she was all alone.

But Simon had no qualms climbing the first few rungs then gliding down the wall. "Look, Sadie, just like *Beauty and the Beast*," he called out, one arm gracefully extended. "Have you ever tried this?"

"No." She crossed her arms over her chest, watching as Simon pushed off again.

"You really want to do that now, don't you?" Ryan asked at her side.

"No," she sharply repeated. And it wasn't a lie. She didn't only *now* want to do it. She'd wanted to do it for years.

Simon slowed to a gradual stop, eyeing the shelves above him. "Hey, Sadie, what's up with that book?"

She followed his gaze but didn't spot anything out of the ordinary. "What do you mean?"

"That book." Simon walked the ladder farther down the wall, then climbed almost to the very top. That's when Sadie noticed the book he was aiming for. Unlike every other book on the shelf, actually every other book in the entire library, the spine wasn't in pristine condition. It was worn and stripped in places. She hadn't noticed it before, but now that Simon pointed it out, she couldn't *not* see it.

"I, um, I don't know," she said.

Simon climbed back down the ladder with the book in hand. Once on the ground, he flipped open the cover.

All the air rushed from Sadie's lungs.

A rectangle had been cut into the pages, and stuffed into the empty space was a stack of folded papers. Papers that were aged in a remarkably similar fashion to the ones they'd found hidden behind the mirror above the mantel.

Simon waited for her to do the honors.

After carefully pulling the pages from the altered book, Sadie then took them to the mahogany desk and spread them over the flat surface. The first page contained a title.

THE CASE OF HARRIETT'S MISSING DIARY

"Holy shit," she muttered.

"Is that . . ." Ryan trailed off, but he didn't need to finish because Sadie did it for him.

"This is the beginning of the manuscript we found behind the mirror."

Sadie had read and reread those pages until she could practically recite them from memory, but nothing about the story made much sense without a beginning. Now it appeared as though she held that very beginning in her hand.

"Like, not to be rude," Simon said delicately, "but how did you *not notice* the one book in this entire library that wasn't like the others?"

"I don't know," she answered, equally stumped. "It was pretty high up."

"Yeah," he replied. "That must be it."

How *had* she not noticed? Now that she examined the book in the light, it was obvious it wasn't just worn over time but that someone had purposely damaged the spine to make it stand out. The only question was *why* . . .

Peering over Sadie's shoulder at the pages, Simon posited, "Would Hazel have left clues around the mansion to be found after her death?"

She tore her eyes away from the conundrum in front of her. "Just because you deal in mysteries for a living doesn't mean this is some type of clue."

"Hear me out, Stockton," Ryan spoke up. "Pieces of a manuscript discovered hidden behind a mirror and now in a purposely manipulated book kind of feels . . . clue-esque, no?"

"Not to mention," Simon added, "the manuscript is a mystery."

Sadie shook her head. "Hazel didn't write mysteries."

Ryan and Simon exchanged a glance.

"*The Case of Harriett's Missing Diary,*" Simon read aloud, hovering over the desk. "You're right, that's probably not a mystery at all."

"Why would Hazel leave clues behind?" she asked. "It doesn't make sense. Clues for *what*?"

Before Simon could reply, the doorbell rang. "Oh, that must be our actors!" He clapped his hands together. "I'll greet them and we'll meet you two in the cellar!"

After carefully gathering the pages, Sadie and Ryan left the library, stopping to tuck the latest discovery safely away in her tote bag before making their way back to the cellar. Emerging at the bottom of the stairwell, Sadie saw Simon standing alongside two strangers and . . . *Charity?*

"Hi!" Sadie greeted the model as she and Ryan joined the circle. "What are you doing here?"

"Well, Simon and I got to talking last night"—Charity, dressed in an oversize white button-up and light-washed denim jeans, paused to air-kiss both of Sadie's cheeks—"and you know I love a good murder mystery. So, here I am. I'm playing a sexy film star." She held her arms out diagonally, putting herself on display. "Think I can handle it?"

Of course this was right up Charity's alley. Sadie should've thought to ask her to participate.

Ryan cleared his throat. "Good to see you again, Charity."

The supermodel's thousand-watt smile beamed even brighter as her eyes flicked back and forth between them. "Oh, it's absolutely *fantastic* to see you again, love."

"All right, let me make proper introductions," Simon spoke up. "Everyone, this is Katie from my improv group." He motioned to a thirtysomething woman with wavy, light brown hair and rosy cheeks. "Katie, meet Ryan and Sadie. And you briefly met Charity upstairs, of course."

"Hi, everyone," Katie said with a bubbly smile. "I'll be playing the victim, Katie Lynn, famous author rumored to be having a torrid affair with someone around town."

"Wait," Sadie interrupted. "Simon, I thought we agreed this wasn't going to be based on Hazel Wilmont."

"It isn't based on Hazel," he said flatly as he adjusted his glasses. "This is a fictitious story about Katie Lynn, famous *adult* novelist. See the difference?"

"Simon!"

"Sadie, you *must* give me some creative liberty here. *It is only an act of fiction!*"

Her narrowed gaze stayed fixed on Simon, but she relented. "Proceed carefully."

"Um, it will be my drink that's poisoned," Katie continued timidly, "so after my dramatic demise during cocktail hour, I'll just be a dead body on the floor."

"Wait," Sadie interrupted again, and she didn't miss Simon's exasperated huff and mumbled, "You've got to be kidding me."

Ignoring him, Sadie addressed Katie. "You're going to lie on the floor pretending to be dead for like . . . *three hours*? You're okay with that?"

"*Okay* with it?" Katie let out a melodic chuckle. "I have three kids under the age of six at home. You want to pay me to take an uninterrupted nap? Don't threaten me with a good time."

"Oh." Sadie nodded, slightly befuddled. "Glad you're able to join us then."

"In addition to Katie, we also have Gabe." Simon motioned to a distinguished gentleman Sadie estimated to be in his late fifties. He wore a navy cardigan and khaki pants, and there was a definite silver fox vibe about him.

"Hello, everyone." The man's voice was surprisingly deep. "I'm playing the role of Gabe Rogers, husband of Katie Lynn, but also rumored to be having a fling of my own with a certain film star." He winked in Charity's direction, and Charity blew him an air kiss. "I've thrown this cocktail party and invited all the known gossips from town in hopes of discovering the identity of my wife's secret lover."

"Now that everyone has met," Simon said with a sharp clap of his hands, "let's get to it!" He led the way to the lounge area, and everyone spread out on the plush sofas and at the high-top tables. "Now, I'll play the role of the butler, because of course every good murder mystery requires a butler. At the end of cocktail hour, Katie will suddenly collapse to the floor, kicking off our game."

Dramatically gripping her neck, Katie slumped over the arm of a sofa.

"All of our guests will be given cards stating their *identities* upon arrival," Simon continued. "So we're not the only ones playing roles here, our twenty guests will be, too. As the butler, it's my duty to ensure our guests are headed in the right direction in terms of discovering clues and asking the right questions. Clues will be planted all throughout the mansion"—he stopped short at the stern look Sadie cast his way—"except for Hazel's writing room, which is strictly off-limits after Sadie's tour."

"And no drinks *anywhere* but the foyer and the cocktail lounge," Sadie cut in. "Just so everyone is aware." She couldn't stomach a Dr Pepper 2.0 incident.

"The killer will change each night, as to not get repetitive," Simon said. "And as much as we prepare for every scenario, these things always involve a little improv. So as much as Gabe, Katie, and I have rehearsed, I want to run through this again in our actual setting. Everyone ready?"

Around the circle, everyone nodded enthusiastically.

Simon smiled, eyes gleaming behind his glasses. "Let's do this."

CHAPTER 19

Opening night was upon them.

Shortly before midnight Friday, the night's guests—a mixture of couples, friend groups, and a mother with her two adult daughters—coalesced in the foyer while Sadie checked tickets and passed each guest their identity notecard. Meanwhile, Ryan and Simon, serving the caramel appletinis, circulated the room.

Sadie's heart thumped erratically, and she couldn't recall a time she had ever been this nervous on the job before. Her hands hadn't trembled as they did now even on her very first tour. The sharp heels of her black over-the-knee boots clicked against the marble floor as she made her way to the head of the group, her hands smoothing down her black boat-neck sweater and gray pleated miniskirt. Jerry asked for the *ambience* to be sexy, so Sadie had chosen what she deemed to be a sexy-enough-without-being-*too*-sexy outfit.

Her fellow hosts for the evening looked pretty sexy themselves. Ryan and Simon both wore white button-ups with black pants and polished oxfords, Ryan opting for a slim black tie while Simon went the route of bow tie, silky black vest, and a slightly askew gray fedora. Sadie wondered how long he debated that choice in the mirror.

Facing the crowd, she pasted on her smile and willed her voice not to shake. "Good evening, everyone, and welcome to the inaugural Wilmont House Mixtures and Murder Tour."

A hush fell over the crowd, everyone casting their attention her way.

"I'm Sadie Stockton, tour guide here at the Wilmont House and one of your hosts for the evening. Please take a few minutes to settle in, enjoy your expertly crafted cocktail, and get to know your fellow patrons. We'll be spending quite a lot of time together over the course of the night."

* * *

Nearly an hour later, Sadie led the night's group through the creaky old door and into Hazel's writing room. Having managed to settle in and suppress her nerves for the past half hour, the shake in her hands now returned, accompanied by the familiar rise of goose bumps that always struck upon entrance into this space. This was the part of her tour she was most uncertain about. Unlike her old historical tours, these guests had paid a hefty ticket price for a murder mystery game, not to hear about Hazel Wilmont's life or writing career.

Taking a steady breath, Hazel's words floated through her mind. *Keep your courage close.*

"All right, everyone," she addressed the group. "We are now standing in the very room where Hazel Wilmont penned every one of her twenty-three published children's books. Right there, at that exact desk."

Low murmurs wafted through the crowd as some stepped

closer to the desk, others perusing the bookshelf display of Hazel's works.

"Careful near the desk," she added. "There's a warped floorboard. Don't trip."

Funny how her subconscious remembered to warn everyone but Ryan.

"Now some might say the most interesting thing about Hazel Wilmont is the rumor she poisoned one, or both, of her husbands. In fact, that likely played a part in bringing you all here tonight. However, for me personally, these books are what inspired my career here at the mansion. And every time I stand in this room, I'm reminded of how truly talented Hazel Wilmont was."

A woman with a sandy blond bob spoke up. "I used to read Hazel's books to Emma and Amelia when they were young." Stacking her hands over her heart, she looked wistfully at her two adult daughters in attendance with her. "They begged me to read the one about the magical fairies over and over again. Even insisted I make them tutus just like the fairies wore, and not just for Halloween. No, they wore those things every single day." The woman laughed as she reminisced, while both her daughters offered embarrassed smiles. Either not picking up on her daughters' discomfort or not caring, the woman added, "Emma even bathed in hers."

"Mom!" one of the daughters blurted, covering her face with her hands.

Sadie laughed along, adding, "I loved that book, too, Emma. But my personal favorite was *The Unicorn Circus.*" Her mind jumped back to the nights spent tucked under her pink comforter, reading and rereading the story of Margaret, a little girl who traveled the world with a magical circus, her mom the renowned trainer of the unicorns. Despite being raised around the mystical creatures, Margaret was terrified of them. But when her mom was injured, she needed Margaret to take over, otherwise the circus might leave them behind. *Keep your courage close,* her mom told her, and despite being afraid, Margaret did it anyway. "The character of Margaret spoke to me the most."

"I remember that one." George, a dapper gentleman visiting from Florida nudged his husband's ribs. "Remember, Jim? We read that one to Hannah when she was little. Back then, I would've given anything to switch it up and have some variety, but now . . ." A far-off look clouded his gray eyes. "Now I'd give anything for her to ask me to read that book one more time."

Jim patted his partner's shoulder as another guest joined in.

"We also read Hazel's books to our children," a sixtysomething woman said, standing next to a man in a navy polo. "Now we read them to our grandchildren. Talk about a full-circle moment."

As the conversation continued, more and more guests shared their personal memories of Hazel's books—even the members of a bachelorette party chiming in. Sadie hadn't planned on this part of the tour being interactive, but once it was happening it felt like the perfect way to honor Hazel in this space. When she next glanced at her watch, they'd gone a full five minutes over the allotted time.

Sadie gently wrapped up the conversation, and as she led the group back downstairs, an enthusiasm blossomed within her that she hadn't felt in quite some time. Hearing others' love of Hazel's stories touched her deeply, and she felt a surge of renewed passion for this home and her role here. And it wasn't until a single tear rolled down her cheek that she realized how close that passion had come to flaming out.

Once everyone was back in the cellar, their guests partook in the second cocktail of the evening—the bloodred rum punch. Meanwhile, Ryan was relentlessly charming as he explained the ingredients and the science behind the drinks they were consuming. The crowd was rapt by his charisma and humor, more than a few persons (and all of the bachelorette party, including the bride-to-be) watching him with obvious lust in their eyes.

Then the floor was handed over to Simon, who greeted the crowd in character, and Sadie snuck upstairs with Ryan to get the absinthe cocktails ready to serve. Ryan moved around the kitchen effortlessly—pouring, stirring, garnishing—but unlike in the controlled environment of his condo, here he was on a time limit, and the kitchen was an absolute mess they'd have to clean up later.

"How did your tour go?" he asked as he darted around the space like a contestant on a high-stakes cooking competition.

"Really well." Sadie wanted to help him, but she had no idea how. "Everyone started sharing their own stories and memories about Hazel's books, and I don't know, it was just really inspiring."

Ryan paused to smile at her but quickly got back to work. "That's really great, Stockton. The night seems to be going well so far. Dare I say we might have a success on our—"

"Do NOT jinx us! It's far too early. The game has yet to even begin."

Ryan's carefree laugh rolled through the room, the sound of it warming her through like the absinthe cocktails he created in front of her. "Okay, fair point. My bad."

She watched him pour champagne into each flute. "Are our guests going to be plastered? Those things destroyed me."

"To be fair, I think you might have the alcohol tolerance of a baby mouse. Also, the guests finished their first cocktail two hours ago and were served their second"—he glanced at his watch—"forty minutes ago. They didn't pound them all within an hour like some people."

She shot her best menacing glare in his direction.

"But I also cut the amount of absinthe in these just to be safe. We can't have our guests thinking they see demon rodent-dogs."

"Hey, that demon rodent-dog was real!" A shudder rolled through her shoulders at the memory of its pointy little chompers. "*Very* real."

Ryan placed each champagne flute onto one of two serving trays. "You ready to take these down?"

Since carrying a tray full of drinks down the cellar steps was sure to end in disaster, they would be using the elevator. Sadie wasn't sure which was more daunting—getting in a nearly century-old box or attempting to not spill all ten drinks on her tray. It had been a long time since she'd waited tables, and it hadn't been at the kind of establishment where anything was served in a champagne flute. "Ready as I'll ever be."

She clutched the tray with both hands, holding it in front of her body like a bomb that might explode. Ryan, far more experienced, held his tray at shoulder height, balanced one-handed on the tips of his fingers. Show-off.

They made their way to the elevator, Sadie moving at the speed of a sloth, Ryan holding the brassy gold doors open with his entire free arm while she caught up. Once inside, she leaned against the wood-paneled wall at her back. Another thing about old elevators is that they're really slow. So when Ryan pressed the button for the cellar, the doors inched together at a snail's pace, eventually meeting before the elevator began its leisurely descent with a low hum.

There was a jolt when the elevator finally came to a stop, the drinks sloshing on her tray but thankfully not tipping over. The doors parted, revealing the dark corner of the cellar. Laughter drifted from the lounge area, and Sadie blew out a breath and followed Ryan back to the crowd.

Once the group had ample time to refuel on cocktails and introduce themselves in character, Simon sent a discreet wink to Katie. At the cue, the actress stood from her seat on a nearby sofa, gripped her neck with both hands and stumbled around, made a few gasping noises, then fell to the floor.

Sadie had to hand it to her, it was quite the performance.

Murmurs broke out among the group, a few patrons applauding.

Wearing a look of absolute terror, Simon rushed to Katie's side and felt for a pulse while frantically repeating, "Wake up, Ms. Lynn. Wake up!" Then he took the glass from her lifeless hand, made a show of examining it and even sniffing it, his suspicious gaze traveling from person to person. With complete seriousness and total dedication to his performance, he slowly drawled, "My apologies, dear guests, but I believe Ms. Katie Lynn has been *poisoned!*"

A collective gasp rose from the group.

Sadie bit her lips together.

It was completely over the top, and yet, as she looked at each of the guests, they were completely enraptured.

Ryan sidled up to her at the periphery of the lounge. "This is pretty good, huh?" he whispered.

"This is pretty *something*, all right."

"Help me take up the empty glasses and bring down some waters?"

"Right behind you."

Moving around the room, Sadie filled her tray with empty glasses as the guests chattered away and fired questions at Simon. When both her tray and Ryan's were full, they headed back to the elevator. The more cleaning they could knock out while the guests were solving the mystery of who poisoned doomed Katie Lynn, the less they'd have to do at the end of the night, and she'd need every minute of sleep—

The elevator jerked to a halt, everything going dark.

"What the FUCK?" Sadie exclaimed.

Overhead, a faint emergency light shone to life.

In the dim glow, Ryan looked as puzzled as she was, kneeling and placing his tray on the floor. As he rose, he pulled his phone from the pocket of his dress pants. "I just got a weather alert. Looks like some storms are rolling in. The power must be out around the city."

That was the very last thing she needed to hear. "This isn't good. Our guests will be confused. And frightened!" Concern morphing into panic, Sadie's voice rose an octave with each word spoken. *"This is going to ruin the tour!"*

Ryan moved toward her, not a far jaunt in the tiny box, and pried the tray from her grip, setting it on the floor next to his. "It isn't going to ruin the tour. Simon's out there with the group and he knows what he's doing."

"What if the power doesn't come back on?"

"Then we'll adapt."

"*We?* In case you didn't notice, *we* are stuck in a fucking box, Pearson!" Sadie's career flashed before her eyes: the day Evelyn hired her, the first time she stepped into Hazel's writing room all alone, the countless number of visitors she'd chatted with about Hazel's books over the years. If she got fired, she'd never get to feel like Belle on that ladder. "You think Simon could manually pry the doors open from the outside?"

Ryan tilted his head, and she knew the answer before he spoke. "We're between floors, it's dark, and Simon isn't a firefighter. And do we want the guests watching a likely unsuccessful and poorly executed rescue attempt, or do we want Simon to do his job and keep them entertained?"

Fuck.

He was right.

"So, what now? We're just *stuck* here?"

Ryan winced. "For the time being, I think so."

Chapter 20

Sadie pinched the bridge of her nose. This was a disaster. If the power didn't come back on, Simon would be left to finish the remaining hours of the tour alone, in the dark, while she and Ryan were stuck in a box no more than four feet wide. This was a little too reminiscent of their utility closet situation, and Ryan emerged from that one with a black eye.

"What are you thinkin' about over there?" Ryan's drawl rudely interrupted her catastrophizing.

Resting her head back against the wall, she said, "How I seem to keep getting trapped in small spaces with you."

Grinning, Ryan tugged at his collar. "*Trapped* feels a little insulting."

"Would you rather I reword? How about . . . I seem to be granted the opportunity—repeatedly—to share a small space with you."

"Yeah, see, that sounds much better." Reclined against the opposite wall, Ryan bent his knee and placed the sole of his shoe against the polished paneling. "*Granted the opportunity* feels like you're blessed to share this space with me. *Trapped* feels like you'd rather be stuck in this elevator with that rodent-dog you felt the need to scream about in the middle of the street."

"Oh, I'd *for sure* take you over the rodent-dog any day. Hands down."

"God, Stockton, you really shouldn't flatter me so much. What I think I hear you saying is that I'm cuter than an innocent puppy."

Unable to suppress the smile that came to her face, Sadie pointed a finger his way. "That thing was neither a puppy nor innocent. You could tell that little demon was itching to bite the shit out of someone with its tiny shark teeth."

The deep, pleasant sound of Ryan's laugh filled the elevator, and warmth reverberated through Sadie in waves.

"What about you, Pearson?" she asked. "What are you thinkin' about over there?"

Unbuttoning his sleeves at the wrist, Ryan took his time rolling each one midway up his forearm. "If you want me to answer that honestly . . . I'm thinking the same thing I've been thinking all night." Next, he loosened the knot of his tie, his eyes performing a slow sweep from the toe of her boots up to the sliver of bare skin below her skirt. "I'm thinking it's damn near impossible to concentrate on anything other than your legs in that skirt and those boots."

"Oh." Butterflies swarmed her stomach, each individual flap of wings felt viscerally.

"And I'm also thinking that we could be here awhile. So maybe it's best to stay"—his eyes locked with hers—"*distracted*."

Sadie swallowed, throat suddenly dry. "I mean . . ."

Ryan's brow arched.

"We are stuck here," she mused. "Indefinitely."

"We are," he agreed.

"And no one else is around."

Ryan shook his head, eyes darkening. "Not a soul."

"And kissing you the other night wasn't awful."

Wearing a smirk, Ryan pushed off the wall and moved toward her. "Not an awful kisser. There you go with that flattery again, Stockton."

"Fine." She bit down on her lower lip. "Maybe it was pretty good."

He stopped in front of her, their shoes toe-to-toe. "Just *good?*"

Any humor was incinerated by the slow heat overtaking her belly. She swallowed again. "Really good."

Leaning closer, Ryan spread his hands on the wall at each side of her head. But he didn't touch her, which felt unbearably cruel. "Tell me *exactly* how good."

Senses heightening, Sadie felt both everything that touched her—the soft brush of her skirt against her thighs, the scratchy material of her bra rubbing against her delicate skin—and everything that wasn't touching her but should be. Ryan's hands. His lips. "So good I think about it in my bed at night."

Ryan's eyes briefly shuttered closed, then refocused on hers with a heat that stoked the flames spreading inside her. "When you think about it, in your bed, do you touch yourself?"

Her answer came without hesitation. "Yes."

"Jesus Christ." Ryan's head fell forward, his breaths heavy on her neck.

"*Do you?*" She may have taken the first vulnerable step, but Sadie desperately needed them on equal footing. "Think about me . . . and you know . . ."

Lifting his head, Ryan's gaze slowly traced the neckline of her sweater, sweeping over her exposed collarbone and up the column of her throat. "*Fuck yes.* Probably ten times since the haunted house."

"That was only two nights ago."

"Yeah," he said as their eyes met. "That's kind of the effect you have on me, Stockton."

Those were easily the hottest words anyone had ever spoken to her. Acting on this attraction was likely not in her best interest, but if Ryan didn't touch her soon she might spontaneously combust from the heat building within.

"Maybe we need to remedy that." Reaching overhead, Sadie grasped his wrist, slid it away from the elevator wall, and settled his palm against her ribs. "Maybe you need to touch me instead."

Ryan stretched his fingers out over her sweater, his grip firm. "If you're trying to torture me, it's working."

His thumb grazed the underside of her breast, and she stifled a moan. "I'd say you can give as good as you get."

"That so?" Leaning in close, his breath was a warm tease over her lips. But he didn't kiss her. And yeah, fucking torture. "You see, Stockton, we have a couple problems here. There are reasons I can't get you out of my head."

"Yeah?" She was practically panting now. "What are those?"

Taking hold of her hips, Ryan pressed her back more firmly against the wall as he crowded her further. "For starters, I can't tell if you want me to like you or hate you. Or if you just really miss the way I used to fuck you."

"Maybe . . . Maybe I'm not sure about that myself." Sadie's heart thudded against her chest wall so forcefully that she wondered if Ryan felt it, too. "What's the other problem?"

"The other problem," he said, entwining their fingers as he pinned her hand to the wall next to her head, "is that I remember."

"Remember what?" she breathed.

"I remember *everything.* I remember the whimpers that came from this throat"—Ryan brushed his lips up the delicate skin at the side of her neck—"when you couldn't hold back anymore. I remember how fucking perfect your tits felt in my hands . . . and in my mouth."

Breaths ragged, it was all Sadie could do to stop herself from begging for all the things he was saying.

Ryan's other hand slid lower and gripped the back of her bare thigh. "I remember how sweet your pussy tasted on my lips, and how unbelievably fucking hot you looked completely naked and writhing on top of me with my cock buried deep inside you. So do I think about us? Lately it's *all* I think about."

Fuck. Slickness accumulated between her legs, a deep flush in her cheeks. She had to touch him. She couldn't stop herself. Curving her free hand around the back of his neck, she kneaded the muscles there. "You know, maybe we could come to an agreement," she proposed.

His lips brushed hers again. "What kind of agreement?"

"An agreement where we act on this."

"Hate to tell you this, Stockton"—Ryan nipped at her lower lip, quickly releasing it before it could turn into a kiss—"but I think we're already acting on it."

Goose bumps raced over her skin, but she needed to focus, at least while she presented this foolproof plan she'd come up with all of ten seconds ago. "Just hear me out."

At those words, Ryan stepped back, hands dropping away from her.

"No, don't . . ." The sudden space between them left her cold. "I don't want you to go anywhere."

"We're trapped in an elevator," he said with a grin. "There's literally nowhere for me to go."

"No, that's not what I—" Sadie gripped his collar with both hands and pulled him close again. "I don't want to stop what we're doing. I'm just saying we should establish some ground rules about what this is. That's all."

"Okay . . ." Ryan's expression remained uncertain. "But you want me to touch you while we do?"

Maybe it was arbitrary, but Sadie needed to have some guardrails in place to ensure they didn't go down the same path they'd been down once before. But she also needed Ryan's hands on her. And she was great at multitasking, it even said so on her résumé. "Yes please."

"Any ground rules about where or how I touch you?" Ryan's eyes held hers. "Because I'm going to need you to tell me where's off-limits."

The statement was so direct, leaving no mistake that he wanted his hands *all over* her. And was there anywhere she didn't want those hands, that mouth? *Nope.* "Touch me anywhere you want."

As if her words melted something within him, Ryan collapsed forward with a heavy sigh, his weight pinning her to the wall, his mouth *finally* claiming hers. He kissed her with an almost frantic need, sucking on her lower lip to the point of near pain before soothing it with gentle sweeps of his tongue. Then a hand slid underneath her sweater, and focusing on anything became one thousand times harder.

As his calloused palm cupped her breast, Sadie broke their kiss and said, "Here's . . . Here's what I'm thinking."

"I'm all ears." Ryan's thumb slowly traced her nipple over her strapless bra, and she bit back a whimper.

"What if," she managed, "just for the time we're working together, we allow ourselves to fully explore this attraction, so to speak?"

"I do love an exploration." His other hand traveled over her hip to the skin between the hem of her skirt and the top of her boots.

"It would be temporary," she continued, breath harder to come by. "And only about physical pleasure."

"Temporary. Physical pleasure. Got it." Fingers moving up her inner thigh, Ryan slightly arched a dark brow, again asking permission for something she'd already consented to. Perhaps he thought she'd change her mind, but there was nothing she was more certain of. Maybe the night at the haunted house was supposed to be a one-off, but why deny what they both so obviously, so *desperately*, wanted?

Sadie slid her legs apart. "It makes sense, doesn't it?"

The way Ryan looked at her in that moment was like she were a toy he'd begged for all year and finally unwrapped on Christmas morning. His hand trailed farther up her thigh, and when he touched her over her underwear, her lower back arched off the wall.

His grin turned wicked. "Whatever you say." Stroking the damp lace between her legs, he applied the lightest amount of pressure, as if he intended to leave her needing more. As if he wanted her to beg him for it. So *fucking* cruel.

But Sadie decided her idea would work. They could act on this—*temporarily!*—and then walk away with no consequences. It was a genius plan, actually. Maybe it hadn't worked out when they were in college, but they'd been acting on youthful impulse then. Now there was a plan in place. Between two mature adults who could keep feelings out of it.

"Besides, you're moving to Charleston, and I don't do serious relationships. And let's be real, us getting along recently is likely a fluke." Why was she still talking? "'Cause I mean, hating each other is what we do, you know. You feel the same way, right?"

That too-sexy smirk twisted Ryan's lips. "Isn't it obvious?" Sweeping her underwear aside, he drug a finger through her slickness. Slowly. Torturously.

"Fuck," she whimpered, twisting his shirt in her hands.

Ryan's smirk split into a wide, devastating smile as his middle finger lingered over her clit. "Hey, Stockton. If you're done talking, can I *please* make you come now?"

Sadie nodded emphatically, winding Ryan's tie around her hand and tugging until his mouth was back on hers. As his tongue swept inside her mouth, his finger fully entered her, and she rocked against his hand, seeking more friction.

"Goddamn, you feel like a fucking dream," Ryan breathed against her lips before kissing her again.

Sadie's hand roamed down his stomach until her palm slid over his erection. Applying pressure, she worked her hand over him, but when she started to undo his belt, Ryan broke their kiss with a gravelly, "You have to stop that."

"You don't want me to touch you, too?" That was confusing. He'd said all those dirty things, and now two of his fingers were currently inside her.

"Of course I *want* you to touch me," he replied, forehead pressed against hers and breaths labored. "I fantasize about it every single fucking day. But only one of us can come in this elevator and it isn't me. Too messy."

Oh. Unless . . . "Not if it's in my mouth."

A shudder ripped through Ryan's shoulders. "Stockton, *please* stop talking. Finally kissing you and touching you has me worked up enough. You saying things like that is almost too much."

The power Sadie felt in that moment was brand new. Ryan wanted her. So badly he looked physically pained trying to keep control of himself.

"Turn around and put your hands on the wall," he suddenly instructed, removing his hand from her underwear.

"*What?*"

"I don't trust you not to torture me while I make you come," he explained, matter-of-fact. "So, turn around and put your hands on the wall."

"Are you ser—"

In one quick movement, Ryan grabbed her hips and spun her around. Then he took hold of her wrists and planted her hands flat against the polished wall above her head. "That's better. Now, where were we . . ."

His hands trekked slowly down her arms, fingers brushing the sides of her breasts on the way to her waist. Then a forearm came around her from behind, hand moving down her lower stomach and beneath the waistband of her skirt. Two fingers slipped back inside her, his thumb gently toying with her clit.

And holy fuck, Sadie could have come from that alone. But Ryan wasn't even close to finished with her. His teeth sank into the back of her neck in a stinging bite that made her internal muscles clench around his fingers. When she moaned, he lifted the back of her skirt and roughly palmed her ass. It was too much and somehow not enough.

"Please," she found herself begging. "I need more. *Please.*"

His hungry mouth made its way to her ear, and her nipples tightened when he sucked her earlobe between his teeth. "Please what?"

"I want those things you said," Sadie moaned, control abandoned. "I want your cock inside me."

There was a muttered curse she couldn't quite make out. Then, "God, I want that, too. But we can't."

"We could, though," she argued. Hand sliding off the wall, she reached back and twisted her fingers in his hair. "No one would know."

The heat of Ryan's mouth lifted away from her neck. Capturing her wrist, he returned her hand to its previous position. "Hands on the wall, baby."

Whimpering now, Sadie's forehead fell forward at the same time Ryan's finger pressed against the perfect spot inside her. "*Please,*" she pleaded. "I remember, too, you know." Maybe she hadn't allowed herself to think about it, but she'd never forgotten how Ryan, even years ago, had given her pleasure so easily, so completely, to the point she often felt his hands knew her body better than her own. "Did you know you're the first guy who ever made me come? With your fingers, and with your mouth, and with your cock."

Ryan groaned like he was in agony. "Respectfully, baby, I'm honored, but I'm also begging you to shut the fuck up." His fingers pumped faster inside her. "You cannot say things like that to me right now."

"I can if you'd get over yourself and just fuck me already."

"Goddammit," he cursed. "Are we seriously gonna argue over whether or not we can fuck in this elevator?"

"It is what we do best," Sadie managed as pressure built in her core.

"Ironically, I would argue that fucking is what we do best," Ryan countered. "But you know we can't do that here. If I fuck you in this elevator, we'll both be completely wrecked. Trust me, everyone will know." He pulled her hips back until the press of his erection slid against her lace panties. Then his hand moved underneath her sweater, tugging the cup of her bra down and pinching her tight nipple.

Pleasure shot through her, and if it wasn't for his strong arm around her, Sadie might have collapsed to the floor. A cry tore from her throat at the sensations, all of them at once. "Then kiss me," she said, turning her head over her shoulder and looking up at him through her lashes. "At least fucking kiss me."

"That I can do." His smile met her lips, finger teasing that sweet spot inside her.

"Right there," she commanded.

Ryan circled the same spot again, pleasure intensifying with each stroke of his fingers. She was so, *so* close—

Harsh light abruptly infiltrated the space.

A second later, the elevator hummed back to life.

Sadie's eyes went wide as Ryan pulled his mouth off hers. They both glanced around in disbelief, and disappointment sucker-punched her right in the sternum.

"No, no, no," Ryan muttered. "*Fuck. That.*" He removed his hand from her sweater, and before she could process what was happening, he leaned away and pulled the emergency stop lever. They lurched to a halt once more.

Returning his attention to her, he said in a low, commanding voice, "We're not leaving here until you come."

There was something so hot about it, about *him*, that it took only seconds before Sadie did just that, her internal muscles clenching around Ryan's fingers, her weak knees almost giving in.

Breaths slowing, her head fell back against Ryan's shoulder. He gently removed his hands from underneath her skirt and sweater and straightened her clothes. Then he pressed a soft kiss to her neck.

After a moment to regain control of themselves, Ryan dropped his arms from around her and moved to the control panel of the elevator. "Let's hope this works." He released the stop lever, and after a delayed jolt, the elevator began to ascend.

As relieved as Sadie was to get out of this box, she wished they'd had a bit more time to recover. "Looks like we're gonna make it out of here after all."

"Didn't I do a good enough job of keeping you distracted?" Ryan teased.

They came to a jerky stop at the first floor.

"Oh, you did very well," she admitted. "But I'd rather be *distracted* in a big plushy bed."

The elevator doors slid open.

Sadie moved to pick up her abandoned tray of glassware, but Ryan stepped in her path and took her face in his hands. He pressed one last kiss to her mouth, then released her and said, "I look forward to taking you up on that invitation."

Chapter 21

As it turned out, Simon had their guests delightfully convinced the power outage was all part of the game. Thinking on his feet, he'd retrieved a few flashlights from the utility closet and they'd continued on, searching for clues throughout the mansion in small groups. As the night wrapped up, their guests seemed to be enjoying themselves as they gathered back in the cellar and started piecing together their discovered evidence.

Working her way around the cocktail lounge—and Katie Lynn's "dead" body, from which she could've sworn she heard a soft snore—Sadie straightened throw pillows and gathered abandoned coasters. But her gaze kept wandering across the room to Ryan, currently enmeshed in conversation with one of the early-twentysomething daughters. Amelia, maybe. Head tilted low, he listened intently as Amelia said something that caused him to grin in that particular way that made his singular dimple appear.

Unable to look away, Sadie's stomach contracted as Amelia pulled her phone from the pocket of her sundress. Was Ryan giving her his *number*? She was maybe twenty-two. Twenty-three, at best. And she was a customer!

Obviously whatever agreement they'd made in the elevator was purely physical. Ryan was free to do whatever (or whomever) he wanted. But did he really need to do it *now*, when his fingers had been inside her only hours ago?

Scooping a throw pillow off the floor, Sadie tossed it on the nearest sofa and discreetly worked her way closer to get within earshot of their conversation. There wasn't much cleaning to do in the area of the cellar where they were huddled, so she pulled a lighter from the drawer of a console table and relit candles that were already burning. It was fine, no one was paying that close attention.

"—an incredible photo," Ryan was saying. So he wasn't giving Amelia his number, she was showing him a picture on her phone. "This is *really* gorgeous stuff, Amelia. The way the light hugs the body in all the right places."

Uh . . . what kind of photo was it exactly?

"Thanks," Amelia replied in a shy voice. "It's a really personal photo, obviously, so that means a lot."

Personal photo?

Wait, was it a photo of *Amelia*?

"Not to mention," Ryan continued, "the way you showcase the legs. And the rounded curves of the chest. Just phenomenal."

Sadie almost choked.

She didn't have a lot of experience with sexting or taking nudes, but did people nowadays actually show them off *in person*? Was that an acceptable thing? At bars across the country, were single people showing off the highlights of their naked photo catalogue like a preview teaser? And no disrespect, but Amelia's mom and sister were all of ten feet away. That was some audacity.

Suddenly realizing the lighter's flame was slowly scalding the tip of her thumb, Sadie dropped it onto the console table with a clatter.

"Hey, Stockton."

Her spine lengthened at Ryan's voice.

"Why don't you stop lighting already lit candles and come look at this."

Shit.

Plastering what she hoped was a self-deprecating, *I'm so tired I didn't notice* smile on her face, Sadie turned toward the pair.

Amelia boldly held her phone up, and as Sadie went to explain that she really shouldn't show just anyone her private photos, she saw the horse on the screen.

Oh.

"This is Muffin." Amelia smiled invitingly as Sadie took the phone for a closer look. It really was a stunning photo. A sunset shot with a fiery orange sky and the last golden rays of sunshine falling over jagged mountains in the background. The dark brown horse ran freely through tall grasses, sunlight gleaming off its body. "I mentioned to Ryan that I dabble in photography and he asked to see my favorite photo I've taken. This is it."

Yeah, that sounded like Ryan. Sadie passed the phone back. "It's incredible. Great work."

Amelia beamed at her praise.

"All right, everyone," Simon's voice boomed over the crowd. "The time has come to figure out who among us is a cold-blooded killer."

"EEEKKKK!" Amelia squealed, bouncing on her feet. "I should go over there. While the lights were out, I snuck away from my group and found a key piece of evidence beside the elevator." She pulled an object from her pocket and held it up in the light. It was a tiny glass bottle, labeled XX POISON XX in red Sharpie. "So cool, right?"

Sadie's gaze darted to Ryan, who looked back at her with amusement crinkling the corners of his eyes.

But Sadie wasn't amused. If Amelia was outside the elevator *during* the power outage, then she and Ryan were *in* that elevator, doing very NSFW things. Was it soundproof? Could Amelia have heard the *things* that were happening inside? That was not the type of show these people paid for, and that kind of Tripadvisor review would ruin them.

Suddenly light-headed, Sadie thought she might pass out.

"Amelia told me that she thought the killer might still be in the elevator," Ryan said, eyes knowing. "But when she realized it wasn't working, she moved on."

"Yep," Amelia confirmed, seemingly oblivious. "But, hey, I still found the poison." She took off toward the rest of the group with the evidence in hand.

Once Amelia was definitely out of earshot, Sadie stepped closer to Ryan and asked quietly, "You're *sure* she didn't hear . . . anything?"

Ryan dipped his head to her ear. "You mean, am I sure she didn't hear you *beg me* to fuck you? Or your moans as you came on my fingers? Yeah. I'm sure." He pulled back, winked, and walked away.

Fuck, she was in over her head.

After a half hour of boisterous and dramatic accusations, the mystery was solved.

The night's killer was George, one of the gentlemen visiting from Florida, playing the role of Katie Lynn's uncle. Unbeknownst to poor, dead Katie Lynn, Uncle George took out a life insurance policy on her just three weeks prior—discovered in the downstairs library by his very own husband, no less!—knowing that once word of her torrid affair got out, she'd be publicly shunned and utterly useless to him in any type of monetary way.

The game ended with Gabe kneeling beside his wife's lifeless body, wiping an actual tear from his eye, and loudly vowing to avenge her.

Very dramatic.

The clock struck five a.m., and Sadie led the group back to the foyer and reminded everyone to please leave a review as their guests gathered their belongings and said their goodbyes. Some of the guests yawned and rubbed at their eyes, but every one of them wore a smile and chatted animatedly about the night's mystery. As soon as the front door closed behind the last guest, Sadie turned back to her two cohosts, as well as Charity, Katie, and Gabe, and let out a huge sigh of relief.

"I think that went really—" Simon couldn't finish his sentence before Sadie threw her arms around his neck, catching him off guard. Catching them *both* off guard. It wasn't in her nature to go around hugging people. But Simon saved their asses tonight.

"You were amazing tonight, Simon." She released his stiff frame. "You somehow kept your cool when the power went out and our guests *fucking loved* you. I'm so proud of you."

Pink crept above Simon's collar. "Just doing my job. Once at *Dinner and Demise*, a guest puked on my shoes and I had to perform barefoot the rest of the night. I'm used to adapting."

"Well, she's right," Ryan added. "This night would've been a disaster without you."

"I'm just sorry you two got stuck in the elevator for so long," Simon apologized. "I wish I could've done something to help."

Sadie's cheeks warmed. "No worries. We made do."

Next to her, Charity mumbled, "I bet you did."

Sadie shot a look to the supermodel, but she only grinned innocently in return.

After profusely thanking the three, Sadie saw Katie, Gabe, and Charity out. Then she turned back to her partners. "All right, we have a lot of cleaning up to do and every minute here is one less minute of sleep I get before I have to be at the bridal shop."

Ryan's head cocked to the side. "You're working at the store *today*?"

"It's Saturday," she replied. "I work every Saturday."

"But you were up all night."

She nodded because he was proving her point for her. "Hence why I'm ready to get home and take a nap."

"But we have to do this all again. *Tonight*."

"Yes, Pearson. I'm aware of the schedule."

Simon's eyes were a pendulum, swinging between the two.

Ryan shoved his hands in his pants pockets. "You can't possibly think it's a good idea to work forty-eight hours in a row with no sleep."

Arms folding over her chest, Sadie's tone sharpened. "I'm twenty-four hours in and doing just fine." That was a lie. Her head felt like it was submerged underwater and her limbs tied down with anchors.

"I'm gonna start that cleanup," Simon interjected, slowly backpedaling out of the foyer.

"You have to sleep," Ryan said, softening his voice. "Surely missing one day isn't that big of a deal. I'm sure Eric would understand. I've met him, he seems like an understanding kind of guy."

"Saturday is the busiest day of the week," Sadie pointed out.

"That's not really helping your case." Ryan took hold of her upper arms, just above her elbows. It was an innocuous touch, but it was oddly comforting. "Sadie, you need rest."

Her heart hit the pause button, then raced to catch up all at once.

It was just that, well, she couldn't remember the last time Ryan called her by her first name. Had he *ever* called her by her first name? The way it sounded—gentle and affectionate and threaded with concern as if he really cared about her well-being—made her eyes sting.

"I'm fine," she said, dropping her watery gaze to the floor. "Really. I'll catch up on sleep as soon as we get through these next twenty-four hours."

She heard Ryan's slow exhale, then he tilted her chin up with his knuckle. With no other choice but to let him see her, Sadie clenched her jaw, willing her expression to remain steady. "Give me the keys to the mansion," he said, studying her. "I'll take care of everything here. Go get as much sleep as possible."

She shook her head. "You don't have to do that. It's not fair for you to do more than me."

"I *want* to do this," he insisted.

"But you don't know the lock-up routine. Which lights to shut off and which to leave on. And you have to ensure every single exterior door is locked 'cause we can't take the chance of—"

"Sadie."

She fell silent. How was she supposed to speak when he kept saying her name like that?

"Trust me to do this. *Please.*"

Exhaustion must really be getting to her because now her throat was thick, too. Afraid she might irrationally burst into tears, she retrieved her tote bag and handed the keys over to him. "Thank you."

He gave her a quick nod. "I'll see you tonight."

"Yeah, um . . ." Hesitating, Sadie considered the acceptable etiquette for parting ways after what happened in the elevator. Certainly a *Thanks for an amazing orgasm* wasn't in order, but there was a wide spectrum between that and nothing.

But Ryan's mouth tipped into a crooked grin like he somehow could hear her inner monologue playing on a speaker. Then he brushed his lips against her temple in a featherlight kiss, mumbled, "Now go," and promptly walked away.

CHAPTER 22

One thing Sadie was grateful for was that her portion of the Mixtures and Murder Tour came at the beginning of the night, because as night two wore on, it became harder to focus on anything other than the aching fatigue that seeped down to her bones. Giving tours was basic muscle memory after all these years, but tonight the details were slipping. She couldn't recall a single one of their guests' names.

Once cursed Katie Lynn kicked the bucket, Sadie traipsed down the second floor hallway, making sure she stayed available to any guest that might need her during their search. As she passed by the former shared bedroom of Hazel and John, an arm encircled her waist from behind, and a sharp yelp emerged from her throat and echoed down the long corridor.

"Shhhh," Ryan whispered next to her ear. "It's just me." He pulled her into the bedroom and closed the door behind them.

"What are you doing?" Sadie asked, slightly breathless.

Shrugging, he settled his hands on her waist and backed her

against the door. "I needed to see you. We've barely spoken all night."

It was true that they'd both been occupied since the moment Sadie arrived half conscious earlier that night. At the least, she'd expected they'd have a few moments alone while Ryan mixed the drinks for cocktail hour, but she'd ended up getting stuck showing a chatty guest to the restroom, scurrying back once the cocktails were ready to be served. "You miss me, Pearson?"

"You have no *fucking* idea." Sinking his hand into her hair, Ryan kissed her soft and slow.

Melting into him, Sadie opened her mouth and took the kiss deep. But unlike the frantic urgency of the night before in the elevator, tonight's kiss was languid and unhurried.

"How are you holding up tonight?" Ryan eventually asked, trailing his kisses lower on her jaw, then down her throat.

"I'm perfectly fine. Just like I said I would be."

His lips met the spot where her shoulder and neck converged. "I think you're lying to me." He nipped her skin and made her gasp. "Do *not* lie to me."

"Fine. I'm spent," she admitted. "I recited my tour from memory with no emotion or enthusiasm. I'm not sure if the guests noticed, but it certainly wasn't my best effort. Now I'm counting down the remaining ninety minutes until this is over." Either exhaustion was making her more truthful than intended or Ryan was slipping past her defenses a little more each and every day. "But this . . . This is a bright spot."

She rose onto her tiptoes to kiss him again, but Ryan pressed against her hips, frowning down at her. "You can't keep this up for another two weekends, Sadie."

As she opened her mouth to inform him that he couldn't tell her what to do, he pressed a finger to her lips.

"I'm not trying to tell you what to do," he said, stealing her words. "I'm only pointing out the obvious because I care."

He *cared*?

What the hell was that supposed to mean?

He cared about her? Or he cared about the project going well? Surely he meant the latter. But she was too tired for any in-depth analysis, and then he kissed her again and any consideration fled her mind.

Ryan cupped her face, thumbs caressing her jaw, his soft sighs slipping into her mouth. Gripping his shirt, Sadie pulled his body closer, all while pushing away the twinge in her chest that told her this drawn-out, sighing kind of kiss was too intimate, too real. Because the rest of her body—her heated skin and her racing pulse and her fluttery stomach—insisted this was *exactly* what she needed.

Outside the bedroom, footsteps thudded down the hallway, accompanied by a loud voice proclaiming, "Did you see the way the husband didn't even flinch when she hit the floor? He has to be guilty."

With one last kiss to the corner of her mouth, Ryan stepped away. "Guess we should get back out there."

"Hey, wait a second." Sadie grabbed his hand before it found the doorknob. "What if you come back to my apartment when we're done here?" Was it weird to ask a guy to come over at five in the morning? Maybe. But this agreement between them came with an expiration date, and she intended to capitalize while she could.

Ryan stroked his knuckle down her cheek. "If I come over, we both know we're not sleeping. And I refuse to contribute to your sleep deprivation."

"Right." She released his hand. "Probably a bad idea anyway."

"Stop it," he drawled, tucking her hair behind her ear. "It isn't a bad idea, and I really want to take you up on it. But how about this instead—text me after you've had at least eight hours of sleep, and if you still want me to come over I'll be there."

After that kiss, she didn't want to wait eight hours. But it was a compromise she was willing to make. "Okay, deal."

The footsteps outside grew louder. Another animated voice said, "My money's on the butler. He seemed a little too quick to determine it was a poisoning."

"All right," Ryan sighed. "Let's go find out who poisoned Katie Lynn tonight."

* * *

Sadie slept hard.

So hard, in fact, that when she checked the time on her phone it was after six p.m. The upside of sleeping nearly twelve hours straight was that she felt revived and clearheaded for the first time in two days. The downside was that she was fucking starving. For more than food.

She leapt from the bed, pulled her skimpiest black lace thong from her dresser drawer, and headed for the shower. Once she was scrubbed clean and her hair was blow-dried and curled, she sent a text to Ryan.

Sadie: Still want to come over?

Then self-doubt made her add:

Sadie: If you have other plans, no big deal.

She chewed her lower lip and stared at the screen. Thankfully his reply came within seconds.

Ry: Thank god. I was beginning to think you changed your mind. On my way now.

Relief surged through her.

Sadie: Just come up when you get here. The code to the gift shop door is 1234.

Ry: Very secure.

Glancing up, Sadie was mildly alarmed by the wide smile she caught on her reflection in the bathroom mirror. She quickly switched off the light and made her way to her closet to debate what to wear. Standing in an oversize tee and her barely-there thong, she stared at her clothes and began to think through every possible scenario that could happen that night.

Ryan understood she was obviously asking him to stay over, right?

Had she made that clear enough?

Just in case, she typed another text.

Sadie: Hey! If you want to bring clothes or whatever, you can stay here tonight. If you want.

Shit. It wasn't until after she'd hit send that she noticed she'd used *if you want* twice. Rookie mistake.

Seconds later, her phone buzzed.

Ry: Will do.

She sat her phone down on her bed. Picked it back up. He surely understood what would likely happen between them if he stayed. Especially after the elevator encounter. But would he bring protection? Or should she have it since she was the one inviting him over?

Sadie: Also . . . Make sure you bring other stuff, too.

She typed a row of winky face emojis, then decided she couldn't pull it off and deleted it. Hopefully he'd decipher what she meant without it. She went back to perusing her wardrobe as if she'd never seen it before. Another text rolled in.

Ry: Other stuff?

Ry: You're going to need to be more specific than that. Dinner? Wine? Dessert? A new security system for your poorly protected door?

Shit. He was making her spell it out for him. Literally. Her cheeks lit up like the Olympic torch.

Sadie: Condoms

Was that too forward? Or offensive? Did she sound like a deviant with a one-track mind set on getting laid?

Ry: Yes ma'am.

Well. That was that.

She'd just decided on an oversize black cardigan and pair of faded boyfriend jeans when a knock at her door broke the silence in her apartment. She scrambled into her jeans, then pulled off her tee and replaced it with the cardigan sans bra, which she hopefully wouldn't be needing anyway. Stomach cinched tight, she padded barefoot across the floor.

"Jeez, Pearson"—she yanked open the door—"did you run h—"

Ryan grabbed her face and crashed his mouth against hers before she got another syllable out.

And *holy shit*, this was actually happening.

She was going to have sex with Ryan Pearson.

He walked them inside her apartment without breaking away, and she was vaguely aware of him kicking her apartment door closed. Of the thick strap of a gym bag sliding off his shoulder. Of a whispered, "Hi," against her mouth.

"Hi," she whispered back.

"You still sure about this?" he asked between kisses.

Was she *sure*? She was clinging to him like a sexually charged koala. "*Very* sure."

He smiled against her lips, hands sliding lower to the curve of her ass. The next thing she knew her thighs were wrapped around his hips as he carried her farther into her apartment.

"God, Sadie." His normally raspy voice was pained in a way she'd never heard before. "I've wanted you for *so fucking long*."

Sadie. Her name on his lips stirred her desire in an unexpected way, but there was also something deeper to it. A familiarity that implied he really *knew* her. That he'd known her for some time, that he'd continue to know her in the future. In some odd way it felt like a promise, and she didn't care for the way it made her hopeful for something she couldn't identify. Something she couldn't put a name to. Something that would always remain just beyond her reach. But she did really love the way it sounded.

Kissing him again, Sadie sucked hard on his bottom lip so he'd stop saying things that made her feel anything beyond the physical. His gravelly moan in response made her wet between her thighs.

"Take this off." She tugged at the shoulder of his long-sleeved henley.

Keeping one arm under her thighs, Ryan bent the other behind his neck and tugged the shirt overhead. Once it was tossed to the floor, she grasped his angular jaw between both hands, urging him back to her, kisses frantic.

"Last night," Ryan said as she moved her mouth lower, "you were jealous when I was talking to Amelia."

Sadie froze, lips stilling against his neck. "I wasn't jealous."

A huff blew against her ear. "I watched you pretend to light the same candle at least five times. You were jealous."

"Okay, you know what?" She lifted her head, only to see Ryan staring back at her with disheveled hair and swollen lips and those earthy green eyes daring her to deny it. The sight alone stole her breath for a moment, until she remembered where she was going with all this. Oh right, denial. "I was only making sure you weren't hitting on a paying customer. That's it."

Ryan's gaze shifted to her mouth and lingered. "I was jealous, too." He kissed her, quick but unexpected, as if he couldn't wait another second. Then he explained, "That night at the bar. When you spent so long in the corner with that model guy. I thought maybe there was something between you two. You have no idea how jealous I was."

Callum? He'd been jealous of Callum? That was laughable.

"Okay, fine." Sadie ran a hand through Ryan's hair just to watch the light brown strands fall back into perfectly disordered chaos. "Maybe I was *slightly* jealous. But literally half the guests on our tours look at you like they want to take you to bed afterward."

One corner of his mouth quirked. "But the only person I want to take to bed is you."

"Then maybe you should stop talking."

She leaned in to kiss him again, but he pulled back. "I wouldn't do that, you know."

"Take me to bed? That's disappointing news in our current state, Pearson."

Ryan squeezed her ass hard enough to make her yelp. "No, smart-ass. I meant I wouldn't flirt with someone else or intentionally try to make you jealous. I'm not looking to be with anyone else while I'm with you."

"To be fair, that's what I thought in college, too, but you had no problem ditching me the second the opportunity arose."

The instant the words escaped her mouth everything stopped. The kissing. The touching. Hell, Ryan even dropped her onto the kitchen counter. Gently, but still . . . She'd clearly fucked up.

"Forget I said anything." Sadie tugged at his shoulders, but he resisted. "It doesn't matter."

Scrubbing a hand over his jaw, Ryan watched her intently. "No, this is important."

Unease unfurled in the pit of her stomach. "Please forget it. I really, *really* don't want to fight with you."

"Hey. No one is fighting here. We're just talking, okay?" He spoke gently. Almost a whisper. "But what do you mean I ditched you? Sadie, I wanted *you* to go to that formal with me. You said no. Please explain this to me."

Looking away, Sadie fidgeted with the sleeve of her cardigan. "I know what I said. And I understand we weren't together or anything so you had every right to do whatever you wanted. But yeah, I was annoyed when you went with Lauren instead, okay? Then you two became a couple, and it was like I never existed."

"Trust me, Sadie, you have *always* existed to me." Ryan eased himself back between her thighs, a hand settling over hers before she could unravel a loose thread. "Can I tell you my perspective on what happened back then?"

Sadie nodded, though she was uncertain she wanted to hear it. This felt like too serious of a conversation, and when adults had serious conversations it led to arguing. And not the harmless jabs she and Ryan usually exchanged, but the wall-shaking shouting and the thundering footsteps and the slamming-front-door kind of arguments she was all too familiar with. Suddenly she felt like a kid again, hiding under her comforter and waiting for the storm inside her own home to subside.

But when Ryan spoke, he didn't sound angry or upset. His voice stayed calm and steady, speaking as if he understood she was skittish, even if he didn't understand why. "Did you know I had the *biggest* crush on you from the very first day we met? It was bad, Sadie, really bad. Everyone knew. All of my friends. Even Old Man Dicky." He huffed a short laugh. "He never kept me more than five minutes all those times I got in trouble for flirting with you in class. I think he felt sorry for me."

Sadie peered at him through narrowed eyes. "A crush? Beyond just wanting to hook up?"

"Christ. You have no idea, do you?" Lifting her hand, Ryan placed a kiss to the center of her palm. "Once we started hanging out after Christmas break, I thought you felt the same. But I remember seeing you on campus not long after classes started back.

I smiled at you, and you looked away like you didn't even recognize me. You made it blatantly clear we were a secret."

It was funny how memories worked. How Sadie hadn't thought about that moment a single time over the years, but when prompted it came back to her with perfect clarity. Ryan enmeshed in a group of coeds, her heading to her last class of the afternoon. He'd looked her way and grinned, and she'd started to smile back—until she noticed his friends' whispers and barely suppressed laughs.

"I assumed you'd want me to pretend nothing was happening." Her voice came out quiet and distant. "You were with your friends. They were all laughing. I didn't want to embarrass you."

"*Embarrass* me?" Ryan cupped her jaw and brought her focus back to him. "Sadie, no. They weren't laughing at you. They were laughing at me because they knew what a fool I turned into when you were around. They knew how I felt about you."

"Oh." She struggled to reconstruct the playback in her head from a different perspective. Without having many friends herself, she'd naturally assumed the role of outsider. Was it possible she misinterpreted his intentions back then simply because he was so different from her? "But if you liked me so much, why did you go with Lauren to the formal?"

"Because after *three months* of sneaking into your room every night, I finally concluded that you were never going to want me in the same way I wanted you. I didn't want us to be a secret. When I asked *you* to go to that formal with me, I was testing the waters. I thought there was a chance you'd agree and we'd finally make things official. When you blew me off, I took that as the final sign you didn't want anything real with me." Ryan's shoulders slumped with the force of his sigh. "I assumed you thought I wasn't good enough for you. I made myself move on."

Something inside Sadie broke. Something buried deep that

until that moment she hadn't realized still existed. Sure, she'd casually dismissed Ryan's invitation to the formal, but she'd gone to *extraordinary* lengths the following couple of weeks to try to come up with enough cash to make it happen. Picking up extra shifts at the restaurant. Skipping her weekly coffee-and-muffin Friday treat. Even making a phone call that she'd tried her best to forget over the years since.

In the end, her efforts weren't enough, and while she'd never admit the full extent of those efforts to Ryan now, she did owe him some honesty. "I, um . . . I wanted to say yes."

"Wait. What?" Confusion slowly swept over Ryan's features. "You *wanted* to go with me?"

Sadie took a steady breath. *God.* Why, even all these years later, was it so hard to talk about her struggles? She knew there was no shame to be had in growing up without money, but it didn't make it any easier to discuss. "I know it may seem like I blew you off, but yes, I did want to go, *with you.* The thing is, I didn't own the right type of formal-worthy dress back then. Or shoes. Or jewelry. And I didn't have the money to go buy those things. I wouldn't have fit in at that party."

The eyes staring back at her immediately filled with regret. "Sadie. *Fuck.*" Taking a step back, Ryan clasped his hands behind his head. "I'm so sorry. It never occurred to me there could be a financial reason, or *any* reason, you said no other than just not wanting to go with me. Then I went with someone else instead. Then I started dating her in a pathetic, immature attempt to get over you. No fucking wonder you hated me, I'm the villain in this story."

"Hey." She pulled at his forearm until he gave her his hand, then she linked her fingers with his. "You aren't the villain. You just didn't consider things like money because you didn't *need* to consider things like money. It's not a bad thing. It's just the way things work."

Silence stretched between them for a moment. Then Ryan said, "Just so you know, I would've rather hung out in your dorm room and watched TV with you than go to some stupid party with anyone else. I wish you could've told me this back then, but I understand why you didn't. I couldn't even work up the courage to tell you how I really felt about you so . . ."

Sadie's chest felt hollow and full at the same time, like she'd swallowed a balloon. She wasn't sure she liked the feeling. "We were college kids. It's no surprise there were things we didn't want to admit to each other. There is no villain in this story."

"Yeah, I guess so." There was something sad to the smile he gave her. "That first time I saw you here in the city after I moved, I couldn't figure out how I got so lucky to run into you after all that time. I waited outside that coffee shop to talk to you, but then you walked out and had this look of . . . disgust. I kind of accepted then how you felt about me."

"To be fair, you really weren't my biggest fan, either," she pointed out. "This hate thing between us worked both ways, you know."

Shaking his head, Ryan spread his fingers wide over the top of her thighs. "Sadie Stockton, I have felt many things for you over the years. Hate has *never* been one of them."

CHAPTER 23

Sadie lunged off the edge of the counter and into Ryan's arms, kissing him with the same intensity he'd had when he burst through her door.

"Sorry," she said as he stumbled backward, "got a little over-enthusiastic there."

"By all means," he replied between slides of their lips, "please keep going."

Hand tangling in her hair, Ryan carried her across the small apartment, breaking their kiss only to place her on her feet at the side of her bed.

"We don't have to do this if you aren't sure," he told her. "We can slow down. Watch TV. Order some food. Whatever you want."

Though Sadie could tell he was sincere, she was confident in what she wanted, and what she wanted was *him*.

"I want this." She slowly unfastened her jeans, pushed them down her hips, and stepped out of them. Then she unbuttoned the front of her cardigan until it hung open, revealing her bare sternum and the outline of her breasts. "I want you, Ryan."

He peered down at her with heavy, hooded lids. "Say that again."

"I want you."

"No. My name."

A soft smile curved her mouth. Placing her hands on his chest, she pushed him down until he sat on the side of her bed and she stood between his thighs. "I want you, Ryan," she said. Slow. Deliberate.

With a low groan, Ryan teased a single knuckle down the skin she'd just revealed to him. From the base of her throat, between her breasts, down her stomach. Shivers rolled through her shoulders when he leaned in and pressed the softest kiss to her sternum. Then he looked up at her, a crooked smile on his face.

"What?" she asked at his expression.

"Look what you're wearing," he said. "TTNB."

"What are you talking about?" she asked, not understanding.

"Remember that first night we were texting?" His smile grew. "TTNB. Tiny thong, no bra. It's exactly what you're wearing right now."

Sadie's head fell back as she laughed. Then she straddled Ryan's lap, smiling still as she framed his jaw in her hands and muttered, "Such a goddamn menace," right before their lips met.

As her tongue explored Ryan's mouth, he pulled her cardigan down her arms, leaving her topless when it fell in a heap to the floor. All at once, Ryan turned as he lifted her, laying her out on the middle of the mattress. He crawled over her, hunger and heat filling his eyes.

Everything slowed down as Ryan took her in. Propping himself up on a forearm, he watched his own hand slide over her thigh, along her stomach, up to her breast. He traced his thumb there, grazing her nipple and watching it tighten beneath his touch. Her head tipped back at the contact, and he took advantage of her exposed throat, kissing and licking and biting his way lower and lower until his mouth reached the upper swells of her breasts. Purposely teasing her, his lips roamed the sides of her breasts and underneath, never fully giving her what she wanted.

When Sadie couldn't take any more, she twisted her fingers in his hair and guided him exactly where she needed him. The wet heat of his mouth enveloped her nipple, sucking and licking and lavishing the taut tip with his tongue. Sensation rippled through her, and a breathy, "Ryan, *please*," fell past her lips.

With another low groan, he sat back on his heels. "You have to let me take my time with you, Sadie. Okay?"

What could she say to that? Absolutely fucking nothing.

Ryan pulled a square wrapper from the pocket of his jeans and tossed it on a pillow. "Eventually," he said with a small grin. Then his eyes tracked every inch of her displayed before him. "Goddamn. You're so beautiful, it's unreal."

While Sadie had been flushed from her cheeks to her chest since the moment he'd burst through her door like she was a glass of water and he'd been stranded in the desert for weeks, lying before him on display in nothing but a tiny triangle of black lace heated her skin until it was unbearable. "*Please* come here."

Ryan settled over her again, and their lips slid together like a lock clicking into place. Their tongues brushed, and needy whimpers rose from Sadie's throat as her hands roamed the contours of Ryan's chest and shoulders and back, anxious to relearn his body.

There was something uncontrolled to it, something slightly frantic, and the next time Ryan pulled back and their gazes met, she knew he felt it, too—the intensity between them she hadn't bargained for. She wanted this, wanted *him*, but she needed to be smart about it if she wanted to come out on the other end without getting hurt. Maybe they'd settled their past grievances, but relationships *always* ended in pain, and heartbreak wasn't for her. So she would tread carefully, keep this focused on physical pleasure and nothing more. That was the agreement.

The problem was that when Ryan switched their positions—pulling her into his lap with her legs wrapped around his waist, her arms folded around his neck, their chests pressed together as he kissed her deeply—it was intimate. More so when his arms tightened around her, holding her so close it was hard to breathe. When he whispered between kisses that he could hold her for days and never tire of it. When her heart twirled in a response unbidden, because those were the most meaningful words any man had ever spoken to her.

But Sadie forced all of that from her mind. Focusing on the physical, she leaned back on an arm and again guided Ryan's mouth to her chest. He wasted no time teasing her, instead sucking on her nipple in a way that twisted pleasure and pain. "Fuck, Ryan," she moaned, tilting her hips so that his erection slid directly against her center. "That feels so good. Don't stop. *Please* don't stop."

Just like she'd asked, Ryan didn't let up, working her nipple with his lips and his tongue and his teeth as she writhed against the hard press of his cock. He had her so worked up she actually groaned when he pulled his mouth away with a wet *pop* and grinned up at her. Then he dipped his head to her other breast.

Sadie's pulse fired so rapidly it might as well have been one continuous beat, and while she'd never heard of anyone passing out from arousal, it certainly seemed possible with how light-headed she felt. Wanting to give Ryan the same pleasure, she skimmed her palm down his stomach and slipped it underneath his waistband, taking his cock in her hand.

Ryan moaned at her touch but his mouth stayed on her chest, the vibration of his voice heightening the sensation. She worked her hand up and down his shaft, relishing the way he thrust into her palm like it was an involuntary action. And when she swiped her thumb over his tip and it came away slightly wet and sticky, she pulled her hand from his jeans, waited until his eyes flicked up to hers, then slowly sucked her thumb clean.

"Fucking hell," he murmured, seemingly mesmerized.

The next second, Sadie was flat on her back, her head at the foot of her bed while Ryan kissed and licked his way down her body. But then he unexpectedly paused at her rib cage and lingered over her tattoo, one she'd gotten in celebration of landing her job at the Wilmont House.

"That's new," he remarked, tracing the tiny cursive words with his fingertip.

Keep your courage close.

"It's from one of Hazel's books," she admitted, suddenly feeling shy. "My favorite one."

Ryan tenderly pressed his lips to the script, and the weird balloon feeling in her chest returned. She pulled in a shuddered breath, swallowed hard, and again pleaded, "Ryan, *please.*"

But when Ryan glanced up, the knowing expression in his eyes suggested he could see right through her. As though this weird emotion she was feeling was tattooed in the same scrawled print across her skin. "Sadie."

She shook her head, determined not to let this veer off course into something more complicated than she was prepared for. "Please keep going. Make me feel good, Ryan."

There was a moment's hesitation, but then he continued his journey down her body, the muscles in his shoulders and upper back shifting and contracting as he kissed her lower stomach before sitting back on his heels. A thumb hooked under each side of her thong, and he pulled the fabric slowly down her thighs, fingers sweeping the length of her legs as he removed the last flimsy piece of her clothing. There was something so erotic about it, the peeling away of the last layer and leaving her completely bare.

Ryan lowered himself between her thighs, and her fingers found their way into his hair, already gripping in anticipation of his mouth.

The first slow slide of his tongue nearly made her see stars.

"*Fuck*, Sadie. You taste even better than I remember." Again, his tongue traced up her center, this time lingering to circle her clit.

Pleasure swelled in her lower belly, and perhaps Ryan could sense how close she was to coming from those touches alone because he eased back and kissed her inner thighs, letting her creep back from the edge.

"Do you know how many times I've fantasized about exactly this?" he asked.

A gentle bite to her thigh made her hips arch. "Really?"

"Fuck yes." Ryan slipped a finger inside her. "Your pussy tastes like dessert."

Sadie clenched around him, and between his finger moving inside her and his mouth sucking at her clit and the dirty things he was saying, it was almost too much to handle. If he was determined to drive her this wild, she could play that game, too. Pushing up on her elbow, she held her hand out for his. "Then let me taste."

Ryan's pupils blew wide as he slid his finger out of her then watched her take that very finger deep in her mouth and taste herself on his skin.

After Sadie thoroughly sucked his finger, she slowly withdrew it from her mouth and said, "Now will you *please* make me come already?"

Some animalistic sound emerged from Ryan's throat as his mouth returned between her legs with reckless abandon. His jaw scratched her inner thighs as he worked to give her pleasure, licking, sucking, *savoring* like she was, in fact, the best dessert he'd ever tasted.

"Yes, Ryan," Sadie moaned when his tongue swept over a spot that was pure bliss.

He flicked the spot again, and her orgasm wound tight.

"Please don't stop. *Please.*"

He gripped her writhing hips to keep her in place, his mouth working the same spot over and over and over again. With one final brush of his tongue, her head fell back, wave after wave rolling through her body, her cries echoing off the walls of her tiny apartment. Good thing no one was downstairs in the gift shop at this hour.

There were orgasms, and then there were orgasms *like that.*

When Sadie opened her eyes, Ryan grinned up at her as he softly kissed her thighs.

"You're so fucking sexy." Moving back up her body, he placed kisses to her skin like he was trying to taste every inch of her he could. "Watching you come like that. *Fuck.* That was the hottest moment of my life."

Reaching her mouth, Ryan kissed her deep, and the taste of herself on his lips immediately stirred her desire again. Sadie grabbed for the condom that had somehow traveled to the center of the bed, needing him inside her like she needed air. "We're not nearly done yet."

While she tore open the package, Ryan kicked off his jeans and boxer briefs. Then she rolled the condom down his shaft. Shifting his weight to one arm, he caressed her jaw and laid his forehead against hers as he slowly sank into her inch by inch.

"You feel so fucking good," he moaned, pausing to take a breath once he filled her completely. "So fucking good."

"You feel good, too." She tightened her arms around his shoulders to keep him close.

"I've wanted this for *so* long, Sadie." His lips moved against her neck. "*So long.*"

She didn't know exactly what to say to that, and it was hard to speak with that uncomfortable pressure filling her chest. But she managed a barely audible, "I'm right here, Ryan."

The pace of his thrusts eventually increased, the pleasure building between them too much to resist, too overwhelming to go slow. Gripping her wrists, Ryan pinned them above her head with one hand, the other slipping lower to tease her clit with his thumb. Her second orgasm sprang all at once as she clutched at the sheet above her head and her cries slipped past her lips and against Ryan's mouth. His touch gentled as she recovered, but then he moved inside her again with intention. He pressed her wrists deeper into the mattress. Buried his face against her neck. Cupped her ass and tilted her hips exactly how he needed them. When she knew he was close, she freed one of her wrists from his grasp and swept her fingernails down his back, murmuring, "Yes, Ryan," until he came deep inside her, his chest heaving against hers.

CHAPTER 24

When they finally dragged themselves from her bed, Sadie invited Ryan to shower with her in her tiny bathroom. An experience that was *not* sexy in the least. Showering together in the movies was made to look steamy and seductive. In reality, it was two naked people taking turns shivering while rotating spots beneath the spray. Also, Sadie had *just* blow-dried her hair before Ryan came over, a feat that was not happening twice in one night, so she piled her thick hair into a messy bun on top of her head and attempted to keep any water below the shoulder line. When they finished, Ryan stepped out first, knotting a towel at his waist and holding another open for her, which he draped around her shoulders as she emerged. And okay, maybe she understood *part* of the shower appeal.

Steam swirled thick and heavy around them, the gold-framed mirror above the sink opaque with fog. Water droplets clung to Ryan's chest and shoulders, his wet hair a thick, matted tangle. He'd never looked more gorgeous.

Sadie hooked an arm around his neck as the other held her

towel in place. She brushed her lips over his, savoring the nearness of him, the anticipation of whatever may come next. A little sigh floated past his lips, and there it was again: that swollen, achy feeling in her chest she didn't know how to put a name to. She ran her tongue over his upper lip, a thrill fizzing through her when he groaned and backed her against the cabinet. And she welcomed it. The heat. The want. The unsatiable desire. All were easier to feel than whatever kept expanding in her chest.

"We need to stop," Ryan said, "or we're going to end up right back in your bed."

"I wasn't aware that was a bad thing." She licked a water droplet off his collarbone.

"Definitely not a bad thing," he said with a shudder, "but have you eaten at all today?"

Come to think of it, she had not. Maybe that's why she got so light-headed earlier. "Uh, no. I am kind of starving."

"That's what I figured." Shifting away from her, Ryan opened the bathroom door and a rush of cool air blew in. "I'll get dressed and go out and grab something. Any requests?"

"Just whatever you can find that's still open."

While he was out, Sadie dressed in leggings and a loose tee, retrieved an opened bottle of white wine from the fridge, and sat down at her kitchen table with her phone to scroll through her mom's texts from the past two days. Texts she was choosing to ignore. It was late, after all, and she didn't want to wake her by replying at this hour. She'd text her back first thing in the morning. Definitely.

Clicking over to Instagram, Sadie pulled up her mom's page, the urge to do a little investigating churning in her gut. When she clicked on her mom's following list, only twenty-two accounts appeared. She scrolled past some names she recognized from her mom's stories about the hospital, a couple of distant relatives, and a few local business pages—including the Wilmont House, which made her smile.

Pausing at the handle KaylaRN99, Sadie clicked over to the page of a young, bubbly-looking blonde and a grid filled with shots of her bright, tightly fitted scrubs prominently displayed as though she were a scrub influencer. Because she was such a mature person, Sadie resisted the urge to send Kayla a friendly DM reminder that Ann Stockton already had a daughter and perhaps suggest she stick to scrub promotion instead of meddling in her mom's love life. Instead, she clicked back to her mom's following list and kept scrolling with one interest in mind.

She discovered the person she was searching for with the next swipe of her thumb. Doug_Reed007.

Well, well, well.

She found him.

And what the fuck was with the 007 obsession?

More concerning, what was with the themed handles? That was one step away from a couple sharing an account. Her mom barely knew this man, for fuck's sake.

The profile photo was a generic sunrise over the ocean (yawn), and when she clicked over to his page, she was met with the taunting notice: This account is private.

"Son of a bitch!" Groaning, Sadie dropped her phone onto the table in a way that definitely wasn't good for it.

"Uh, pizza not okay?"

She startled at Ryan's voice. Having been so engrossed in her mission, she hadn't noticed her door open again.

"It was the only place still open nearby," he continued. "I bought more wine, too."

She turned in her chair. "Sorry, that wasn't about you. Pizza is good."

Ryan stored the wine and a six-pack of beer in her fridge, removing one bottle and popping the cap on the edge of her counter. He carried the pizza and his beer over to the table and sank into the seat next to her. "Who's the son of a bitch then?"

"Douglas Reed 007." Sadie downed the last of her wine.

"I'm confused." Ryan flipped open the cardboard box, revealing a thin-crust pepperoni pizza. "Is that a real person or an MI6 agent?"

"Exactly!" Angling her phone, she showed him the private account banner on her screen. "Like who does this guy think he is making his account private? As if he's *so* important or something."

"The fucking nerve of some people," Ryan deadpanned. "Who is this guy, Sadie? And if you tell me this is someone you swiped right on after what just took place in your bed, I'm taking my pizza and going home."

While his tone was light enough, she didn't miss the flash of uncertainty in his eyes. "Oh, nothing like that. Well, not *nothing* like that. I didn't meet Mr. Douglas Reed 007 on a dating app, my mom did. Now she wants me to meet him. Can you even believe that bullshit?"

"Christ, that's terrible." Confusion replaced the concern blinking back at her. "What's the problem here? What am I missing?"

Sadie pulled a slice of pizza from the box and forcefully chewed off a piece so large her mouth was too full to immediately answer. Hangriness definitely wasn't helping the situation. After she managed to swallow without choking, she began firing off her unfiltered thoughts one by one. "You wanna know what the problem is? I'll tell you what the problem is. The problem is *Kayla*, this new grad nurse my mom has been working with at the hospital. I don't even think she's there to help the sick people, Ryan. I think she's just looking for an in with the scrub influencer community. And since she obviously doesn't care if her patients live or die, she spends her time at work convincing *my mom* that she needs to be on Instagram and dating apps and, and, and . . ." Dropping the remainder of her slice back into the box, she held her phone aloft as evidence. "And go on dates with guys named Douglas Reed 007!"

Ryan's gaze shifted to the screen. "I think his name is just Doug."

Her eyes narrowed like laser beams.

"Okay, that clearly doesn't matter at the moment," he corrected.

"You don't get it," she continued. "My mom doesn't date. Ever. Not once since my dad left us. She. Doesn't. Date."

Having yet to touch their food, Ryan sat back in his chair with a thoughtful look about him. "Okay, if that's true, and now she's seeing someone she wants you to meet, don't you think he must be important to her?"

"That's the problem!" Sadie rubbed her palm across her forehead as a headache began to throb at her temples. "The last thing she needs is for some mediocre man to break her heart."

"Why do you assume that will happen?"

A shift was taking place in the conversation. One that ventured dangerously close to the things she didn't talk about. With anyone.

When she didn't answer, Ryan moved his chair closer to hers. He leaned forward, elbows on his knees. "I get being protective of your mom. But why is your natural inclination to assume she'll get her heart broken?"

"Because it was *really bad* the first time!" The words escaped her lips before she could silence them.

As heat spread through her cheeks, Ryan softly gripped her thigh. "Will you tell me about it?"

Sadie wanted this night to be sexy and fun and carefree, not spent on the verge of tears debating whether it was safe to pour her heart out to a man who had let her down once before.

But then he added a low, *"Please?"* and that broke her remaining resolve.

So she took a deep breath and started with the basic facts: "My father, like yours, is an absolute dickwad."

When Ryan's mouth quirked, she relaxed the slightest bit.

"That night in the closet I told you how he cheated on my mom their entire marriage. With multiple women. He'd meet them at work, in the neighborhood, at the local bar, even at church. More than one of them at church, actually. Who would've guessed that would be the hookup hotspot before apps came along. Anyway, as you can imagine, there was *a lot* of arguing. And what I didn't tell you that night in the closet was that I think my mom kept herself in that situation for so long because of me."

Sadie didn't pretend to know all the reasons her mom stayed as long as she did, but what she had learned over the years was that when adults chose to "stick it out for the kids," they weren't fooling anyone. Least of all the kids living under the same roof. The trauma was still there, probably even more so than watching their parents separate and move on to individual, happy lives.

"While they were yelling and fighting every night after I was supposedly asleep, that's when I would read Hazel's books and tell myself to keep my courage close, just like my favorite character, Margaret."

Ryan rubbed soothing circles against her legging-clad thigh. "But you were so little."

"Yeah, I was." The weight of Ryan's hand on her leg felt like an anchor, holding her in place, keeping her secure. She placed her own hand over his so he wouldn't be tempted to move it away. Instead, he flipped his over and entwined their fingers, and suddenly she felt far more vulnerable than at any point in her bed earlier. "They finally divorced and my father moved to Florida with one of his affair partners. Turns out she was pregnant with twins, and I'm assuming that was the final nail in the coffin of my parents' marriage. Can't really ignore that one, you know. So he moved away and started a whole new life, and my mom never saw a dime from him. Because of the custody arrangement, I had to go visit a couple times over summer break. But he stopped pursuing visitation when his child support bills racked up."

"You're right," Ryan offered with a consoling smile. "That's some real dickwad behavior right there."

"For sure," she agreed, appreciative of his attempt to lighten the conversation. "Who knows, my father might even beat yours out in the dickwad Olympics."

Ryan threw his head back and laughed, loud and open, and Sadie felt weightless.

"Don't get cocky now," he said. "My father is a solid competitor." With a tug of his hand, Sadie was suddenly out of her chair and in his lap, and she could have resisted but the comfort of his arms was too enticing. "Seriously though, I'm sorry for all that you went through back then. But if this Doug guy makes your mom happy after all these years, and after what *she* went through, don't you want that for her?"

"I don't want to see her hurt again," she justified. "After my dad left, there was a long period where instead of overhearing them arguing at night I'd hear her crying, and that was even worse. And it's not like she's alone all the time. She has her job, and she has bad-influence coworkers, and she has *me*."

Ryan didn't need to say anything. The more she tried to convince him the less she convinced herself.

"You think I'm being selfish." Translation: She knew she was being selfish.

"No." His forearm flexed around her. "I think you're being . . . understandably cautious."

"But you think I should meet him?"

"I think you obviously love your mom a lot. And she must love you an awful lot, too. So if she wants you to meet someone who's become important to her, then yeah, I think you should."

"And if this Douglas guy hurts her precious little heart again?" she posited, fingers fidgeting with the collar of Ryan's T-shirt.

"Then you'll be there for your mom no matter what happens." He pressed a light kiss to her jaw. "But I think you already know the right answer here."

This gentle, compassionate, thoughtful side of Ryan stirred things within her. Things that made her forget how hungry she was and this Douglas dilemma.

Leaning closer, Sadie began planting slow, openmouthed kisses along Ryan's throat in a route headed for that luscious lower lip of his. Before she made it even halfway to her intended destination, he gripped the back of her neck and brought her mouth to his, the hunger in his kiss momentarily surprising her before she matched it.

"We haven't finished eating," he pointed out, not bothering to pull away.

"Consider it taking a break."

"Whatever you say."

He stood, taking her with him as they stumbled backward until haphazardly tumbling onto her mattress, Ryan catching himself with one arm just before his full weight landed on top of her.

"Don't break my bed," she warned as he wrestled her shirt up and over her head.

"Why would I ever do that?" He tossed the shirt somewhere behind him. "I think it's my new favorite place."

CHAPTER 25

Sadie woke the next day expecting to feel the warmth of Ryan's body at her side.

Instead, when she slid an arm to the other side of her bed, all that greeted her were cool, empty sheets. She opened her eyes and confirmed that she was, in fact, alone.

Alone in her bed.

Alone in her entire apartment.

What the hell? Had Ryan just *left*? Without a word?

It wasn't as though she expected him to stick around all day or anything, but hooking up (several times!) and subsequently leaving without saying goodbye felt unnecessarily rude. Especially after she told him things she didn't tell anyone. Then again, maybe that was the problem. Maybe her vulnerability freaked him out and he left without a word to ensure she knew where they stood. At the time, it seemed that Ryan wanted to hear about her past. But looking back on it, maybe she'd read the situation entirely wrong and made it awkward by oversharing. Maybe his interest was his way of being polite. He'd signed up for a physical fling, not a therapy session, after all.

Even if her lack of ability to read one-on-one social situations was beyond mortifying, Sadie certainly wasn't going to sit around pining over him. If Ryan wanted to escape as soon as the sun was up, that was his prerogative.

Determined to forget last night as easily as Ryan apparently had, Sadie climbed from bed, yanked some clothes from her dresser, and headed for the shower. But as she stood under the hot spray, her achy muscles forced snippets from the night before to replay in her head like a movie. Sore arms? Oh, those were from squeezing Ryan's shoulders while he came apart. Red marks on her hips? Oh yeah, Ryan's fingerprints from when he clutched her while she writhed on top of him. Worn-out thighs? Well, there was an exponentially long list of guilty culprits for that one.

But there were other, gentler moments she couldn't stop picturing, either. After they had sex for the second time, she'd emerged from the bathroom to find Ryan in sweatpants and a pair of black-framed glasses. She must have looked at him curiously, because he said, *What? I wear contacts during the day now.* It had taken all of her willpower not to drag him back to bed that very instant for round three.

Instead, they'd set up camp on her couch and finally eaten pizza sometime around two a.m. They drank wine straight from the bottle and watched an unreasonable number of *Jeopardy!* reruns. She'd explained to him why it was her comfort show, something she'd grown up having on in the background to break the silence of an empty house while she did homework after school. And, as much as it pained her to admit, Ryan was a formidable

Jeopardy! opponent. She might have swept the history- and literature-related categories, but he easily took music and pop culture. Neither of them fucked with physics though.

At some point, she must have dozed off because she was roused by Ryan's gentle drawl coaxing, "Come on, baby, let's get you to bed."

Sadie recalled stripping down to her T-shirt and underwear, sliding between the sheets, watching Ryan undress and slide in next to her. It was so late it was early, and when Ryan's arm settled around her waist and pulled her back against the solid comfort of his chest, she'd tried to fall asleep again. She really, really had tried.

But as the minutes ticked by, she became more and more aware of his body pressed against hers in the tangle of sheets, the every so often flex of his forearm to hold her tighter. Eventually, she'd whispered into the dark, "Hey . . . You still awake?"

A deep, sleepy voice replied, "Is that your refined version of instigating a sexual encounter?"

Laughter bursting out of her, she'd rolled over and said, "Yes, that's exactly what it is," before kissing him deep.

Overall, it was kind of nice to have company for once. Someone to talk with and joke with and just *be present* with. It had all been so good, or at least *she* thought so anyway. So even if she had awkwardly overshared some things about her childhood, Ryan leaving this morning with no explanation felt . . . off. But that's what men did. They left, reasoning be damned, and she was a fool to expect anything different because of one good night.

Sadie shut off the water with an aggrieved huff then toweled off and dressed in an old tee and pajama shorts. Yanking the bathroom door open, she startled at the sight of Ryan at her kitchen table, casually sipping from a to-go coffee cup and scrolling on his phone.

"Jesus Christ!" she exclaimed. "You scared me. I thought you'd gone home."

Ryan looked up from his screen, brow furrowed. "Gone home? Didn't you see my note?" He held up last night's pizza receipt.

Sadie moved closer to the table, the scrawled message coming into view.

> *Gone for coffee.*
>
> *Back soon.*
>
> *—R*

"Oh. I didn't see it."

Head tilting, Ryan's gaze sharpened. "My stuff was still here."

Casting a quick look to the floor at the end of her bed, Sadie only now noticed the black gym bag with the white Nike swoosh partially concealed by her comforter. She crossed her arms over her chest, defenses rising against the undertone of accusation in his voice. "Obviously, I didn't notice that, either."

"So . . . what?" he asked. "You woke up, assumed I'd left, and went about your day?"

"What was I supposed to do?" she countered. "Stay in bed, pining for your return?"

Ryan emphasized the cell phone in his hand. "Or perhaps text me and ask where I went instead of automatically assuming I'd bailed?"

"Look, you're the one sneaking out as soon as the sun is up so I don't—"

"As soon as the sun is up? Sadie, it's two in the afternoon."

Oh.

Well, that was news.

"I didn't want to wake you." Sighing, Ryan set his phone down and ran a hand through his hair. "I just wanted caffeine so I didn't end up with a headache. Were you *hoping* I'd gone home?"

The way Sadie saw it, she had two choices here. She could admit the idea he'd left so abruptly had bothered her. Or she could double down and pretend it didn't matter in the slightest. He might not have bailed on her, *yet*, but the seed had been planted, so she chose the latter. "We don't need to do this. You don't owe me any explanation. This is just a temporary hookup, remember?"

Ryan flinched, and she immediately felt like an asshole, even though she was only speaking the truth.

Before she could say anything else, there was a rhythmic knock on her door. Odd, considering there were only a handful of people with the code to the gift shop.

"I should . . ." She pointed to the door, and Ryan stiffly nodded.

The moment Sadie opened the door, her mom floated in like a feather on the breeze. "Well, would you look at that! My daughter isn't dead in a ditch after all!"

One thing about Ann Stockton was that she *always* assumed if someone didn't answer their phone they were surely deceased, and, inevitably, in a ditch. She likely had a map of the city's drainage system with every ditch in a ten-mile radius highlighted in bold yellow.

Before Sadie could reply, her mom's expression shifted from concern with a hint of annoyance to blatant disbelief with a hefty dose of curiosity. It happened as soon as her eyes landed on Ryan sitting at the kitchen table.

"Oh. So sorry to barge in, Sadie-bug. Didn't realize you had *company*."

"Maybe you should've called first," Sadie pointed out.

The tight smile that formed on her mom's face told Sadie she had it coming. "I *did* call first, dear. Unfortunately, it went straight to voice mail. And as my loving, usually thoughtful daughter hasn't bothered returning my texts in *days*, I was concerned."

"Oh, uh . . ." Sadie shot a glance to her nightstand, where her phone currently sat next to the charging cord but wasn't plugged in. It must have died sometime overnight. "Sorry about that."

But alas, there was a sight much worse than her dead phone. Because on that very nightstand also sat last night's open box of condoms, perfectly angled toward them with the brand name boldly on display like they were in a condom commercial. Adding insult to injury, a discarded foil square sat next to the box, the top ripped open to ensure there was absolutely no mistaking that those condoms had in fact been used.

Sadie's cheeks flamed with the fire of a thousand hells.

Horrified, she could only watch as her mom's eyes traveled over the condoms, then to the Nike gym bag at the foot of her bed. Then she whipped around with a smile so saccharine it made Sadie's stomach turn. "Well, aren't you going to introduce me?"

A strangled, "Uh . . ." was as far as Sadie got before Ryan stood and circled the table with his hand extended.

"Hi, ma'am," he said with a kind, charming smile. "I'm Ryan Pearson. It's a pleasure to meet you."

Her mom enthusiastically took his hand. "Ann Stockton. Sadie's mom. And trust me, the pleasure is all mine."

"Sadie looks exactly like you," Ryan said, his natural charisma taking over. "Same exact eyes and everything."

Speechless, Sadie watched the two of them fall into easy conversation, her mom's smile as wide as a jack-o'-lantern's from simply discussing the weather. It was the dimple. It worked every goddamn time.

"Again, I'm sorry for interrupting," her mom eventually said. "Now that I know my daughter is alive and *certainly doing well*, it seems, I'll get out of here and leave you two alone."

"Absolutely not," Ryan said with a determined shake of his head. "You came to check on your daughter, so *I'm* going to get out of here and let you do that. Sadie's so lucky to have a mom who cares as much as you do."

Sadie watched her mom's eyes fill with adoration as though Ryan had just helped an old lady cross a busy street and rescued an abandoned kitten along the way. "Thank you for saying that," she uttered in a voice filled with gratitude. "Sadie doesn't always appreciate my concern."

"Mom," Sadie warned, "not now, please."

Ryan's gaze slid over to meet hers, and there was so much she wanted to say but couldn't. Mainly that she didn't want him to go, especially after the way their conversation had ended, but she couldn't fix it with her mom right there watching. Hell, she wasn't certain she could fix it at all. In that case, maybe him leaving was for the best. But that didn't stop her heart from silently sinking as Ryan collected his gym bag (and awkwardly avoided any contact with the condom display as he plugged her phone into the charger).

Striding into the kitchen once more, Ryan said, "Again, it was really nice to meet you," to her mom. Then he directed his attention Sadie's way and, for unknown reasons, she held her breath. "I know it's late but I thought you might want breakfast anyway." He nodded his head toward the countertop next to the fridge. An iced coffee sat next to a brown paper bag with the top folded over. Without opening it, she knew there was a blueberry muffin inside.

There was so much more behind the gesture than what appeared on the surface, and guilt pummeled her chest with the subtlety of a jackhammer. "Thank you," she managed.

With one last glance, Ryan moved past her, the latch of the front door clicking into place a moment later. As his footsteps echoed down the stairs, Sadie wondered if he would ever step foot in her apartment again.

But that thought was soon broken by the ruffling of a paper bag as her mom took out Sadie's blueberry muffin, had a seat at the table, removed the wrapper, and broke it in half. "Come tell me *everything* about Mr. Pearson."

Sadie dawdled over to the table, picking up her iced coffee on the way. "There's not much to tell."

"Well, I don't believe that for one second." Her mom passed a muffin-half over, which Sadie eagerly accepted. "Want to try again?"

"We're just hanging out while we work on this project together. That's it."

Sharp blue eyes cut to the condom exhibit on her nightstand. "*Hanging out?* Is that what you kids call it these days?"

"Mom!"

"What? There's no shame in a healthy sex life as long as you're being safe." She smiled conspiratorially. "Which it very clearly appears you are."

Sadie dropped her forehead into her palm, her entire face burning. "I don't need a sex talk. I'm a grown adult."

"Fine, fine. But honestly, Ryan seems lovely. Why can't there be more than *hanging out*?"

"Because we don't feel that way about each other." Sadie took a bite of muffin, not bothering to wipe away the crumbs that tumbled down her chin. "And he's moving to Charleston to expand his pub crawl empire so it doesn't matter. We're just having fun for a bit." Although the current heaviness in her chest wasn't that *fun*, if she were honest. "Anyway, I'm sorry I worried you, but as you can see, I'm fine."

"Are you fine though?" her mom pressed, leaning in across the table. "You keep canceling our Monday dinners, and I know you're busy with work and other *things*, but it's not like you to be this distant."

"I know." Sadie stood from the table and threw away the muffin wrapper and crumbs. "And I'm sorry about that, too. I'll do better, I promise."

As she passed by her mom's chair, a soft hand wrapped around her forearm. "Is this about Doug?"

Well, there it was.

"Sadie-bug, you better tell me the truth." She tugged Sadie's arm, forcing her into the chair at her side.

"I mean . . ." Sadie hesitated. "Maybe it's *a little* about him."

Clarity overtook her mom's features in the form of a soft smile. "Okay, I know it must come as a surprise that I'm dating after all this time—"

Well, at least she could acknowledge that.

"—and I don't mean to pressure you, but I'm *really* excited about this guy I've come to care about meeting the most important person in my life."

Phrased that way, Sadie felt like an absolute dickwad. Perhaps she'd get a special guest invitation to the Dickwad Social Club where she could sip whiskey and smoke cigars alongside her father and Ryan's. "You like him that much, huh?"

Scrunching her nose, Ann Stockton full-on blushed. In that moment, she looked so youthful. So happy. "I really do."

"Just promise me you'll take things slow, okay?" Sadie urged. "I don't want to see you get hurt again."

The giddy smile on her mom's face wavered. "You know, sweetheart, I appreciate your concern, I do. But I'm also a grown adult. You don't need to be worried about me getting hurt. I'll be okay."

"Well, you weren't okay the last time." *Shit.* Sadie hadn't meant to say that. Perhaps her new semi-nocturnal schedule was interfering with her inner filters. "I'm sorry. I didn't mean it. Let's just forget I said that."

"Uh, no." Her mom's face transformed to something stern, eyes perplexed. "I don't think we can."

"Mom, really. We don't need to do this."

"No, I want to know what you meant by that."

As her mom folded her arms across her middle and sat straight in her chair, Sadie realized there was no use trying to escape this conversation; she was too deep to backpaddle to shore. So she took a breath and then blurted, "Look, we both know how Dad was. And I don't just mean that he left us and started a new family. I mean the years and years before that when he cheated on you constantly. When every single night was a new argument. Maybe you thought I was too young to remember most of that, but I remember it all. I was little, but I still knew what was happening."

Sadie watched her mom's face drain of color, and maybe she should've stopped there, but if she was going to be forced to talk about it, she might as well put it all out there.

"I remember when we stopped going to church on Sundays because he had an affair with the organist. I remember being too scared to make any friends after he had an affair with Elizabeth's mom from our neighborhood. I even remember the argument about that one, and deciding I'd hate them both, Elizabeth and her mom, out of loyalty to you. Then after he left, I remember how hard it was for you to support us. How you worked all the time and picked up as many overtime shifts as you could. How you never had a social life or friends or did anything for yourself. I don't want to watch you go through something like that all over again."

"Oh, Sadie-bug." Posture slowly deflating, her mom appeared shell-shocked. "I guess it was naïve of me to think you were too young to know what was happening under your own roof." She slipped into a thoughtful silence for a moment, and then, "Why didn't you ever mention this before now?"

In a way, it was probably an attempt to protect her mom from any further hurt. She'd gone through enough without feeling like she'd messed up as a parent. "I didn't see a point in bringing up painful memories. And I know you did the best you could. I don't want you to feel like you failed me or something."

"Maybe I did."

"No. See, this is exactly why I didn't want to talk about this." Sadie's voice rose with frustration she couldn't suppress. She didn't want her mom's apologies, especially when the one person who should be apologizing to them both never would. "You shouldn't be taking any blame for the way things happened back then. Dad was the asshole here, not you."

"Let me finish," her mom sternly replied. "No matter what your father did, it was still my responsibility to protect you, and I didn't do a good enough job of that. I'm sorry."

Sadie looked away.

"But somewhere along the line, it seems you've confused who the parent is supposed to be here. You are *not* responsible for protecting my feelings. And you certainly aren't responsible for ensuring I never get my heart broken again. If you want to know the truth, the reason I never dated all those years had nothing to do with your father or swearing off men after the divorce."

Sadie glanced up again. "It didn't?"

"Honestly." She clasped Sadie's hand and gave a firm squeeze.

"I was busy working and raising my child and dating wasn't a priority I wanted to seek out. But more than that, I was *happy* on my own. I got married so young, and after the divorce was the first time I ever had my own house and supported myself. I had a full life with you and my job, and sure, those days were tough financially, but we also had a lot of good times, didn't we?"

It was true those uninterrupted times they spent together, whether watching movies on the couch in their pj's or cooking boxed macaroni and cheese for dinner, were always special to Sadie. "Yeah. We did."

"I like to think that if the right person would have come along back then, I would've pursued it," she continued. "But a lot of relationships come down to timing. And I'm in a place now where I have the time. And Doug is a good guy."

"Fine," Sadie sighed, her arguments deflating one by one like popped balloons. "I'll meet him."

"Great!" Her mom's radiant smile reappeared in an instant, and maybe it would be worth suffering through one dinner to see her this happy. "Next Monday. I'll make a reservation somewhere. And no backing out this time!"

"I won't. I promise."

Rising from the table, her mom bounded toward the door with an extra skip in her step. "All right, I have to go now. Since you ignored all my messages, I assumed that was a *no* for dinner tonight so Doug is taking me on a sunset cruise instead."

"On the ocean?" Sadie didn't like that one bit. "That doesn't seem entirely safe."

"Sweetheart, didn't I just tell you who the parent is in this relationship?"

Sadie met her mom at the door. "Fine. But wear a life jacket, okay? And don't drink too much. Alcohol and open water don't mix."

Her mom pulled her into a tight goodbye hug. "Whatever you say, sweetheart." Stepping back, she studied Sadie for a moment before she added, "Should I make that reservation for three . . . or for four?"

Sadie's stomach twisted. "Um, just three. I told you things with me and Ryan aren't like that."

"Oh-kay," her mom replied, clearly unconvinced. "But do me a favor, bug. Instead of spending so much energy worrying about *my* relationship, maybe spend some time reflecting on how the past might be affecting *yours*."

Then she lovingly tapped Sadie's cheek before practically dancing down the stairs.

CHAPTER 26

"There are four. Fingers crossed." Simon leaned forward in his chair at their shared table, his face all but disappearing behind his laptop screen. He was referring to the online reviews for the Mixtures and Murder Tour, and four was approximately what Sadie had expected after only one weekend. Most people didn't leave reviews. Even if you asked them to.

Seated across from him, Sadie anxiously tapped her foot underneath the table as she awaited whatever Simon was about to reveal. Next to her, Ryan sat stoic. They hadn't spoken since he left her apartment yesterday, though she'd typed out at least a dozen texts before deleting them all. If he was nervous about the reviews, he didn't show it. If he was still upset with her, he didn't show that, either. From the moment he'd walked into the restaurant and sank into the chair at her side, Sadie couldn't get any type of read on him at all.

"This first review is from Tom." Simon's voice drifted over the screen. "Do we remember a Tom?"

"The bald guy with the tattoo sleeve from Saturday night?" Sadie guessed.

"Nope," Ryan chimed in. "That was Theo. Tom was the older gentleman from Saturday who was with his wife, Jill. In town for their wedding anniversary. Jill surprised him with tickets because he's always reading mystery novels and rewatching *Clue*."

Of course Ryan, the person who spent the least amount of time with their guests on the tour, would be the one to get to know them the most.

The top half of Simon's face peeked above the laptop screen. "How does he do that?"

The question was directed at Sadie, and she shrugged. "No clue. It's annoying though, right?"

Ryan didn't react. Not even a scoff or snide comment.

Simon's gaze dipped below the glowing screen once more. "Tom says, 'This murder mystery tour was the best thing my wife and I did on our weekend trip to Sutton Island. I even discovered a clue in the dining room—yes, *the* dining room! Highly recommend.'"

Simon's eyes popped up again, brimming with joy behind his frames. "Tom loved it!"

Sadie wasn't relieved just yet. "Tom is only one person. Keep reading."

The next review was cowritten by the gentlemen visiting from Florida, Jim and George. It was equally complimentary, even noting their favorite part of the night was seeing Hazel Wilmont's writing room where she created the stories they used to read to their daughter.

Throat swelling as Simon read aloud, Sadie took a long swig of Diet Coke to clear it. It was then that she felt Ryan's eyes on her for the first time, and when she looked his way, he gave her a small smile. "You did good," he mouthed.

That acknowledgment meant something to her, but all she could do was return his smile and regret how she'd messed things up between them.

Simon read off the third review from Amelia, which might as well have been an ode to Ryan. *Ryan made the best cocktails ever! Ryan was soooo funny! Ryan made the experience so much more than just any old murder mystery game!!*

While Simon continued to read the lengthy tribute, Sadie gathered her nerve and whispered to Ryan, "Guess you did pretty good, too."

He smiled her way again, but it didn't reach his eyes this time.

"The last one is from a Kimberly." Simon's eyes popped over his screen. "Do we remember a Kimberly?"

"Saturday night," Ryan answered. "The group of three women on a girls' trip who started drinking long before the tour started."

"Oh shit." A sinking feeling spread through Sadie's stomach as she recalled the trio Ryan referred to. They hadn't been a problem, per se, just the type anyone who ever worked in the hospitality industry immediately knew *could* become a problem. Inebriated on arrival, the women had interrupted her walk-through of the dining room several times with loud outbursts proclaiming, *Bastard had it coming!* and *Maybe I'll serve Mark a special ham this Easter!* before bursting into raucous laughter while the other guests exchanged knowing looks.

Sadie had kept things moving, situations like those were nothing new to her after all, but once her walk-through wrapped up, she warned both Ryan and Simon about the trio. Ryan then made the decision not to serve them and kindly, privately offered them mocktails instead. At the time they seemed okay with it, even charmed by Ryan's attention and concern, and the night went on uninterrupted.

Now Sadie held her breath and wondered if Drunk Kimberly had sobered up and decided to go scorched earth on them in a Tripadvisor review.

"It's two stars," Simon preemptively warned. "'The Mixtures and Murder Tour is one you could and *should* skip. The night starts with a historical tour of the mansion, which is basically . . .'" Simon's face rose above the screen, contorted in a grimace. "You know what, I think we should skip this one."

"No fucking way," Sadie said. Reviews might be painful, but she didn't have the willpower not to read something that could make or break her career. "Keep reading."

Face disappearing again, Simon spoke lower when he continued, as if that would make the review more digestible. "'The night starts with a historical tour of the mansion, which is basically a snoozefest led by a rigid, stuck-up guide.'"

Sadie audibly gasped.

Simon popped back up again. "Sorry, Sadie."

"Just keep going," she instructed.

"'Next was cocktail hour,'" Simon continued. "'If you can even call it that. The drinks were weak AF.'"

"Wait." Ryan shifted forward in his seat. "She actually said 'weak AF'?"

"She did," Simon confirmed.

Ryan blew out a gusty sigh. "Of course they were *weak*. They didn't have alcohol."

"Guess she forgot that detail," Simon offered. "Then she says, 'The only somewhat cool portion of the night was the murder mystery, but the clues were hard to follow.'"

"That happens when you're plastered," Ryan muttered.

"'I'm giving it two stars, though, because the bartender was extremely hot. Maybe he should try bartending shirtless. Now that'd be worth the money.'"

Sadie gasped again.

Ryan's arm shot across the table, one finger pressing the back of the screen until the laptop snapped closed. "I think we're done with these reviews."

No longer obstructed, Simon's nervous smile faded as he tucked his laptop away in a leather bag perched on the empty chair at his side.

Before anyone said anything, a waiter dropped off their food, but Sadie suddenly wasn't hungry for the BBQ chicken flatbread she'd ordered. Both Ryan and Simon seemed less fazed, digging into their food as if all was well in the world. Picking up her fork, Sadie took a small bite as she waited for someone to say something. Anything. She couldn't be the only one stewing over Kimberly's audacity.

But when no one offered anything beyond bewildered silence, she placed her fork back down. "Okay, what the *actual fuck* was that?"

Ryan wiped his mouth with a paper napkin. "She has no idea what she's talking about."

"Clearly. But it doesn't bother you? I mean, it's one thing to be called stuck-up, it's another to have someone publicly suggest you should do your job half naked."

"Yeah, I don't love it," Ryan replied, far calmer than she thought he should be. "But I've built a career working around alcohol, you think I'm not used to being objectified?"

Something powerful roared to life in her chest. Something that felt awfully close to protectiveness. "That doesn't make it okay. We should respond."

"And say what?" Simon spoke up. "'You were trashed, Kimberly'? I don't think that'd be a good look."

Sadie's thoughts jumbled together as she tried to come up with something they could reply with. Maybe then this loud, unsettling, protective feeling she'd developed over Ryan in the past thirty seconds would quiet a little bit. "We could say that her review is offensive to our talented bartender who cared enough about her safety and well-being not to serve her and her stupid friends." She shrugged. "I mean, *maybe* we leave out the stupid friends part if we have to, but you get it."

"Listen, I appreciate your urge to defend my honor," Ryan said, "but Simon's right. Anyone who reads these four reviews should be able to sparse out that Kimberly was the problem."

"But what if Jerry reads that review?" she countered. "'Snoozefest' and 'stuck-up' aren't exactly ringing endorsements for me, either."

Simon dipped a fry in a container of ranch dressing. "There are three other glowing reviews. That's seventy-five percent. And more reviews will come in over the next two weekends and Kimberly's nonsense will eventually be drowned out amid all the great things others have to say."

"You really think so?"

"I do." Simon popped the French fry into his mouth.

Sadie wasn't so sure, but only time would tell.

* * *

After dinner, the three split up. Sadie had hoped to get a moment to talk to Ryan alone, but he'd mentioned he was heading out to go shadow a new Pearson's guide on their first solo pub crawl. So she went back to her apartment alone, changed into Ryan's sweater she still hadn't returned to him (and possibly hid in the back of her closet while he'd been at her place so he wouldn't be tempted to take it back), and sat down at her table to reread the pages of Hazel's manuscript.

Now that she had a beginning, the story itself made more sense. Two sisters, Harriett and Alice, grew up with distant parents and were sent off to boarding school for the majority of the year. When a classmate starts rumors that Harriett cheated on a science project for which she was awarded a coveted prize, all their friends turn on her, and Harriett is expelled from school and sent home to their terrible parents. Alice is left behind to clear her sister's name in hopes Harriett will be allowed to return to school. In order to do that, Alice needs to find her sister's diary, where Harriett journaled daily about her work on the project. But it's harder than expected to locate the diary since Harriett kept it hidden so others couldn't copy her work.

But there were other things about the story that didn't make *any* sense. Mainly, Hazel Wilmont didn't write mysteries. Her works were about fantastical places and magical animals and whimsical characters. This story was outside Hazel's norm, yet the voice was unmistakably hers. There was also the issue of why it was found hidden in pieces around the mansion. And did an ending even exist? There was a whole collection of Hazel's unfinished manuscripts, so there was no guarantee this one was ever completed. Either way, Sadie should probably turn all this over to Mindy, but kind of like Ryan's sweater, she wasn't yet ready to part ways.

After flipping through the pages one more time and gaining no more clarity than she had previously, Sadie placed the manuscript back in an unused drawer of her nightstand and crawled into bed. Unfortunately, her sleep schedule was now thoroughly fucked and she wasn't tired. As she lay in bed *not* sleeping, her mom's voice echoed in her head. She should spend time *reflecting* on how the past might be affecting her relationship? What did that even mean? She wasn't in a relationship! There was nothing to reflect on!

Frankly, it was rude of her mom to just show up (uninvited!) and drop some kind of coded bomb (unprompted!) and then scutter off to go wine and dine (on a *fucking yacht!*) with Douglas. Besides, she was so clearly in the wrong here. Sadie didn't let the painful pieces of her past shape her life now. Sure, she worked at the home of her favorite childhood author whose books happened to be her lifeline back then, but that was because of her eternal love for Hazel's words, not because she was a masochist who wanted daily reminders of her past. And okay, she didn't really do the whole relationship thing, but most single guys her age were terrible anyway, a fact beyond her control.

She was happy with her life.

Things were quiet.

And calm.

And stable.

Giving up on sleep, Sadie flipped on her bedside lamp, grabbed her phone, and went straight to her mom's Instagram page. Time for a little check-in. A new photo posted late last night greeted her—a fancy charcuterie board and two glasses of sparkling champagne, the sunset casting golden beams across the ocean in the background. There was one comment on the photo from KaylaRN99.

LOVE being a part of this journey!!!

That was it. Sadie was *this close* to using the World Wide Web to *her* advantage to start finding out information about Kayla's parents. Maybe her mom was single and needed a new bestie to pressure her into bad decisions. Or maybe her father was single . . . The possibilities there were endless. Before she started stalking Kayla's page, she managed a double tap on her mom's photo even though she didn't fully feel it in her soul.

But something else did stir in her soul, and instead of clicking Kayla's username, Sadie found herself navigating to Ryan's page and slowly scrolling through his photos of the city. She paused on a shot of him surrounded by a few other pub crawl guides—all of them wearing the Pearson's T-shirts that for some reason now made her smile instead of scowl. Curiosity transformed to longing as she stared down at his grin, and she scrolled to the top of the grid, finger hovering over the follow button.

It shouldn't be weird to follow someone on social media who was inside her less than forty-eight hours ago. Nevertheless, nervous flutters overtook her stomach like the first time Ryan asked for her number in Fundamentals of American Government.

She held her breath and pressed follow.

Nothing happened.

Of course nothing happened! Did she expect her phone to suddenly burst into flames in her hand? God, she needed to get a grip. And get her mom's words out of her head while she was at it.

Sadie rolled over to plug her phone back in and get back to staring at the ceiling some more. But then it happened. Not a combustion, of course, but a quick vibration against her palm that alerted her to a notification. Ryan followed her back.

It was absolutely ridiculous, but a thrill shot through her like they were the first two people to ever mutually follow each other on a social media app. Before she could determine if his return follow warranted any further action on her part, her phone vibrated again. This time a text.

Ry: Hi.

Maybe he'd taken her follow as an olive branch. Maybe that's exactly what it was.

Sadie: Hi.

She waited, but when nothing else came in after a few minutes, she realized she was going to have to do the heavy lifting here. Which, after the way she'd acted, was fair.

Sadie: I'm sorry.

Ry: For?

Sadie: For acting like I didn't care when I thought you left without saying anything.

Ry: So you did care?

Well, he wasn't going to make this easy on her.

Sadie: Yes. A lot actually.

Three blinking dots flashed across her screen then disappeared. A second later her phone lit up with an incoming FaceTime. *Shit.* She'd already taken off all her makeup, her hair was piled in a bun that leaned more rat's nest than adorable mess, and she was in bed in *his* sweater. But she really wanted to talk to him, so she hit accept anyway.

Ryan appeared on her screen, bouncing in the frame as he walked out of someplace she didn't recognize, loud music blaring in the background.

"Sorry about that," he said, coming to a stop in the parking lot and leaning against a brick wall.

"If you're working, I can let you go," she offered, even though he'd been the one to call her. "I don't want to be a bother if you're busy."

Ryan shook his head once, gaze sweeping over the screen. "Not busy and never a bother."

Sadie was unsure what to say next. The truth was that even if things were temporary between them, she couldn't deny the night they spent together meant something to her. Finally she went with, "I really am sorry. I had a great time with you, but then I got in my head about it. I convinced myself that maybe you left because I'd overshared about my past and made things weird."

"Sadie. No." Despite the low light outside the bar, she could see Ryan's eyes soften. "I had a great time, too. And I'm happy you talked to me about those things. I asked you to tell me, remember?"

"Yeah, but I don't know . . . I just thought maybe I'd made this more complicated than what you were expecting. You signed up for a physical fling, not to listen to me whine about the details of my past."

"Sadie, this is whatever we want it to be. There are no rules on what we can or can't talk about when we're together."

"No, I know," she said. "I just don't want things to be weird between us, that's all." She gave him a small smile. "I'm kind of enjoying what we're doing here, and I don't really want it to stop before it has to."

"I'm kind of enjoying what we're doing here, too." Ryan wet his lips. "Also, just so I make it abundantly clear, there's no fucking way I would have left *after that* without a word."

Heat infused her belly. "We're pretty good together, huh?"

"Pretty good?" Ryan scoffed, scratched at his chin. "Fuck, Sadie, you're the best I've ever had. There's no comparison."

Sadie's thighs reflexively squeezed together. He had no right turning her on so easily. "You could come over," she suggested. "When you're done working."

"I wish I could but I'm still gonna be a while. And you have work in the morning." Eyes sweeping down the screen, he added, "You look fucking adorable, by the way."

She did *not* look adorable by any far stretch of the imagination. "Now you're just lying to me, Pearson."

"I swear to you, I'm not." His grin spread. "The messy-hair look suits you. You should lean into it. Hey . . . is that my sweater?"

"Maybe."

"Christ, that's sexy as hell."

"Are you *sure* you can't come over?" she pleaded. "I would thoroughly enjoy having you in these sheets next to me."

Heat flared in his eyes. "If there was any way I possibly could, I'd already be there."

The want in his voice was obvious, and it created a courage she didn't normally possess. "If you were here . . ." She swept her tongue over her lower lip. "What would you do to me?"

"Sadie." Ryan's eyes darted above the screen, tracking right to left as though watching someone walk by. "That's not fair and you know it. I'm in a public parking lot."

"If you don't want to play, I can let you go." Sitting up, she pulled his sweater over her head before lying back against her pillows wearing only her underwear and a smirk. "I'll just continue to play on my own."

"*No, no, no!* Wait!" The image on her screen jostled around. When it steadied again, Ryan had an AirPod in one ear. "Okay, that's better. Please don't hang up."

"So if you were here . . . what would we be doing?" Holding her phone aloft, Sadie skimmed her other hand along her collarbone then down to the curve of her breast. "Would you be touching me?"

"Yes. God yes." Ryan spoke in a pained voice, gaze glued to the screen.

Since there was only so much he could say out loud if people were walking by, Sadie gave him a little mercy. "Would you touch me here?" Her middle finger circled her nipple, the peak perking at her touch.

"Yes." Again his eyes briefly flashed upward before returning to her. "Absolutely."

"I remember how good it felt the other night." Moving her hand to her other breast, she rolled the tip between thumb and forefinger, gave a pinch that shot pleasure to every nerve ending she possessed. "*You* felt good, Ryan. Your hands. Your mouth."

Part of her couldn't believe what she was doing. *Was she really about to masturbate with Ryan watching over FaceTime?* But the other part of her was drowning in the flood of desire, and for some reason she trusted that doing this, *with him*, was safe.

"Sadie, you're uh, making things really hard for me." Desperation was etched in his features.

"You want me to stop?"

"No, no. I definitely think you should finish what you started." Ryan's gaze briefly lifted and he gave a small nod of acknowledgment to someone offscreen. Then his attention refocused on her. "Stay the course, you know."

A quiet laugh slipped past her lips. "I definitely don't want to be labeled a quitter." Her hand trailed teasingly over her stomach, down to the waistband of her silky black underwear. She dipped a finger inside, gently stroked her clit, and didn't bother suppressing the soft moan the action drew from her.

"I'm going to need you to remove . . . the barrier."

Realizing what Ryan was trying to communicate, Sadie pushed her underwear down her hips, kicking away the covers and angling the phone to show as much of her body as possible. Then she returned her hand between her legs, sweeping her finger up and down, grazing her clit but not lingering there. Yet.

"Goddammit," Ryan muttered under his breath. "This isn't fair."

"If it helps," she said, "I wish it was you here touching me as much as you do."

"That's really nice to hear, baby, but it definitely doesn't help."

Breaths deepening, Sadie slid her middle finger inside. "I'm so wet already, Ryan." She wasn't just saying that, either. It was almost impossible how turned on she was from this. Perhaps she'd just discovered a performance kink.

"Keep going," he encouraged, voice gritty.

Sliding a second finger inside, she moved her thumb to her clit. This time she allowed the pleasure to build there as she traced circles just the way she liked. "Ryan," she moaned, eyes closing.

"You're doing so good. So fucking good."

His praise pushed her further toward the edge. "I want you, Ryan." Her voice was a pleading whimper now. "I want you here, inside me, *so fucking* bad."

"God, I want you, too, baby. So much it's painful." Perhaps no one was walking by at that moment, or perhaps Ryan no longer cared. "I want to watch you come, Sadie." Okay, so definitely alone then. "I want to watch you come on your fingers knowing that you're wishing they were mine."

Holy fucking hell. That did it. In the next second, every muscle in her lower body clenched tight as she bit her lower lip and let her orgasm crash over her.

After the last sparks of pleasure faded, Sadie opened her eyes to Ryan's perfect, grinning face on her screen. "Good girl," he said, hoarse.

Despite everything she'd just done, she reached for the top sheet and pulled it up over her chest, suddenly shy. "I should let you get back to work now."

Ryan sank a hand in his hair and blew out a heavy breath. "I'm gonna need to jog around the block a time or twenty before I can go back inside and speak words to my new employee and his tour group."

Scrunching her nose, Sadie said, "I'll make it up to you."

"And how do you plan on doing that?"

"Hmm . . . What do you want?"

Ryan's brow arched. "Anything?"

She considered it. There wasn't much she wasn't willing to do with him, so how bad could it be? "Anything."

The grin on Ryan's face turned downright devious. "Have dinner with me tomorrow night."

"*Dinner?*" That wasn't at all what she'd anticipated his response would be.

"Dinner," he confirmed. "You said anything, and that's what I want."

"But—"

"I've gotta go. Pick you up at seven."

CHAPTER 27

Sadie paced back and forth, heels click-clacking against the hardwood floors as she awaited Eric's arrival. If there was one thing she knew for certain, it's that Eric would pry the truth about Ryan out of her one way or another. Best to come out with it forthright, calmly state the facts, downplay any reaction he might have. That was the plan.

However, as soon as the door chimed and Sadie spun around to see his handsome, unassuming face, the words burst forth at once. "I think I have a date with Ryan Pearson!"

Before Eric could say anything, Charity—who'd been perfectly hidden behind Eric's muscular frame—appeared out of nowhere with eager, gossip-seeking eyes. "WHAT? Tell me everything!"

Sadie was dragged to the couch in a flurry, Charity sinking next to her and Eric perching on the coffee table in front of them.

"Start from the beginning," Charity instructed. "No skip-sies."

Where did her beginning with Ryan even start? Probably the first day of Old Man Dicky's class, but she didn't go back that far. Instead, she hit the highlights of cocktail tasting at Ryan's place,

Charity's birthday house-of-horror show (much of which they'd witnessed), and how getting stuck (and handsy) in the elevator led to a hasty hookup arrangement and Ryan spending the night at her apartment. Then she told the couple how she'd agreed to dinner with Ryan tonight (skipping over the whole FaceTime masturbation thing, obviously).

"How's the sexual chemistry?" Charity asked at the same time Eric said, "Why are you freaking out about it?"

The two exchanged glances, and a silent debate took place. "Fine," Charity eventually huffed. "I'll let E ask his boring therapist questions."

"Thanks, babe," Eric deadpanned, and Charity blew an air kiss his way. "As I was saying, why are you freaking out?"

"I'm not *freaking out,*" Sadie replied, but all three of them knew that wasn't true. "But this guy was my enemy and now we're going to dinner? And is it even a date? He didn't call it a date, so perhaps I'm getting ahead of myself. Perhaps he just wants to try out a new restaurant and wants company or something, you know? As a friend. Maybe that's all he meant by it. You know what I mean?"

"Oh, it's definitely a date," Eric stated.

"For sure," Charity agreed.

"But why do you say that?" Sadie pondered why her voice sounded tight and squeaky. "How do you know?"

Shaking his head, Eric shot a pitying, *Isn't she clueless?* look to Charity. "Because I saw how he looked at you at the bar. And the entire night that followed."

"And the entire weekend on the tours," Charity threw in. "I didn't know you two got busy in the elevator—*hot,* by the way—but everyone in that mansion could tell something's going on between you two. Even lifeless Katie, who spent most of the night with her eyes closed."

"This Ryan guy has it bad for you," Eric said. "And I think you have it bad for him, too."

Sadie thought carefully before responding. "I can admit that I like spending time with him. But at the end of the day, we both know it's temporary. So whatever tonight is, it isn't a *real* date. I don't do relationships. He's moving. That's that."

Eric shrugged as though everything she'd said was trivial at best. "Charleston is what, a few hours away? You're sitting in the presence of a couple who has made it work between Sutton Island and New York for years now."

"Well, to be fair—" Sadie quickly stopped herself from finishing a sentence that could be taken the wrong way.

But Eric wasn't having it. "Say it."

Shit. The last thing she needed right now was to make the only two people she could talk to about all of this mad at her. "Look, I think you two are the closest thing in existence to a perfect couple if there was one," she prefaced.

"But . . ." he urged.

"But your road hasn't exactly been easy." She looked back and forth between the couple, both staring at her expectantly. "It just makes me think that if two people who obviously love each other *so* much have struggled to make it work, then no one stands a chance."

The couple exchanged another look.

"Okay, first of all," Eric said, leaning in, "do not use us as an example to justify whatever misguided conceptions you have about relationships or whatever. Second of all—"

"Babe, not so harsh." Charity's perfectly manicured fingers spread over Sadie's knee. "I think what he's trying to say is that we were really young when we met, and we both had priorities of establishing our careers in separate cities. Of course we had our obstacles, but now that we're older and in a really good place, I can honestly say it was all worth it. Those times made us stronger."

"She's right." Eric looked at Charity with complete adoration. "We may not have always been together, but there hasn't been a single day in the past eight years that I haven't been completely in love with this woman. I think we both knew we'd always find our way back to each other when the time was right. So I don't want to see you cling to this Charleston thing as the reason you keep yourself from investing."

That wasn't what she was doing. There were a plethora of reasons for not getting invested. Charleston was only one of them. "There's nothing wrong with keeping things casual," Sadie muttered.

"Right, right." Eric nodded, but it was the sarcastic kind of nod that was the opposite of agreeing with her. Sadie didn't care for it. "Because in all the time I've known you, I've never seen you hung up on someone like this. But I'm sure it means nothing. Super casual."

"Damn, babe." Charity's big brown eyes darted between them like pinballs. "She told us she's going to dinner with this guy. That's a big step."

"It is *a step*, sure." Eric's shoulders relaxed as his posture softened. "Look, I don't know what happened between you two in college, but is there a chance that maybe you've downplayed how much you were hurt by it?"

"No," Sadie automatically replied. "It wasn't a big deal. We were just hooking up. He didn't owe me anything. I wasn't hurt. He didn't *hurt* me."

"If you say so. But you two seem really into each other now, so don't self-sabotage this before it even begins."

Sadie didn't have a reply. This was the second time in as many days that someone in her life called her out on her aversion to relationships. Were her issues that transparent to everyone but her?

"Let's talk about something else." Charity squeezed Sadie's knee in a show of support. "How was the rest of your weekend? Weren't you exhausted?"

While Sadie appreciated the conversational pivot, this wasn't a topic she wanted to discuss, either. "It might've been a little tougher than I imagined." *A little tougher* was quite the understatement. "But nothing I can't handle for two more weekends."

Charity and Eric exchanged looks again.

"I don't care for that, by the way." Sadie swiped her finger between the two. "These silent, judgmental conversations you two have right in front of me."

"Sorry about that," Charity said, swinging her focus back to Sadie. "It's just that after helping with the tours myself this weekend, I don't know how you managed to drag your ass in here on Saturday. And I was telling Eric that and . . ."

Sadie didn't like where this appeared to be heading. "What are you two scheming?"

Eric leaned in again, mouth opening and closing once before he finally said, "I'm banning you from the store the next two Fridays and Saturdays."

"WHAT?" Sadie exclaimed.

"See, I told you," Charity whispered to Eric, though her eyes were pinned on Sadie. "As predicted, she's defensive. And you thought *banned* was the best word choice? That's not how we practiced it at home."

"I know, I know." Eric raised his hands in defense. "I panicked."

"Okay, really, I am *right fucking here!*" Sadie blew out an exasperated breath, shifting on the couch. "Eric, is this some kind of punishment? Did I do something wrong this past weekend?"

"Not at all," he assured, calm demeanor returning. "But I won't be able to live with myself if I have to spend two more weekends watching you come in here halfway comatose. Believe it or not, I care about my friends. And I can't see you that miserable. Please take the time off. You'll be doing *me* a favor."

Sadie wanted to say no, but it always made her feel good whenever Eric called her his friend. She didn't want to ruin the moment by continuing to push back. "Okay," she reluctantly agreed. "Just for the next two weekends."

* * *

Because it would've deviated too far from his penchant for perfection to be anything but prompt, Ryan was right on time for their maybe-date. Speaking of perfection, he'd shown up at her door looking like a goddamn dream in a white dress shirt and an olive green tie that enhanced all the subtle, earthy shades in his eyes.

What had caught Sadie off guard, though, was the bouquet of soft pink calla lilies he clutched in one hand. Since the moment she'd spotted the delicate flowers, she'd found it increasingly harder to breathe as she searched her kitchen for something sturdy enough to support the weight of the bouquet. A vase was something she'd never thought to purchase—fresh flowers a luxury she'd never grown up with or thought much about in adulthood.

Once the calla lilies were secured in her stainless steel utensil holder—cooking utensils scattered across her countertop—she turned from her sink with a blush warming her face. They were all of five minutes into this date and it was obvious that no one had ever bought her flowers before. But Ryan simply kissed her cheek and complimented her floral-print dress, and somehow calmed the insecurity building within.

Thunderstorms were expected throughout the night, and dark, ominous clouds covered the sky as Ryan drove them to an old inn and restaurant that Sadie knew to be uber fancy and upscale. By the time they found nearby street parking, heavy raindrops pelted the windshield, and Ryan came around his SUV with an umbrella ready, opening her door and extending a hand to assist her step.

It was all so formal.

More so when they were seated in a dining room with sparkling chandeliers scattered above white-clothed tables while melodic piano notes swirled with the conversational hum of the well-dressed patrons. Immediately, a waiter filled crystal glasses with ice water and asked if they'd like anything else to drink while they perused the gold-embossed menus. Ryan ordered an old-fashioned, but Sadie didn't want to be judged for ordering the wrong wine or cocktail at a place like this, so she declined.

"You're quiet tonight," Ryan observed once the waiter was gone. "What's wrong?"

"Nothing's wrong." She smiled to reassure him. Because nothing *was* actually wrong. The restaurant was lovely, even if upscale places made her uneasy. A feeling compounded by the fact she didn't understand why Ryan would go to all this trouble. Maybe he felt bad about what happened in college and was trying to make it up to her in some way. Regardless of his motives, she couldn't stand the idea of Ryan thinking he messed up because he what? Had been too thoughtful in bringing her flowers? Too chivalrous in opening her door and pulling out her chair? Too eager by bringing her to a really nice restaurant? "It's beautiful in here. Thank you for all of this."

The waiter returned and provided them an in-depth rundown on the menu selections for each course, because it was the type of place that had *courses*. Many of the ingredients he spouted off were things Sadie had only heard of from cooking shows. So when the waiter wrapped up his superfluous descriptions and looked her way expectantly, she said, "I'll just have whatever he's having."

Placing his menu on the table, Ryan smiled politely at the waiter. "Could you give us another moment, please?" With a nod, the waiter scurried away. Alone again, Ryan tapped his fingers against the table. "I think I messed up."

Sadie, mid-sip, set her crystal glass down. "What do you mean?"

"You're uncomfortable. I should have kept things more casual."

Was it that obvious how much she didn't belong at a place like this? "No," she said. "It's perfect. Really."

Ryan tilted his head. "Don't lie to me, Sadie."

"Okay, it's a little more upscale than what I'm used to," she admitted. "But I truly appreciate you bringing me here. I just don't frequent places like this, and I don't really know how to act."

"I don't think there's any certain way you need to act. It's just a restaurant."

She pointedly dropped her gaze to the table. "Ryan, I have four separate forks in front of me right now."

Clarity washed over his face as he sat back in his chair. "Yeah, this is my fault." His eyes scanned the room. "Hold on, I'll fix this."

Alarmed, she said, "No, you don't need to do anything. Really. It's fine."

"It's not fine. I don't want you to be uncomfortable." Ryan motioned to the waiter, who promptly returned to their table. "My apologies, but we need to leave unexpectedly. Could we get the check?"

The waiter nodded and replied, "Of course, sir," and then was off to take care of Ryan's request.

Sadie felt horrible. "You didn't have to do that. Really. I swear it's fine."

Reaching across the table, Ryan took her hand. "I don't want tonight to be *fine*. I want it to be perfect."

"But the waiter probably hates us. All we had was your drink, which you didn't even finish."

"I'll leave an astronomical tip and I'm sure he'll be okay with it."

"Are you sure?" she asked, not feeling any better about the situation.

"Sadie, I swear to you. The most important thing is that you enjoy tonight, and I will do whatever it takes to make that happen."

The waiter returned, and Ryan paid their bill. Then he led her through the restaurant with his hand gently resting at the small of her back. Outside the rain had picked up, and lightning flashed in twisted streaks across the dark sky. Avoiding puddles as they rushed to the car, Ryan attempted to keep her covered with the umbrella, but he lost that battle to the harsh bursts of wind. By the time Sadie was seated in the passenger seat and Ryan pulled the driver's side door shut, they were both drenched from head to toe, clothes soaked through.

Ryan turned to her, hair dripping rain down his forehead, and they both burst out laughing. "Christ," he said, slicking his hair back. "I did *not* pull any part of this night off smoothly."

Sweeping her hair over one shoulder, Sadie tried her best to keep it from dripping onto the expensive leather interior. "Please. A little rain never hurt anyone."

Reaching across the console, Ryan softly stroked her cheek. "Come home with me?"

She blinked up at him, appreciative that he asked and didn't assume, despite her overnight bag sitting in his back seat. "Of course."

After starting the ignition, Ryan pulled away from the curb, but he left one hand resting on her thigh the entire drive.

Chapter 28

They parked near Ryan's building and didn't bother with the umbrella as they made a semi-run for it across the street and up the steps to the covered front porch. The same gentleman Sadie had noticed on her previous visit sat in a rocking chair on the neighboring porch with a cat curled in his lap—the shade of its gray fur strikingly similar to the man's scattered wisps of hair—both watching the storm roll in.

"Evening, Ryan," the man said with a wave of his hand, attention on the skies.

"How's it going, Nelson?" Ryan fitted his key into the knob. "Beautiful evening, huh?"

The man looked their way and smiled broadly, as if an inside joke was being referenced Sadie didn't understand. "You know I love a good storm."

"I know you do, Nelson. By the way, this is Sadie. And Sadie, this is Nelson Dean, my favorite neighbor."

"I'm his *only* neighbor," the man said with a deep, booming laugh. "Pleasure to meet you, ma'am."

"You, too, sir," Sadie replied with a polite smile.

Ryan pushed the front door open and laid a hand on her lower back. "We're going to go get out of these wet clothes, but you be careful out here, all right?"

"Now you know that's not necessary," the gentleman said with a dismissive wave.

"Nelson," Ryan drawled, looking back at his neighbor.

"Yeah, yeah. I hear you." The man stroked a hand down the cat's back.

"We're still on for breakfast next week?" Ryan added.

Sadie smiled to herself at the accuracy with which she'd nailed her assumptions of this relationship on her first visit.

"Don't forget it's my turn to pick the restaurant," Nelson replied. "Y'all have a nice evening now."

Once inside the condo, they began to make their way to the second floor, somewhere Sadie hadn't explored on her first visit. "What was that about?" she asked. "Why does your neighbor need to be careful?"

Ryan followed her up the stairs. "Nelson has a fascination with storms."

"So . . . what's wrong with that?"

"He doesn't always take proper safety precautions while storm chasing. He's been struck by lightning two and a half times."

Sadie stopped mid-step. "Wait. *What?*"

When she peered over her shoulder, Ryan shrugged. "It's true. He's been on the local news and everything. Other than being a little shaken up, he was perfectly fine. Now he thinks he's immune."

"Immune?" she huffed. "To *lightning*?"

"Yep."

Sadie started up the stairs once more then abruptly stopped again. "How does someone get struck by lightning a half of a time?"

"Technically, Winston was directly struck one of the times. But Nelson was holding him so it still counts." At her surely baffled expression, Ryan clarified, "Winston is the cat. Nelson says they're both immune now."

"Has anyone told him it doesn't work that way?" she asked. "It's fucking lightning, for Chrissake."

With an affectionate grin, Ryan pressed a kiss to her mouth. "I appreciate your concern for Nelson and Winston. But do you want to go back downstairs and debate my neighbor on the scientific facts of lightning—a debate, mind you, that you will certainly lose because the man has been struck two and a half times and walked away without a scratch and you can't argue with that—or would you like to go upstairs"—he kissed her again, letting his lips linger over hers—"and get out of these clothes?"

She didn't need further convincing. "Upstairs."

They fumbled the rest of the way to his bedroom, Ryan's mouth on the back of her neck and his arm tight around her waist. When they crossed the threshold, Sadie wanted to study his room like one of Michelangelo's sculptures. A person's bedroom was intimate, and she wanted to absorb every detail of the space he'd created for himself. But the only details she could ascertain between heated kisses were the creamy white walls, the king-size bed covered in a grayish-green comforter, and the upholstered bench at the foot where he dropped her overnight bag without even looking.

Then she was in an attached bathroom with white marble floors and a clawfoot tub. As Ryan's kisses trailed to her neck, Sadie noticed the shower. Not just any shower. A shower that took up one entire wall of the bathroom. They stumbled in that direction, and Ryan opened one of *two* glass doors and turned on one of *two* showerheads.

"What are we doing?" she asked.

"Warming you up. You're shaking."

For the first time, Sadie felt the trembles that rolled through her shoulders down into her hands. Ryan turned on the second shower-head, fingers testing the water's temperature. He kicked off his shoes, so she followed suit and stepped out of her heels. With the loss of his body heat against her, her teeth chattered.

"It's warm now." Ryan undid his tie, pulled his belt free from his pants, and tossed them both to the floor, the buckle clanging against marble. Then he stepped into the shower, fully clothed, and stood directly under the spray. "You coming?" he asked, lips twisting in a playful smirk.

"In my dress?" Sadie glanced down and back up, and Ryan's expression echoed what she already knew—it couldn't possibly get more drenched.

"Let me take it off you when I'm ready." He extended a hand, and she slipped her palm against his and let him pull her into the shower and underneath the spray. Reaching overhead, he angled both the showerheads in their direction to keep them both warm at the same time, and now she finally understood the appeal of shower sex.

But Ryan didn't so much as kiss her before dropping to his knees, hands disappearing under her dress, tugging her underwear down her legs a moment later. "All I've been able to think about for the past twenty-four hours is watching you get yourself off last night." He peered up at her as he tossed her thong over his shoulder. "I've been counting down the minutes until I can get my hands on you. My mouth on you."

His deep green eyes worshipped her from top to bottom, hanging on her chest where her tight nipples were easily revealed through the drenched, see-through fabric, then moving farther down her legs as his fingers brushed over her calves. He encircled her ankles and guided them apart.

"Hold this." He lifted the front hem of her dress, and she cinched it near her hips.

Water trailed down the front of her thighs, and Ryan caught a drop with his tongue and followed it all the way up to her center. The direct spray from the showerhead revealed every slight muscle contraction underneath his white dress shirt as he went to work between her legs with purpose, as if he needed her orgasm more than she did. It was frenzied and unrestrained. Explosive. When she came, it was hard and fast and loud, her thighs shaking violently.

Ryan rose to his feet with a hunger in his eyes she was desperate to satisfy. But when he said, "I need you, Sadie," his voice was all vulnerability and softness. A tone she'd never heard before.

Gripping the center of his sopping wet shirt, Sadie pulled him close. "You have me," she said as their lips met. In that moment, kissing Ryan felt brand new. She didn't know why. There was no logic behind it. She'd kissed this man dozens—probably even hundreds—of times before. But the way their lips worked together in perfect tandem, the way he breathed her in like she was the singular element of his awareness, the way her heart ached painfully in her chest, it was an entirely new experience.

When she pulled away, she rested her head back against the tile, eyes closed, the moment something too intense to witness. But that only heightened the brush of Ryan's fingers slipping the strap of her dress off one shoulder, of the scattering of kisses across her collarbone that followed, of the hot water steaming up the room and the press of his lips to her skin and the booming thunder that rattled through the walls every so often.

Opening her eyes, Sadie hurried to untuck Ryan's shirt and unfasten his pants and slip her hand inside. Ryan sighed heavily—maybe in relief, maybe in the pain of holding back—as she wrapped her fist fully around his shaft, slowly stroking up and down. His weight collapsed against her, but she managed to hitch her leg around his hip and guide him against her center.

With a strangled groan, Ryan lifted his head off her shoulder. "I don't have a condom in here. Let me go grab one."

"Ryan." Sadie tightened her leg around him, keeping him in place. "I want you like this."

A beat passed while he searched her eyes. "Are you sure?"

Sadie was certain. It wasn't a careless decision made in the heat of the moment, though the moment was definitely a scorcher. It was a decision made because she trusted him. Because she knew him. Because no matter what she told herself, he wasn't just some random guy. "I'm sure. I'm on the pill."

Ryan's hand slid into her hair as he kissed her, the other clutching her thigh as he pressed inside her slowly, skin to skin.

Once he was fully inside, he paused to blow out a deep breath, as if he didn't take a moment to calm down he might come right then and there. "Christ," he mumbled. "You're so perfect. So fucking perfect." He started moving again in a slow rhythm. "So smart. So incredible. So goddamn beautiful."

Sadie wasn't sure Ryan was fully aware of the things he was saying—his gaze cast down to where he slid in and out of her, his words barely audible—but she clocked every utterance, every syllable.

"You're pretty perfect yourself, you know," she said, needing to give something back to him.

His eyes lifted then, focused and full of clarity. "No, you don't understand."

Curling her hand around his jaw, Sadie brushed her thumb along his cheekbone. "What don't I understand?"

Ryan looked as though he wanted to answer but at the last moment decided against it, covering her mouth with his instead. His pace increased, and every thrust pressed deeper and deeper inside her. They both came apart within minutes, clinging to each other with limbs heavy from exertion and the weight of drenched clothing. But as good as it all felt, as *great* as it all felt, Sadie couldn't help but wonder what it was that Ryan had wanted to say but didn't.

* * *

After they dressed in comfy sweats and T-shirts, Sadie sat at Ryan's kitchen island while he made them both a grilled cheese on the stove—the kind of comfort food that put her at ease. Even so, she hoped he wasn't silently judging her for passing up a multi-course meal at the top-rated restaurant in town for what was probably the top-rated food among six-year-olds.

"I still feel bad about ruining dinner," she admitted, chewing at her thumbnail while she watched him work.

"Trust me, you didn't *ruin* anything." Ryan turned the stove off and plated their sandwiches. Then he came around the island and took a seat in the barstool beside her. "It was my fault. I wanted to impress you and of course my first instinct was to take you to the fanciest restaurant in the city." He pushed a plate toward her. "It was such a dickwad move. Completely out of my father's playbook."

"Hey, no, it wasn't a dickwad move." Angling her body toward his, she loosely entwined their ankles. "It was a really sweet and thoughtful move. Do you know how many people in this city would kill to have Ryan Pearson take them to a fancy restaurant? Thousands, likely."

"You're just saying that to make me feel better." His trademark smirk appeared. "It's probably only in the hundreds."

Laughing, she nudged his shoulder with her own. "It isn't like you to sell yourself short, Pearson."

Ryan returned her smile and kissed her forehead. "Really, though, I should have known you would prefer something more low-key."

Twisting back around on her stool, Sadie left her ankles threaded through his while she took a large bite of gooey, melty cheese. Maybe it was no meal from a Michelin-starred restaurant, but no one could convince her the combination of bread, butter, and cheese wasn't a delicacy.

"This is really good," she told him after swallowing her first bite. "Thank you."

Ryan took a large bite out of his own sandwich. "Just don't use me for my grilled cheese skills, okay?"

"No promises." Sucking melted cheddar from the tip of her thumb, she added, "But if I were going to use you for something, it'd probably be your remarkable talent for making me repeatedly come."

Something in his expression faltered, his grin turning forced. "I do what I can."

Sadie didn't know how or why, but the tone in the room shifted. She tried a different topic. "So, what you said about the fancy restaurant being a move from your father's playbook. What did you mean?"

"That's something he does a lot," he said with a shrug. "The only way he knows how to gain favor with someone is by impressing them. One time when I was failing chemistry in high school, he sent my teacher a fancy bottle of wine and a letter inviting her to come tour the science labs on campus. And, of course, also inferring that this would earn me extra credit in her class. As if that was all that was needed to fix the fact that I was in a class I couldn't keep up with. But he didn't want to hear that."

Feeling a sharp twinge in her chest, Sadie set the remainder of her sandwich back on the plate. "I'm sorry you struggled with school. And I'm sorry your father's such a dickwad. And I'm mostly sorry I assumed that just because you didn't have the same struggles I did, that you didn't have any at all."

"I don't want your apologies, Sadie." Picking up her hand, Ryan kissed the back of it before returning it to the table between them. "It was a long time ago."

"Well, you're getting them anyway. But I'm still having a hard time wrapping my head around this whole thing with your father. You're a good person and you've created a successful business. What else could anyone possibly want from their adult child?"

After a long swig from his beer bottle, Ryan answered. "Let me clear it up for you. I'm a good person—meaning I pay my employees more than my father thinks I should because it's more important to me that they have a decent paycheck than it is to increase my bottom line. I created a successful small business—but no matter how successful it is, he'll never get over the fact that it's *just a pub crawl*. Even worse, I put our family name on it, which he assumes was purely a move meant to embarrass him among his academic colleagues. And I don't know, maybe it was a little bit."

Unable to continue without offering some type of comfort, Sadie began rubbing circles over his shoulder blades. "And your mom and sister? Do they feel the same?"

Tension seeped from Ryan as though her touch was the only thing he needed to unload the heavy weight he'd been carrying. "My mom just tries to keep the peace by avoidance. And my sister, Rachel, knows how he is, but unlike me, she *was* cut out for academic life. And she actually *enjoyed* it. She followed in my mom's footsteps and is a law professor in Florida now. Definitely not a disappointment. So as sympathetic as the two were to my struggles with school, neither could understand them. It always felt like everything came so easy to everyone but me."

Guilt crashed over Sadie, making her slightly dizzy. It was the exact thing she'd always assumed about Ryan. Everything came so easy to him. His charisma, his numerous talents, his ability to create tours that sold out months in advance. Looking back on it now, she'd been so jealous of all of those qualities that she couldn't recognize they actually had a lot in common.

Now she hugged his side and propped her chin on his shoulder. "I wish your father saw what I see in you."

A curious furrow appeared on Ryan's brow. "Yeah? How do you see me, Sadie?"

In that moment, it was far more important that Ryan hear the truth than it was for her to hold back because of how much that truth might scare her. "Well . . . I see a guy who managed to build the most successful tour company on Sutton Island—no small feat, as I should know—after being fearless enough to turn down the security of his family's money and leave school in order to pursue what he really wanted to do with his life. I see a guy who is *so fucking good* with people that everyone wants to tell him their whole life story within two minutes of meeting him. I see a guy who cares about others deeply, whether it's his employees or his lightning-immune neighbor."

As Ryan's grin slowly grew, Sadie's heart expanded along with it.

"And I see a guy who I firmly believe is capable and dependable and intelligent. Someone I now know I'd want on my team in any situation because he *will* accomplish anything he sets his mind to."

Ryan's hand worked its way into her hair as he pulled her in and kissed her long and hard. "I think that's the nicest thing anyone's ever said to me."

Sadie's heart seized. "Then I think that's a goddamn shame."

Chapter 29

The storms continued over the next couple of days, and when weekend two of the tours kicked off Friday night, Sadie spent the first several minutes collecting rain jackets and umbrellas from the visitors who braved the severe weather. She'd worried all day they'd have several no-shows due to the storms, but as the clock struck midnight all twenty patrons were present and accounted for, even if drenched and windblown and definitely in need of that first cocktail.

Sadie's portion of the tour went well—admittedly, taking the day off from the bridal shop had done wonders for her mental clarity, though she'd still called Eric three times to check in.

Ryan had slept at her place last night, and they'd stayed up as late as possible in an attempt to switch to a nocturnal schedule once again. Perhaps she should be more cautious with how much time she was spending with him, but every time she got that heavy feeling in her chest that told her to tap the brakes, she reminded herself that things between them were temporary, and it couldn't hurt to enjoy it while it lasted.

As she led the night's group downstairs for cocktail hour, she tried to push all thoughts of Ryan out of her mind—an extraordinarily difficult task knowing he was waiting downstairs in the dress shirt and tie she'd watched him put on earlier and would be taking off him as soon as this night was over. When they emerged into the cocktail lounge downstairs, he looked her way and winked, and she reflexively smiled like she'd just won an award.

Their guests partook in the second cocktail of the evening, slinking onto the sofas and armchairs as Ryan took control and explained the ingredients in the drink before them. This routine was becoming more comfortable to each of them, it seemed, the tour more effortless.

At least that's what she thought until the moment glass shattered behind her.

Sadie spun toward the commotion as a collective gasp rose from their patrons.

Broken shards of a martini glass lay spread out at Simon's feet.

"Excuse my clumsiness, everyone." Simon knelt down to attend to the mess.

Sadie looked around for the nearest stack of napkins, but a yelp of pain yanked her attention back to Simon, bright red blood now oozing from his palm. For a moment she assumed it was part of the game, that Simon had switched up the script and it was food coloring or dye trickling down his hand. But then the color began to drain from his face. Actor or not, he couldn't fake that.

"Oh god." Rushing over, Sadie dropped to her knees in front of him, careful to avoid the jagged pieces of glass.

"Please excuse me for one moment," Ryan said to their guests. Then he, too, made his way over and knelt down at her side.

Hopefully they were blocking their guests' view of Simon's mangled hand, but Sadie heard the murmurs that broke out among them as they also tried to figure out if this was part of the show.

"Are you okay?" After grabbing some napkins off the nearby console table, Sadie pressed them to the wound. Blood immediately seeped through. "What happened?"

"There was a piece of the glass I didn't see, and I put my hand down directly on it," Simon replied, panicked. "Guys, I don't do well with blood. *This is going to ruin the tour!*"

"No, no. It's going to be fine," Ryan soothed. "Focus on breathing. In and out."

Simon closed his eyes, nostrils flaring as he pulled in deep breaths. And that's when Ryan shot her a wide-eyed look that said *I don't know if this is going to be fine at all.*

"Okay, okay, okay . . ." Sadie's mind raced through scenarios of how to deal with the situation. "There's a first aid kit upstairs in the bathroom. You think you can make it up if we take the elevator?"

"Yeah, of course." Simon's weak, quivering voice didn't inspire confidence.

Sadie looked at Ryan. "I'll get him patched up if you'll stay with the guests." What she didn't vocalize was that they couldn't afford another bad review after Drunk Kimberly, and a bleeding host/butler wasn't the thing five-star reviews were made of. "*Please,*" she emphasized. "Just keep talking cocktails and, you know, whatever you talk about on your pub crawls."

Ryan must have read the desperation in her eyes because he didn't argue. "All right. Up you go." He took Simon's good hand and helped him to his feet, ensuring he was steady before letting go.

Sadie slipped Simon's arm around her shoulder, just in case, and they hobbled to the elevator.

"I'm so sorry, Sadie," Simon repeated as the tiny elevator ascended. "I'm so sorry."

"There's nothing to be sorry for. Accidents happen. We just need to make sure you're okay."

The doors opened onto the first floor, and Sadie led the way down the hall to the bathroom. Once inside, Simon sank to the floor.

"Stay here, I'll find some food or juice or something." Darting to the kitchen, Sadie picked out a green apple from a bowl on the counter (likely intended for tomorrow night's appletinis) and grabbed a bottled water from the fridge. Returning to the bathroom, she thrust the items at Simon. "Here. We can't have you passing out."

Simon held his bloody hand aloft. "Will you twist the lid off?"

"Right, right." She opened the water and handed it over.

Simon drained half the bottle before setting it to his side.

"Eat this apple. It'll help stabilize your blood sugar." The ability to spew medical knowledge that she had no idea the factual basis of was truly a talent she'd never known she'd possessed until then. But Simon took the apple and sank his teeth into the side.

Rummaging through the antique armoire in the corner where they stored bathroom supplies, Sadie located the first aid kit and unzipped the top, unsure what was in it or when it had last been used. An assortment of bandages and rolled tape spilled onto the floor. She scooped up some square-shaped gauze pads and wet them at the sink. Then she knelt at Simon's side.

"Give me your hand," she instructed. "But don't look. And keep eating that apple."

Simon held his hand out to her, squeezing his eyes closed and turning his face away. "Is it bad?"

She peeled away the useless, blood-soaked napkins. "Um . . ." It wasn't *good.* The deep gash immediately bubbled up with fresh blood. If her babysitter's first aid course as a teenager had taught her anything, it's that this was beyond her skill set. "So I think maybe we should find an urgent care. Or an ER."

"No!" Simon's head jerked around, but he caught one glimpse of his hand and quickly turned away again. "I have the murder mystery to lead. I can't *leave.* I'm the butler. Everyone knows the butler is the most vital role!"

Sadie pressed the gauze over the cut, doing her best to clean the area without inflicting pain. Would only water be good enough, though? There wasn't any rubbing alcohol at her disposal. Should she grab a bottle of liquor from the kitchen and pour it over the wound? No, she decided, that felt extreme. "I appreciate your dedication, Simon. But we'll explain the situation, call it a night, and refund our guests' money." That was the only logical choice. It's not like she or Ryan could step in and provide the murder mystery experience these people paid for.

"Unacceptable," Simon argued. "Just tape some bandages on there and I'll push through."

Unable to argue and perform medical miracles at the same time, Sadie fell silent as she applied fresh, dry gauze to the wound, taped the bandages in place, then rolled Simon's sleeve up and wrapped his entire hand and forearm in a self-adhering stretchy wrap that went all the way to his elbow. When she finished, she sat back on her heels and blew out a gusty breath. It wasn't perfect, but it would do. Hopefully. "If you bleed through all of that, we're going to the ER. No ifs, ands, or buts about it. Understood?"

"Yes, ma'am."

Sadie threw away the bloody debris and washed her hands before returning to the floor, her back against the opposite wall so she could watch for any signs her patient may lose consciousness.

Simon made a move to stand. "We should get back down there."

"Don't you dare." She snapped her fingers and pointed to the floor. "Sit your ass back down and finish your apple. We're not moving until you're less pale."

Simon complied, but it wasn't without protest. "I need to do my job, Sadie."

"Ryan can handle it for a few minutes. He probably has the group eating out of his palm already." Eyeing Simon's bandaged hand, she realized perhaps that wasn't the best metaphor at the moment. "We've got some time."

"You're probably right about that." Simon relaxed back against the wall. "He probably winked once and they forgot the two of us even exist."

God, wasn't that the truth. "Or he grinned at them in that way where his dimple pops."

"For sure he's done that at least three times by now." A weak laugh escaped as Simon chucked the remaining apple core into the wastebasket. "You ever notice how his accent thickens when he turns on the charm? I honestly don't even think he's aware."

What Sadie couldn't say was that Ryan's accent also thickened in bed. So yeah, she'd noticed. "You're starting to look better," she said, swiftly changing the subject. "Less gray."

A shy smile wavered along the edges of his mouth. "Thanks for taking care of me."

"Thanks for not passing out on me."

"Well, I do what I can." There was a quiet moment before he spoke again. "I've really enjoyed working here this past month, just so you know. Back in New Orleans I had a lot of close friends and really loved my job there. Giving all that up to move here was pretty hard, and I was starting to think I might not find anything close to the life I had there." Another beat passed. "I, uh, sometimes struggle with depression, and Adam's been working so much because of the transition. It's been difficult, being in a brand-new city with no friends. But these tours have made me feel like I'm doing something worthwhile for the first time since I moved here. So even though you're not thrilled about all this, thanks for having me here."

Sadie couldn't deny she'd enjoyed getting to know Simon, despite not loving the idea of why he was here. And at least he (mostly) respected her requests and boundaries when it came to Hazel Wilmont. "I'm glad you're here, Simon. And truthfully, I don't have many friends, either. I could certainly use another."

He pushed his glasses up the bridge of his nose. "Yeah?"

"Yeah." Sadie didn't mention how impressed she was by Simon's ability to put himself out there. That he'd managed to accomplish in one conversation what she couldn't accomplish in weeks or months of knowing someone. That internally she was celebrating the fact her friend count was now up to two! "So how'd you get into the business of murder mystery acting?" she asked. It was something she'd wondered since the day they met. "Seems pretty niche."

"Says the woman who works as a tour guide in the home of a deceased author and potential murderess."

"Hazel didn't kill her husband."

"Hmm."

Sadie shot Simon a look to convey how much she didn't care for that noncommittal sound.

"Anyway," he moved on, "I wanted to be an actor from the time I was seven and got cast in a community production of *Peter*

Pan. Then in high school and college, the theater department was where I felt at home. Where I made friends. After college, I moved to New York for a year, convinced I was gonna make it big on Broadway. In twelve months, I didn't get a single callback from any audition I went on. I returned home, broke and defeated. And really lonely. Then one of my friends told me about *Dinner and Demise*, and one thing led to another."

"But you felt fulfilled there, right?" Sadie asked. "Performing in New Orleans?"

"I really did." A wistful smile came to his lips. "I realized I never needed to be a superstar, I just wanted the opportunity to keep doing what I loved. You know?"

"I get that," she replied, thinking about her own career at the Wilmont House. How she'd do nearly anything to keep working around Hazel's books every day. How devastated she'd be if it was all taken away.

"Come on, friend." Using his good hand, Simon pushed off the floor and slowly rose to his feet. "I've got a murder to solve."

After stuffing the scattered bandages and supplies back into the first aid kit, Sadie returned it to the armoire, but when she went to close the drawer, it wouldn't shut. The kit was a smidge too large.

"What's wrong?" Simon asked over her shoulder.

"Nothing." Trying again, she used more force, as if that would magically solve the problem. But nope. "I can't get this back in the drawer. It's weird."

Sidling up next to her, Simon peered down at her dilemma. "You got it out of the drawer on the left, not the right. Problem solved."

"That doesn't . . ." She opened the identical drawer next to the one she was currently befuddled with. "It's the exact same size, if it doesn't fit in this one"—she moved the first aid kit to the opposite drawer—"it isn't going to fit—"

Simon pressed a finger to the drawer on the left. It slid closed. Easily.

"That doesn't make sense," she said. "They're the same."

"Unless . . ." Gaze sharpening, Simon moved his attention to the drawer on the right, and Sadie watched the wheels spinning in his brain. "Unless things aren't as they appear."

"What's that mean?"

"Is this piece of furniture original to the home?"

"Of course."

"And has it always been located here in the restroom?"

"As far as I know," Sadie answered. "But this space was only converted into a bathroom when they renovated the house into a public museum. This room was originally a formal sitting area intended for guests to have a drink while awaiting their host. Kind of pointless, because Hazel didn't entertain. Anyway, what does any of that have to do with this?"

"Is it possible—" Sliding his unmangled palm into the drawer, Simon felt along the sides and across the bottom. Then his thumb caught in a divot at the front edge, and before Sadie could figure out what was happening, he lifted the piece of wood out of the drawer, revealing a secret compartment. "Just as I thought. *Classic* false bottom. How have you never noticed this?"

But she couldn't answer, because there in the hidden space were more loose papers. Papers that could only be— "That has to be the rest of Hazel's manuscript."

Sadie scooped them up (likely not as carefully as she should in her excitement) and let her eyes scan the first few sentences. Sure enough, it picked up right where the middle of the story had left off. She didn't have time to read them now with their guests waiting downstairs, but she quickly flipped to the back to ensure she had the ending this time. And once she'd determined she was now in possession of the *full* manuscript of *The Case of Harriett's Missing Diary,* she squealed like a barn owl and threw her arms around Simon's neck.

"This is it!" she proclaimed, jumping up and down while Simon patted her back with his wrapped forearm and said, "Okay, we can't have you getting injured, too."

"You're right." But remaining calm was a true feat with her heart galloping against her ribs. "How have you worked here *a month* and already discovered all of these secret hiding spots?"

Simon snorted. "I think the better question is, How have *you* worked here for five years and not discovered any of them?"

It was a fair question. "I don't know, Simon. You make up clues for a living. But I don't go through my everyday life looking for slightly askew mirrors or a suspicious book or a false bottom in a drawer."

"Maybe you should." His gaze dipped to the papers in her hand. "Sometimes the most obvious things are hidden in plain sight."

* * *

When the night wrapped up, Ryan insisted on driving Simon to get his hand checked out. So Sadie returned to her apartment alone, showered, then sat down at her kitchen table with the remaining pages of Hazel's manuscript. But once she finished reading, she had as many questions as she did answers. Not about the story, that part all wrapped up nicely. Alice followed Harriett's clues and eventually found the diary, then took it to the headmistress and presented the evidence of her sister's work. The expulsion was reversed, and Harriett was allowed to return to school. The story ended with a joyful reunion between the sisters. That all made sense.

What didn't make sense was why this manuscript was hidden. Or why Hazel wrote a mystery in the first place. It wasn't unlike authors to write in more than one genre, and it was still a children's book. But to go from fantastical creatures in faraway lands to a contemporary mystery set at a boarding school? It was . . . odd. But Sadie wasn't going to figure it out in her current state of exhaustion, so she tucked the pages safely away with the others then slipped into bed.

A couple hours later, she was awakened by the sounds of Ryan's movements as he entered her apartment and began to undress.

"How'd it go?" she asked, voice thick with sleep.

"Ten sutures across his palm."

"Oh my god!" Rubbing her eyes, Sadie squinted against the daylight breaking through the curtains. "That's *a lot* worse than I expected."

Ryan pulled off his shirt and laid it across the top of her dresser. "You're telling me. He almost passed out three different times."

"That sounds awful. Poor Simon."

Down to his low-slung boxer briefs, Ryan peeled back the covers and slid into the cool cotton sheets next to her. "Poor *Simon*? I'm the one whose hand is nearly broken from how hard he squeezed it. Where's my sympathy?"

"Oh, you poor thing," she said, injecting faux sympathy into her voice. "That must have been *so hard* for you."

In one deft movement, Ryan rolled on top of her, her laugh compressed from her chest accordion-style. "Very, *very* hard." Dipping his head, he planted kisses along the curve of her neck, his erection soon pressing between her legs.

"You should let me remedy that for you." She swept her fingernails down the planes of his back. "I'm practically a pro at medical emergencies now."

"Definitely." His lips grazed the shell of her ear. "The ER doctor couldn't stop talking about what a great job you did with Simon's bandage. Said it looked like the work of someone with a lot of first aid training."

"*Really?*" Holy shit! Maybe she'd retained more from that babysitter's course than she'd initially given herself credit for. "The doctor said it was that good?"

Ryan pulled back, wearing a crooked grin. "No, Sadie. He said we should have come immediately."

"You're an asshole!" she declared, though she was already laughing again. "How dare you inflate my ego like that. You know who isn't going to be coming immediately? *You.*"

But it was an empty threat as she lifted her shoulders so he could pull off her T-shirt.

"Oh, it's like that, is it?" Ryan's palm skated up her ribs as she settled against the pillows, savoring the feel of his hands on her skin. "Well, not to worry. I'm in no rush. I can do this all day long."

As his lips met hers, Sadie was overcome with how *good* it all felt. If it was always like this . . . well, she could understand the desire some people had for committed relationships. This closeness was a powerful high, so much so that she found herself asking, "Do you want to come with me to dinner Monday night? With my mom and her new . . . friend?"

Putting a few inches of space between them, Ryan, eyes gray-green in the early morning light, studied her closely. "Are you sure?"

Though the invitation had sprung forth without much consideration, she didn't regret it. "I'm sure."

A quick press of his lips to hers before he said, "Then I would love to."

For the briefest of moments as Sadie smiled up at him, she couldn't keep herself from envisioning it: the two of them going to bed together, waking up together, doing mundane daily tasks together. But that was a make-believe world with all of the highs and none of the lows, so she didn't dwell on it for long before she pushed the fictional images out of mind.

Pulling the top sheet over their heads, Ryan cocooned them together in the comfort of her bed, blocking out the rest of the world so all that remained was the two of them.

CHAPTER 30

Monday arrived, and Sadie had doubts. Big ones. Ones that had her typing out a lie about another case of food poisoning in the text thread with her mom, the send button the only thing standing between her and an escape from this fiasco. Would it make her the worst daughter in the world to cancel last minute? Possibly. Was she still highly considering it? Absolutely.

"What are you doing?" Ryan slid behind her as she stood at the bathroom counter with her makeup halfway finished, staring down at her phone. Tilting the screen, she allowed him to read it over her shoulder. After a pause, he sighed. "Sadie, no. You can't cancel. We're supposed to meet them in less than an hour."

"Hear me out." She placed her phone on the counter and spun around. "I could cancel and then we could stay here and do *other* things." Draping an arm over Ryan's shoulder, she rose onto her tiptoes and kissed the pulse point in his neck. "Things that involve sexual encounters."

"No you don't." Ryan twisted away from her. "You are *not* seducing me right now. You made a promise to your mom, and I intend on making sure you keep it."

Perhaps inviting him had been a mistake after all. If he weren't here, she'd be free to stand her mom up and worry about the consequences later. "I can do whatever I want," she said petulantly.

"It's only dinner." Hands settling on her hips, he reeled her back into his personal space. "What are you worried is going to happen?"

Truthfully, she didn't have an answer to that, only an ominous sense of foreboding deep in her gut.

When she didn't reply, Ryan said, "Why don't we leave early and I'll buy you a drink at the bar before they arrive?"

Sadie nodded, but she was going to need far more than a stiff drink.

The downtown restaurant her mother had chosen for the momentous occasion hadn't quite filled up yet when she and Ryan arrived and took a seat at the polished bar. Over the next half hour she sipped a rum and Coke and listened as Ryan rambled about their upcoming week. While she appreciated his effort to keep her distracted, it wasn't working.

The longer she sat there, the more she was convinced this was a bad idea. If her mom had been happy all these years without a relationship, why change the status quo? Didn't she remember how terrible things were with Sadie's father? Didn't she remember the arguing and the lies and the repetitive cycle of heartbreak? Didn't she remember the embarrassment he caused them both when he moved away and started a brand-new family as if they were so easily replaceable? If this sudden change of heart was about companionship, or what Sadie really didn't want to consider—sex—she could find those things without a relationship.

And maybe it was selfish, but Sadie didn't want to share her mom. Not with Douglas. Not with new-grad Kayla. Not with anyone.

Then she spotted them.

Dressed in tight jeans and a cowl-neck sweater, her mom lingered just inside the doorway next to a dark-haired man in a gray blazer.

"Oh god. Oh god. Oh god." Sadie glanced around for the bathroom, suddenly queasy.

Locked in on her every movement, Ryan turned his upper body toward the entrance and waved at her mom, drawing her attention. As she and Douglas made their way over, Ryan set a hand on Sadie's knee. "Breathe, Sadie. Everything's going to be okay."

That's all there was time for before the pair were within earshot, and Ryan rose off his barstool and greeted them both while Sadie sat stiffly frozen. At least until her mom leaned in and hugged her—or pretended to hug her—while she whispered, "Say something, Sadie-bug. You're being weird."

That broke the spell, somewhat, and she stood and addressed Douglas for the first time. "I'm Sadie. Ann's daughter. But you already know that."

"It's so nice to meet you, Sadie." Douglas proffered a hand, which she shook. Reluctantly. His palm wasn't sticky, so that was one small point in his favor. "I'm Doug."

"Nice to meet you, too, Douglas."

He gave her an odd look like maybe she'd misheard him. "Oh, just Doug is fine."

"Shall we head to our table?" her mom cut in.

A hostess seated them near the windows, which meant Sadie could watch the passersby on the busy sidewalk instead of maintaining eye contact with Douglas, seated directly across from her. When the waiter came, she and Ryan each ordered another cocktail while Douglas and her mom decided to split a bottle of merlot—*so adorable!*

Then it was silent.

Deathly so.

"Ryan," her mom eventually spoke up, "so glad you could join us tonight. Tell me how the tours are going. I barely get any details out of Sadie."

Ryan recounted Saturday night's tour, telling them how eight of the guests had been a group of seventy-year-old women who had gone to the same high school and remained close enough friends that they still took a yearly trip together. The women had been a hoot—literally. They nicknamed themselves the Blue Owls after their school's mascot and had a series of communicative *hoots* used to draw each other's attention while they searched the mansion for clues. It was one of the most memorable tour groups Sadie had ever hosted, and she couldn't wait to see if any of the Blue Owls left a review.

But that was for another night. All Sadie could do at the current moment was listen as her mom and Ryan carried the night's conversation, and she was more than happy to quietly sit back and sink into her assessment of Douglas.

He wore thin, wire-rimmed glasses that made him look like an advertisement for thin, wire-rimmed glasses. His dark hair was cut short and speckled with gray at the temples, and he had a prominent Adam's apple that bobbed every time he swallowed a sip of water, which was quite frequent (*too* frequent?). His fingernails were short and neat, and a nice-looking gold watch peeked from under the sleeve of his blazer, although she didn't know enough about watches to make a determination on its estimated cost. The arm that wasn't sporting the maybe-expensive watch rested along the back of her mom's chair, and she was certain she didn't like the bold public statement that action implied.

"Isn't that right, Sadie?"

Startled by Ryan's question, she boldly agreed, "Yep, that's right," though she had no idea what she was affirming.

Thankfully the meaningless small talk kept up, and Sadie began to think maybe she could survive this dinner unscathed. Perhaps without having to say more than a handful of sentences even. But once their food arrived, Douglas cleared his throat, and her stomach lurched, somehow knowing what was coming.

"So, Sadie . . ." He spoke timidly (*too* timidly?). "Ann talks about you so much, I feel like I already know you."

He chuckled.

She didn't.

Truly, she didn't know where this animosity came from. While she hadn't been thrilled about tonight's dinner from the get-go, she hadn't expected to feel this kind of unexplainable anger brewing and expanding, threatening to pour out of her. As if Ryan could sense she was creeping closer to the edge of a precipice, he settled a hand on her thigh, fingers warm and firm against the sleek material of the black vested jumpsuit she'd selected for the occasion.

"Ann tells me you weren't too thrilled about putting on this murder mystery tour," Douglas continued. "It must be challenging to oversee a project you weren't happy about in the first place."

"Not really," she replied. "There are a lot of things I'm not happy about, Douglas."

Ryan squeezed her thigh.

Her mom's eyes narrowed.

Both actions a warning.

"Right, of course." Looking thrown, Douglas cut a piece of

salmon with the side of his fork. "Well, are there any questions you have about me? I realize it's been a while since your mom has dated, so if you want to grill me, feel free." He gave another little chuckle, but Sadie was going to take the offer at face value.

"Okay then." She set her own fork down and folded her hands along the edge of the table. "Are you married?"

Douglas's face contorted. "What?"

"Do you have *a wife*, Douglas?"

"No!" he exclaimed. "I'm not—I'm not married!"

Dropping a cloth napkin onto the table, her mom rolled her eyes. "Sadie, *really*?"

"What?" Sadie replied, defensive. "He wouldn't be the first and only man on a dating app that's married. Always good to be direct about it."

Clearing his throat, Ryan slid his chair backward. "Sadie, show me where the restrooms are."

"They're right over there." She pointed to a large RESTROOMS sign hanging over an alcove along the far wall.

"I don't see them. Show me." Fingers firmly encircling her wrist, Ryan tugged until she was up from the table and they were headed toward the sign—which he clearly saw just fine.

Once they'd turned into the alcove and were out of view from the tables, he spun around. "*What* are you doing?"

"What do you mean?" she deflected. "And obviously you didn't need me to show you where the restrooms are."

"No, Sadie, I didn't. I was saving us all from that shitshow taking place at the table. Really, what're you doing? Doug is just trying to talk to you and you're being incredibly rude."

Annoyed at being called out, she folded her arms over the buttoned bodice of her jumpsuit. "I don't like him. He's . . ."

"He's *what*? He's literally said two sentences to you."

"See, I knew this whole thing was a mistake. He's going to hurt her, Ryan. I can tell."

Ryan exhaled slowly, as though working through how to best state something she didn't want to hear. Then he said, "Sadie, the only person hurting your mom right now is *you*. I see her flinch every single time you call him Douglas when he's told you to call him Doug. And asking if he's *married*? Come on. I can't sit back and watch you act this way."

He wasn't wrong, she was being childish. But maybe if she ran Douglas off now, she'd save her mom the heartbreak in the end, and wasn't that the better alternative? Being a little lonely now and then was surely better than nights spent crying yourself to sleep.

"Take it from someone who has a tenuous—to put it mildly—relationship with both parents," Ryan continued. "Don't mess up your relationship with your mom. It's obvious how much she loves you. This is important to her."

"Fine." It was as close to an admission of guilt as she was willing to give. "But can we agree that he has a smug face? Like one that will remain unnervingly calm when my mom confronts him about his second family she's discovered? Or one that wouldn't look out of place on the FBI's most wanted list when it turns out he's not really an *accountant*?"

Ryan blinked a few times, a myriad of expressions passing over his features. "His face is fine. Just behave better."

He led her back to the table, and she made up her mind to be more pleasant over dessert. So she switched on the practiced smile she used when giving tours, and as she slid back into her chair, she said, "Well, *Doug*, tell me about the world of *accounting*."

Sadie didn't miss the relief on her mom's face, or the look of gratitude she directed to Ryan.

Doug talked about his "work," and Sadie kept her mouth too full of banana pudding to offer any commentary other than polite nods. When the waiter brought the check, Doug was insistent on paying for everyone (*too* insistent?), and the end to this nightmare was finally in sight. But before she could fake-yawn and officially call it a night, her mom announced she was running to the restroom before they headed out.

Torn, Sadie debated her best move: go with her mom and face her one-on-one after her less-than-stellar behavior, or stay at the table with Doug. Inaction chose for her as she watched her mom swiftly navigate the long stretch between the tables and the bar without her. This option was likely best anyway, she still had Ryan to do the conversing for them both.

"Sadie, I'm actually glad we have a moment alone," Doug said then, tone serious in a way that immediately put her on edge. *More* on edge. Dangerously close to tumbling *over* the edge. Was he about to yell at her for her behavior? *He wasn't her father!* "I know you don't know me very well yet, but I want to assure you that I care a lot about your mom."

"Okay . . ." Queasiness turned her stomach. She reached for Ryan's hand under the table and found it was already right there waiting.

"I just . . ." Doug's voice wavered. "Well, I wanted to ask . . ."

"Yes?" She twisted Ryan's fingers in a way that was surely painful, but he didn't pull away.

"I know we haven't been dating all that long." Doug fidgeted with his napkin, a sheen of sweat suddenly glistening across his forehead. "But I'm in love with your mom, Sadie, and I want to propose."

"Propose what?"

"Marriage," Doug clarified. "I want to marry your mom."

All the air was sucked from the room.

Sadie couldn't breathe.

Couldn't react.

The clatter and commotion of the busy restaurant faded into a vacuum, the only thing she was vaguely aware of was Ryan's murmured, "Jesus, Doug, read the room," under his breath. But she was frozen. Empty. Void.

God only knows how much time passed before she snapped out of it, but it took Ryan squeezing her hand and repeating her name multiple times. The first thing she did was reach for the bottle of merlot that wasn't quite empty. The wine slid down her throat, and if any eyebrows were raised at the woman guzzling wine straight from a bottle in the middle of a crowded restaurant, well, she didn't give a single fuck.

"Again, I know it's soon." Speaking rapidly now, Doug's eyes darted in the direction of the restrooms. "But when you know, you know. And I've never been more sure of anything in my life."

"Uh . . ." It felt as though her vocal cords were caught in a clamp. She placed the now-empty bottle on the table and swiped the back of her hand across her mouth. "It's been what? A couple *months*?"

"Three as of next week."

"Oh!" A sardonic laugh floated through her lips. "My mistake. That makes all the difference then, Douglas." Beside her, Ryan sighed wearily. "By all means, marry my mom and ride off into the goddamn sunset if it's been *three entire months*!"

Doug winced. "Perhaps tonight wasn't the best time to bring this up."

"Perhaps not," Ryan answered on her behalf.

Doug's eyes widened as her mother emerged from the restroom and headed back their way. Leaning forward, he pulled his wallet from his back pocket in a rush, removed a business card, and placed it on the table in front of her. "Here's my number. We can talk whenever you're ready and I'll answer anything you want. Just consider it, Sadie. Please? I'd love your blessing before I ask."

Sadie was speechless.

Ryan picked up Doug's card and dropped it into her tote bag hanging on the back of her chair.

"What'd I miss?" her mom asked upon return to a silent table.

"Doug was saying his meter is almost up," Ryan offered when both Sadie and Doug remained quiet. "I guess we should call it a night then, huh?"

Sadie glanced at Ryan, who was desperately doing everything he could to get her out of this situation, and gratitude filled her heart.

"He's right," Doug said. "We should get going."

Her mom glanced at each of the men, then her suspicious gaze landed squarely and directly on Sadie. While Sadie had no idea what her face conveyed in the moment, Ann Stockton was no dummy. "All right then," she said, clearly aware *something* had gone down. "Guess we'll head out."

Moving on autopilot, Sadie allowed Ryan to lead her by the hand through the crowded restaurant to the sidewalk outside.

Doug hadn't parked far off, and they stopped beside his Volvo to say their goodbyes.

Sadie watched as her mom warmly embraced Ryan as if they were the bestest of friends. "Ryan, dear," she said, "it was so great seeing you again."

"You, too, ma'am," he courteously replied.

Then she turned her attention on Sadie. "And Sadie-bug, it was . . . Well, it was *something*."

That was it.

No hug. No kiss on the cheek. No warm words of maternal affection.

Doug opened the passenger door and her mom climbed in, then he gave them an awkward wave as he circled the car to the driver's side. They pulled away from the curb and drove off into the balmy October night, and Sadie was left behind on the sidewalk wondering what the fuck had just happened.

Chapter 31

They made it all the way back to her apartment before Ryan said, "Are we gonna talk about it?"

"No." Sadie kicked off her heels and pulled Ryan's sweater from where it now permanently resided on the top of her dresser. "You know what the thing is? Who has the audacity to ask someone a question like that the first time they meet?" Deepening her voice, she did a poor imitation of Douglas. "Hi, Sadie, I'm Douglas. Can I marry your mom even though you know nothing about me?" She rolled her eyes. "And I'm sorry but 'when you know, you know' is such cliché bullshit. Tell that to the what, sixty percent of couples that get divorced? I'm sure they just *knew*, too, right? Three fucking months, Ryan. Three!"

While Sadie whipped her jumpsuit off and pulled the sweater over her head, Ryan stepped out of his shoes and neatly tucked them under her bed. Then he lay across her comforter and turned up on his side facing her. "Does it make you feel any better at all that he does seem to genuinely love her?"

"Of course he loves her, Ryan. She's highly lovable." She

unzipped the collar of the sweater as far as it would go—now was not the time to have anything brushing against the front of her throat—then tugged on a pair of plaid pajama shorts and some knee-high socks and flopped down on the bed beside him. "But how much can you really know about a person in a few months? They probably haven't even had a real argument yet. But they will. Arguments are inevitable. Then what?"

Ryan peered down at her. "Just because Doug wants to propose doesn't mean your mom is going to say yes. Maybe she thinks it's too soon as well."

"Hopefully she doesn't get asked because I have no intention of giving Douglas my blessing."

Ryan bit his lips together.

"What?" she prompted. "Just say it."

"I think you're walking a dangerous line here." His hand found hers resting on her lower stomach, and their fingers twined and traced and twisted together in constant motion. "Maybe it's best to let your mom make her own decisions. If Doug proposes and she says yes, then you talk to her about your concerns. If he proposes and she says no, problem solved. Either way, don't you think it's better than Doug *not* proposing and her finding out it's because you kept him from it?"

She scowled up at him. "Whose side are you on here?"

"Yours." Ryan leaned down and kissed her, soft and chaste. "Always and completely yours. That's why I want you to consider how whatever action you choose will affect your relationship with your mom. That's the most important thing here."

As he brushed her hair away from her face, Sadie was overcome with that feeling of expanding warmth she couldn't name. "Thank you," she said. "For tonight. I wouldn't have survived it without you there."

"Honestly, *you* would have been fine." The grin that came to Ryan's face was soft and easy and achingly familiar. "It's *Doug* I would've been worried about."

Somehow, amid everything, Sadie managed a genuine smile.

"Thanks for inviting me." Ryan kissed her once more before glancing at his watch. "It's still early. What do you want to do the rest of the night?"

"Hmm . . ." She bit her lip, considering. Usually within five minutes of being alone together they were stripping off each other's clothes. But sex was the very last thing on her mind tonight, and she hoped Ryan would be okay with just hanging out together. "You know what sounds perfect, actually?"

He studied her for a moment. "It's *Jeopardy!* reruns, isn't it?"

"Nope." Rising from the bed, Sadie headed to the kitchen. She pulled a carton of moose tracks from the freezer, grabbed two spoons, then returned to him. "It's *Jeopardy!* reruns in bed *with* ice cream."

"Perfection," Ryan softly sighed as she shuffled back onto the bed and rejoined him.

* * *

The next morning Sadie was back at the bridal shop earlier than normal to ensure the weekend had gone okay in her absence. Walking the aisles, she searched for any signs of chaos or disruption, but the dresses were all hung perfectly spaced on the racks, shoeboxes organized on the shelf in ascending size order, tiaras sparkling in the glass display case.

One pearl necklace was slightly askew for her liking, so she unlocked the case and was straightening the milky white beads when Eric strolled through the front door wearing a thick gray cardigan over his staple V-neck. Sadie knew this had more to do with the calendar than the actual temperature outside, which certainly didn't necessitate thick cardigan usage. But that was the thing with Southerners, at some point they tried to will the cooler fall season into existence with their wardrobes, even if it left them miserable and sweaty for the majority of the day. Eric would abandon that cardigan by noon, guaranteed.

"You're early," he observed, chucking a pointed glance at his watch for good measure.

"I wanted to make sure the shop was okay after the weekend," she replied, sliding the display case closed. "How did Friday and Saturday go? Really?"

"As I told you when you called—*thrice*—" He arched a disapproving brow as he circled the counter. "It was fine. I do know how to run my own store."

Sadie was well aware of his abilities, but she still viewed them as a team. Where Eric was the face and creative genius of his store, she was the one who kept up with the day-to-day tasks and mundane details he was too busy for. Had he ever emptied their trash cans in the past seven years? Doubtful. But when she looked down at the wastebasket tucked in the corner near the register, it was, in fact, empty. "No, I know that. Of course you do."

"So, how'd last night go?" Eric logged into the iPad that kept track of his consultation appointments. "It was dinner with your mom and her new man, right?"

"Oh, that." Damn it. She'd forgotten she'd mentioned it to him. "Yeah, so that was a complete fucking disaster."

When he dropped the iPad and looked up expectantly, Sadie launched into the full account, ugly details and all.

When she finished, Eric smiled mischievously. "So are you going to call Doug *Dad* or *Papa*?"

She bumped his shoulder with her own. "How *dare* you."

He gave a lighthearted chuckle before switching into advice mode. "If you want my opinion, I think Ryan's right. I think you have to let Doug propose and see what your mom chooses to do. You don't want to step into the middle of this."

Sadie had feared he would say that. But wasn't it Doug who forced her into the middle by asking in the first place? That was another point deducted from his likability.

"If she does say yes, hypothetically speaking . . ." Eric's thoughtful gaze drifted to the ceiling, wheels turning. Hopefully he was about to say something deeply profound that would help her out of this crisis. "I envision Ann in a classic mermaid style. Simple. Elegant. No heavy beading or lace or embroidery. Just clean lines, silk buttons."

Appalled, Sadie protested, "Stop dressing my mom!"

"Calm down." His eyes did a quick sweep over her. "I'll dress you, too, of course. Assuming Ann wants you in the bridal party, that is. How do you feel about an off-the-shoulder neckline?"

"I don't need a dress! There isn't going to be a wedding!"

"It sounds like there might be. And I wouldn't be a good friend if I didn't tell you to at least consider the possibility."

Just like the night before, Sadie's entire stomach ached. Of course, Eric couldn't possibly understand the extent of her distress on this subject, she'd never told him about her parents' marriage. She'd never told anyone. Well, anyone other than Ryan.

She leaned against the display case, letting it support her. "No. I don't see it happening."

"Whatever you say." Eric picked up the iPad once more, and Sadie assumed the conversation was over until, without looking up, he mused, "You and Ryan seem to be getting serious if you're taking him to dinner with your mom."

The ache swelled, rising into her chest. "Uh, no. I mean, it was just dinner. Not a big deal."

Eric hummed a noncommittal sound and pecked away at the screen.

"If anyone's getting serious, it's you and Charity," she deflected. "How are you feeling about everything?"

Lowering the screen, he took a moment to think before he spoke. "I think this might really be it this time. Genuinely. I think we've both figured out our shit and it might just last this time around."

"I'm really happy for you," Sadie said, even if she had her doubts. "And I hope you didn't take offense to what I said the other day, because I do think you two are great together."

"No offense taken. I know when you started working here we both thought that all of this"—he waved a hand at the symbols of eternal love surrounding them—"wasn't something either of us saw in our futures. But I don't know . . . Lately, it doesn't feel so far off, you know?"

"Speak for yourself, okay?" Sadie injected humor into her tone despite the swollen, balloon feeling beneath her ribs. "Some of us are still perfectly content to keep our relationships casual and carefree."

"Mmhmm." His sharp eyes cut to hers, and she thought he was going to press the issue. But he stood up and headed for the front door. "Just think about that neckline, okay?"

* * *

The rest of Sadie's week passed in a peculiar way–without a single call or text from her mom. Normally she texted daily. Stories about where the cheating neurologist and his resident snuck off to this time or who she ran into at the grocery store and insisted Sadie must remember even though she never did. But ever since Monday night's dinner, it was radio silence.

Of course, Sadie could've reached out herself, but something stopped her every time she picked up her phone. Besides, she had a lot on her plate at the moment. The final trial tours were this weekend, and thanks to an abundance of positive reviews from the Blue Owls, things were looking hopeful. Evelyn even fielded a few phone calls during the week inquiring when more tickets might be available online.

There was a challenge though. Jerry and Mindy would be attending the final tour Saturday night to determine for themselves how it went. Needless to say, Sadie's nerves were shot to hell. If she could just finish this project off on a good note, she'd deal with her mom and Douglas afterward.

Friday night's tour started off routinely: Sadie checked tickets at the door, Simon made small talk in the foyer with the arriving guests, and Ryan retrieved more appletinis from the kitchen. A soft breeze drifted in through the open front door, and the last two guests of the evening—an attractive couple in their early sixties—made their way up the staircase to the porch. The man wore a gray suit, the woman a cashmere sweater and a black silk skirt that rippled in the breeze.

"Good evening," Sadie greeted once they reached the doorway. "Welcome to the Wilmont House Mixtures and Murder Tour. May I check your tickets?"

The woman unsnapped a clutch and presented her phone to Sadie with the mobile tickets onscreen. It wasn't until Sadie went to match the names on the tickets to the names on her list that she paid any attention to the names themselves. When she did, she might as well have run full speed into a brick wall. *Pearson.* The names on her list were Preston and Julie Pearson.

Her stomach fell to her feet. How had she not noticed this before now? Likely because their names were in the middle of eighteen others, and she hadn't read over the night's list prior to their guests arriving. Now she stood frozen—*in front of Ryan's parents!*—unsure what to say or do.

"Uh . . ." She blinked up at the couple before her. "All good, please come on in."

With a stern nod, the man moved past her into the foyer, followed by his wife.

"Here are your identity cards for the evening." Sadie handed both of them a small notecard, which they each studied with a look of displeasure as though she'd passed them a handful of wet spaghetti noodles instead. "Please take a few moments to mingle with your fellow guests. The tour will begin shortly."

Blood rushed through Sadie's ears, but she had to get to Ryan before he walked in and saw his parents with no warning. She twisted her way through the bodies crowding the foyer, desperate to get to the kitchen before it was too late. As soon as she made it to the hallway, Ryan appeared, headed in her direction, a tray of appletinis perched at shoulder height.

"Hey there!" She stepped directly in his path. "There you are!"

A curious grin formed on Ryan's mouth. "Where else would I be?"

"Good point." There was no way to know how Ryan would react to his parents being there, though she could venture a guess it wouldn't be taken as good news. "Um, I need to tell you something."

"Right now?"

"Yep, right now."

His brows knitted. "Okay . . ."

"Your, um, your parents . . ." She nervously picked at a fingernail. "They're *here*."

For a moment, Ryan didn't react, other than the slightest narrowing of his eyes. "Is that a joke?" he finally said. "'Cause I don't really get it."

"Ryan." She shook her head. "It's not a joke."

As he studied her, something in her expression must have confirmed it. All at once he moved around her to peer into the foyer. She followed, watching closely as his jaw clenched when he spotted the couple among the crowd.

"Now this," he muttered through a humorless laugh, eyes glued to the couple. "*This* is going to ruin the tour."

"Why do you think they're here?" she whispered.

"No *fucking* idea. But I'm about to find out."

Ryan entered the foyer, charismatic smile returning to his face. But Sadie knew him well enough now to see the tension in his shoulders, the ever-so-often tic of his jaw. Not knowing what else to do, she watched as he passed cocktails to their guests, briefly chatting and exchanging pleasantries as he headed in the direction of his parents.

Moving swiftly, Sadie darted through the crowd to try to get close enough to hear whatever was about to go down.

Thankfully, Charity, in a sparkly miniskirt, stood near the couple, posing for a selfie with one of their guests. As soon as the photo was snapped, Sadie interrupted. "Charity, can I talk to you?"

Charity shot her an odd look. "Yeah, sure." Then to the young woman who looked absolutely starstruck, Charity smiled and said, "I'll catch up with you a little later, okay?"

Once the guest had sauntered off, Sadie quietly explained her dilemma. "I don't really need to talk to you. I just need to be close enough to hear what's about to go down. The man in the expensive suit and the woman in the silk skirt are Ryan's parents."

"Shouldn't you say hi? It's nice of them—"

"No, I don't think this is going to be a positive interaction." Sadie wasn't about to spill Ryan's personal business, so she left it at that.

"Oh." Understanding washed over Charity's face.

With only two cocktails left on his tray, Ryan approached his parents. Sadie watched intently over Charity's shoulder while the supermodel pretended to talk about the weather. She spoke in a low enough voice that Sadie was able to hear when the first thing out of Ryan's mouth was, "What are you two doing here?"

"Good to see you, too, son," the elder male Pearson replied, sarcasm thick. Taking both appletinis from the tray, he passed one to his wife and held the other up in the light. "Back to bartending, I see."

"I am *consulting* on this tour," Ryan answered.

"Consulting?" Preston Pearson scoffed derisively. "Is that what you're calling this?"

Helpless, Sadie watched Ryan swallow hard, barely holding back his anger. Ryan had been the one thing to get her through that disastrous dinner with her mom and Douglas, and she wanted more than anything to be a support for him now. But she wasn't good in social situations, and the last thing she wanted was to misstep somehow and make it worse for him.

"Can't you two get along for one night?" Mrs. Pearson spoke with something like defeat in her voice. Or maybe exhaustion. And Sadie could understand that being married to such a dickwad would be draining. "Your father is a guest lecturer in Savannah next week, so when Rachel mentioned you were working on a tour at the Wilmont House, we decided to come to the island first and surprise you. You haven't been home in ages."

"Well, congrats," Ryan said. "I'm certainly surprised. Now if you'll excuse me—"

"See, what I can't figure out is *why* you're bartending in this . . . murder mystery or whatever shenanigan this is," his father cut in. Sadie swallowed the urge to yell, *It's an act of fiction, actually!* "Is something wrong with the business you haven't told me about?"

A choked laugh emerged from deep in Ryan's throat. It was the only laugh of his Sadie had ever heard that she didn't like. "Of course your first inclination is to assume my business is failing," he said. "Of course it is."

Guilt pummeled Sadie right in the sternum, recalling how she'd suggested the very same thing the day she'd found out about this project.

"But," Ryan went on, "since Pearson's Pub Crawls is nothing but an embarrassment to you, I'm baffled as to why you'd care if it wasn't doing well. At least if it fails, you'll get the immense satisfaction of saying I told you so."

"While I may not love the idea of you making your living off of pub crawls," Preston Pearson replied, "bartending in a gaudy, low-budget murder mystery is a new low even for you, son."

"Right. Got it." Disdain dripped from Ryan's voice. "Thanks, *Dad*."

"Now, sweetheart," Julie Pearson said, positioning herself between the two men. "Your father means well. We both only want what's best for you."

"It's okay, Julie," Ryan's father interrupted again. "Our son has never appreciated all the ways in which I look out for him."

"*Look out for me?* Is that what you call showing up unannounced and insulting me?" Ryan's shoulders slumped, an air of defeat settling over him. "Look, stay or don't stay. Either way, I have work to do." He swiftly exited the foyer.

Sadie wanted more than anything to follow Ryan and ensure he was okay, but it was well past time for her to begin the tour, and Simon kept shooting her inquisitive glances from across the room. So instead, she squeezed Charity's arm in a show of gratitude, then she climbed the first few steps of the grand stairwell and pitched her voice over the chatter. "Good evening, everyone. My name is Sadie Stockton."

CHAPTER 32

Trying to get time alone with Ryan proved to be increasingly difficult as the night wore on. Thanks to a guest stopping her to ask questions about Hazel's books, which on any other night she would have greatly appreciated, Sadie didn't make it to the kitchen to help Ryan with the absinthe cocktails until they were ready to be served. And once the drinks were distributed, he quickly disappeared again.

When unfortunate Katie Lynn hit the floor, Sadie seized the opportunity and searched everywhere for him. He wasn't in the kitchen, or the library, or in any of the numerous bedrooms that stretched down the second-floor corridor. It wasn't until she passed by Hazel's writing room and noticed the door slightly ajar that she finally found him, standing at the bookshelf with his back to her.

"Searching for your next read?" Sadie strolled into the room, goose bumps—like always—pebbling her skin.

Ryan looked over his shoulder then back to the shelf. "Kind of. I'm looking for yours."

"Mine?"

"The one that's your favorite. That your tattoo came from."

Without warning, her heart twisted uncomfortably. "Ah. Well, that would be down here." At his side, she bent to a lower shelf, fingers seeking out *The Unicorn Circus* and handing it over.

Ryan laid the book open on the shelf before him and thumbed through the pages. Stopping on one particular page Sadie knew by heart, he ran his fingertip over the words *Keep your courage close*. It was the same way he'd traced them on her skin, reverently and with awe. "Just like yours," he whispered. "Just like *you*."

The pressure in her chest was too much, and even more so when Ryan leaned over and pressed his lips against hers in an achingly tender kiss.

When he stepped back, Sadie took a beat to gather herself, then said, "You want to talk about it?"

Ryan closed *The Unicorn Circus* and placed it back on its proper shelf. "Talk about what?"

"Oh, you know"—moving close, Sadie linked her arms around his neck—"your parents showing up, the fact that you're hiding out in this room, or just what you want for breakfast later. Any or all of the above."

His palms skated along her ribs. "If I admit something to you, do you promise not to make fun of me for it?"

"Please. It's me." Then she added a wry, "So no promises."

His lips curled into a smirk. "Guess I'll have to take my chances."

"No, really," she encouraged, fingers threading through the hair above his nape. "Please tell me."

"The very first night I came through the square and saw you at the mansion was a total fluke," he said. "I'd never intended this place to be one of the stops on my pub crawl, but some of the sidewalks on my usual route were closed off for construction so I cut through the square. Then I saw you. It was maybe a few months after our coffee shop encounter, and you were standing at the entrance gate talking to some of your guests. I don't even think you saw me, and I certainly wasn't going to try to talk to you. But I looked up the house the next day and learned the rumors about Hazel, so that's when I added it to my tour. It made for an interesting stop, but mostly I just wanted more chances to see you."

Sadie's breath hitched, lungs unable to expand. "Really?"

Nodding, Ryan's demeanor seemed uncharacteristically shy. "I didn't know how much you hate random tour groups exploiting the rumors about this place. Now that I do, I'll stop bringing my pub crawls by here."

"No, don't stop." She was surprised at how quickly her reply sprang forth. But lots of tour companies included the mansion on their routes. It wasn't fair to ask Ryan not to. "Will you just mention Hazel's books, too?"

"Of course." Ryan's lips met hers, their kiss lingering longer than before.

As much as Sadie wanted to get lost in the moment, now wasn't the time. "We should get back to our guests," she said. "Including your parents."

"Yeah," he stiffly replied, and she felt the tension return to his shoulders. "You're right."

It was clear Ryan didn't want to talk about them. But Sadie couldn't pretend she hadn't heard what she did earlier, even if she'd only heard it because she was eavesdropping. "I, um, I hope you're not mad, but I heard what they said to you. Earlier in the foyer. You can talk to me about it, you know."

He looked at her for a moment, and she couldn't decipher what he was thinking. Was he about to tell her it was none of her business? Because honestly, it wasn't. Just because she'd opened up to him about her familial woes didn't mean he had to do the same. Maybe he didn't want to talk about something so personal when a month from now they'd be back to nothing more than acquaintances. Finally, he pressed his lips to her forehead. "Not mad. But later, okay? Right now I just want to get through this fucking night."

The door creaked open then, Simon sliding into the room a second later and declaring, "There you two are. We have a couple problems." Sadie instantly separated herself from Ryan, only for Simon to huff a loud, "Please. Everyone knows you two are fucking, don't try and hide it on my account."

Well then. Sadie placed a hand along her collarbone, feeling the heat rise to the surface of her skin. "Um . . . What are the problems?"

"First"—Simon held up a finger—"no offense, Ryan, but your dad is kind of a dick. He's ruining the vibe."

"No offense taken," Ryan said. "You're not telling me anything I don't know. You need me to handle him?"

"No, no." Simon gave him a sympathetic look. "I'll deal with him. I'm sure you have enough daddy trauma without adding to it." He shifted his focus and put up another finger. "But Sadie, the second problem is Ms. Pendleton. She keeps touching the artwork despite my many warnings."

Sadie felt her previous Dr Pepper aneurysm return. "Touching it? *With her fingers?*"

"Right on the canvas," Simon confirmed. "And that's not the worst part."

"Oh god . . ."

"She also snuck in Cheetos in her pocket." Wincing, Simon gritted his teeth as he delivered the horrendous news. "I fear there may be Cheeto residue on every painting in the third-floor corridor."

She gasped. "Even the Georgia O'Keeffe?"

"*Especially* the Georgia O'Keeffe."

"Oh, for fuck's sake!" She turned to Ryan. "Are you going to be okay? I need to go deal with this."

"I'm good," Ryan said. "Go take care of Ms. Pendleton and her Cheetos."

Grasping his shoulder, Sadie rose on her tiptoes and pressed a quick kiss to his cheek, then sprinted out the door and down the hall.

* * *

Even after confiscating Ms. Pendleton's Cheetos and issuing another stern warning to keep all hands off the artwork, Sadie stayed on the woman's tail the remainder of the tour. Therefore, she didn't see Ryan again the rest of the night. Maybe he was avoiding his parents—who stayed for the duration of the tour, though every time Sadie spotted them they both looked like they'd rather be literally anyplace else—and if so, she couldn't blame him. But as the hours passed, the more concerned she grew.

If there was one steadfast quality about Ryan, it was his ability to remain cool and collected. Seeing him off-kilter was uncharted territory, and she was the last person in the world with the skills to navigate it. But once Ms. Pendleton and the rest of the group coalesced back in the cellar to solve the mystery of who poisoned ill-fated Katie Lynn, Sadie slipped up the stairwell to the main floor.

She found him in the kitchen tossing back a shot of vodka. From his messy hair and bloodshot eyes, she could guess it wasn't his first (or second, or third). His tie hung undone, his collar unbuttoned.

"Hey, you." She approached him with a gentle smile. "Having a party in here without me?"

When Ryan glanced her way, the relief that filled his eyes was so glaringly apparent even she couldn't deny it.

"I would never," he said, words slightly slurred. "You're invited to every party with me. All of them. Consider it a standing invitation."

"Ryan." Taking the vodka from his hand, she screwed the top on and moved it out of reach.

"I know, I know," he sighed. "I've disappointed everyone tonight, including you. But that's what I do, you know. I disappoint. Just ask my father if he's still around, he'll be more than happy to tell you all about it. Probably has a spreadsheet saved somewhere detailing the times and dates for every instance I've let him down." Gripping the edge of the counter, he leaned his weight into his arms and hung his head in shame. "It doesn't matter what I do. It doesn't matter what my company does. I've never been smart enough. I've never been resourceful enough. I've never been hardworking enough. *I'm* never enough."

Dipping underneath one of his arms, Sadie positioned herself between him and the counter. Then she took ahold of his face and forced him to look up at her. "Hey. That isn't true. I don't care what your father thinks. You are far *more* than enough."

Conflicting emotions warred in his eyes. "Sadie, I—"

"Is this a bad time?"

They both turned at the voice of Julie Pearson, who stood in the entranceway, flanked by her husband.

"We were heading out," she continued. "I wanted to say goodbye."

Well, this was awkward.

Pushing away from the counter, Ryan stood to his full height.

"Mom, Dad, this is Sadie Stockton. Sadie, these are my parents, Preston and Julie Pearson."

Sadie offered a forced smile. "Hello." She wasn't about to say *Nice to meet you* because nothing about meeting them had, in fact, been nice.

"This makes *some* sense now," Preston Pearson muttered. "Son, if you're participating in this as a favor for your girlfriend, you could have just said that. Although, I wouldn't advise taking time away from your own company to be here doing *this*. When you're a business owner, that has to be your top priority at all times."

"Oh, so you're a business owner, too, then?" Sadie said innocently, knowing full well the answer.

"No." Preston Pearson swallowed. "I'm a professor with a PhD in business administration."

"So you study other people's successful businesses. I see."

"Sadie," Ryan said, but she ignored him. It was well past time someone put this man in his place, and she felt up to the task.

"You know"—she tapped her chin for effect—"perhaps you should have Ryan come speak to your classes then. Since he has real-world experience and all."

Preston smiled smarmily. "I don't think my students are looking to get into the pub crawl business, Ms. Stockton."

"Why not, Mr. Pearson?" she asked, unruffled. "Do they hate joy as much as you seem to?"

Preston shot a perplexed look to his wife. "I'm sorry, didn't we just meet?"

"Unfortunately, yes. Although it really hasn't been a pleasure, Professor." Sadie had no idea where this brazenness was flowing from but she chose to fully embrace it.

"Sa—" Ryan grabbed for her hand, wobbling slightly off balance in the process. "Sadie, you don't—"

"For fuck's sake, son." Preston's voice rose, setting Sadie on edge. "Are you *drunk*?"

And there went the last thread of her restraint. This man was not going to come into her house and insult her . . . well, whatever Ryan was to her, and then raise his voice to intimidate them both.

"Can you blame him?" she shot back. "I'd be throwing them back, too, if my father showed up at my place of employment just to criticize my entire life." Of course that would mean her father cared enough to know what she did for a living, which he didn't, but that wasn't the point at the moment. "That is a real dickwad vibe, Mr. Pearson."

"Look, this doesn't really involve you," Preston said. "This is a family matter."

"Don't talk to—" Ryan began, but he was in no condition to stand up for himself right now, much less her. And she didn't need his help anyway.

"Actually it *does* involve me because I seem to be the only person in this room who cares about your son and actually sees him for the kind, intelligent, charismatic person he is." Sadie slid her hand into Ryan's, wrapping her other around his biceps to keep him steady. "Do you even know that people *gravitate* toward Ryan because he makes every person he's around feel special? That's a quality you can't teach at your overpriced college. And I don't care what he does for a living and neither should you. If you can't be proud of him for being the caring, empathetic, and thoughtful person that he already is, then *you're* the problem. Not him."

Sadie turned her attention to Ryan's mother. "And I don't know where you fall in all of this, but if you want to see your son more often maybe you should stand up for him once in a while. Now if you'll excuse us, *we're* leaving." Her angry gaze flicked back to Ryan's father. "Good day, Professor."

Sadie pulled Ryan straight past the couple and into the foyer, where the last of the night's guests were gathering their belongings.

Simon grimaced when his gaze landed on Ryan. "He okay?" he asked, making his way over.

"He will be," she replied, holding tightly to Ryan's hand. "I'll get him settled at my apartment then I'll be back to help clean up."

"Sure thing, boss."

Ryan staggered along behind her through the front courtyard to the guesthouse. Inside her apartment, Sadie led him to her bed. With him sitting on the edge, she knelt down and unlaced his shoes.

"I'm so sorry," he whispered. "I'm so, so sorry."

"Don't be. You didn't do anything wrong." Once his shoes were off, she slipped his tie from his collar and started unfastening the buttons on his shirt.

"The last thing I want is to fuck this up for you, Sadie."

"Nothing's fucked up." At least, she hoped not. It hadn't seemed their guests had noticed Ryan's absence for significant portions of the night, but Sadie learned a long time ago there was no predicting what people paid attention to and would say in a review. She slipped his shirt down his arms. "There. Lie down and get some rest."

Sadie slipped away momentarily to grab a glass of water, but when she returned Ryan still sat on the edge of the mattress, shoulders hunched forward, head downcast. She set the glass on the nightstand.

"I don't usually let him get to me like that." Ryan spoke so softly Sadie barely made out the words. "I can usually ignore him, you know."

"The things he said to you were pretty awful. No one should be spoken to that way, especially by someone who is supposed to love them."

Looking up, Ryan took ahold of her hips and guided her between his thighs. "Do you really mean what you said about me tonight?"

It broke her heart that he even needed to ask. All this time she'd assumed Ryan was the poster boy for confidence, but he was just a regular person with his own insecurities, someone who needed and deserved affirmation. "Absolutely I do."

He pulled her close then, his forearms tight around her waist and his cheek pressed against her stomach. As he hugged her to him, that unexplainable pressure in her chest returned. Stronger than before.

Ryan peered up at her. "Sadie, I need to say something."

She quickly shook her head, somehow knowing that whatever he wanted to say would only inflate the pressure under her ribs instead of alleviate it. "No, you need to rest, and I need to go back and help Simon. I'll be back soon, okay?"

Ryan looked as though he wanted to protest, but then he finally lay back on her bed.

Sadie leaned over and kissed his cheek, but it wasn't until she was outside her apartment with the door closed that she fully exhaled.

Chapter 33

This was it.

The final night of the tours.

The culmination of all the work they'd put in over the past five weeks.

Jerry and Mindy arrived last of the night's guests, while Sadie shuffled around the foyer making small talk with those who bothered to arrive on time and were already halfway through their appletinis. As she mingled, she also kept a close eye on Ryan, who had slept off his hangover all afternoon and then rushed to get ready, leaving them no time to talk about anything that had transpired the night before.

Not that Sadie necessarily wanted to talk about any of it. Not the things she'd said to his parents. Not the tour drawing to a close. Definitely not whatever he was about to drunkenly say to her this morning before she scrambled for an escape. The fact was that tonight was the end. The end of the tours. The end of their arrangement. Likely the end of her job at the bridal shop when she was named director of the Wilmont House. The stakes were high, and she didn't want to think or examine any of it. She wanted to coast through this night on autopilot, achieve the career success she'd been working toward for years, and deal with everything else later.

As if delaying their start time wasn't enough, Jerry boldly spoke up before Sadie could begin her introduction, announcing himself and Mindy as the mansion's owners. Sadie wasn't sure what purpose that served, other than making himself feel important and making everyone else feel awkward. Talk about someone who couldn't read a room. He'd get on fabulously with Douglas.

Despite her annoyance, Sadie's voice wavered with nerves as she began the tour. As always, she started on the third floor and worked her way down, discussing the artwork—that miraculously remained undamaged after Ms. Pendleton's Cheeto incident—and infusing stories from Hazel's life along the way. By the time they reached Hazel's writing room, Sadie had relaxed enough that her voice was smooth and round.

"Watch your step," she announced. "There's an uneven floorboard near Hazel's desk." Images of Ryan repeatedly tripping worked their way into her head, and she wondered if she was now destined to think of him every single time she entered this room.

The group spread deeper into the space with Jerry and Mindy bringing up the rear, both appearing thoroughly bored.

While Sadie slipped into her memorized spiel on Hazel's writing career—normally the highlight of her night—her attention kept drawing to Jerry, who checked his watch repeatedly. Did he have somewhere more important to be at one in the morning?

Eventually, Sadie made her way to the bookshelf and held aloft *The Unicorn Circus,* as had become her habit since the first night of the tour, and explained to the group that of all of Hazel's works it was the one most personally meaningful to her. Then she asked if anyone else had a favorite they'd like to share. A few spoke up. A middle-aged woman named Pam said she read all of Hazel's books as a child but couldn't remember the details of them now. A young couple in their twenties said the series set in a magical forest with talking trees inspired the theme of the nursery they were currently painting for their baby on the way.

But every person who spoke cast a glance at Jerry and Mindy, as if this was a quiz to be passed instead of a relaxed, engaging conversation. Since Jerry and Mindy weren't doing anything to fit into the group or put the others at ease, Sadie made a hasty decision to acknowledge them. "Since we happen to have Hazel's own great-niece with us tonight"—*shit*, was it great-niece or great-*great*-niece?—"Mindy, would you care to share any stories about Hazel's books or which might be your personal favorite?"

Mindy gave a sheepish smile. "Oh, that's okay."

"Are you sure? I know everyone would be fascinated to hear you say a few words about Hazel."

Mindy blinked several times. "I never read them."

A literal record scratch couldn't have silenced the room more.

The back of Sadie's neck flushed hot. "Oh. My apologies for putting you on the spot like that." While Mindy nodded and appeared slightly annoyed, it was Jerry whose jaw clenched. He was furious. "Let's head downstairs, shall we?"

Panic set in as Sadie rushed through the remainder of her walk-through, and both Simon and Ryan looked perplexed and slightly alarmed when the group emerged into the cocktail lounge a full ten minutes before the usual time. Luckily, the tumblers of rum punch were ready and waiting, so their early entrance went unnoticed by anyone other than the three of them and the other actors.

Ryan's lesson in cocktails passed with a few loud punches of laughter from Jerry, meanwhile Sadie did her best to dissolve into the crowd. Once Ryan turned the floor over to Simon, Sadie quietly accompanied him as they made their way to the elevator. As soon as the doors slid shut, the words burst forth. "She hasn't even read the goddamn books!"

Ryan's brows jumped toward his hairline. "What? *Who?*"

"Mindy! Can you believe that? I asked if she could share any insights as Hazel's great-niece, great-great-niece, grand-niece, whatever the fuck she is, and she couldn't! Because she hasn't read them!" The elevator doors opened again, and she continued her rant as they trekked to the kitchen and Ryan got to work. "I mean, how does someone who is *related* to one of the most famous authors of all time not read their books? And they were published before Mindy was even born so it's not like she hasn't had the time."

"I agree it's weird, but does it really matter?" Ryan asked as he arranged crystal champagne flutes onto two serving trays. "She's the owner, but she's not really hands-on."

"True," Sadie agreed. "But when I'm director, how can I present ideas to someone who has no knowledge of the subject matter? Then again, after the look on Jerry's face, I'm never getting the job. I should probably call Eric up now and let him know he's stuck with me until we both retire."

"I don't think you need to worry about one comment, you know?" Ryan skillfully swirled each glass in a circular motion, coating the inside with absinthe before pouring the remainder into the sink, performing what Sadie now knew to call an absinthe rinse. "Maybe it was awkward, but you can't be faulted for not knowing she hasn't read them. And who else would they possibly hire? No one knows this place like you do, and you're the one who made this project a success."

"Yeah, I guess." Her nerves settled a little bit.

On the elevator ride back down, Sadie remembered that this

wasn't only a big night for her career, but for Ryan's as well. "I assume you'll pitch Jerry tonight on investing in Pearson's? For your expansion?"

"Uh . . ." He hesitated, gaze dropping somewhere between them. "About that. We need to talk."

Sadie's stomach twisted. She supposed this would be "the talk" where they'd officially end their situationship. He'd say they'd stay friends. She'd agree. Then he'd move off to Charleston and forget all about her, the way people always did when they started a brand-new life in a brand-new town and left everything and everyone else behind.

The elevator opened up to the cellar, and Ryan looked her way with a guarded smile. "Later, okay?"

She nodded, throat too thick to speak, then stepped off the elevator and pasted on her own smile.

As cocktail hour continued, she felt the distance from Ryan already growing. He didn't make eye contact with her even once, and it felt intentional.

Sadie made her way around the lounge, collecting empty glasses and exchanging small talk with their guests, but the entire time her mind was elsewhere. It was scary not knowing what her life would look like when all of this was over and the debris of her shaken-snow-globe reality finally settled. But it was more than the promotion that she may or may not get, changing her everyday life either way. For the first time ever, her relationship with her mom seemed to be on shaky ground, and she didn't know how to fix it. Then there was her friendship with Eric and the looming fear it wouldn't survive if she left her job at the bridal shop and was no longer a part of his daily life.

Beyond all of that, it was the recurring memory in her head of Ryan sitting on her bed the morning before, drunk and dejected and looking up at her as though she was the only person who could make it better. That image might as well have been a massive boulder pressing on her sternum, preventing her from taking a breath without searing pain radiating throughout her entire chest.

This thing between them was always temporary, she'd known that from the start. But that didn't detract from how close they'd become or how much she'd relied on him lately. Going their separate ways was a certainty, but despite her foolproof plan, it seemed she could no longer pretend it wasn't going to hurt.

The rest of the night passed in a blur, her thoughts and emotions scattered.

Before the guests parted ways, Jerry made one final declaration to the group as they gathered their belongings in the grand foyer. "I'm not sure everyone is aware," he said, voice booming over the crowd, "but this is the final night of The Mixtures and Murder Tour."

The group collectively murmured its displeasure.

"Unless . . ." Jerry propped a hand on his hip, the other stroking his chin. "Unless you all think we should make it a permanent staple here at the Wilmont House? I don't know . . . What do you say?"

What a flair Jerry had for the dramatic.

But the group applauded, and Jerry flashed his unnervingly bright smile. "That settles it then. Tell all your friends about us, we'll be back."

Sadie's heart rate spiked. Was that it? Had she done it? Instinctively, her gaze traveled to Ryan. He winked and mouthed, "Well done."

The group trickled out the front door, soon followed by Charity and Katie and Gabe.

Then Jerry said to the three of them, "Let's speak in the dining room."

Hope sprouted in Sadie's chest. She'd pulled off this entire murder mystery tour with two weeks' notice and made it a success, and now she was on the verge of landing the job she'd coveted since she was a kid.

In the dining room, Mindy and Jerry stood on one side of the table while Simon, Ryan, and Sadie lined up on the other.

Jerry cut right to the chase. "It's evident the guests had a great time here this evening and I've kept track of the online reviews, which have been mostly exceptional."

Sadie wondered if by *mostly* he was referring to Drunk Kimberly's rant.

As his mouth lifted in a broad smile, Jerry's overly white veneers reflected rays of light bouncing off the chandelier. "I think it's fair to call this idea of mine an overwhelming success."

Of course the first person Jerry would acknowledge would be himself. When no one said anything, probably he was expecting congratulations or applause, he spun on his heel and paced the length of the rosewood table. Mindy stepped back to clear his path.

"There are some things we need to discuss moving forward, however," he continued, tucking his hands into his pants pockets. "Simon, how difficult will it be for us to hire actors on a permanent basis?"

Simon stepped forward. All that was missing was a spotlight and they might have been contestants on a reality TV show, waiting to find out who was moving forward in the competition.

"There are a few acting troupes in town," Simon answered. "I can't imagine it would be too much of a challenge."

"Good, good." Jerry kept pacing and Simon stepped back into

line. "Ryan, how long until you could get a bartender up to speed with what we're doing here? Of course it will be impossible to find someone who can bring your level of expertise, but I want someone who can at least come close."

"Training someone won't be difficult," Ryan spoke up. "But there are other challenges. One, you're going to have to pay someone extremely well to get them to give up weekend shifts where they could be earning a lot in tips."

Jerry stopped pacing. "Of course. This is a high-end guest experience." *Tell that to Preston Pearson,* Sadie thought. "All staff will be well paid."

"The second issue I see," Ryan continued, "is bar access. Or lack thereof. If you want this to be a high-end experience, I suggest having an actual bar constructed in the cellar. It's too cumbersome to bring drinks down from the kitchen. A real bar would allow for a drink menu not just predetermined cocktails, and it would add to the cocktail lounge *ambience* you're looking for."

Sadie bit the corner of her mouth to stop her grin from spreading, watching how easily Ryan used all of Jerry's own keywords to persuade him, knowing it would inflate his ego and there would be no chance of him shutting down the ideas, lest he look like he was shutting down his own requests.

"I was thinking all the same things," Jerry said. *Predictable.* "I knew getting you on board as a consultant was the right move." Then he looked her way. "Sadie, how long will it take to make all of this happen?"

Like Simon, Sadie stepped forward at being called upon, then felt ridiculous for doing so, then decided it would be too weird to step back again. "Realistically, I'd say it depends on how quickly we can get construction on the bar underway."

"Construction won't be a problem," Jerry confidently replied. "Plenty of contractors in this city owe me favors."

"Another thing to consider is that tourism on the island drops off significantly in January and February," she continued, trying to portray confidence. "But it picks back up pretty quickly in the spring. I think March would be ideal for an expected launch. Tickets would need to go on sale first thing in January."

"Excellent." While Jerry scrubbed a hand over his jaw and considered her words, Sadie stepped back in line, relieved.

But what did this all mean, though?

Was this Jerry's way of acknowledging that she would be taking over for Evelyn?

That had to be what it meant.

Surely.

Ryan subtly nudged her with his elbow. A nudge she knew meant *Ask!*

She stepped forward again, but just as her mouth opened, Jerry said, "Oh, and Sadie, there's one other thing I need from you."

"Oh, okay. What's that, sir?"

"With Evelyn's retirement coming up, we'll need a new director here at the estate."

It was happening!

"Yes, sir." She swallowed. "I'm aware."

"After tonight"—his words blurred together in slow motion—"we've decided that person is going to be Mindy."

Chapter 34

Mindy?" The name burst from Sadie's lips like an accusation. To her right, there was a small gasp from Simon. To her left, a muffled *Fuck* from Ryan.

Mindy stepped forward with a meek smile. "Upstairs, you reminded me that I don't know very much about my great-aunt, and I think it's time I learned."

This was because of her own stupid comment during the tour? She somehow inspired Mindy to take over running the estate? All because Mindy never read the books her own relative wrote? "But . . . But . . ." Sadie didn't know where to start. This wasn't even the last thing she saw coming, this had never been a possibility in her mind. "Being director of this estate is a full-time job."

"Oh, I know!" Mindy spoke with eagerness and enthusiasm, as though they were discussing a vacation to the Italian Riviera, not working a forty-hour-per-week day job. "Jerry and I talked about it, and I'm prepared to give up my committee role at the tennis club *and* step back as lead chair for the annual Sutton Island Regatta Gala."

"Well, as long as you're serious about it then."

Neither Mindy nor Jerry picked up on the sarcasm in Sadie's voice. Mindy just nodded. "Very serious. I'm also cutting back my hours volunteering at the stables."

"But, Mindy . . ." Simon spoke up. "What about . . . What about the horses? Who will care for *the horses* if not you?"

If this situation weren't so utterly devastating to her entire future, Sadie might have laughed at how absurd this all was.

"Oh, don't worry." Mindy spread a dainty hand over her heart. "There are other volunteers. I would never *abandon* the horses."

"Needless to say," Jerry interjected, "Mindy will need help learning all that goes on here. Sadie, she'll be relying on you until she's fully up to speed."

Un-fucking-believable.

Not only was she not getting the promotion, but she'd have to train the person who was. A person who had likely never had a real job before.

"I think that covers it," Jerry said, clearly growing bored with this conversation. "Excellent work, everyone."

"See you next week, Sadie!" Mindy chirped.

And with that, the couple saw themselves out.

Dizzy, Sadie pulled an antique chair from the dining room table and sank onto the wobbly frame, no longer giving a fuck about the house rules.

"Sadie, I'm so sorry." Simon's hand landed on her shoulder. "I did *not* see that coming."

"Yeah. Me, either."

Ryan cleared his throat. "Simon, do you mind giving us a minute?"

"No problem." Simon pointed over his shoulder. "In fact, I'm gonna take off. I'll talk with you both later."

When the front door closed and it was only the two of them, Ryan knelt in front of her chair. "What can I do?"

Sadie didn't respond. There was nothing he could do. There was nothing *anyone* could do.

"Maybe if I talked to Jerry or—"

"Ryan, no." She lifted her eyes to his. "I appreciate it, but there's nothing you can do about this." Silence fell between them for a moment, then she asked, "Did you pitch Jerry on the expansion?"

"What?" Ryan's brows knit before he swiftly shook his head and cleared any expression away. "We don't need to talk about that right now."

Yes, they did. Because if everything else was collapsing, Sadie might as well finish this off while she was at it. There was no need for Ryan to comfort her now, to act out a fictitious role they both knew was ending. "Earlier, you said we needed to talk. Well, what is it?"

"I don't want to do this right now, Sadie."

"Well, I do." Each beat of her heart felt like someone pressing on a bruise. "Just say it."

Shaking his head, Ryan's eyes fell to her lap as he refused to look at her. "You're upset. Understandably so. Let's do this later. I'm begging you."

"Fine, I'll say it." Best to rip the Band-Aid off all at once. "We're not going to do this later, because we both know there *isn't* a later for us. The tours are over now. And if I'm correct in my assumption, I'm guessing you spoke with Jerry at some point tonight and he agreed to invest in Pearson's. Now you need to tell me that you're leaving town soon, but you really don't want to after what just happened." Throat raw, each word burned as if chased with a shot of vodka. "But really, it's *fine* because that was the expectation all along. So I'm happy for you. We don't have to drag this out."

"That's not what happened." Finally tilting his head up, Ryan's green eyes locked with hers. "I never pitched Jerry."

"What? Why not?" Confusion inserted itself into the litany of emotions warring inside her. "That was the *entire* reason you took on this project." When he hesitated to respond, she pressed, "Why not, Ryan?"

He took a measured breath, wet each lip in turn. "Because things have changed and I'm no longer pursuing that avenue."

"*Pursuing that avenue*?" Sadie scoffed. "Jesus, Ryan, stop talking in code and just tell me already."

"Fine," he said, voice deepening with resolve. "If you want to know the truth, sometime during this past month I fell in love with you again, Sadie. Actually, that's probably inaccurate. I probably fell in love with you again the second I saw you in that coffee shop years ago. Either way, I am. In love with you. So leaving town no longer feels right. I've been trying to find a way to tell you that."

Sadie tilted her head, certain she'd heard the words right but baffled they'd been spoken. He must be confused. *Love?* That wasn't what *this* was.

"I really didn't want to do this after what just happened," Ryan continued. A relief because Sadie was all out of words at the moment. "But you want me to be honest with you, and I don't know how to do that without telling you that I love you." He covered her hand with his own. "And please, *please* don't panic because there is no expectation for you to say it back. I just needed to be truthful about my feelings for you because I messed up in college by not telling you how I felt, and I don't want to do that again."

Stricken, Sadie searched his eyes as if she might discover the real reason he was saying these things, but all that reflected back at her was vulnerability. "Ryan." She spoke softly, carefully. "You aren't *in love* with me. I don't understand why you're saying that you are. Is this some kind of joke?"

Hurt crumpled his expression. "Why would being in love with you be a joke? Have you not felt *anything* for me over the past month?"

"Of course I have," she admitted. There was simply no denying feelings had become involved. "But *love*? Ryan, this was supposed to be temporary."

"What about the past month felt temporary to you, Sadie?" Ryan's tone morphed into something defensive, something guarded. "Spending every single night together? Meeting your friends? Going to dinner with your mom? You defending me to my parents? We took care of each other. What about any of those things says temporary?"

"We agreed."

"Well, things changed." He paused, voice softening when he went on to say, "At least they did for me. I thought they had for you, too."

This was too much. Too serious. Too overwhelming.

Her stomach churned and her heart physically *hurt*. She wasn't prepared for this. Standing abruptly, she put some distance between them, as if that would possibly help. "Look, you can't change your plans for your business or your life because of me."

Rising from his crouched position, Ryan stepped around the chair she'd vacated, but he maintained the space between them. "A while ago you asked if I was doing this expansion for me or to prove something to my father. And you were right. I love *this* city, and I'm happy with Pearson's the way it is. When my parents showed up last night, I realized with complete clarity that I don't want to chase more and more and more in order to feel like I'm enough. I want to be the person you described, Sadie. The one who's already enough. And I want to make the person I love my top priority. I want to make *you* my top priority."

"Please stop saying that." Eyes burning, Sadie blinked away the tears accumulating at the edges of her vision. When had this gotten so out of hand? Was it the first time she'd invited him back to her apartment? Or sooner, when they'd given in to their attraction and kissed at the haunted house? Or maybe even before that, at the bar when she'd pretended Ryan was her boyfriend. Maybe neither of them had remembered to stop fucking pretending since that night.

"Why is it so awful to hear?" Ryan dragged a hand through his hair. "I knew after things went so wrong at dinner with your mom and Doug that it was going to have an effect on us, I just didn't know it would be this profound."

"This doesn't have anything to do with that."

"Doesn't it?"

Disbelief was etched in Ryan's features, and Sadie hated it. Hated how everyone in her life kept making these bold claims about the way things affected her. She knew what they all thought: She was damaged from her childhood and couldn't move on. But it wasn't true. It wasn't! She was capable of moving on, but that didn't mean she would forget. And the one thing being proven to her in the very moment was that relationships could last only so long before reality set in and the arguments started.

"Look, I'm not Doug." Ryan took a tentative step forward. "I'm not asking you to marry me. I'm only asking you to be with me. Without conditions. Without a time limit. Things have been so fucking great between us, and if I'm not going anywhere, why does that have to change? Right now, we could go back to your apartment and crawl into bed together like we've done nearly every day for weeks now. It doesn't have to be any more complicated than that, Sadie."

He made it sound so simple. And it would have been easy to listen to him. Easy to pretend this night never happened and take him home and let him soothe her with his words and his touch. And if it wasn't for the hopeful sadness in his eyes, or the goddamn boulder on her chest, or if he just hadn't said those particular three words, then maybe she could have done it.

Instead, she took a shaky breath. "I'm really sorry I let things get carried away, but I can't do this."

Eyes pleading with her, Ryan lifted a shoulder in a hopeless shrug. "You said I was enough. And I believed you."

"You *are*." The fact he questioned otherwise threatened to be her breaking point. But she had to hold firm and do what was best for them both. "It's not about that. I just . . . I don't know how to do relationships."

"Is that so?" Slowly shaking his head, Ryan blew out a long, defeated sigh. "Well, you sure fooled me." He strode past her toward the grand foyer, and the worst possible sense of déjà vu descended as he called over his shoulder, "See you around, Stockton."

CHAPTER 35

Sunday passed.

Then most of Monday passed.

And Sadie stayed in bed, cut off from the world outside.

No, that wasn't exactly true. Texts came in from Simon and Eric and even her mom. Because despite her mom's current anger with her, she of course still cared about something as important to Sadie as her job. Yet Sadie couldn't bring herself to admit the truth to either Eric or her mom. If she did, they would want to talk, and Sadie couldn't handle that right now. So she replied to both inquiries with a vague, Good! We'll talk later!

The only person she hadn't heard from was Ryan, not since he walked out of the front door of the Wilmont House after proclaiming his love for her, which by now he surely realized wasn't really *love* at all.

Sadie thought he might have texted by now to tell her she was right, that he'd been confused, that he was sorry for making such a big mistake. But nothing. No texts. No calls. No updates to his social media—which she limited herself to checking once per hour.

So time moved on but Sadie didn't. She emerged from bed only to eat a bowl of cereal on occasion. Breakfast, lunch, dinner, it didn't matter. She subsisted on Apple Jacks or Cinnamon Toast Crunch, and deciding between the two was almost too much to bear. She couldn't watch TV anymore. There was too much of a chance she'd scroll through a *Jeopardy!* rerun and then the painful ache in her chest would flare anew, her onetime comfort show now just another reminder of *him*.

Instead, she spent her waking hours scrolling on her phone as the sunlight rose and faded in her apartment, and when she couldn't stand lying in bed another second, she'd sit at her kitchen table with Hazel's manuscript, reading and rereading and unsuccessfully trying to figure out what wasn't clicking into place about the book.

But whenever she read Hazel's words her thoughts naturally drifted to her job at the mansion, whatever that even was anymore. Instead of a unicorn trainer, she'd be a Mindy trainer, and that thought made her cackle aloud . . . until she recalled Ryan's fingertip tracing the words, *Keep your courage close* as he said, "Just like you." Then a sharp pang struck deep in her abdomen, and suddenly nothing was funny anymore.

Goddammit.

What the hell was wrong with her?

Whatever it was, she'd pull herself together tomorrow. Tomorrow, she'd go to work at the bridal shop and she'd figure out her new life going forward. Tomorrow.

Then Tuesday came and went, along with Wednesday and Thursday and Friday, and the only thing she accomplished was texting Eric and Evelyn to lie about picking up a virus and saying she'd be out the rest of the week. She knew neither of them believed her, and the guilt over disappointing them both only added to the weight relentlessly crushing her chest, but she couldn't muster up the energy to face either of them.

Then a week had passed and she hadn't left her apartment once. She wasn't sure the last time she'd showered, and she had to switch to eating Pop-Tarts when the milk expired. She told herself this hole she was in was because of the job, but when she tried to sleep at night it was Ryan's dark green eyes and his easy grin and that one fucking dimple that kept her awake, consuming her every thought.

And the worst part was that she had no one to blame but herself. In the weeks they were together, she'd lowered her guard too far. She'd let Ryan really see her, really *know* her, and there was no way to undo that now. They'd played their roles so well that they'd both ended up fooled. But that's all it was . . . an act of fiction, as Simon would say. The fact it hurt now was all the more proof she'd made the right call. If it felt this bad when it wasn't even real, she couldn't imagine the heartbreak if it had been.

Sunday night, Sadie stood in her kitchen debating between cherry or blueberry Pop-Tarts when a loud knock at her door broke the endless silence. She checked the time on her microwave. Nine o'clock. While not entirely alarming that someone—likely her mom or Eric—had finally come to check on her in person, the late hour made her take pause. Then it occurred to her that it could, perhaps, be Ryan, and with equal parts hope and dread—dread because seeing him would definitely set her back at least another week, hope because despite everything else, she really, really missed his fucking face—she rushed to the door.

When she yanked it open, heart galloping, her jaw fell open. "*Douglas?* What are you doing here?"

Dressed in faded jeans and an old sweatshirt, her mother's boyfriend blinked rapidly behind his wire-rimmed frames as though he was about as comfortable standing on her doorstep as she was with him being on it. He coughed. "It's Doug."

"Right. What are you doing here, Doug? And how'd you get in?" Curiosity turned to panic as numerous horrific scenarios flashed through her mind. *"Oh my god, is my mom okay?"*

"She's fine," Doug immediately reassured, lifting his shifty gaze for the first time. "There was a tour guide in the courtyard who gave me the code when I told him who I was looking for."

While unsettled Matt had given out the gift shop code with no questions asked, that was an issue for later.

"Can I come in?" he asked. "I'd like to talk."

Sadie motioned him inside and closed the door. "Can I get you anything? Water or something?"

"No, I'm okay." Stopping just inside the kitchen, he turned to her. "Sadie, I need to apologize. I see now that bringing up a proposal the first time we met was inexcusable. I shouldn't have overstepped like that."

"Okay. So why did you?" she asked. "Or better yet, why are you even thinking about proposing this soon anyway? It's only been a few months. What's the rush?"

A thin smile formed on his lips. "You're right. It's impractical. But Ann is so funny and so smart and so incredible, and when we're together, it's just . . . it's just the happiest I've *ever* been. It's like I've been given this unexpected gift of falling in love again, and I don't want to waste a single second." As he paused, his smile faded away. "I never had children of my own—probably one of the reasons I've messed things up so badly here—but I was married once before. I was in my thirties, and it lasted for almost seven years."

"What happened?" If Doug was about to admit he'd had a secret family and his wife found out, she couldn't promise he was going to walk out of here.

"She had an affair."

Sadie winced.

"With my lifelong best friend and business partner at my accounting firm."

Sadie winced harder. "Yikes. That must've *really* sucked." God. Her people-ing skills were off the charts tonight.

To her relief, Doug huffed a short, surprised laugh. "Yes, it certainly sucked."

While Sadie could have sympathy for the man's past, it didn't change how she felt about him proposing so soon. Hell, if anything, it affirmed her concerns over the two moving so quickly when they barely knew anything about each other. "So you came here to tell me that you and my mom have both been cheated on, so I should trust that you won't hurt her?"

"Not exactly," he replied with a subtle shake of his head. "I didn't come here to talk about what your mom and I have in common. I came to talk to you about what *me and you* have in common."

That caught her off guard. "What do you mean?"

"I know our situations aren't exactly the same," Doug said, "but I'm willing to bet our lack of trust in people is fairly similar. I not only lost my wife when she cheated, I lost my best friend, too. And from what your mom has shared with me about your father's affairs, it seems it wasn't only your father who hurt you both, but some other people she, *and you*, both trusted."

A thick lump formed in Sadie's throat. She pictured the pretty organist at church who always wore a bright smile and had extra strawberry bubblegum in her purse. Then she thought of her friend Elizabeth's mom, and the time she found the two girls playing in her makeup drawer. Instead of getting angry, the woman threw them a makeup party and helped the girls put on sparkly eye shadow and bright pink lipstick. Sadie had always thought she was the coolest, most beautiful mom on the block. Then she was shameful and guilt-ridden for the very thought once she overheard her parents argument about that one. "Oh," she said now, "that was all a long time ago."

"Sure," Doug agreed. "But Sadie, it would be completely understandable for you to have a tough time trusting people in any capacity after that. I would know. I know I *did*. I had to work on my own issues for a very long time."

She didn't know what to say.

Doug straightened. "Anyway, I just came here to say that I should have known better than to put you in the situation that I did. So again, I'm sorry." He dipped his head in acknowledgment then moved toward the door.

"Hey, Doug," Sadie called out. "You really love her, huh?"

He turned back her way. "More than anything."

Well, that was another thing they had in common.

"Fine," she sighed. "You have my blessing to propose." Then, for clarity's sake, she added, "But even if you two get married, I'm not calling you Dad. Or Papa."

"I, uh—" Doug coughed, clearly taken aback. "I wouldn't expect you to. However, it's a little late for proposing. I just want her to take me back."

Take him back? "What do you mean?"

Doug blinked away. "Ann ended things. After the dinner last week. She said the timing wasn't right. I thought she'd come around after some time but . . ."

Instead of feeling any relief at this news, all Sadie felt was shame. This had nothing to do with timing and everything to do with her behavior. Now it made sense why her mom had barely reached out all week. It wasn't because she was mad—well, maybe she was *a little* mad—but because she was hurting after breaking up with Doug.

"Shit, shit, shit!" Sadie rubbed her forehead as the beginning of a headache sprang up behind her eyes. "And you still came here even though she ended things?"

"I wanted to apologize, regardless."

Sadie had to respect the man for that. Coming to her apartment couldn't have been easy. "By the way, how'd you know where I live?"

A smile transformed Doug's face, wide and kind of goofy. Kind of charming. "I wasn't lying when I said she talks about you all the time. I know every school you attended. I know you work with Eric Andreas and that he was on *Runway Wars*, and I've now watched his entire season. I know that your favorite color is gray, you're terrified of any animal smaller than a house cat, and your favorite food is a tie between cereal and Pop-Tarts—but only the frosted kind."

Damn. She wasn't sure if she should be flattered or embarrassed. "Well, I mean, what kind of weirdo eats unfrosted Pop-Tarts, you know."

Doug's smile wavered.

"Oh shit." Sadie slapped a hand over her mouth. "You do, don't you?"

"I do, actually," Doug quietly muttered. "It's just the healthier option."

A slow sigh slipped through her lips, somehow transforming into a soft laugh. "I'm gonna try *really hard* not to hold that against you, Doug." As the humor faded, she added, "It sounds like you know a lot more about me than I do you."

"Yeah. I, uh, wish we could've had time to change that." He pushed his glasses up the bridge of his nose. "I hoped that once you got to know me, you'd realize I'm not a bad guy. I may love Ann more than anything in this world, but I understand that she loves *you* more than anything in this world. I never wanted to come between that, Sadie. I only wanted the chance to be in her life, too."

Well. What could she possibly say to that other than, "I'll talk to her."

Doug's eyes lit with hope. "*Really?*"

"Really. And I'm sorry if my behavior ruined things in the first place."

"Again, I never should've brought up a proposal so soon. It was my fault."

A smirk came to her face. "If we're being totally honest, I was kind of being an asshole *before* you brought it up."

"If we're being totally honest . . ." Doug paused, mouth tipping up. "Yeah, you definitely were."

"Fair enough," Sadie replied. "I'll be sure to own up to that when I talk to her."

"Thank you, Sadie. Really."

After she saw Doug out, Sadie sent a text to her mom.

Sadie: Dinner tomorrow. Six o'clock. My place.

Instead of skulking back to bed, Sadie grabbed the box of (frosted!) blueberry Pop-Tarts and a Diet Coke and slid into a chair at her kitchen table. Then she reached for Hazel Wilmont's manuscript and flipped to the first page.

CHAPTER 36

By the time the sun rose Monday morning, Sadie could no longer avoid the inevitable.

She climbed from bed, showered, and dressed in something other than pajama shorts and Ryan's sweater for the first time in a week. She even put on a bra.

After waking with a sense of clarity that morning, she'd texted Evelyn to meet her at the estate, then meandered across the courtyard and let herself into the mansion. She walked the familiar halls, bright and airy and empty, taking in each piece of artwork, each unique architectural detail.

When Evelyn arrived, Sadie was lingering in Hazel's writing room, which somehow felt like the appropriate place for what she needed to do.

"I hope you're feeling better," Evelyn said as she strolled in, though it was unclear if she was referring to Sadie's made-up illness or the fact Mindy had commandeered her promotion.

"Thank you, I'm okay. Listen, I'm sure you're aware that Mindy will be taking over as director and because of that—"

"If you called me here to hand in your resignation, keep it."

Sadie almost smiled. Evelyn was always two steps ahead.

"I'm well aware this isn't how you wanted things to go," Evelyn continued. "This isn't the way *I* wanted things to go, either. But I also know how much passion you have for Hazel's books. It would be a tragedy to lose your expertise and care. *You* are the irreplaceable one here, more so than I am."

The sting of emotion burned behind Sadie's eyes. "Thank you, Evelyn. That means a lot."

Dressed down in a cream-colored sweater and black slacks, Evelyn tucked a strand of gray hair behind her ear. "I know none of this is ideal, but Friday is my last day, and without you here to steer the ship, even if it's not in the official role of director, I hate to think what will happen to this place."

"Me, too," Sadie admitted. It was the exact reason this decision was so tough. "But I'm not doing this because I'm angry. I'm doing this because I have no other choice. Jerry wants me to be Mindy's right-hand person, and I can't do that and work at the bridal shop. It was one thing to give up my job there if I became director, but I'm not willing to do it if that isn't going to happen."

"Ah." Evelyn nodded once. "Well, that I understand. What about your living arrangements?"

That was yet another thing Sadie would be losing. She *loved* her apartment. But she couldn't stay there if she wasn't on staff, and there was no way to delay the inevitable. "If you would tell Mindy that I'll be out by the end of November. I included it in my resignation letter, but I think we both know she isn't going to read that."

Evelyn's lips twitched as she held off a smile. "This really isn't how I expected things to go."

"I know," Sadie sighed. "Me, either." Slipping the strap of her tote bag off her shoulder, she eyed the envelope containing her resignation letter tucked next to Hazel's manuscript. She'd had every intention of handing them both over, but in the midst of losing everything else, she decided to hang on to this secret a little longer. She took out only the envelope and passed it over.

Reluctantly, Evelyn accepted the letter, turning it over in her hand. "I'm not going to give this to Mindy yet."

"But—"

"I'm going to hold on to this, and you're going to take some of the massive amount of vacation time you've accumulated. My retirement party is on Saturday and I expect you'll be there. Think about this long and hard this week, and if you still want to do this then, I'll fully support that."

In a rare move, the estate was closing to the public next Saturday night in order to throw Evelyn a goodbye party, something well deserved after forty years, though Sadie had suspicions Evelyn probably planned it herself since Sadie had been busy with the tours. The idea of seeing Jerry and Mindy again turned her stomach, but there was no way she couldn't show up after everything Evelyn had done for her over the years, including hiring her in the first place. And it was that sentiment that made her say, "Okay, I'll think about it."

After Evelyn left, Sadie walked through the home she knew so well, emotion cinching her throat. But when she looked around at the place in which she'd spent countless hours of her life over the past five years—at the paintings and tapestries she could recite monologues about, at the furniture layout she could navigate with her eyes closed—it was only her memories made here over the past month that came to mind. Memories made with Ryan and Simon.

Simon had surprised her—not only with his talent, but also

with his dry humor and wit. And if it wasn't for him, she'd never have known Hazel's hidden manuscript existed. The way his brain created clues and pieced together puzzles was unreal. In fact—

Stopping in the middle of the first-floor hallway, Sadie pulled the manuscript from her tote bag and studied the title page. She might be an expert on Hazel Wilmont, but the pieces of this puzzle weren't clicking into place. And if there was one person who could figure it out . . .

Rushing to the library, Sadie dropped her belongings on the oversize desk. Then she grabbed her phone and sent a text to Simon.

Sadie: Any chance you could meet me at the mansion? I need your help with a mystery.

His response came within a minute.

Simon: Be there in half an hour.

While she waited, Sadie spread the manuscript out on the desk, chapter by chapter, hoping to gain clarity on what kept irking her about this story. When Simon arrived sometime later, she was pacing back and forth, fingers steepled in front of her chin.

"I hear there's a mystery to be solved." Simon leaned a shoulder against the expansive doorframe, arms folded over his chest. "I think I can help with that."

It took a few seconds for it to dawn on her why Simon looked different. He was dressed casually in jeans and a plain black tee, no vest or starchy dress shirt in sight. "Look at you dressed down," she teased. "Did you run out of vests?"

"Never." Grinning, he strode into the library. "But it's nine a.m. and I'm with a friend so this is what you get."

A friend.

She liked the way it sounded.

"So what's going on?" His eyes scanned the pages spread over the desk.

"I keep going over and over this manuscript and something is still bothering me about it. Forgetting the fact it was hidden in pieces around the mansion—which, *odd*—it still doesn't make sense that Hazel Wilmont wrote it in the first place. She wrote about mythical creatures and made-up worlds from a fantasy. This is a contemporary children's mystery. It doesn't fit. *Unless* it was written for a purpose, and I can't figure out what that purpose might be."

With a slight tilt of his head, Simon clicked his tongue, contemplating. "You said Hazel became a recluse after the death of husband number two, correct?"

"His name was John Wilmont. And yeah, pretty much."

"Hmm. Okay, tell me what happens in this story."

Sadie talked him through a synopsis about the sisters, Harriett and Alice, and Alice's mission to find Harriett's diary in order to clear her sister's name.

"Let me see if I understand correctly," Simon mused. "Harriett journaled about her science project in this diary, and she kept it hidden so other students didn't steal her work. When the students accused her of cheating and she was expelled, she left clues so her sister, Alice, could find the diary and know she was innocent. But why didn't Harriett just show the diary to her teachers when she was accused?"

"It was a pride thing," Sadie answered. "Harriett didn't think she should have to defend herself against baseless accusations. The only opinion she cared about was Alice's."

A gleam sparked in Simon's eyes. "You see the correlation here, right?"

"What do you mean?"

"Baseless rumors about Harriett. Baseless rumors about Hazel. Tell me, what was Hazel's sister's name? Mindy's grandmother?"

"Um . . ." Sadie's heart raced and she didn't know why. But it felt like they were on the verge of . . . something. "Addie. Her name was Addie!"

"Harriett and Hazel. Alice and Addie." Simon regarded her expectantly. "You see what I'm saying now, right?"

"Kind of," she lied. "But why don't you explain it to me anyway."

"What if Hazel did write this book for a purpose? Or not exactly a purpose, but a *person*. What if that person was Addie? What if she wrote this book and left it for her sister to find after her death? The same way Harriett did for Alice after she was expelled."

Sadie peered up at him with wide eyes. "Simon, you're a genius!"

"Call me a genius when we find what we're looking for."

"I thought we just figured it out," she said, confusion returning.

"We figured out *part* of it," Simon corrected. "But if all of this is right, then this manuscript was meant to lead Addie to something bigger . . . Perhaps a diary?"

"Holy shit."

"Yeah, holy shit." His hands spread wide along the desk as he leaned over the pages. "Now, tell me where the clues were hidden in the book."

"Um, um, um," she spouted, trying to focus. "The first one was hidden in a dresser drawer."

"Similar to the armoire," Simon mused. "The others?"

"An unused fireplace in the dormitory! And, and, and . . . Behind some books in the stacks in the library!"

"Similar to the mirror above the mantel and the book in *this* library."

Sadie nodded, all of it finally clicking into place.

"Here's the biggest question," Simon continued, eyes focused and sharp. "Where did Alice find Harriett's diary in the story?"

"Hidden in a vent."

Simon took a deep breath, exhaled slowly. "I don't think it will be exactly the same, but similar. Just like the others. So think about this house you know so well, Sadie. Think walls, think pipes, think floor, think—"

Simon kept talking, but he didn't need to. As soon as he said *floor,* the image of Ryan tripping over the warped floorboard in Hazel's writing room hit her like a ton of bricks. "The floorboard, Simon! It's the floorboard!"

Clarity washed over his face.

Without another word, they took off at full speed, running side by side up the grand stairwell and down the second-floor corridor, bursting through the door to Hazel's writing room and dropping to their knees next to each other at the misshaped floorboard. Sadie took a minute to catch her breath while Simon ran his hand over the plank, thumb slipping under the warped edge that had given Ryan hell for the past month. Sure enough, with a generous amount of effort, it popped out of place. Underneath, the subfloor had been sawed through, its jagged edges revealing nothing but a dark gap.

"You should have the honor," Simon said.

Sadie raised a brow. "The honor of sticking my arm into a hole where any number of bugs, spiders, or rodents could reside?"

"Yeah, it sure as hell isn't gonna be me."

Sadie rolled her eyes. But then she held her breath and slowly slipped her hand into the space, ready to retreat if she felt anything silky, slimy, or furry. Her wrist disappeared, and then her forearm.

"I don't feel anything." She circled her arm in every direction but there was nothing other than wooden beams. Until she went to retract her arm, and her fingers brushed something worn and soft, something like leather. "Wait." As more of the object came into reach, her thumb jabbed a sharp corner that could only be thick pages of paper. Heart skipping at least three beats—*maybe four!*—she pulled a leather-bound journal from the hole in the floor.

Sitting back on her heels, Sadie dusted off the cover as best she could with her palm. Then she flipped through the pages, each one a dated entry. "Simon," she uttered, breathless. "I think we just discovered Hazel Wilmont's diary."

Chapter 37

The knock on her apartment door came precisely at six.

Swiping her hands on her leggings, Sadie made her way from the stovetop to the door, pulling it open to reveal her mom's familiar face, though it lacked its normal warm smile. "Hi," she offered, demure.

A bottle of pinot was thrust her way, along with a return, "Hello."

"Thanks." Sadie accepted the offering and motioned her mom inside. "Come in."

Placing the wine on the counter, Sadie moved back to the stove and stirred the pot of boiling pasta. It was unnatural, things feeling this strained between them. It didn't help matters that she was already off-kilter after the discovery of Hazel's journal, after which Simon had insisted upon taking her to brunch to celebrate with bottomless mimosas. Though with the careful way Simon tiptoed around the subjects of both Ryan and her lack of promotion, Sadie guessed his ulterior motive was more about keeping her mind off things for a little while. It also made her aware that Simon had spoken with Ryan at some point, and it took every ounce of her restraint not to ask about him. Needless to say, it was no surprise her *one* mimosa had, in fact, turned bottomless, and she'd walked home tipsy and warm, then fallen asleep until an hour ago.

"I'm making pasta and marinara." Sadie wasn't much of a cook but she hadn't wanted to have this conversation in public. "Just have a seat. It'll be done in a few minutes."

Once the pasta was finished, Sadie made two plates and carried them to the table. Then she brought over silverware and poured two glasses of pinot.

With a slow breath, she sank into a chair and handed a glass to her mom, whose eyes were sharp and expectant over the rim.

"About the dinner with Doug," Sadie started, "it's inexcusable the way I behaved, and the last thing I want to do is mess this up for you if he makes you happy."

Ignoring the food, her mom lifted her glass to her rose-painted lips, sipping long and slow before she replied. "Really? Because it seems that was exactly what you intended to do."

Ouch. But okay, she deserved that. "I admit it was harder than expected to see you with him. I really don't know why exactly. I *do* want you to be happy, but I just . . . I don't know. I freaked out."

Expression softening on a sigh, her mom set her wine aside. "You know me making room in my life for someone else doesn't mean there's less room for you, right?"

"Please, Mom, I'm not a child. You don't have to explain to me that I'm still your special girl or something." Though Sadie wasn't opposed to hearing it if it was what her mom really wanted to say.

"Actually, I think I do. You may not be a child, but this was never a conversation we had back then. Maybe you do need to hear it now. Sadie," she stated firmly, "no one is going to take me away from you or replace you in my life. *No one*."

"Even if you marry Doug?" As soon as she said it, she realized she probably wasn't supposed to mention the whole marriage thing, but her mom didn't appear surprised.

"Even if I marry Doug."

"Wait. You knew he was going to propose?"

A weary smile curved her mom's mouth. "Doug and I swore to each other very early on that we'd never lie to one another, so after that horrendous dinner, I asked what happened while I was in the restroom and he told me. And I'm sorry, too, because it shouldn't have happened that way."

"Is that why you ended things?" To clarify, Sadie added, "Doug came by here last night. He told me you broke up with him."

Brows rising, her mom pointed to the floor. "He came *here*? Without a bodyguard?"

"Very funny," Sadie said, a smile pulling at her lips. "He loves you a lot, you know."

"I do know. But I realized that just because I'm ready after all this time doesn't mean that you are, and it's not fair to expect you to be okay with me suddenly getting engaged when we've barely discussed any of this. So I thought it was best to cool things off for a while."

There was no question about it, Sadie was the asshole here. Her mom ended things with Doug for no reason other than her adult daughter's petulance and immaturity. And from the way she spoke, it was clear that if it wasn't for Sadie, she would have said yes to Doug's proposal.

"Mom, please don't end things with him because of me. I'm sorry I wasn't on board then but I am now, or I'll get there eventually. I should've given Doug more of a chance. He was really sad when he was here last night."

Skeptical blue eyes blinked back at her. "Are you *sure?*"

Sadie couldn't blame her for sounding doubtful. "I'm sure. A man doesn't show up on the doorstep of his girlfriend's temperamental daughter to try and make things right unless he really loves her."

Her mom's cheeks flushed a deep pink as she covered a shy smile with both hands, her soft laugh floating through her fingers. "I can't believe he did that."

"Trust me, it came as quite the shock to me, too." Sadie took a sip of wine, then said, "I'll learn to be okay with this, I swear."

Reaching into a cross-body bag stowed on an empty chair, her mom took out a business card and slid it across the table. "There's something else I didn't mention to you."

Embossed in black lettering was a name: **REBECCA THURSTON, LMFT**. Underneath, a phone number.

"What's this?" Sadie asked.

"Something I should have done a long time ago. I made some mistakes back then, and one of those was not recognizing how much you were affected by what happened with your father. I should've gotten us both into counseling. Sorry I'm a couple decades late."

"To be fair," Sadie countered, "it's not like you had the time or money to spend on therapy. I think food and clothing were a bigger necessity at the time."

"Maybe so. But I should have worked harder to figure something out." Gaze landing on the card between them, she went on to explain how she'd started therapy a year ago, when she first thought about dating again. And how that therapy had been beneficial in helping her recognize issues she hadn't even realized were still affecting her after all that time.

"So new-grad Kayla didn't peddle you onto the World Wide Web against your will?" Sadie asked.

The sharp crackle of laughter she got in response was warm and loud and beautiful. "No, Kayla didn't peddle me anywhere."

Sadie picked up the business card. "Why are you giving this to me?"

Her mom's laughter faded into a sigh. "Because I think talking with a professional would be beneficial to you. We could go together and do a family session if you want, or if you want to go alone, that's okay, too. Or if you'd rather find someone else who doesn't see me. Whatever you want."

Sadie rotated the card between her middle finger and thumb, tapping each side against the tabletop. Talking about the past, with a stranger no less, sounded like a special type of slow, methodical torture. But when she thought about the past week she'd had, that felt like torture as well. Maybe it wouldn't be the worst thing to try this therapy thing out and see if it might help. "I'll think about it."

"Good!" Picking up her fork, her mom swirled the pasta on her plate. "Now where's that handsome boyfriend of yours? I figured he might be joining us."

The stabbing pain between her ribs struck so quick and so forceful that Sadie had to make a conscious effort not to whimper. Though she was unaware of whatever happened with her face, it clearly alarmed her mother, whose eyes immediately filled with sympathy.

"Oh, sweetheart, what happened?"

"He, uh, he was never my boyfriend." Tucking her knees into her chest, Sadie wrapped both arms around her legs. Maybe making herself small might lessen the hurt. "It was a temporary thing. It's over now."

A long pause ensued before her mom spoke up again. "Excuse me for pressing if this is a sore subject, but it doesn't seem like bringing someone to dinner to meet your mom's boyfriend is something you do with someone who is *temporary*. That feels like something you do with someone you trust, someone who makes difficult situations easier."

When Sadie didn't say anything, her mom came around the table and embraced her. And with that one simple action, the floodgates opened as if they'd been knocked off their hinges. Sadie suddenly and openly sobbed while her mom stroked her hair and whispered over and over that everything would be okay.

When her tears eventually subsided, Sadie sank back in her chair, wiping at her tearstained cheeks. "I, um, I just got caught up in it, I think. But it's for the best this way. I don't want a relationship."

"Mmhmm," her mom murmured, eyes falling to Ryan's sweater that Sadie wore. "I didn't want a relationship, either. Until I did." Then she tapped a fingernail against Rebecca Thurston's card. "Use it."

All Sadie could do was nod.

"Now, let's talk about something happier, shall we?" Her mom's voice rose a few octaves higher. "You mentioned the last weekend of the murder mystery tours went well, tell me all about it!"

Fresh tears burst forth all over again. "I think—" Sadie could barely get the words out. "I think I might need to move back home."

"Oh dear." Ann Stockton rose from the table. "Let me refill my wine."

CHAPTER 38

Tuesday morning was a cool, crisp, picture-perfect day as Sadie made her triumphant return to Eric Andreas Designs. Okay, there was nothing *triumphant* about it exactly, other than the fact she'd made it there of her own accord and looked halfway decent in a periwinkle sweater and gray pencil skirt, even if her makeup was minimal and her under-eyes puffy.

When she unlocked the front door and made her way inside, Eric already sat behind the counter, pecking away at the iPad. Doing her best to maintain a neutral expression, she made her way over and sat their coffees down before him.

"Morning," she greeted, then silently applauded herself for how casual she'd made the one word sound.

"Glad to see you're back among the land of the living." He didn't look up. "A whole week to recover? Must've been some serious illness."

"Mmhmm," she replied, guilt practically choking her. "I'm really sorry about that. I hope it wasn't too bad here. If you need me to stay over tonight to help catch up on anything I'll be happy to."

Eric lowered the iPad, dark eyes locking with hers. "We don't have a lot of time so I'm going to cut to the chase. Obviously you weren't sick for an entire week. I'm assuming something went wrong with the last weekend of the tours, which is the only reason I've given you some space. But now that you're back, what the hell happened?"

Placing her tote bag on the counter beside their coffee cups, Sadie quietly admitted, "I didn't get the promotion at the estate. Mindy decided she wants to play director so I hope you have no plans of getting rid of me anytime soon."

"Oh shit." Shock washed over Eric's face. "I didn't see that coming."

"Literally *no one* did! I don't even think Mindy did until that very night."

"God. I'm sorry."

Sadie attempted a half-hearted smile. "I gave Evelyn my resignation letter yesterday. She won't give it to Mindy until after this weekend though. Just in case I change my mind."

Putting away the iPad, Eric pulled the lid off his coffee. A thin curl of steam swirled up between them. "You're sure you want to go as far as quitting? I know you love that house."

"I do. But Jerry wants me to help Mindy implement the murder mystery tours on a permanent basis. We're talking hiring staff and overseeing the construction of a bar, not to mention all the daily tasks the director already handles like scheduling and marketing. I can't do all of that and work here, too."

"Mmm."

A single syllable, yet Sadie didn't care for his tone. "What's that supposed to mean?"

Eric tapped his fingers against the glass. "You sure you're quitting the right job?"

"What?" Her heart tripped. "You don't want me working here anymore?"

"Of course I do," he rushed. "But working at the Wilmont House is your childhood dream, and I can't compete with that. If you can only do one, I guess I'm not sure why you're picking this one."

Sadie felt like discarded fruit in a juicer—twisted, drained, and completely wrung out. "I don't understand."

"As much as I love having you work here, if you need to leave to pursue other things, I'll understand." Eric's eyes were soft, words gentle. "I won't love it, but that's for selfish reasons. I'd never want you to feel obligated to keep working here because of our friendship."

She glanced down at the necklaces and earrings and tiaras in the display case, shiny and obnoxiously sparkly. Who would straighten them every day if it wasn't her? Someone who didn't care nearly as much as she did, that's for damn sure. And what if Eric hired someone else and that person became his new friend and she was replaced altogether?

Avoiding eye contact, she timidly asked, "Eric, do you think we'd still be friends if I didn't work here?"

A prolonged silence caused Sadie to lift her eyes.

Eric's brows were furrowed, mouth pursed. "Why would you even suggest otherwise?"

Her cheeks heated, the price of being vulnerable. "I know we'd still be *friendly*, but what I mean is, would we still be friends actively? If we didn't see each other here every day, wouldn't we slowly fade from each other's lives?"

"Is that why you're so weird about taking time off?" His

expression slowly morphed as if he'd figured out a riddle that had taken seven years to solve. "You think if you're not my steadfast employee we'll no longer be friends?"

"Out of sight, out of mind, right?"

Leaning across the counter, he settled his large palms on her shoulders. "Sadie Stockton, you will always have a job here if you want it. No matter what. But if you decide to move on, that's okay, too, because there's no possibility I'm ever going to let you just fade from my life or whatever nonsense you just said. It's not going to happen. If you leave here, we'll make it a priority to see each other outside of work. I guess I'll have to get my own coffee, which, quite frankly, sucks, but we can meet up there in the mornings. And we can have weekly dinners. Better yet, weekly shopping trips because we can't let your wardrobe become a victim of this decision, either. I refuse to let you slip back into the dark days of waterproof sandals."

A grin came to her face as his assurances made her chest feel warm and fuzzy. "I still maintain they were cute *and* functional."

"You can maintain it all you want, doesn't make it true." His hands slipped away from her shoulders. "But seriously, Evelyn's right to make you think about this. Despite Mindy being the new director in title, someone has to actually run that place. And if I know you at all, you want it to be you."

In truth, Sadie *did* want it to be her. The idea of Mindy's inexperience running the place into the ground haunted her. What if another guest spilled Dr Pepper? There was zero chance Mindy would know which rug restoration company to call. Or what if someone put their snacky fingers on the artwork again? And if the rugs and art weren't properly cared for, that was a slippery slope to the whole mansion falling into ruin. "You might be right about that."

"So what are you going to do about it?"

If Sadie was going to stay on at the estate, Jerry and Mindy would first have to agree to a few conditions or it simply wouldn't be feasible. A hefty raise, for one. Clear oversight in hiring and staffing, another. The couple would be at Evelyn's retirement party Saturday night, so that gave her time to prepare exactly what to say.

Instead of answering Eric's question, she asked, "Would you and Charity want to tag along to this party at the estate on Saturday? I could use a date, and two is better than one."

Eric smirked. "I'm sure she'll be up for a party. Although I have to ask, where's Ryan?"

Wow. Sadie was not prepared for that question, and she flinched at the sound of his name. "I . . . Uh . . . That's over."

"Fuck. I'm sorry," Eric apologized with a wince. "You ready to talk about it?"

Throat clamped tight, she shook her head.

"All right. Not now, but soon."

* * *

After Sadie left the bridal shop that evening, she made the last-minute decision to stop into a market in order to restock her milk and Pop-Tart supply. Inside, she grabbed a basket and roamed the aisles, finding it hard to concentrate on locating her items. Then again, it was hard to concentrate on *anything* lately. But it's not like she had anywhere else to be or anyone waiting for her, so she allowed herself to meander like a sad, unmotivated snail.

But when she turned into the wine aisle, she stopped in her tracks.

Halfway down the aisle, Ryan stood in a black hoodie and gray sweatpants, arms crossed over the wide expanse of his chest as he chewed his lower lip and scanned bottles of the fancy, expensive shit that had its own refrigerated section. Before Sadie could process that he was actually there, in person, standing less than twenty feet away from her, her eyes slid to a petite woman at his side. She had light blue eyes and dark brown hair pulled into a tight ponytail, and she wore a matching hot-pink yoga set.

And Sadie couldn't breathe.

She took one step backward, then another. But her feet didn't move fast enough, because Ryan turned to say something to his companion, and his eyes landed directly on her. There was a moment where neither of them reacted, then Ryan's eyes widened as he blinked to the woman at his side and then back to Sadie.

Sadie's heart, which seemed to have momentarily ceased beating, now thudded back to life like it was trying to break free of her chest wall. Moving faster, she turned and hightailed it toward the front of the store.

"*Sadie!*" Ryan's desperate voice called from behind her, but she kept moving, body numb other than her pounding heart. "Sadie! Please wait!"

A hand landed on her arm before she could make her escape, and she had no choice other than to turn and look up into Ryan's green eyes. Up close, they were red-rimmed, dark circles staining each under-eye. "Sadie," he said again, urgent. "That's not what you think. That's my sister, Rachel. She came into town for a couple days. I couldn't let you think . . ."

The immediate, intense relief that descended upon Sadie wasn't a comfort. Only confirmation of how deep she'd let herself get into this messy situation. "It doesn't matter what I think. You don't owe—"

"Do *not* say I don't owe you an explanation," Ryan interrupted.

"I absolutely do owe you that, and it very much matters what you think."

Just then, Ryan's sister rounded the end corner of the aisle with a wide smile. "Wait, did I hear you say Sadie? Is this *the* Sadie?" Stopping at her brother's side, the woman's blue eyes lit as they landed on her. "I'm Ryan's sister, Rachel. I've heard so much about you. It's so nice to meet you in person!"

Sadie smiled politely, but her attention drifted back to Ryan. He didn't meet her gaze. "Nice to meet you, too," she said, focusing again on Rachel.

"Not only has this one talked my ear off about you"—Rachel nudged Ryan in the ribs—"but I've heard about you from my father, too. And, if I'm being honest, I think he might be a little afraid of you, which automatically makes you one of my favorite people. Can you please come to all of our family holidays?"

"Rach," Ryan warned.

"Or better yet," Rachel continued, ignoring her brother, "can you come with me when I break the news that I quit my job *without* having another one lined up? I'll pay for your travel and accommodations. From what I've heard, you can go toe-to-toe with the good professor, and I need that kind of energy—"

"Jesus Christ, Rachel!" Ryan scrubbed both hands down his face. "Please not now."

"Fine!" she exclaimed. "I shall return myself to the wine aisle. But Sadie, just think about it, okay? It could even be a Zoom."

With that, Rachel winked at her and then took off as quickly as she'd appeared.

"I'm so sorry," Ryan apologized. "She's a bit of a whirlwind."

"She seems really fantastic, actually," Sadie said with a small grin. "Glad you have her in your corner."

"Yeah. Uh, anyway, I'll leave you alone now. I just wanted to clear that up so you didn't think the worst of me." Ryan lingered for a moment, as though waiting for her to say something to stop him from leaving. But what was there to say? And if perfect words for that moment did exist, Sadie certainly didn't have them. "Good to see you, Stockton."

Then he was gone before she could even say goodbye.

CHAPTER 39

When Sadie entered her apartment ten minutes later, it felt . . . empty.

And so were her hands, because after seeing Ryan, she'd left the market with no milk and no Pop-Tarts.

Again, she cursed herself for ever allowing him into her life. Everything had been perfectly fine until he came around. And she knew, *eventually*, everything would be fine again. But what she couldn't undo was the way he'd made her consider the possibility of more than fine, or the way she now knew how it felt to rely on him and share everyday life with him. He'd brought into question her steadfast decision that relationships weren't for her. And even if it was just the tiniest crack in her armor, she feared it would never hold up in battle again.

Right now, there was only one thing that would distract her.

Hazel Wilmont's diary sat on her kitchen table, exactly where she'd left it before work this morning. After last night's dinner with her mom, she'd been too emotionally wiped to dive in, but now she had the whole evening before her. Grabbing a Diet Coke from the fridge, she cracked open the top, then sat at the table and began to read.

By the time Sadie closed the leather-bound journal sometime later, she'd read the diary cover to cover twice, only stopping when her tears fell so rapidly she could no longer wipe them away before they splattered onto the time-weathered pages. Pushing the journal away, she dropped her forehead onto her folded arms and sobbed at her kitchen table.

Hazel started writing the diary the year before her death, when she'd been diagnosed with a terminal illness and knew her time left on earth was limited. The diary confirmed what she and Simon had figured out the day before: it was written for her sister, Addie, along with the manuscript they'd discovered in the mansion. Hazel began the diary with a letter to Addie, recalling their younger days when they would make a game out of creating clues for each other that would lead to a hidden prize. The sisters were incredibly close growing up, but when Hazel's affair came to light, followed by the scandalous rumors she'd poisoned her husband, her entire family shunned her. Including Addie.

According to the diary, Hazel never blamed Addie for that decision, though. Addie was married and had young children at the time, and Hazel understood that if Addie kept in touch, she, too, would risk being cut off from not only their parents, but her husband and children as well. So Hazel never attempted to contact her sister. Instead, she wrote her life story within the pages of the journal so that Addie would one day know the full truth. Then Hazel created one last mystery for her sister to solve and left the very first clue—a photograph of the main library where they'd discovered the beginning of Hazel's manuscript—in an unmarked envelope to be delivered to Addie upon Hazel's death.

But Addie never discovered the manuscript or the journal—whether by choice or by circumstance remained unclear—and that would undoubtedly eat away at Sadie for eternity, but not every story got the ending it deserved. And Hazel Wilmont definitely deserved a better ending to her story. Hazel stated within those pages that she never poisoned her first husband, William Eubanks. In fact, she was at John Wilmont's home that very night ensuring he was okay after the morning's public scuffle. She wasn't even aware William had returned to the mansion until she walked in that night and found him keeled over on the dining room floor, Easter ham on the table next to his brandy. The coroner determined there was no foul play, hence why Hazel Wilmont was never a serious suspect. But despite the facts of the matter, society loved a good scandal, and Hazel wasn't bothered enough to defend her reputation.

But as interesting as all of that was, it wasn't the part of Hazel's diary that got to Sadie the most. No, the part that had her tears overflowing and her heart aching was the way in which Hazel wrote about John Wilmont and the incredible love they shared before his unfortunate passing. John had captivated Hazel's attention from their very first meeting at the print shop, but she'd dismissed the chemistry between them because she was a legally married woman who had sworn off any real chance at love. But John didn't give up, and Hazel slowly lowered her defenses.

One night John dropped off some bound manuscripts, and the two shared their first kiss. It happened in the elevator—which made Sadie smile, knowing what she and Ryan had done together in that very same place. Hazel wrote about how well John treated her, how he encouraged her writing in a way no one in her family ever had. But they both understood their situation for what it was: Hazel was married to a wealthy man whom society held in high esteem, and John was a working-class guy with very little to his name. No matter what they *wanted,* they were resigned to a life where Hazel stayed married to William, and the most they could hope for was that William stayed away and the two could be together out on the island.

Then William died and everything changed. Free to be together, the two married within weeks and started their life in the very home where it had all begun. The following year with John was the happiest time in Hazel's life, the love she never expected consuming her heart, mind, and soul.

After that first year together, John began having episodes, and Hazel would often find him pale and out of breath. The town doctor came to the mansion and examined him, but there was no need. John came from a long line of men in his family who had a rare heart condition, none of them living beyond age thirty. The doctor offered some pills, but they all knew what these symptoms meant. John was afflicted with the same condition, his heart already getting weaker, and there wasn't anything that could be done about it.

A year later he was gone, and Hazel was overwhelmed with grief.

With no one to lean on, she became fully immersed in her writing, escaping into the worlds she created on the page.

The same worlds Sadie escaped to as a child.

But what pained Sadie the most, what made her weep uncontrollably there at the kitchen table, was Hazel's written words proclaiming that no matter the heartbreak she went through, the heartbreak she never recovered from, she'd endure it all again if it meant even one single day with John. How her only regret was that it took her so long to let him into her life, and she only wished she could go back to the months she spent denying her feelings for him and accept that she'd fallen for him the first time she visited that print shop.

Eventually, Sadie lifted her head and wiped her cheeks. Had she made a huge mistake with Ryan? Would she one day regret pushing him out of her life?

Crossing the room to her dresser, she quickly undressed out of her work clothes and pulled on the oversize quarter-zip sweater. This time she zipped it all the way up the collar, wanting Ryan's scent to envelop her. She crawled into bed and opened her text thread with him. There were no new messages of course, but rereading all the old ones made those questions swirling in her head even louder.

But Sadie couldn't be uncertain. If there was anything she understood now, it was that things between her and Ryan would be all or nothing, there would be no halfway about it. And she refused to further hurt him, so she wouldn't ask Ryan to be in her life again if she wasn't completely sure she was ready. Until then, she'd get on with sorting out her life, and maybe, just maybe, the answer would come to her.

But she couldn't resist typing out one message.

Sadie: Good to see you too, Pearson.

She hit send.

* * *

Sadie had always assumed any decent therapist would have a couch. So as she sat in an overstuffed armchair in Rebecca Thurston's tastefully decorated but couchless office, she doubted how *beneficial* any of this could possibly be. What if she was overcome with emotion and needed to lie down a moment? Was she supposed to stay *vertical* during her time of distress? It seemed that if Rebecca Thurston, LMFT, hadn't considered her patients' comfort, was she really someone who could help Sadie with trust issues? Doubtful. So Sadie let her mom do most of the talking from the armchair next to hers.

Speaking about the period of time directly after Sadie's father left, her mom was saying that despite how bad things had been in her marriage, she'd feared she wasn't strong enough to do it all on her own—the same fear that had kept her from leaving for far longer than it should have.

Therapist Rebecca looked directly at Sadie then with a pensive expression. "What about you, Sadie?" she asked. "How did you feel during that time?"

"Um . . ." When she glanced at her mom there was nothing but encouragement in her eyes, so Sadie decided to stop deflecting for once in her life. "To be honest, I felt . . . *relieved.* Relieved there wouldn't be any more arguments. Relieved I might get to sleep through a single night without being awoken by hushed attempts at shouting that eventually stopped trying to be quiet. Relieved I wouldn't feel the need to examine every overheard word to determine if this was going to be the argument that ended everything once and for all."

Rebecca leaned forward in her chair across from them, arms folded over a legal pad in her lap. "Can you tell me a little about your relationship with your father after the divorce?"

"There isn't much to say," Sadie answered. "He moved out of state before it was even final. I had to go visit a couple times, but that ended once he remarried and the twins were born. Instead of pursuing visitation, he'd call every couple months or so. He'd ask about school and I'd say it was fine. He'd tell me about the twins saying their first words or taking their first steps, and I never figured out what I was supposed to say to that. God, those calls were awkward. And I think he felt it, too, because they eventually faded to holidays and my birthday. Then those faded to cards. Sometime in high school he started missing my birthday altogether."

Scrawling something on her legal pad, Rebecca asked, "So all communication stopped at that point? In high school?"

"Basically." Again, Sadie glanced at her mom in her peripheral vision. "And there was one time I reached out when I was older. In college."

As expected, her mom's brows pinched with confusion before she quickly smoothed out her expression.

"I called him and asked if he could help with money," Sadie explained. "Just a couple hundred dollars or so. I had been invited to this formal on campus, but I didn't have the type of dress it required. I worked extra shifts for a couple weeks and saved up what I could, but then my car had a flat tire and that was that. I thought that since I'd never asked for *anything* from him in all those years, maybe that one time he'd help out."

Even years later, Sadie recalled that stilted phone call with perfect clarity. "But he said it wasn't a good time. That the twins both needed ballet costumes for their upcoming recital." She blinked down to her lap, hands fidgeting with the hem of her blouse. "He chuckled like it was a joke. That his two daughters were draining all his money, seemingly forgetting *I* was his daughter, too. The daughter he hadn't bothered supporting in years. And there was no asking about my life, about school, about the fact that I'd picked up the phone for the first time in years. Nothing but a casual dismissal of my request as if we would chat again next week." She cleared the sudden shake from her voice. "That was the last time I ever spoke to him."

"That must have been a really important formal for you to make that phone call," Rebecca observed.

"No," Sadie said with a single shake of her head. Because it occurred to her in that moment that maybe she hadn't actually compartmentalized her relationship with Ryan as well as she'd given herself credit for back then. Maybe even in college she'd been lying to herself about her feelings for him. "The formal was just another dumb college party. It was more about the person who had invited me."

"Ah. I see." After a beat, Rebecca then said, "Backing up a little, you said your father casually dismissed this request that was obviously very important to you. Can you expand on how you felt hanging up the phone that day?"

Sadie racked her brain, trying to articulate what had festered inside her for so long now. "Disappointed. Unsurprised. Mostly . . . replaceable." Saying the word aloud plucked a familiar string within her. It's exactly what she'd been afraid of when it came to leaving her job with Eric. The two situations weren't anything alike, but the fear was the same: being forgotten, being replaced, being slowly but surely abandoned. "I felt . . . I felt like if one of my own parents had no hesitation leaving me out of their new life, what does that say about *me*, you know? I wasn't important enough that my father cared about being a dad, but the twins were. Suddenly he could be present. Suddenly he could hold down a job. Suddenly he could do all the things that he didn't care about doing for me . . . So maybe I was the problem."

A Kleenex appeared before her, courtesy of her mom, and that's when Sadie realized her eyes were wet.

Goddammit, she could really use a couch.

Rebecca went on to say some professional, therapist-sounding stuff about self-worth and dealing with past hurts. Sadie was sure it was all very insightful and encouraging, but she couldn't focus on the words anymore.

She was drained.

And so fucking tired.

But also . . . a little less heavy.

CHAPTER 40

Nope. Not that one."

Those were the first words from Eric's mouth when Sadie opened her door dressed in the floor-length black gown she wore to all the fancy soirées at the mansion. Eric and Charity stood side by side across the threshold, Eric in a white tux and Charity in a crimson red gown with a thigh-high slit.

"Really?" Sadie spun around to show him the lace detailing on the back, but she was certain Eric had been with her when she'd purchased this dress years ago.

"It's tired," he remarked flippantly. "And you wear that every time there's a formal event."

"So sorry I don't have multiple evening gowns in my closet."

"Say no more."

Until that moment, Sadie hadn't paid attention to the awkward way Eric and Charity stood shoulder to shoulder with their hands behind their backs. Then Eric brought an arm forward, revealing a garment bag they'd kept hidden.

"What's this?" Sadie asked.

"What do you think it is?" Eric supported the bag with both arms, holding it like he'd carry a body. "It's a dress. Now let us in."

Stepping out of the doorway, Sadie let the couple into her apartment, exchanging air kisses with Charity as she passed by. "That's for me? You made me a dress?"

"Not exactly." Going straight to her closet, Eric shoved some clothes aside to make room for the hanger. "It's from my *Runway Wars* days, but I thought it would be perfect for tonight."

Unzipping the garment bag, he revealed a floor-length, emerald green silk gown. The dress had thin, barely-there straps, a drop waist, and a dangerously low-cut open back.

It was quite possibly the most beautiful dress Sadie had ever seen. "Eric, it's absolutely stunning. But this cannot be for me, right? It's too much."

Something earnest brewed in his dark eyes. "Several weeks ago you said to me that sometimes a dress is really important. I may not know what that was about, but I do know that tonight felt like an occasion for an important dress."

Without speaking another word, Sadie went to him and hugged him tightly.

From across the room, Charity called out, "Guys! Don't make me cry. I spent an eternity on my makeup."

Sadie stepped back, her own eyes damp. Which seemed to be a habit lately.

Eric squeezed her shoulders. "You've got this."

Sadie wasn't sure about that. Demanding a raise and permission to implement some of her ideas at the mansion felt like a big ask. But she'd made up her mind, and if it meant leaving the estate in her past, well, she was pretty sure Hazel Wilmont would have understood.

A *ping* chimed from where she'd left her phone on the kitchen table. She made her way over and checked the message.

Simon: Are you SURE I chose the right tux?

Yesterday, when Simon texted her photos of three different tux options, Sadie realized that he and Ryan had been included on tonight's guest list. Ever since, she'd been debating with herself if Ryan would show up or not.

"Why do you suddenly look pale?" Charity asked, pulling a bottle of wine from Sadie's fridge.

Another message rolled in.

Simon: The lavender jacket is too much, isn't it?!?

She typed a quick reply.

Sadie: It isn't too much! You'll look great!! See you there!!!

That was at least three too many exclamation points, but at the moment she didn't care.

Sadie dropped her phone back onto the table. "It's just that there's a small chance . . ."

"Ryan might be there tonight," Eric supplied.

"He probably won't come, right?" Sadie asked, nervously chewing a thumbnail. It's not that she didn't want to see him—of course she wanted to see him. She *always* wanted to see him. She just didn't know if she was strong enough to see him again. His devastated, red-rimmed eyes at the market were still burned into her brain every time she closed her eyes.

Leaving the dress, Eric joined her and Charity at the table. "You never said what happened between the two of you. As your friend, if I need to have strong words with him tonight for hurting you, I'll do it."

Charity snorted as she tipped the wine bottle to her lips.

"*Excuse me.*" Offense was written all over Eric's face. "I can have strong words."

"Of course you can, babe," Charity replied with a conspiratorial wink at Sadie.

"Don't worry," Sadie assured. "It's nothing that warrants strong words from Eric Andreas."

"Then tell us," Eric prodded, pulling out a chair and plopping himself down. "What happened that was so bad you had to end things?"

She cleared her throat. "He . . . um . . . told me that he loved me."

The weight of Eric's judgment was heavy in the seconds that followed, brows furrowing, then rising, then furrowing again. "By all means," he deadpanned, "let me kick his ass then. What. A. Dick."

"Okay, okay." Sadie rolled her eyes. "I get it. But this was supposed to be temporary, then he's telling me he's no longer moving to Charleston because he wants to be with me, because he *loves* me. That's a lot of fucking pressure. I mean, obviously I care about him, but *love*?"

"Now I'm just an outside observer here," Eric said, "but it seems like you were really happy when you two were hanging out or whatever you're choosing to call it. And the Sadie Stockton I know doesn't fake sick and call in to work *for an entire week*. Unless maybe . . ."

"Maybe what?"

Eric shot one of his *Can you even believe this?* looks to Charity, who mouthed, "Spell it out for her, babe," back at him.

"Unless maybe you have some pretty strong feelings of your own," Eric clarified.

"Oh."

"Just because you don't want to say the word doesn't mean you don't feel it."

Wait. Could he be right? Could she have already fallen *in love* with Ryan?

It was true that she missed him.

God, she missed him so *fucking* much.

After her therapy session with her mom, she'd realized it didn't take a genius to figure out the root of her issues with forming relationships. She never trusted anyone to stick around, to find her worthy of sticking around for. But Ryan had changed his future plans in order to do just that. Without her even asking, he'd decided being close to her was more important than his business or anything else. He'd shown her how determined he was to stick around, *begged her* to let him stick around, and what had she done? She'd made him feel like he wasn't enough for her. Just like so many others in his life.

Eric was right. She was in love with Ryan. There was no way to keep denying it, and she wasn't sure she even wanted to. She'd spent the past two weeks sick over the fact she wasn't sure she was ready to let herself fall for him. But the joke was on her the whole time, because she'd already fallen, ready or not. So the decision wasn't whether or not to love Ryan, it was what to do about it now that she did.

"Go get dressed." Eric stood, politely pushing in his chair. "We have a party to disrupt."

* * *

Sadie held her breath and Eric's forearm as the three walked into the grand foyer of the Wilmont House, her eyes already scanning the crowd for Ryan. In the opposite hand, she carried a clutch that had only one item in it: Hazel Wilmont's journal. No matter how the night ended, the time had come to hand it over to Mindy.

"Can you ease up?" Eric muttered under his breath. "You're wrinkling the fabric."

"Sorry." Sadie was only halfway listening, but she eased her grip on his arm. "I don't see him."

A plethora of familiar faces were scattered throughout the foyer and the infamous dining room. Some staff members were huddled in a small group, and Matt was there with his girlfriend whose name Sadie couldn't remember. She was fairly certain the woman bent over harshly whispering to an elementary-age kid was Evelyn's daughter, Grace. But wherever Sadie looked, there was no sign of Ryan.

"It's still early," Charity reminded her, arm slung through Eric's on the opposite side. Sadie had never been accompanied by two more beautiful people, and she certainly wasn't used to all the heads that turned their way and the excited whispers of "Is that Charity Chase?" that trailed behind them.

Deeper in the foyer, Sadie's gaze lifted to the grand staircase, where Jerry and Mindy were in conversation with someone—was that the mayor?—midway up the steps, as if that wasn't the most inconvenient spot to hold a conversation.

"I don't think I'm ready." Sadie turned to Eric and Charity. "I need more time. What if I forget all of my demands and cave?"

"You won't," Eric reassured. "We practiced."

"What if I clam up and forget everything though?"

"Again," he said calmly, "you've got this."

"What if—"

"I think you're out of time." Eric's eyes darted pointedly to a spot behind her.

When Sadie peered over her shoulder, Jerry and Mindy were headed their way.

"Shit," she uttered.

"I have nothing but faith in you," Eric said quickly before putting a wide smile on his face for the approaching duo. Somehow, that was exactly what she needed to hear though, because if Eric had faith in her then surely she could have a little in herself.

"Well, well, well." Jerry's voice echoed from behind her, his normal conversational volume loud enough to easily drown out the piano notes.

Sadie turned to the couple with a practiced smile, quickly taking in Jerry's classic tux, Mindy's flapper-style, black-and-gold-sequined gown.

"Sadie, you never told us you knew all these celebrities," Jerry continued, not looking at her. He extended a hand to Eric. "I met Charity on the tour but I don't believe we've met. Jerry Whitlock. What a pleasant surprise to have you both join us this evening."

"Eric Andreas," Eric said, shaking Jerry's hand. "Sadie and I have been friends now for what, seven years or so?"

Sadie nodded. "Sounds right."

"In fact," Eric continued, "Sadie's the first person I hired at my store. She's been an integral part of my success."

An integral part of his success?

Okay, while she appreciated what he was doing, that was bullshit of the highest order. So much so she had to clear her throat to keep from laughing.

"Is that right?" Jerry's gaze narrowed in on her. "I have to say, we were thrilled the murder mystery tours were such a success."

And there it was, the opening she needed. Ignoring her racing heart, she said, "About that, could we perhaps talk somewhere private?"

Jerry's brow lifted, but he gave a single nod. "Lead the way."

Sadie looked to Eric and Charity.

"We're gonna check out the buffet," Eric said. "Don't worry about us."

Sadie led Jerry and Mindy to the first-floor library, which they always closed off during parties. After pulling the sliding double doors together to drown out the hum, Sadie preemptively cleared any waver in her voice. Then she approached the couple and cut to the chase. "I'm considering resigning my position here at the Wilmont House. I think I—"

"What? *Why?*" Mindy suddenly hunched forward, supporting herself with a stiff arm propped on the corner of the oversize desk. "No, no, no, no. We can't have that. Why would you want to leave? You can't *leave*!"

Jerry stuffed his hands in his pants pockets, expression contorting at his wife's reaction.

"Um." Sadie looked back and forth between the pair, thrown. "The thing is, I assumed when Evelyn retired, I would take over as director. Since that isn't going to happen, it may be time to move on. However, I do really love this house, and I won't go into the details about why Hazel Wilmont means so much to me, other than to say her books were an instrumental part of my childhood. Because of that, I would prefer to stay on, but I do have a few conditions."

"Conditions?" Jerry snorted.

"We'll meet them," Mindy said firmly. "Whatever they are, we'll meet them."

"Christ, Bunny." Jerry ran a hand through his sandy blond hair. "You might want to hear what they are first!"

While Sadie had expected this meeting to be awkward, she hadn't expected it to be this particular type of awkward. "A raise, for starters. A significant one. I want the equivalent to the director's salary."

"Done." Mindy didn't even look at Jerry, nor did she flinch.

"Okay . . ." Sadie didn't understand what was happening, it wasn't supposed to be this easy. "And I want final say on the staff hired for the murder mystery tour. Actually, *all* staff hired at the mansion."

"You've got it," Mindy replied.

Jerry paced back and forth, muttering to himself.

"I also have some proposals I want to implement," Sadie continued. "Starting with the gift shop hours. While I won't get into it all now, I do want those proposals to be seriously considered."

Mindy nodded. "I understand."

Jerry sidled up to his wife again. "Bunny, don't you think we should at least discuss this privately before you go agreeing to *everything*?"

"No." Mindy's one-word response was sharp, decisive. Then her voice softened as she addressed Sadie. "All of that is doable. *Please* don't leave."

"Uh, Mindy . . ." Sadie might regret this later, but she had to ask. "Is everything okay? I wasn't expecting you to be so agreeable."

Back turned, Jerry scoffed in a *You and me both* kind of way.

Ignoring him, Mindy tucked a loose tendril of hair that had escaped her updo behind her ear. "Working with Evelyn this past week, I realized I may be in over my head. I think I got defensive during the tour when it was made obvious that I don't know, well, *anything* about Hazel. But the truth is, I also don't know the first thing about running this place."

"And I am *so sorry* about the tour," Sadie apologized. "I never meant my question to be a slight."

Mindy waved away her apology. "I know that. The thing is, Hazel was a really painful topic for my grandmother. While I don't know what happened between them, I do know they never repaired their relationship before Hazel passed, which my grandmother very much regretted. Because of that, Hazel wasn't really spoken of in our home unfortunately. And her books weren't, either."

After reading how close the two sisters were growing up, Sadie could understand that. "Mindy, I'm sorry. Families are complicated. I shouldn't have assumed anything about yours."

"It's okay. I'm actually grateful because taking your tour taught me so many things I never knew about Hazel, and it made me realize how much more I want to learn." She offered a timid smile. "But I got a little overzealous in naming myself the new director of the estate. I'm not ready for that role, that much has become obvious this past week."

Sparks of hope ignited in Sadie's chest. "What are you saying?"

"I'm saying the role of director is yours. Assuming you still want it."

In Sadie's peripheral vision, Jerry's jaw flexed as he bit back his commentary, but Mindy didn't seem to give a fuck about Jerry's opinion at the moment so neither did she. "I would love to accept that position. It's been a dream of mine since childhood."

"*Thank god* that's settled." Mindy blew out a breath as though a tremendous weight had been lifted from her shoulders. "But Sadie, I really would like to be around more. And I'd really like to learn about Hazel. Can you help me with that?"

"I can absolutely do that. In fact, I know the exact place to start." Unsnapping her clutch, she took out Hazel's journal and passed it over to Mindy. "I'll be in touch next week."

Sadie left Mindy and Jerry in the library, both hunched over Hazel's words.

Chapter 41

Sadie rushed through the halls, searching for Eric and Charity to tell them the good news. Or bittersweet news, rather, since leaving the bridal shop after seven years certainly wouldn't be easy. But she was choosing to trust that Eric meant what he said about remaining in her life.

She spotted the couple in the kitchen, both holding glasses filled with bubbly champagne and chatting with Simon and Adam. She rushed over to the group.

"I'm the new director!" she announced, interrupting whatever conversation they were in the midst of, but she had a feeling they wouldn't mind.

"Wait, what about Mindy?" Simon asked, and Sadie rushed through what had taken place in the library.

When she finished, Simon pulled her into a firm hug, crushing her cheek against his velvet jacket. "That's amazing! And I'm so fucking relieved for Mindy's horses."

Laughter bubbled out of her as she hugged him back.

"That's really great, Sadie," Adam said once Simon released her. "Congratulations."

Eric winked at her. "Really proud of you."

"*So* proud," Charity added, tipping her champagne flute.

"Thanks, guys."

Sadie turned her attention back to Simon. One thing she'd realized when reading Hazel Wilmont's diary was that Hazel likely would have *loved* that a mystery game was taking place in her home. Maybe people came because of the dead husband(s), but the tour was also the perfect way to honor both Hazel and her sister. And there was only one person Sadie wanted in charge. The truth was, there was a reason Jerry brought Simon on board as a consultant, and she would give credit where it was due. Simon was the best at what he did. There was no one funnier, no better storyteller, no one with a bigger heart than Simon Winchester.

"And now for my first official act as director," Sadie continued. "Simon, I'd like to offer you the permanent position as lead actor on the Mixtures and Murder Tour. *Please* say you'll accept. No one can play the butler like you can, we both know that."

Mouth forming a sly grin, Simon tapped his chin pensively. "Hmm, it could be tough to fit into my busy schedule . . . Just kidding! Of course I say yes!" Again, Sadie was crushed against his jacket, her laugh muffled. "We're gonna have so much fun together!"

"Okay, okay. Enough." Sadie pulled out of his embrace.

"Well, this night is turning out perfectly." Charity clinked her champagne flute against Eric's.

Sadie's smile fell. It wasn't nearly perfect. Not yet.

"Have you seen him yet?" Eric asked, clearly following where Sadie's mind went.

She shook her head.

"If you're talking about who I think you're talking about," Simon softly intoned, "he isn't coming. I talked to him earlier. He didn't think showing up would be a good idea so he's working instead. I think he's trying to stay busy."

Sadie's heart sank, eyes automatically tearing up. On some level, she'd thought maybe Ryan would take the opportunity to see her, despite everything. But it sounded as though he was moving on. It may have only been a couple of weeks ago, but perhaps when you tell someone you love them and they completely shut you down, it's all the closure you need.

"I'm sorry, Sadie," Simon added.

"It's fine," she said, though it wasn't fine at all.

"You okay?" Eric asked.

"I will be. I just hoped I'd find him and everything would work out and it would be this magical night. Stupid adrenaline. And stupid optimism."

"Maybe it could still work out that way," Adam spoke up. "In the beginning of all this, Simon mentioned you didn't care for Ryan because he brought his pub crawls by the mansion. So if he's working, won't he be coming by here?"

A tiny thread of hope wrapped around her heart.

"That's a great point," Simon said. "Sadie, if you want to wait around after the party, we'll stay with you."

"Really?" she asked, touched by the offer. "It's usually after eleven when he comes through the square, you don't mind staying that late?"

"Such a grandma," Eric muttered under his breath.

"It'll be your *grand gesture!*" Charity added with an enthusiastic lilt to her voice. "It's perfect!"

Sadie wasn't sure about that. "I don't know. I'm not sure waiting on a sidewalk is really grand-gesture material."

"Excuse me." Eric motioned a hand down the length of her. "*That dress* is a grand gesture. Do you think just anyone gets to wear an Eric Andreas original from the set of *Runway Wars*?"

Sadie looked down at the green silk. He wasn't wrong, the dress was fucking fantastic, and far more beautiful than anything she'd ever worn before. Sure, it was only a dress, but it gave her the confidence needed to say, "Okay, I'll wait for him."

* * *

The party was over and the caterers packed up by ten o'clock, so Sadie spent the remaining hour quietly running through made-up scenarios in her head while Eric and Charity engaged in boisterous conversation with Simon and Adam.

When the clock finally neared eleven, she made her way outside and paced in front of the entrance gate, curious as to what the others scattered throughout the square—a few pedestrians and a couple small tour groups—must think of the woman in a formal ballgown traipsing up and down the sidewalk.

As much as she'd tried to plan what she was going to say, she hadn't been successful. Her adrenaline was too high to focus, her mind bouncing like a rubber ball from one thought to the next. She'd have to figure it out when she saw him. *If* she saw him.

The night had a crisp chill in the air, and her bare shoulders shivered whenever the breeze skated across her skin. She paced and paced, unsure of how much time had passed, and her hope began to fade with each turn of her heels against brick.

Then she heard it.

Ryan's voice, cadence and drawl unmistakable, projected loud enough for an entire group of pub crawlers to hear. Sadie spun as though that voice were a magnet, and sure enough, Ryan rounded the corner nearest her, wearing that stupid Pearson's T-shirt she actually loved as he led his tour group down the block.

It took a moment, but when Ryan saw her standing in the middle of the sidewalk he stopped in his tracks, his sentence abandoned. His green eyes narrowed, like he couldn't quite figure out if it was actually her. But he was Ryan Pearson, so he regained composure at record speed.

Sadie couldn't say the same. Her breaths came in shallow bursts, and she clutched her hands together to stop them from shaking, or at least make it less noticeable. Every step closer Ryan drew reverberated throughout her entire body.

"Everyone, this is the Wilmont House," Ryan said as the group came to a stop outside the gates, his eyes focused only on her. Sadie felt the questioning gazes of his pub crawlers on her, too—likely wondering why a woman in a fan-fucking-tastic dress was standing speechless on the sidewalk in front of them. "Former home of famed children's author Hazel Wilmont. Now, many of you might associate Hazel with the rumors that she poisoned her first husband in this home, and possibly her second husband, too. But I don't believe any of that."

Sadie waited with bated breath for whatever he said next.

"Unfortunately, people spread rumors and create gossip regardless of the truth. But I get the sense that Hazel Wilmont cared far more about her work than what people thought of her. And while people were busy spreading false stories, she was busy creating her legacy through her books." Ryan let the statement hang in the air for a moment, then said, "Everyone, this is Sadie Stockton. She works here at the Wilmont House."

For the first time, Sadie acknowledged the group. "Actually, I'm the director of the Wilmont House." Surprise flickered across Ryan's face. "And I think Ryan is exactly right. In fact, Hazel's diary was recently discovered here in the mansion, and it confirms that Hazel never poisoned anyone. If you'd like to hear more about Hazel and her books, I hope you'll find time to give us a visit while you're in town."

"Hello, friends!" Simon's voice called out from behind her. "Hate to interrupt, but I'm the lead actor on the Mixtures and Murder Tour here at the mansion, and I was wondering if you all might want to come in and look around for a few minutes? If your guide is okay with that, of course."

Sadie smiled at Simon over her shoulder and mouthed "Thank you" before turning back to Ryan, hoping he'd pick up the clues that she needed to talk to him. Alone.

A few enthusiastic *yes*es rang out from the pub crawlers, and after a moment that felt like an eternity, Ryan nodded. "Yeah, sure. Why not."

"Excellent." Simon motioned for the group to follow his lead. "Right this way, everyone. Follow me."

Sadie watched them go, clutching their plastic cups as they traipsed through the front courtyard and up the porch steps. Part of her yearned to scream out, *No drinks upstairs!* but now wasn't the time.

"So, what's this about a diary?" Ryan asked sheepishly, shoving his hands deep in his pockets. "And you're the director now? Congrat—"

"*I love you!*" Sadie didn't know how much time they had so everything else could wait. The only thing that mattered was saying what she should have realized weeks ago. "I do. I love you, Ryan." His lips parted slightly, but she rushed to keep talking before he could say anything to throw her off course. "I don't know if I'll ever forgive myself for pushing you away when you told me how you felt, or for making you feel in any way that you weren't enough for me. Because you are enough. And I *did* fall in love with you. It just took me a while to recognize it because it's never happened to me before. Not like this."

"Sadie." Everything about Ryan softened with that one word: voice, posture, expression. But she couldn't decipher if it was in an *I still love you, too* way or an *I'm about to gently decimate your heart* way.

Uncertain, she continued pleading her case. "Actually, no, it has happened to me once before. Because I think I loved you in college, too. I mean, why else call up my father, who I hadn't spoken to in years, just to ask for money for a dress so I could try to go to some party with this guy who was maybe a lot more important to me than I realized?"

"Wait." Head tilting, Ryan studied her, eyes filling with emotion. "You *did* that?"

When she nodded, he started to move toward her, quickly closing the distance between them. "I want to be with you," she continued. "And not temporarily. I may not be great at this relationship thing, *yet*, but I swear I'm working on it. And I really don't want to lose the only guy I've ever loved, twice now it would appear, so please tell me it's not too—"

Before she could get another word out, Ryan reached her, took her face in his hands, and crashed his mouth against hers, kissing her as though he'd been dreaming of nothing else the entire time they'd been apart. Sadie met his eagerness and need with her own, relief consuming her as their bodies melted together there on the public sidewalk, in the very spot they'd had so many exchanges over the years.

"Sadie," Ryan rasped against her mouth, hands firm on her cheeks.

"Yeah?"

"That dress is fucking unreal."

"I know."

His soft laughter puffed against her lips. "You wanna know something else?"

"What's that?"

"I'm so fucking relieved you're standing here." Then Ryan pulled back, searching her eyes. "But are you *sure* this is what you want? This past two weeks has been absolute hell, and I need you to be sure."

"I know." She placed both hands on his chest, wanting nothing more than to linger in the comfort of his arms. "And I'm sure. I swear to you, I'm so fucking sure."

"Good, because I'm *so* in love with you, Sadie." Ryan's lips were warm and soft when they met hers again, and he took his time with the kiss, letting it root them to the moment, creating another memory in what had always been Sadie's favorite place on Earth.

Eventually they ended the kiss before it bordered on public indecency, Sadie wearing a wide smile that stretched her cheeks. "Sorry I had to interrupt your pub crawl."

"I'm not." Ryan rubbed warmth into her upper arms as a cool breeze whipped around them and rippled her dress. "I'm only sorry I still have to finish this goddamn pub crawl instead of going up to your apartment and methodically taking this dress off of you."

A shiver rolled through her shoulders, but this time it wasn't from the breeze. "How much longer will you be?"

"We have one more stop. But why don't you come along?"

"On your pub crawl?"

Ryan shrugged a shoulder. "Why not? We've got one more bar, I'll wrap things up, then we can come back here and I'll spend the rest of the night showing you how much I missed you."

Seeing Ryan in his element was something Sadie couldn't pass up. "Can my friends tag along, too?" As she spoke, it wasn't lost on her that she'd used the plural form of the word. Because not only had she opened up her life to Ryan over the past month, she'd also opened up her circle to Charity and Simon and Adam, too. And it felt really, *really* nice to have new friends.

Ryan kissed her tenderly. "Absolutely."

"Should I run upstairs and change really quick?"

"Absolutely not."

* * *

The last stop of the night on Ryan's pub crawl was a local staple in town, Sutton's Irish Pub. Sadie had passed the whitewashed brick building with a notable green awning more times than she could count over the years, but she'd never ventured inside. (Perhaps Eric was right about her grandma status.) Now she followed Eric up to the bar while he explained to Simon and Adam that they must try some shot that tasted like maple syrup and was served with a biscuit. Sliding onto a barstool, Sadie snuck another glance out to the patio where Ryan was finishing up with his group, likely telling them all about the establishment and what drinks he recommends.

Watching him now, it was hard to believe she'd ever denied that she was in love with him. Once she'd allowed herself to be open to the possibility, it was so blatantly obvious. He'd done everything right. He'd shown up for her when she needed him. He'd helped her through one of the most stressful periods of her life. And he was willing to change his plans to be near her. When she expected people to walk out of her life and never look back, Ryan had already proven he wanted to be with her, whatever it took.

Notes from a pop song Sadie didn't recognize blared from the speakers as Charity slid onto the stool next to her and leaned in to be heard over the music. "So listen, I know you and Eric are besties, and I'm totally here for that. Really. But I'm hoping since I'll be spending more time in town, maybe *we* can have our own girl time, too?"

If Sadie wasn't mistaken, the briefest flicker of uncertainty crossed Charity's face. Could it be possible that even a supermodel might struggle with putting themselves out there to try to make a new friend? Of course it was possible, no one is immune from vulnerability. Sadie smiled. "I'd *really* love that."

"All right, everyone." Eric's voice rose above the rest as a bartender placed a tray of shots and a bowl full of buttermilk biscuits in front of him. "What are we toasting to tonight?"

"How about Sadie's promotion?" Adam suggested, lifting a shot from the tray.

"Um, excuse me, how about *my* new job?" Simon shot a pointed look to Adam. "*I'm* your husband."

"I think you're all forgetting the most important thing that happened tonight." Charity lifted her own shot glass high in the air. "I say we toast to Sadie and her new man."

"I'll toast to that." Ryan's arm slid around her waist as he joined the group.

Sadie smiled before turning her head and giving him a quick kiss. Looking around the group, warmth radiated from the very center of her chest outward, fizzy sparks crackling like the remnants of a fading firework. And it wasn't only because she'd gotten the job she'd always wanted, or even because she'd finally admitted she was in love with Ryan. Her heart overflowed because for the first time in her life she stood among a circle of friends, *true* friends, and that filled her up in a way she couldn't put words to. A way that made her vision blur with tears and her throat cinch tight.

"Okay, *I've* got it." Eric picked up two more shots and passed one to Sadie and one to Ryan. When everyone was ready with their glasses aloft, he said, "Tonight we toast to new beginnings. Whether that's a new job, a new romance, a new friendship—or maybe an old one that might look a little different in the future but will *always* remain important." He winked at her, a knowing smile on his lips. "Cheers to love, in all its forms. Because in the wise and extremely heartfelt words of one Sadie Marie Stockton, *I just really* love *love*."

Epilogue

I now pronounce you husband and wife. You may kiss the bride."

A tear fell down Sadie's cheek as she watched Doug pull her mom in for a long kiss in front of the thirty guests gathered in the courtyard of the Wilmont House on a balmy Saturday afternoon in April. Ann Stockton looked stunning, of course, in a custom mermaid-style gown designed by the one and only Eric Andreas.

Only five months had passed since Doug showed up on Sadie's doorstep, and she'd be lying if she said she had absolutely no reservations about how fast the engagement and wedding came afterward. But Sadie kept going to therapy, now by herself instead of with her mom, and she was learning to manage those concerns without creating a rift between the two. Spending more time around Doug had helped as well, and she could now admit that he (probably) didn't have a secret second family.

The holidays had been especially interesting, not only incorporating Doug into the Stockton traditions, but Ryan as well. Overall, Christmas had gone relatively smoothly, though Sadie didn't care for the Santa hat Doug wore all Christmas Day without once taking it off, not even when he got down on one knee in front of the Christmas tree to pop the question to her mom. But whatever, if Doug didn't care about looking ridiculous in all their engagement photos, then why should Sadie care.

As the newlyweds headed down the aisle, Sadie's gaze drifted to find Ryan standing alongside Eric and Charity among the rows of white chairs. Charity's arm was looped through Eric's, her own massive diamond ring sparkling in the afternoon sunlight. Only a couple months ago, Sadie had shown up at the bridal shop after receiving an emergent text from Eric, only to find the store closed and Eric waiting outside. When Sadie asked what was going on, he'd replied, *I guess I fully bought into the bullshit.* He led her inside, where Charity stood in front of a trifold mirror in the wedding gown with the light pink embroidery that Eric completed months back. Charity was absolutely stunning, smile radiant.

The couple had scheduled an appointment to get married at the courthouse, and Sadie was their one invited guest. The simplicity of it all didn't surprise Sadie in the least. If there was ever a couple whose calm, quiet love Sadie fully believed in, it was Eric and Charity.

Now Ryan caught her gaze and winked, and Sadie smiled as she linked arms with Doug's best man—one of his accounting firm partners (though not the one who'd fucked his ex-wife, obviously)—and made her way up the aisle.

Afternoon turned to evening as the reception wound on underneath a tent in the courtyard, the loving newlyweds cutting the cake and sharing their first dance. Sadie stayed busy throughout, her duties as maid of honor and director of the Wilmont House keeping her hopping from one task to the next, ensuring everything went perfectly for her mom's big day. But once the party started to wrap up and Doug and her mom made their exit in a rented convertible, Sadie went in search of her boyfriend.

Before she could find him, she stumbled—literally—into Simon as she pushed through the back door to the garden. "There you are!" he said, dusting off his suit jacket. "Do you think we could show Adam our little discovery later?"

"Simon!" she chastised. "We agreed to never speak of that again."

"We don't have to speak about it, we can just show him. Please, Sadie, please?"

In preparation for today's nuptials, last week Simon helped her search the attic for the antique candleholders they used as centerpieces for fancy events at the estate. In true Simon fashion, his curiosity had him digging through boxes that hadn't been opened in decades. Which then led him to discover a small wooden box tucked away in the very back corner of the attic, inside a single syringe and a bottle of pesticide with a powdery substance coating the glass.

"I already told you," Sadie muttered quietly so no one else could hear. "It doesn't mean anything. Hazel likely had a rat problem in the attic."

"And she dosed each little mousey with some pesticide from a syringe?" Simon let out a bark of laughter. "Be so for real right now, friend."

The truth was, Sadie didn't know what the truth was anymore. All she knew for certain was that sometimes the line between truth and fiction blurred, and the only person who would ever know Hazel Wilmont's full story was Hazel Wilmont. "Simon, I said no."

"I swear to god you never let me have any fun."

Simon sulked away, and Sadie continued on her search. She finally spotted Ryan near the cake table, sipping champagne and chatting with some pretty blonde in a summery floral dress who looked vaguely familiar. Halfway across the lawn, it dawned on her—New Grad Kayla. Reaching the two, Sadie went to Ryan's side, his arm naturally wrapping around her shoulders as she fitted herself against him. "Ah, there you are," he said, dropping a quick kiss to her temple. "I was just telling Kayla about the Mixtures and Murder Tour here at the mansion."

"Yeah, it sounds *super* fun," Kayla replied, blue eyes lighting. "I'd never heard about it before."

"Oh," Sadie said, surprised. "I thought my mom would have mentioned it."

Kayla's head tilted. "Your mom?"

"Oh, I'm sorry. I didn't introduce myself. I'm Sadie."

"Nice to meet you, Sadie," Kayla said, confusion still woven through her voice. "But forgive me, who is your mom?"

Now Sadie was confused, too. "Ann Stockton is my mom. You know, the bride."

"OH!" Kayla let out a frilly little laugh and placed her fingers on Sadie's arm. "I'm so sorry. It's just that Ann's never mentioned you by name."

Ryan took her hand and squeezed tightly. "Kayla, it was nice meeting you," he said, "but I haven't gotten a chance to dance with my girlfriend all night so if you'll excuse us . . ."

"Of course!" Kayla smiled brightly. "Nice meeting you, Sadie!"

Sadie nodded as Ryan pulled her in the direction of the parquet dance floor where the band was playing a cover of an Elvis ballad.

"There's no way my mom doesn't talk about me at work!" Sadie shout-whispered as soon as they were out of earshot.

"Of course she talks about you, baby."

"I know she does because she tells me she talks about me all the time! And Doug said she talks about me all the time! Plus, I'm the maid of honor! Clearly, Kayla is trying to steal my mom."

"Mmhmm. Clearly." Stepping onto the dance floor, Ryan pulled her into his arms. "How are you doing?"

"Well, I'll definitely be talking about what Kayla just said in therapy on Monday, but other than that—"

"Sadie." Ryan gently shook his head. "Forget Kayla. How are you really doing? Your mom just got *married*."

Yeah, there was that. "I think I'm doing *okay*." She said it like a question because that's exactly what it was. "I mean, I still think they rushed things. But I do think Doug has good intentions and loves her. So I'm still going to worry about her, but she did look really happy today."

"Yeah, she really did."

Ryan pulled her closer, and Sadie closed her eyes and nuzzled her forehead against his neck while they swayed, his woodsy scent invoking feelings of comfort and safety. Her mom wasn't the only one who was really happy. In the past five months Ryan had continued to show up for her, be patient with her, and love her unconditionally. It was hard to imagine there was ever a period of time when she bristled at the mention of his name or the sight of him across the square, when now he was the most important person in her life.

The night she'd realized she was in love with him had certainly been a cataclysmic event. Despite that, all of her walls hadn't fallen at once. Her issues weren't resolved overnight. That's just not the way things worked in real life. She still had a lot of work to do on herself, but she was still a person deserving of love, even if she wasn't perfect.

As they moved with the music, Sadie tried to picture what a wedding might look like for the two of them. They'd have it at the mansion, of course. And they'd keep it small, just their close friends and family. It would be a day filled with love and happiness, not unlike the very day they'd just had.

"What are you thinking about?" Ryan softly coaxed.

Sadie lifted her head. "How six months ago I thought I couldn't stand you."

Dropping an arm from around her, Ryan covered his heart as if he'd been wounded. "Wow. Thanks, baby."

"You didn't let me finish." She tugged his hand away from his chest and guided it back around her waist. "I was also thinking about how much I *love* you now."

"Okay, that's better," he teased. "Keep going."

They began to sway again, and Sadie's fingers slipped into the soft hair above his nape. "I was thinking about how much I've come to rely on you and trust you, which is such a huge thing for me."

His lips brushed her forehead. "I rely on you, too, you know."

"And then I was thinking . . ." Hesitating, she stopped swaying and met Ryan's gaze. "I was thinking that *maybe* we might have a wedding of our own one day."

"Really?"

The surprise in Ryan's voice didn't surprise Sadie in the least. He'd spent the past five months moving at her pace, never speaking too much about the future in case it freaked her out. Yes, they loved each other. Yes, they were committed to each other. Yes, he reassured her over and over again that he wasn't going anywhere. But broaching the topic of an engagement or marriage—even far in the future—was one step she could tell he was skittish of, and it had everything to do with her and nothing to do with him.

"I mean, don't get down on one knee right here or anything," she said. "But just so you know, I don't want you to be afraid to have those conversations with me, either. And maybe . . ."

"Yeah?" he encouraged.

She swallowed back her nerves. "Maybe . . . only if you want me to . . . maybe I could move into your place soon. We're there every night anyway, and my apartment is too small for all of our stuff. I don't know, it was just a thought."

The differing shades of green in Ryan's eyes all lit up as he cradled her face and pulled her in for a kiss. "Sadie," he whispered against her lips, "I would *love* for you to live with me. But are you sure you'd be okay giving up your apartment? I know how much you love your place."

In therapy Sadie was learning that she didn't always have to cling *so hard* to the things she loved out of fear they might slip away. Yes, she loved her apartment. But she loved Ryan more. And he'd given up expanding his business to stay near her, so she wanted to do this for him. Besides, she already worked at the Wilmont House—she didn't need to live there, too. "I'm sure."

Ryan stroked her cheek, eyes soft. "And just so *you* know, I'll marry you today, tomorrow, ten years from now, or never at all if it's not what you want. I only need a life with you in it. Every day. That's all I ask."

Sadie kissed him again, letting it linger until she pulled back to say, "*That* I can definitely do."

ACKNOWLEDGMENTS

A lot of authors will say that the sophomore novel is the hardest to write, and in this instance, that holds very true. This book took on a few different versions, *a lot* of revisions, and plenty of tears throughout the writing process. Somehow, I think that made me love Sadie and Ryan even more. So if you picked up this book, thank you for spending your time with them, and I hope you loved them, too.

My utmost thanks and gratitude to my brilliant editor, Esi Sogah, who helped me shape this story and these characters into their very best versions. Working with you has been nothing short of a dream come true. Thank you also to Naira Mirza, Anika Bates, Kristin Cipolla, Genni Eccles, and everyone at Berkley for the work you do every day. I appreciate you all immensely.

To the incredibly talented Liza Rusalskaya, thank you for another beautiful cover that I spend an embarrassing amount of time just staring at. I am blown away by your talent for capturing the exact vibe of these stories and then turning it into gorgeous art.

To Jessi, thank you for showing up for me, whether that's in the Eras Tour Ticketmaster queue or driving to a different state to attend my events. To Katie and Cassandra, thank you for our dinner and ice cream nights. To Dr. Carol Esmark Jones, thanks for answering all my college-life questions, and for three decades of friendship, too.

I'm blessed to say there are so many people in the romance writing community that I need to thank that it becomes nearly impossible to do so in a few paragraphs. However, I absolutely must express my gratitude to the following: Alicia Thompson, not only for your friendship and advice over the years but also for being the kind of friend who hops on a plane to come celebrate the launch of my debut with me. Your light just keeps getting brighter, my friend. Amanda Hopkins, I'm so thankful for the time we spent together in three different cities this year, even if my feet have never hurt as much as they did after we trekked all over NYC. Heather McBreen, getting a five-minute voice note from you is a truly delightful experience that can only be topped by getting a second five-minute voice note from you while I'm still listening to the first. Seriously, I wouldn't have made it through this year without you. Amy Buchanan, thank you for being one of the very first people to lay eyes on the early chapters of this book and also for just being a really good friend. Audrey Goldberg, I thank my lucky stars that you agreed to read my work a long time ago and now you're stuck with me. I'm so glad we became friends. Amanda Wilson, thank you for being the *very first* reader of a significant portion of this book—your early feedback was invaluable. Heather Frances, thank you for dropping everything to read this book when I was spiraling, and also for the answers to my basic tech questions, which probably everyone else knows. Sarah T. Dubb, thank you for reading both of my books and for being a positive light and source of reassurance when I need it the most.

I also want to send my heartfelt gratitude to every author who took time to write blurbs for both this book and my debut. It's still hard to believe that authors I hold in such high esteem actually read my words and then wrote nice things about them. That's always going to feel super surreal.

To all the librarians and booksellers out there, thank you for getting books into the hands of readers in a time when it's most needed. The work you do every day is invaluable. And a special shout-out to my local independent bookstore, Good Girl Books, whose unwavering support has meant everything to me!

The last time I wrote acknowledgments I didn't have a book out in the world yet, so I had no idea what to expect. I can now say that the readers have easily made this experience worth all of those difficult days when the words don't come and the insecurities get heavy. I cannot overstate the joy I feel when someone reaches out to say that they loved the story, or that they connected with a character, or that they now want to travel to a new place because they were inspired. Please know that if you have read, reviewed, or posted about one of my books, I am *so* appreciative.

Finally, to my family (you know who you are), thank you for being super cool about all this. I'm lucky to have each and every one of you in my corner. And to my husband, I'll just leave it at *I love you* because I already dedicated this book to you. What more do you want? *XO*

ACKNOWLEDGMENTS

[illegible]

Image by Danika Corrall Designs

Megan Oliver is a writer, an avid romance reader, and a travel enthusiast whose vacation mishaps provide plenty of inspiration for her characters on the page. She lives with her husband, two dogs who refuse to cuddle as much as she'd prefer, and a cat who barely tolerates the presence of any and all of the above.

VISIT MEGAN OLIVER ONLINE

meganoliverbooks.com